THE EAGLE

SOPHIE HARDING

DISCLAIMER

THIS BOOK CONTAINS THEMES THAT SOME READERS MAY FIND DISTRESSING.

WHILE REAL PLACES AND LOCATIONS HAVE BEEN REFERENCED IN THIS BOOK, ALL OF THOSE DEPICTED HAVE NO RELATION TO PAST OR CURRENT PEOPLE AND EVENTS. NOR HAS THE AUTHOR INTENDED TO SLANDER OR REBUKE ANY OF THE LOCATIONS OR ESTABLISHMENTS REFERENCED.

ACKNOWLEDGEMENTS

To Mum – for being bit of a thriller expert and taking me through the entire plot, telling me which bits were good and which bits to change. Thank you for watching all of those crime/thriller TV shows. Your knowledge was invaluable.

To all of my online chums – thank you for listening to my endless voice notes, where I laugh about a bit I thought was hilarious, and for answering incredibly random questions such as 'does someone need a passport to fly from Inverness to London?'.

CONTENTS

THE EAGLE

CHAPTER ONE

Time of death: 7:47am

The words tear me apart as I hear them. I stand next to her body, looking down at her lifeless eyes. The eyes that were always filled with warmth and courage, now they are just a shadow of a woman who brought me so much joy. I collect her hand in mine, placing it gently on her stomach. I step away from her, understanding all too suddenly that my life will no longer be the same. She was my world. No, that's too cliché. She was the soothing tune you play when the world seems to be ending. She was the homecooked meal after a stressful rainy day, cold and alone. She was everything a mother should be. I turn my head slowly, clocking eyes with my father.

I watch him. I watch his eyes. They don't move. They are frozen, gazing down at the woman he called wife. Our driver and my father's assistant, Francis, makes his way into the room. I check to see what he was carrying; it is a brown, leather briefcase. This is the briefcase my father always keeps close. He will never tell me what is in there. The man is a cloud of secrets. He never trusts me with the truth; he always says that I am too young. I guess sixteen is too young to learn about the dark underbelly of your father's profession.

"Evelyn, we need to move." My father barks, clearing his throat. Clearing his throat is always my father's way of telling me he is losing his patience. And he never calls me the name my mother used to call me. Evie. Not Evelyn. Evie. I don't understand the man. I don't understand why he is so indifferent about the situation. Of course, I will understand eventually. But it will be too late. If I could foresee the future and offer myself some advice, it would be to cut ties with my father. Here and now. I should leave. I should run for the hills. But I can't. I'm now completely dependent on the man. My father isn't violent or abusive; you need emotions for that. He is just a wall, completely made of stone. And I have no idea what would happen if that wall collapsed. "I won't ask again, Evelyn." My father snaps, making me jump. I then jump again at the crash of the door slamming behind me. Finally, I am alone. I yearn for solitude, the moments of inner peace, even if it is to bid my mother a final goodbye. "What do I do, Mum?" I ask the still woman who used to make me smile every day. "You always told me what to do, and now I'm hopeless." I whisper, forgetting that I shouldn't have expected a response. "Mum, I'm so scared..."

"Evelyn!" My father bellows from beyond the door. I scowl, holding my tongue. I clutch my mother's hand, only making it worse for myself, as the realisation pours through my skin and into my blood, straight to my wrinkling heart.

"Goodbye, Mum." I gather whatever strength I can and kiss her falsely pink, icy cheeks. I wipe my tears and leave the room, closing the door of happiness forever.

I walk to the car, mournfully following my father. Francis holds open the rear door of our glossed, black Mercedes Benz C-

Class. I take one final look at the Royal London hospital before lowering myself onto the cream leather seat. Francis closes my door and travels to the other side, opening the door for my father, who soon sits beside me. Immediately, my father retrieves his phone from his trouser pocket as Francis sits in the driver's seat. On a large touchscreen on the centre console, Francis has inputted a new destination. I squint my eyes, trying to read the ETA. "Twelve hours? Where are we going?" I ask. Francis doesn't respond to my question; he just glances at me in the rear-view mirror. My father ignores me completely as he makes a call. I spin my head to face him, but he just roars orders down the phone. I lean my head back against the headrest. I am to be trapped in this car for twelve hours. Sure, I am trapped in a very pleasant Mercedes, but I have just lost my mother. I have just lost my life as I knew it. No golden cage will improve this situation.

"I don't care how you get it done, just get it done. Connelly has paid you a small fortune for this, and trust me, what Connelly wants, he gets. Don't waste my time and don't phone me again until you have what Connelly asked for." My father angrily presses his thumb against the screen of his phone, stroking his chin in thought.

"Who's Connelly?" I continue asking questions. I'm probably opening a rather large Pandora's Box. My father ignores me yet again.

"You might want to get some sleep, Miss Norman. It's a long car ride." Francis takes the executive decision to change the subject. I'm sure my father was giving him a look in the mirror, silently instructing him to do so.

"A long car ride to where?" I scowl at Francis. He stutters slightly before turning his gaze to my father in the mirror.

"Evelyn, do us a favour. Shut up or sleep." My father finally snaps at me, full of iciness and malice. I stare into his dark brown eyes, which are shaded by his stern, groomed eyebrows. A frown line is forming on his forehead. He isn't old-looking; he is only just past forty. But his permanent glowering has left its mark on his features. Not a single chocolate hair on his head is out of place. And dark stubble rests on his jaw and neck. My father always wears a black designer suit; he is a connoisseur of fashionable business wear. On the days that are too hot for a full suit, he usually wears tailored trousers and a white shirt. He never wears colour. He's a tall man, standing at 6'2, and of a mesomorphic build. He's strong and could easily lift me like I was just a bag of rice. I inherited most of my own physical traits from my mother. My eyes are a sky blue. She always told me they were my best feature. They're striking, especially when compared to my dark brown hair, almost black. I'm slim and relatively short, standing at 5'2. I assume I'm still growing. I hope I am.

Around half an hour later, I am leaning my head against the window and closing my eyes, half asleep, half listening to whatever conversation Francis and my father are having. We're still in London and traffic is heavy.

"Sir, are we stopping anywhere along the way?" Francis asks. I continue to fake my sleep.

"I think that'd be wise. Anywhere suitable should be fine." My father orders. I can just about hear the constant tapping against his phone.

"Sir." Francis accepts the instruction. I like Francis. He isn't overly talkative but he always seems like an ally of mine. One might even say a friend. "Sir, forgive me if I am crossing a line, but it might be worth asking Miss Norman if she needs anything from you."

"What could she possibly need?" The cluelessness in my father's voice wounds me. I am used to it, though. My whole life, he has been cold. Distant.

"Again, pardon my free speech, sir, but she is your daughter. And she has just lost her mother." The more Francis talks, the more I listen. I know what he's implying. He's basically telling my father to stop being an inhuman robot.

"Just focus on getting us there, Francis. I'll speak to Evelyn." My father clears his throat. I sigh, growing bored of faking sleep. With a huff, I leap awake to my father's surprise.

"God, I hate long car rides." I unbuckle my seatbelt before reaching into the boot of the car and opening my favourite backpack. I can hear my father sigh irritably. "Francis, you're clever. Where did I put my wireless headphones?" I reach my hand into the backpack and rest my stomach on the back of the seat, keeping me steady.

"Side pocket, Miss Norman." Francis replies and I can practically hear the smile on his face. I finally find them, stuffed into the side pocket, just like he said. I bounce back onto my seat and buckle myself back in. From my back jeans pocket, I grab my phone. One of the advantages of your father being a bad-tempered secret millionaire is all of the upgraded tech. I scroll and scroll for the perfect song to listen to.

"Evelyn, need I remind you of the dangers of taking your belt off in a moving vehicle?" My father drones as I begin to place my headphones over my ears.

"And need I remind you that my name is not Evelyn? It's Evie." I don't care about my tone. "Besides, Francis is racing ahead at a grand speed of..." I lean forward to check the speedometer. "Oh, wow, 12mph. Trust me, I was fine. Anyway, this is an ironclad way of making sure I shut up." I speak the last sentence with a certain callousness. My father rips the headphones from my head and clutches them in his hands, startling me. I look into his vicious eyes.

"May I make a small suggestion?" He practically foams at the mouth. I scoff derisively at him. "Either you speak to me with a little more respect or you don't speak to me at all. That tone may have been fine with your mother but is it not going to last long with me. And as for your name, Evelyn is the name on your birth certificate. It is the name we gave you, and it is the name I will use. Is any of this in any way unclear?" My father hisses. I can't look at him. I can feel tears accumulate in my eyes. He's always had a way of making me feel so small.

"No." I whisper resentfully. My father drops my headphones onto the middle seat between us. I take them forcefully and wrap them around my ears. My bottom lip trembles as I look at the city outside. Tears fall and I quickly wipe them, not wanting either my father or Francis to see me crying. Crying in front of my father is a big no-no. It is weak. Emotional. Pathetic. My eyes glance at Francis, who is frowning at me, not through anger but through something I haven't really seen in him for a long time. He is frowning in sympathy. Francis squints his eyes briefly, silently asking if I am alright. I nod and continue to look outside. I rest the side of my head against the glass, thinking about everything. I haven't really had time to grieve my mother. Everything happened too fast. From the hospital room to the car, it was like a bullet. However, now, I have nothing but time to finally realise what has happened. And, god, it's hitting me hard. It's hitting me like a punch to the chest. And it all comes out. I sob. I hold my eyes shut and sob. I feel like I'm going to stop breathing. I panic, so many emotions are going through me all at once. I feel the pain of losing her. I feel the shame of crying in front of my father. I feel lost and alone. I feel like my whole world is ending. I am certain my father is going to snap at me with some remark about how feeble I am. But he doesn't. In the corner of my eye, I see him offer me something. I can just about see his hand and in it is a piece of tissue paper. I stare back at him, floored by the gesture. My father doesn't say anything. Instead, he raises his eyebrows, urging me to take the tissue. So I do. I pat it against my soaked cheeks, wiping the streams of tears falling down them as well as my mascara. I fall into a moment of despair, realising I'm going to be crying for hours, maybe even days. Maybe even weeks.

I wake up to a stinging sensation against my cheeks and the feeling of my dried tears. My eyes can barely open. They feel swollen and irritated. But I don't feel the movement of the car. It's a relatively quiet drive anyway, but it almost feels like we've stopped. I finally manage to open my eyes to see if we have stopped. All I see is a crowd of stationary cars. We're in a small car park and the cacophony of a nearby motorway is the only sound. I unlock my phone and check the in-built GPS system. We are somewhere just beyond Birmingham. I must've been asleep for a decent amount of time. I slowly turn my heavy head to the side. Just outside of the car is my father, barking orders down the phone. I can't really hear what he's saying. But it's probably the same old, angry discourse. I take my headphones off and clutch the door handle, desperately needing some fresh air.

My father seems surprised to see me out of the car. I stretch my arms up, looking around me. We're at a services. Even though it is the middle of May, there is a chill in the air. I take a long, deep breath. The last thing I remember before sleeping was practically hyperventilating. Almost choking. I exhale and begin to trek away.

"Evelyn." My father snaps.

"Just going for a walk." I don't face him. I don't even really regard him as I take heavy steps away from the car. My legs feel stiff. They need movement.

"We're leaving in five minutes." My father informs me. I don't reply. I just salute in a gesture of contempt, still not looking at him. Five minutes is enough. I'll take any time I can get. I am desperate to be away from that car. I am desperate to be away from my father. I could run away. I could sprint to a nearby A-road and hitchhike. I have no real love for my father. I have no real want to spend any time with him. In a year and two months, I'm eighteen. And then I'll be able to do what I want. But, for now, I am stuck with him. And, I guess, he's stuck with me.

My father chews his sandwich as he scrolls absentmindedly on his phone. I swear it's like his second brain. The day I see my father go a whole hour without the use of his phone, I'll be impressed. I rarely use mine. I must be the only sixteen-year-old in existence who doesn't really use their phone. I have music and social media but that's it. I haven't really had a chance to say goodbye to any of my friends back in London. I don't know how long we're away for, but it feels pretty permanent. As I scroll through my music app, my phone begins to ring. It's my best friend, Samantha. I briefly glance at my father before answering the call and bringing the phone to my ear.

"Hi, Sam." I speak quietly.

"Evie, where are you?" Sam seems flustered.

"I'm, uh, in a car." I look at my father again, not actually knowing if I'm allowed to talk about the situation. "Look, I don't know when I'll be back. My Mum died…" My voice becomes a weak whisper. My father exhales.

"Evie, I'm so sorry to hear that. If you need anything…" Sam is genuine. She is kind, sympathetic and I could really use a hug from her right now.

"Thanks, Sam. I'll, um, I'll call you when we get to wherever the hell we're going." I nod tearfully, appreciating her friendship.

"Alright, Evie. Speak soon."

"Bye." I close my eyes and end the call, leaning my head back. A sudden realisation hits me. I don't know if I'll ever see Sam again.

"Evelyn." My father pushes his phone into his trouser pocket.

"Yes?" My voice is practically inaudible as I stare out the window.

"Eat your sandwich." He refers to the unopened ham and cheese sandwich lying in the middle seat. The last thing I want right now is food. The thought of eating something makes me want to vomit.

"Thank you, but I'm not hungry in the slightest." I mumble, still watching the cars trail past. I clock eyes with a toddler, sitting in his little car seat. I smile at him and it looks as if he is giggling. I observe the other people in the car. His parents are sitting in the front, laughing and full of merriment. God, I'd sell my soul to the devil to switch places with that toddler. "It wasn't a polite request." My father breaks the hopeful silence. I close my eyes. "Dad, if I eat that sandwich, I will puke. So, unless you want vomit all over these nice, leather seats, it's going uneaten." There is so much scorn in my voice. But today, I'm not scared of him. I am numb to his bullshit. I am numb in general. "Look, I'm not saying that to be difficult. The last thing I want right now is food." I try to settle the situation before he gets a chance to hit me with yet another icy comment. He doesn't respond. He just nods slowly, finally understanding. He's actually accepting a decision I've made. Alert the authorities.

"Do you have any questions?" He asks calmly. It takes me by surprise. He's willing to shed some light on the situation. I look at Francis in the rear-view mirror, seeing if he shares my scepticism. He does, it seems.

"Where are we going?" I place all of the questions I have in a queue in my head.

"Scotland."

"Why?"

"To stay with your aunt."

"Aunt Joan?" For the first time since my mother died, I sound uplifted. I love Joan.

"Mm-hmm." My father collects a bottle of water from the cupholder beside him and sips some slowly. I decide to do the same, retrieving my own bottle of my water from my cupholder. We sip in unison.

"How long for?" I tighten the lid on the bottle once I am done drinking.

"Indefinitely." He puts his own bottle down.

"Are we ever going back to London?" I look down. My father looks at me. I can't see his eyes. He is about to answer me but is interrupted by the familiar chime of his mobile phone. He makes an irritated noise before answering the call.

"What?" He pauses. "Friday?" Another pause. "That's not good enough. I don't want Connelly there." Another pause. "Well, I don't care if it's impossible." He looks at me briefly. "We are moving to Scotland for a reason. Make sure Connelly stays in London." He hangs up.

"I'll take that as a no." I whisper to myself, leaning the side of my head against the window. I cross my arms, practically hugging myself. I feel the tears build. The moment is silent. It's torture.

"Evelyn, look at me." There is an unfamiliar warmth in his voice. I barely recognise it as I gradually turn my gaze to his. "I apologise. But we are never living in London again. Do you understand me?" A frown appears on his face, making me nod. I look back out the window, resting my head on my palm. My other hand chucks the sandwich into the boot. I then rest it on the middle seat, tapping my fingers nervously. A sudden feeling around my hand makes me jump. I look at it. He's holding it. He isn't looking at me but his hand is holding mine. My mouth is agape in blind astonishment. This is the most comforting thing he's done in, well, forever. In a moment of madness, I unbuckle my seatbelt and shuffle towards him, making my way across the wide seats. He looks down at me in confusion as I rest my head against his arm, silently praying that he'll show me some affection. I need it. Today of all days, I need it. After a lingering amount of time, I am about to give up on my quest for fondness. But then his arm moves. He wraps it around me. He's hugging me back. There's no emotion in it at all. And I know he's probably doing it more out of duty than anything else. But still, it's the most comforting thing he's done in my sixteen years. To anyone else, this wouldn't be a shock. But to me, it's a milestone.

"Evelyn, wake up." My father's voice startles me awake. I'm still leaning against him, drowsy and clouded. The car isn't moving. I twist my head up to see my father. This is the closest I have ever been to his face, and I can see his brown eyes in more detail. There is a tiny streak of blue in one of them. I never noticed that before.

"Where are we?" I croak, my voice weak and drained.

"Fort William. I took the liberty of fastening your seatbelt, since you decided to remove it." His snide remark causes me to feel something digging against my neck.

"Oh, so that's why I feel like I'm being strangled." I pull the belt away from my throat and move away from my father. I've been lying against him all the way from Birmingham to Fort William. Poor guy. "Why did you wake me up?" I ask, rubbing the sleep out of my eyes.

"Because I need to leave the car. Stay here, Evelyn." He clutches the handle and leaves the vehicle.

"But I've got to pee." I mutter to myself. I then look ahead. Francis is still in the car with me. I'd love to be a fly on the wall inside his head. He's just witnessed me receive a morsel of affection from Gregory Norman. He's probably going into shock.

"Forgive me for speaking out of turn, Miss Norman…"

"Evie." I roll my eyes.

"Miss Norman." He reiterates firmly. "But that was a lovely sight."

"If you say so. I heard what you said to him earlier. Thanks for trying." I shrug, about to clutch the door handle. "Be right back."

"Miss Norman, your father said to stay…" His voice is muted once I reach the outside of the car and close the door.

I stroll aimlessly stroll through the supermarket, looking for the lavatory. I find it and make my way towards it. If we're in Fort William, that must mean I slept for hours. And it feels like it too. My head is a boulder. Being in Fort William means we're only a couple of hours from my Aunt Joan's. She lives on the Isle of Skye, in a little village called Kyleakin. I've been to her house quite a few times but I haven't been there in years. I adore it. I adore the mountains. I adore the smell of the lochs surrounding the island. I even adore the Scottish.

"I thought I told you to stay in the car." The low, commanding voice of my father fills my ears as I approach the entrance to the public restrooms. I stop and turn my head to see him emerging from the men's.

"I have to pee." I offer him look of mock confusion and continue my journey to the loos.

"Evelyn." He sounds impatient. I roll my eyes. My needs are significantly greater than his right now.

"Dad, seriously, can this wait?" I look at him, almost desperately. It takes him a million years but he finally nods. "Thank you." I hurry away.

When I leave the restrooms, my father's stood there, waiting for me. That's not a surprise. As cold as the man is, he's always been extremely overprotective. There's a solid reason I've never had a boyfriend and that's Gregory Norman. There is an irritated shadow in his eyes as we walk together through the supermarket.

"Evelyn, when I tell you stay in a car, you stay in that car." He begins a reprimand.

"I needed to pee."

"Then you tell me first. Don't just leave, am I clear?"

"Yes." I sigh and look down as I walk. I want to ask him a question but I am so timid around him. I think I've spoken more to him in the last five hours than in the last sixteen years. I need to be braver. "Dad?"

"Hmm."

"You know you said we can never live in London again?" I attempt to begin my question, smothered by shyness.

"Mm-hmm."

"Did you mean forever?"

"I'm not a fortune teller, Evelyn. I don't know where you'll be in five, ten years but while you are living with me, we stay away from London." His response isn't chilly. But it is guarded.

"Is there a particular reason why?" My question causes him to stop walking. Maybe it was a bit too brave. He looks down at me, his eyes narrowed in caution and deep thought.

"There is. But that's something only I need to know. I don't want any more questions about why we're here, understood?" His stare is enough to make me comply.

"Yeah."

"Good." He continues walking, collecting his phone from his pocket and scrolling through it. I grudgingly follow, disappointed in his unwillingness to communicate with me. He's always been secretive. And I still don't actually know what he does for a job. I know it pays well. I'm hoping he tells me everything one day. But I don't see that happening for a while.

"I spy with my little eye, something beginning with... M." I drone, doing anything I can to fill the journey. I lean my head back, waiting patiently for either of them to offer up an answer. My father isn't entertaining the game at all, but is instead, typing on his phone. Francis is staring ahead at the road. "God, you guys are the worst road trip companions."

"Mountains." My father mutters unenthusiastically, not taking his eyes off the screen. He is the last person I would expect to participate in my little activity.

"Lucky guess." I roll my eyes. "Oh, that reminds me. We need to do our Norman tradition." I unbuckle my seatbelt yet again and lean forwards, towards the centre console of the car. I use the touchscreen to connect my phone to the Bluetooth.

"Evelyn Dawn Elizabeth Norman, that's the last time you take off your seatbelt." My father scolds. My eyes widen.

"Oh, shit, he used my full name." I groan as I push myself back into my seat, buckling myself back in. I can see a glimmer of amusement on Francis' face in the mirror.

"And you can axe the colourful language." My father continues. I ignore him as I open the music app on my phone and wait for it to pair with the car. After a second, traditional Celtic music begins to fill the space around us. I snicker happily and gleam at my father, who is trying his hardest to hide a smile.

"Oh, my god." I glare at him in mock horror.

"What?" He asks.

20

"You're smiling." I comment dryly. "Gregory Norman is smiling. Tell the pope!" I yell lightly. Francis chuckles. I giggle until I see my father's face. "Oh, never mind, he's not anymore."

"Evelyn, turn off the music." He instructs, donning his usual cloak of irritation.

"Dad, come on. We used to do this all the time, driving up to Aunt Joan's. The moment we passed Glen Coe, Mum would put the music on, you remember?" I implore him to remember. I implore him to think back to the good times. We have such good memories of this place.

"I won't ask again. And you know I hate repeating myself." His expression is alarming.

"Dad, please."

"Evelyn, I said switch it off!" He practically roars. How Francis hasn't crashed the car, I will never know. I scowl at my father and use my phone to turn the music off.

"You know what? I really hate you." I huff and twist my body, so I am facing the window. The mountains fly by like they're weightless. I was too hopeful. For a brief moment, I thought my father had some humanity. I'll never make that mistake again.

CHAPTER TWO

At around 8pm, we reach Kyleakin. I love it here. It feels like home. I look around at the village. I look at the houses, the loch, the harbour. The Skye bridge. I spot the little ruin of Castle Moil, resting on a hill. I used to climb up there all the time when I was a child. I close my eyes and listen, feeling the almost arctic air bring goosebumps to my skin. I suddenly hear the slamming of the car boot. It shatters all illusion.

My father holds open the door and I walk into Joan's house. The first sound I hear is the excited barking of a Husky. I prepare myself for his attack. The moment I see him, I grin. He rushes to me, barking and wagging his tail. I am propelled backwards, landing on my back as he licks my face.

"Max, get off me!" I giggle, trying to push him away. My father closes the front door behind him once Francis has entered with our suitcases.

"Max, here. Leave Evie alone." The warmest, kindest voice echoes against the walls. I look up as Max rushes back to Aunt Joan. I get to my feet as she opens her arms and I leap into them, closing my eyes and forcing the tears back.

"Hi, Aunt Joan." My voice is merely a whimper.

"Evie, sweetheart. It's so good to see you again." She strokes my back. "Oh, let me look at you." Joan holds my head in her hands, scanning my face. I can't do anything but smile tearfully. "Oh, you're still the prettiest thing in the world."

"Thanks, Aunt Joan." I nod gratefully.

"Gregory." She lets me go and approaches my father, slowly wrapping her arms around him. He returns the hug, completely full of love for his sister. It's bizarre. He's an affectionate man. I know he's capable of it. I've seen him act lovingly towards my mother, and now Aunt Joan. The only person he isn't remotely affectionate towards is me.

"So good to see you, Jo." My father mutters sincerely, still holding my aunt.

"Anything you need, Greg. Anything at all." Joan places a hand against his face and kisses his cheek. "How was the journey up?" She spins to face me.

"Uneventful." My father interjects. I scoff quietly.

"Tea? Coffee?" Joan changes the subject.

"I'd love a coffee, Jo, thanks." My father is different around Joan. He's more casual. More normal.

"And you, Evie?" Joan grins at me.

"Nothing for me, thanks." I shake my head shyly.

"Why don't you go up to your room and get settled in? Do you remember which one it is?" She asks and I nod.

"Come on, Max." I tap my knees and Max joins me as I begin to climb the staircase.

Joan's house is larger than it used to be. She's had an extension built onto the side of it. That was never the case before. There are five bedrooms in total. Two family bathrooms. Her and my father's room have en-suites. Francis is staying with us too and has been given his own bedroom. I look at the photographs hanging on the walls as I reach the upstairs floor. There are so many. Some are from Joan and my father's childhood, standing with my grandparents. My paternal grandparents died before I was born and I never met them. Joan would always tell me what wonderful people they were and how pleasant her and my father's upbringing was. It makes sense. Joan is the kindest person in the world. I am incredibly thankful for her.

As I wander through the upper floor, I pass several doors. Max follows me diligently as I aimlessly stroll through the house. I stop when I pass a certain door, left slightly ajar. I frown and take small steps back, leaning my head back to look inside. It's an office. This wasn't here when I visited last time. I press my hand flat on the door and open it wider, taking cautious steps inside. It all feels very forbidden. I look down at the desk and the laptop resting on it.

"Evie." Joan's voice makes me jump. I spin to face her and she is standing in the doorway. "Sorry, I forgot to lock this door. Come on out." She calmly instructs and I obey, leaving the office. Once I am out, Joan takes a key from her pocket and locks the door.

"Prohibited, understood?"

"What is it?" I ask innocently.

"Your father's office. Don't ever let him catch you in there." Her expression turns serious. I nod. "I've left your bedroom exactly how you had it. That was a few years ago, though, so your tastes may have changed." She leads me to another room. My bedroom. With a beaming smile, Joan opens the door. A wave of nostalgia instantly hits me. There is a double bed, covered in blankets, teddy bears and purple fluffy pillows. A dressing table rests in front of the window and a double-door wardrobe stands against the wall, covered in little photographs. I stroll to the window, looking out to the harbour and the mountains.

"It's perfect." I whisper.

"Come downstairs. I've made us all some dinner." Joan walks away from the bedroom. The thought of food makes me queasy, and I know I'm going to have to repeat the conversation I had with my father earlier. Nevertheless, I appreciate Joan's hospitality. Before leaving the room, I notice a note on the bed. I pick it up.

Evie
You'll be alright. I promise. Anything you need, you need only ask.
All my love
Aunt Joan

With a tear in my eye and a fullness in my heart, I sit on the bed. I sigh, close my eyes and fall back. It's going to be weird staying here without Mum. I don't even know how long we're here for. The lack of certainty troubles me and I hate being kept in the dark.

I pick at my dinner. It looks amazing; a salmon dish. But as lovely as it looks, I can't eat a bite. My father and Joan are having a pleasant discussion, and Francis is sitting with us. I catch his eye now and again, and he offers me a friendly nod. I slouch in my seat, feeling a wave of sombreness. The last time I sat at a dinner table, my mother was alive. She'd cooked for us. That was the last time I ate something.

"Is there something wrong with the salmon, Evie?" Joan asks, bringing a forkful to her mouth. I sink into a feeling of guilt.

"It's not the food. I'm sure it's really nice." I look down, gently stabbing the baby potatoes with my fork.

"Try and eat something, sweetheart. I know it's hard." She regards me with the most affectionate understanding. I look at my father, who is chewing and staring at me. After a long sigh, I pick up a small potato and slowly eat it. Satisfied that I'm actually eating something, my father stops staring. "Your appetite will come back, I promise. And when it does, we'll have a Mexican night. Just like we used to." Joan giggles sentimentally. I remember her little themed dinners. Mexican night. Indian night. Italian night. Joan was the best host.

"Dad, I know it's late but…" My sudden speech makes my father look at me. "After dinner, can I go for a walk? Just to the harbour and back?" I wait for his response.

"No."

"Dad, I just spent twelve hours in a car." I argue softly.

"I said no, Evelyn." My father clears his throat.

"I'll take her, Greg. Max needs to go for a walk anyway." Joan jumps to my aid. I can't help but smile at her camaraderie. My father leans back in his chair, still chewing, clearly full of indecision.

"Harbour and back." He states firmly. I grin, looking at Joan, who offers me a wink.

I pull my denim jacket tighter around my body as we walk. I forgot how cold it is up here, even in the middle of May. Max walks ahead, sniffing anything and everything. Joan walks beside me, her face illuminated by the full moon. It lights up the water beside the harbour. After a moment, Joan stops walking and looks out at the loch.

26

"I thought it'd be nice for us to get some girl time. Some alone time, so we can talk about things." Joan mutters carefully as I stand beside her. "I know this question is ridiculous but how are you?"

"I don't know. I miss her. I still haven't really realised what's happening." I look down, trying to force the tears back. "He won't tell me why we're here. He won't tell me how she died. He won't tell me anything." I shake my head, succumbing to the flood in my eyes.

"Oh, sweetheart. Come here." Joan pulls me into an incredibly affectionate embrace. I sob in her arms, releasing all of my grief. "I hate him, Jo. I hate him."

"No, you don't, Evie. I promise you, you don't." Joan pulls me out of the hug and stares into my eyes. Hers are the same brown as my father's.

"Why is he always so horrible to me? It's like he hates me."

"No, sweetheart. He loves you." She strokes the tears away from my face.

"No, he doesn't."

"Yes, he does." She reiterates, a desperation in her voice. "He doesn't show it awfully well, granted. But he adores you. He lost his wife, Evie. I know the man was never the warmest person, but he is grieving, just like you are. And while you're allowed to be vulnerable, he isn't. He has to stay strong. And that's so difficult." Joan takes my hands, imploring me to consider her words. I understand what she's saying. I know my father is going through the same horrors I am.

"What do I do?" I shrug, visibly clueless.

"Have you ever tried speaking to him? I mean, really speaking to him?"

"Once, I think. He just wanted the conversation to end. I could see it. He was getting really impatient." I roll my eyes.

"Speak to him, Evie. What harm could it do?" Joan is full of wisdom.

"Is that a trick question?" I offer her a look of mock suspicion.

"Evie." Joan chuckles, stroking my face. "Speak to him. He may surprise you."

"Fine. Thank you for letting us stay with you, by the way." I change the subject, hoping to relieve the heaviness in the air.

"My pleasure, sweetheart. Family looks after family. Besides, I've missed you so much. Tomorrow, we'll go for a little drive. Go to Portree, maybe. No Francis. No Gregory. Just you and me. Would you like that?" Joan's offer fills me with elation.

"I'd love that." I nod tearfully.

"We'll leave at ten." She winks at me. Max begins to bark. "Oh, Max, stop your noise, it's late." Joan walks away to sort out the dog. I stay where I am. Thinking. Almost brooding. Maybe I do need to try and understand my father more. I endlessly complain about him but Joan is right, the man is probably struggling with his own grief. Before we leave for Portree, I am going to try and have a conversation with my father.

I'm ready for the day. I'm ready for a pleasant experience with my aunt. I'm showered, clothed. I'm doing my best to look as human as I can. As I sit at the dressing table, I notice my eyes. Deep, dark bags lie beneath them. I didn't really sleep. I'd done nothing but sleep in the car, so I was endlessly tossing and turning. And crying. God, they look irritated. I pluck up my courage. I can do this. I can speak to my father. It shouldn't be difficult. Awkward as hell, but not difficult.

I stroll around the house, looking for him. He's nowhere to be seen. As I approach the kitchen, Joan is making herself a cup of coffee. When she sees me, she smiles.

"Good morning, sweetheart. I've just got to let Max out for a while and then we can make tracks. Have some breakfast." She explains as she stirs the coffee.

"I don't eat breakfast."

"Oh, no, of course you don't. I forgot. Well, there's tea and coffee if you want some."

"Thanks. Have you seen Dad?" Once I ask, Joan pauses for a second.

"In his office. Knock, Evie." She warns.

"I will." I offer her a polite smile and make my way out of the kitchen. He's in the mysterious office. I feel a wave of apprehension.

As I stand before the office door, my heart is beating a thousand times a minute. All I need to do is knock. But it's taking so much time. It's taking so much willpower. I close my eyes and mutter words of encouragement to myself. God, I am so scared. So timid. But I can't be timid. My father doesn't respect timid. I chide myself for being such a wuss and knock thrice on the door. There is a long stretch of silence. The longer it goes on, the more I want to abandon this quest. Maybe this wasn't such a good idea after all. I spin, about to walk away but the door flies open.

"Evelyn." My father sounds surprised. I slowly turn to face him. He is standing in the doorway, keeping the door nearly closed.

"Hi. Um… are you busy?" My fingers fidget.

"When am I not busy?" His rhetorical question irks me.

"I'll rephrase." I can't hide the annoyance in my voice. "Have you got time for a quick talk?" My words are slow and nervous. My father inhales deeply and thoughtfully. He glances back into his office before nodding.

"Not here." He fully emerges from the office, locking the door behind him. "Has Joan told you the rules around my office?" He pockets the key as he follows me down the stairs.

"Trespassers will be shot on sight?" I quip as I reach the bottom step. I laugh to myself before looking back at my father. He isn't amused. "Sorry." My smile disappears.

I stroll tentatively into the kitchen and my father makes a beeline for the coffee machine. I look down at the floor as he switches it on.

"Do you want one?" He glances back at me as he places a mug under the coffee outlet. I suddenly look up and shake my head.

"Have you eaten breakfast?"

"Dad, I haven't eaten breakfast in four years." I mutter as I sit on a counter. The only noise is the whirring of the coffee machine. It's awkward. It's uncomfortable.

"What did you want to talk to me about?" My father gets to brass tacks, putting his hands in his pockets as he faces me. I'm suddenly rendered completely mute. I've rehearsed this little speech in my head several times but now I'm centre stage, I can't find the words.

"Uh…" I stammer and scoff, drowning in hesitation.

"Evelyn, this was your idea. I'm waiting." My father crosses his arms and leans back against the counter, his eyebrow raised. It only makes me feel smaller.

30

"Okay, here goes." I take a deep breath, grabbing whatever confidence I can. "I can talk to you about anything, right? I mean, if I had a problem, I could come to you?" It takes me about forty years to say it but I do. I'm so nervous. I've never been able to talk to my father. Whenever I needed advice, I always went to my mother.

"Of course you can." There is a glimmer of kindness in his eyes. It comes as a shock.

"Okay, good to, uh, good to know." I nod slowly.

"Is there a problem you wish to discuss?" My father takes a sip of his newly-made coffee. His question seems absurd. Of course there are problems I wish to discuss.

"Uh, well, yeah…"

"What is it?"

"Well… when Mum died, you didn't really…" Oh, god, I've lost the words again. I can see a hint of impatience on my father's face. "For fuck's sake, I had it."

"Language, Evelyn." He scolds.

"Shit, sorry. Ah, bollocks. Oh, for…" I close my eyes, telling myself to start again. "Um, okay, so when Mum died, you didn't really seem to… um…"

"Evelyn."

"You didn't really seem to care." I close my eyes tightly, opening one to check his reaction. His expression is a wall. It's a poker face. I then see him frown. "I didn't mean it like that." I hurry to explain. "I just meant that, for the whole car journey, you just seemed really, well… um…"

"I'm losing my patience, Evelyn." That's incredibly clear. I take a deep breath.

"You know what? Screw it. I'm just going to say it." I don't know where this courage has come from. "You don't need to pretend that you're fine all the time. You're not fine and that's okay. Joan told me how difficult this must be for you. And I just want you to know that I'm here, okay? I'm, like, here for you or whatever." I jump off the counter and walk aimlessly around the room, not able to stop the awkward feeling. I can't look at him.

"Evelyn."

"What?" I huff, still turned away from my father.

"Look at me." His voice is a mix of irritation but also concern. I sigh and face him, not really wanting to. "You're right. I'm not fine. My wife of twenty years died. The mother of my child. You're only sixteen years old, you couldn't possibly understand what I'm going through. And I'll be honest, Evelyn, I don't really care if I'm not fine. There's only one thing I care about right now."

"Your job?" I mutter under my breath, full of contempt. My father doesn't immediately respond but he definitely heard it.

"That's honestly what you think?" He seems offended.

"Well, it's hard not to, Dad. You dragged me away from London. I have no friends. No school. No idea why we're here in the first place. And all you've done since Mum died is roar orders down a phone and treat me like…" I don't continue. I was falling into a rabbit hole, spewing words I didn't mean. I was about to put my foot right in my mouth.

"Finish that sentence, Evelyn." He commands. "You want to be able to talk to me, then say exactly what's on your mind." He is almost pressuring me to speak. I don't like it. It's too much pressure.

"Dad…"

"Finish the sentence, Evelyn."

"Alright. You've been treating me like shit. Pardon my Latin." I sigh, shaking my head.

"Is that what you think?" He is still expressionless.

"Yes. Look, I need my Dad. I will never need you more than I need you right now. I need a hug. I need you to fucking tell me that everything is going to be okay. Again, pardon my Latin." I hold my hands up by way of apology. I get ready for the cold, heartless reprimand. But it doesn't come. I wait and wait. Finally, I look at him. He is staring at me in deep thought. He sighs and puts his coffee mug down before taking long, slow steps towards me. I'm a rabbit in headlights. Oh, Christ, is he going to hug me? My father holds out a hand as if he is going to but he stops himself and rests it on my shoulder instead.

"Everything is going to be okay, Evelyn." My father speaks softly. I feel the slightest sense of comfort.

"Thank you." I offer him an awkward smile.

"And I can see that I'm going to need to make a swear jar." He jokes. It catches me off guard. I begin to laugh. Then I hear a sound I haven't heard in a long time. My father chuckles. It's low and quiet.

"Dad, can I ask you a question?" My merriment makes way for something serious.

"Yes." My father turns and makes his way back to his coffee mug. Once he has it, he sips patiently.

"When you told me to turn off the music in the car, was it because of Mum? Did it remind you of her or something?" I look down at my nervous fingers.

"Yes." He answers honestly and freely.

"I'm sorry. That was probably a bit insensitive of me." I nod in understanding.

"It was a bit, but I'll let it slide."

"And I'm... sorry for telling you I hated you." I hate apologising. It makes me want to sink into the floor.

"You're forgiven." He curtly nods. "Look, I need to get back to work. Are you going to be alright?" My father takes another sip.

"Yeah, I'll be fine. Joan is taking me to Portree." I inform him and he nearly spits out his coffee. I frown, floored by his reaction.

"Why?" The irritation in his eyes is back.

"I don't know. She wants to give me a nice day out. What's the problem?" I ask, clearly oblivious. My father slams his mug down. "Dad, what...?" He completely ignores me as he walks out of the room with determination.

"It's not safe, Jo!" My father and Joan are taking part in an incredibly heated discussion in the dining room. I stand outside the door, resting my ear against it. Max sits beside me, watching me as I eavesdrop.

"Gregory, she has just lost her mother! She is sixteen years old! She deserves some fucking happiness." Joan argues. We're going to need a bigger swear jar.

"I know she does, Jo. But listen to me when I tell you it's not safe."

"Why not? When are you going to tell me what's going on?"

"I will. I promise. I just need to sort some things out with Connelly." The mention of my father's elusive boss catches my attention.

"He's in Scotland, isn't he?"

34

"He arrives on Friday. He's invited us to a gathering."

"What kind of gathering?"

"A celebration of the company. We're all invited. You. Me. And Evelyn. He wants to meet her."

"Gregory, you cannot introduce that man to your daughter."

"What choice do I have, Jo? The man has me by a string!" I can hear the distinct sound of my father losing his cool. "He says jump and I have no choice but to ask how high. You think I want Evelyn anywhere near him?"

"You always have a choice, Greg. When it comes to protecting your daughter from the likes of someone like him, you always have a choice!"

"Joan, he is the one thing I can't protect her from." There is a gloominess in my father's voice, like a deep regret. As I listen, Max starts to become wired. He jumps up and leans against my hips. I stumble slightly as his claws scratch at my sides.

"Max, that bloody hurts. Stop." I speak in incredibly hushed tones but he starts barking. "Max! No! Be quiet." I whisper urgently, still pressing my ear against the door. He continues to bark. I am about to speak to him again but the door suddenly flies open. I fall forwards, landing right against my father, who catches me. I slowly look up at him. Oh, god, he's furious.

"I was just, uh, trying to… um…" I genuinely have no excuse for this.

"Evie, how much of that did you hear?" Joan obviously notices my panic.

"All of it?" I grimace, full of guilt and shame. My father lets out a long, angry sigh. He releases my arms and shuts the door.

"Sit down." My father orders firmly. I immediately obey, sitting myself down on one of the dining chairs. Joan sits in the seat next to mine. My father takes a seat directly opposite me. He interlocks his fingers on the table, clearly ruminating what to say. I don't look at him. He's an eagle and I'm a mouse.

"Before we begin, can I get anyone a cup of tea?" Joan offers, trying to warm the chilliness in the air. My father doesn't stop staring at me.

"No, thank you." He snaps calmly.

"Dad, look, I didn't mean to…"

"Evelyn, I think it would wise of you to make the executive decision to not speak."

"Yeah, you're probably right." I sink into my chair.

"I'm rarely not. As you probably know, our conversation, the one you eavesdropped on…" He frowns as he accentuates the word 'eavesdropped'. "It was regarding a man named Connelly. Now, you asked about him in the car. I am not willing to tell you anything about this man. I won't even entertain any questions you have about him, because the less you know about him, the better."

"Greg…" Joan attempts to protest but he silences her with a look.

"Now, as you also probably heard, we are going to a dinner of sorts. Formal. Incredibly exclusive. Connelly will be hosting it at the hotel he's staying in. I'm not happy about it. Not in the slightest, but I think we can be certain that it's not optional." My father chooses his next words carefully. "Evelyn, while we are at this event, you do not leave my side. You do not leave my sight. Am I clear?"

"Yeah." I nod.

"Good. Connelly arrives in Skeabost on Friday. He's staying in the Skeabost House Hotel. That's when and where the event is. Francis will drive us there and back. Now, I am aware you have no evening attire, so I will allow Joan to take you to Portree today to find something. Joan, let Francis drive you both. Don't take your car. Use my AmEx to get anything you need." His expression softens a touch.

"When is Connelly leaving?" Joan re-enters the conversation.

"Tuesday. After he has left Scotland, I will also need to pop back to London." My father answers.

"Why?" I interject. My father hesitates before answering.

"Business. I will be gone for two days. I'll be leaving here Tuesday late morning." There is yet another stern frown above his eyes. "Evelyn, while I am gone, you do not leave this house." He states firmly.

"What? Why?" I grimace in confusion.

"Evelyn…"

"No, Dad, that's not fair. I can't stay stuck in this house for two days." I argue.

"Evelyn, it wasn't a polite request. You will not take one step out of this house until I get back, am I clear?" His fuse is about to blow but I don't care.

"Is it because of this Connelly guy? Are you scared of him or something?" I scoff.

"I said no questions about Connelly." My father stands. "And I think you should revise your tone when you speak to me."

"Fuck my tone." I snap.

"Evelyn…" His eyes burn with fury.

"No, I have lost everything, Dad." I sob. "You don't get to treat me like this."

"I'm your father, Evelyn. This is exactly how I should treat you."

"Even after I've lost my Mum?! Even after losing the most important person in my world? After losing my school, my friends? My whole damn life? My world is falling apart, Dad. So, why can't you just be a human being for once in your fucking life and understand how I feel?!" I stand and rush out of the room.

"Evelyn!" I can hear my father order me to come back but I'm already halfway up the staircase. I throw open my bedroom door and slam it shut behind me. I pace across the room, panting and staring at the floor. That was probably a bad idea. But I don't care. I'm in this situation because of him and his choices. And now I am going to meet Connelly. I kick the mattress and yell angrily. My anger turns into sheer despair as I sit on the edge of my bed and cry into my hands.

CHAPTER THREE

Joan and I are walking through a quaint dress shop in Portree. I
haven't seen my father since my little outburst in the dining room.
Joan hasn't mentioned it. She didn't talk about it at all in the car. I
don't think it needs discussing. I run my hands over the different
dresses but I haven't got the faintest clue what to get. I've never
been overly into fashion and I've always been a bit of a tomboy.
Besides, I've never been to a formal event before. My mother and
father always left me with a nanny when they would go to
business parties. Oh, god I have no idea what to wear. It's a good
job Joan is here to help me.

"Right, I've just had a text from your father." Joan appears next to
me, reading the screen of her mobile. "It's a black tie event. That
means you're going to want a long evening gown, something
black, silver or purple."

"Is he still mad about this morning?" I cross my arms.

"Well, you did say some rather colourful things to him, Evie." She
gazes into my eyes. "Black would be best, I think. It would really
bring out your eyes."

"You know a lot about this." I observe.

"It's all due to my mother. She was such a fashionable woman."
Joan speaks as she rummages through the hangers of dresses. She

collects a black, sleeveless evening gown. She shakes her head and puts it back.

"Joan, just grab any dress. It doesn't matter what I wear." I'm growing bored of being in this shop. I hate shopping for clothes.

"That's where you're wrong, sweetheart. You can tell a lot about a woman by what she wears. And on Friday, we need to send a certain message." She winks.

"What message?"

"Well, I think it would be beneficial to send a message to Connelly, telling him that you are completely off-limits." Joan collects another dress.

"Off-limits?" There is a worried confusion in my tone. Joan puts the dress back and looks at me. She looks concerned.

"Connelly is a dangerous man, Evie. Your father won't answer questions about him but I will. Any question you have. If I know the answer, I'll tell you." Joan collects another dress and peruses it. "He had a thing for your mother. One could even say a slight obsession. Once the man wants something, Evie, he gets it. He has these little obsessions now and again."

"Obsessions?"

"Like I said, the man is dangerous. Deplorable." She puts the dress back. "So, we need to find a dress that tells him to back the fuck off." Joan winks and picks up one final dress. A massive smile spreads across her face. It is a black long-sleeve dress with a mermaid silhouette and a rounded neckline, covered in sparkles. I don't normally enjoy dressing up, but it's gorgeous. "Are you still a size 8?"

"Yeah." I nod.

"Then this is the one." Joan wraps the dress around her arm.

"Isn't it a bit Morticia Addams?" I comment as she makes her way to a jewellery cabinet.

"Not at all, sweetheart."

"Alright, I'll take your word for it." I follow her to the cabinet.

"You won't need a necklace but a nice big pair of earrings will look lovely. We'll need some black heels too. Oh, I'll do your hair for you as well. This is all rather exciting, isn't it?" Joan makes a noise of giddy elation. It warms my heart.

"What are you wearing?" I ask.

"I've got something at home. It rarely gets worn but it'll be perfect for Friday." Joan gestures politely to the shop assistant, who soon joins us. "Could I please have a look at those earrings? The ones with the rubies?" She points an index finger to a pair of Gothic-style drop earrings, covered in red gemstones.

"My birthstone." I think aloud. Joan offers me a smile as the shop assistant unlocks the cabinet and places the earrings in her hand.

"These are perfect. Evie, go and try the dress on for me." She instructs and I take the dress from over her arm. Once I have found the changing rooms and put the dress on, I do a double take as I look in the mirror. I look like her. I look like my mother. She used to always wear gowns like this to business events with my father. She was always the most beautiful woman there.

"Evie, how is it?" Joan asks from beyond the curtain. I open it and invite her in to have a look. The moment she sees me, she places a hand on her heart. "Oh, sweetheart, you look just like…"

"Mum." I state, letting a tear fall. "Maybe this dress isn't the best idea, Joan."

"Why not?"

"Connelly. If I look like Mum, then…" All kinds of unwanted thoughts enter my mind. If he was obsessed with her, then maybe looking like her isn't a great idea.

"Don't you worry, Evie. This dress is perfect. And it's made even more perfect by the fact you look like your mother. She was a beautiful woman. And we all need to remember her in our own way." Joan places a hand on my cheek, wiping the tears away. "Every time I look at you on Friday, I'll see her, and nothing would bring me more joy. I loved your mother, like she was my own sister. We're buying this dress and don't you worry about Connelly. He'll have to fight me before getting his hands on you, and I promise, that is a fight he will not win." Her statement makes me giggle. I look at myself again. I feel a glow of confidence. I feel like my mother, the strongest woman I know. She's with me. And she'll be with me at this party.

Our time in the shop is at an end. Joan passes our purchases to Francis, who stores them in the Mercedes. Once he's put the shopping away, Joan looks at her watch before turning to face me. "Shall we get some lunch?" She suggests. "Hopefully, your appetite has come back."

"Not completely." I confess.

"That's fine. I'd still like to stop somewhere though, just to get you a little something to eat. I don't mean to be rude, sweetheart, but you're looking a little peaky." Joan gently clutches my cheeks and observes my face.

"Thanks for the passive insult." I mutter, my voice distorted and my lips pursed.

"Come on. I know a lovely place." Joan strokes my cheek and walks away, further into the town. I follow. We stroll down a small street, surrounded by little independent shops and cafes. This is one of the reasons I love Skye. There's no mass-produced consumerism. No real capitalism. Life is simple. All of a sudden, Joan stops walking. I look at her face. There is a slight panic in her eyes as she stares ahead. In the distance, a couple of men in suits stand outside a coffee shop. "Evie, go back to the car. Right now."

"Who are they?" My curiosity will be my downfall.

"Come on." Joan gently takes my arm and spins me to face the path we just trekked. I can't help but look back as I am walked to the car. One of the men clocks me before bringing a phone to his ear. I instantly turn my head back to the front.

"Aunt Joan, who are they? Do they work with Dad?" I ask.

"Yes and no. Let's just get you home."

There is an urgency to Joan's movements as she opens the front door to her house. I hate being kept oblivious to stuff like this. But I'm not dumb. I have the power of deduction. And I can confidently deduce that those men were something to do with Connelly. As I walk through the doorway, I am greeted by Max, who welcomes me enthusiastically. Francis gives me the bag of purchases.

"Evie, go and hang the dress up, darling. I'm going to pop out for a moment." Joan approaches the front door.

"Where are you going?"

"Just to get some bits and bobs. Make sure you hang the dress up or it'll wrinkle like an old man." She smiles at me and leaves. I'm left slightly stumped.

I climb the staircase to take the dress to my room, aimlessly scrolling on my phone. As I walk across the landing, I bump into someone. I look up to see my father emerging from his office. He closes the door.

"Sorry." I mutter shyly. My father just clears his throat. I offer him a smile of genuine regret before continuing towards my room, stowing my phone in my jeans pocket.

"Did you get a dress?" Once I hear his voice, I stop and spin to face him.

"No. We went to a fancy dress shop. I'm going as a nun." I attempt some humour. I can't tell if he's amused or not. When he doesn't respond, I raise my brows and head back to my room.

"Evelyn." Once again, I am stopped. I roll my eyes and look at him once more. "We should discuss what you said this morning."

"Do we have to?" I can't hide the reluctance in my tone.

"Yes. Living room. Ten minutes." My father goes back into his office, closing the door behind him.

"Whoopee." I drone and drag myself to my bedroom. Once I am there, I open the wardrobe and take the dress out of its covering. I smile as I hang it up neatly, making sure there are no little specks of fabric out of place. It'll be my own personal battle dress. It's my armour against the evils of the world. On Friday, I will wear it with pride.

The walk to the living room is full of anxiety. I'm not scared but I would rather walk through a pit of lava than have this conversation. I need to think of some things to say. I try to remember what I actually said in the dining room this morning. It was something along the lines of 'Dad, you're an inhuman monster'. I think that was the general gist of it. And I have no excuses for it. I am not happy about him being a cold, heartless robot but I definitely shouldn't have said that to his face. I groan

44

audibly before opening the living room door. When I open it, I see him, sat on a sofa, scrolling through his phone.

"Take a seat." He doesn't look at me but he taps the seat next to him.

"Did you know that looking at a phone screen for too long makes you go blind?" I close the door and make my way to the spot beside him, sitting down so slowly. I wait and wait for him to regard me. I smile awkwardly, looking around the room. My father finally tucks his phone into his trouser pocket. He then clears his throat and looks ahead.

"Now, Evelyn, why are we sat in this room together?" Oh, yay, rhetorical questions.

"My foot *in* mouth disease?" I lean back, commenting dryly.

"Something like that, yes. But before we begin…" He reaches to the side of the sofa and collects something. When I see it, I stifle a laugh. It's a glass jar. "I believe you swore at me four times this morning."

"Actually, it was seven times. Five in the kitchen. Two in the dining room." I nod slowly. "By the way, I don't have cash. Do you take contactless?" I do all I can to bring some humour to the situation.

"In that case, may I suggest you either abstain from swearing or find yourself a cash point and start paying up?" My father raises a brow and puts the jar down.

"Whatever." I sink into my seat.

"Look, Evelyn, I am very aware that you are not happy. Your mother has died. You had to leave a home you've lived in all your life. But believe me when I say that I am not happy either. Now,

I'm hopeful that's human enough for you." My father frowns at me, clearly still wounded by my words.

"Dad, we really don't need to have this conversation." I cross my arms and pray that the floor opens up.

"I disagree."

"Oh, yay." I mumble sarcastically.

"I understand how you feel. Believe me, I do. And I am trying my hardest to make sure you are happy here. But you have to understand, Evelyn, that we are not in the best of circumstances right now." He leans back. "I'm not willing to answer any questions about my occupation. All you need to know is that it pays incredibly well, it is flexible and I'm my own boss, of sorts."

"I thought Connelly was your boss." I frown.

"He's more of a client than a boss. I do still work for myself." I'm surprised he answered my question. "For reasons you will never know, my job is risky. And that's all I'm willing to disclose about what I do."

"Can I ask…?"

"No."

"But, Dad…"

"No."

"Fine." I slouch in my seat.

"I apologise, Evelyn, if you think I've been cold. But I'm your father. My job is to teach you and keep you safe. It is not my job to be your best friend." His words wound me. I feel the familiar sting in my eyes as I well up.

"Mum didn't feel the same way." I mumble.

"I am not your mother." My father remarks. "She was a wonderful person, full of warmth. I can't give that to you. I will never be anything like your mother. And I apologise." He seems genuinely regretful. I quickly wipe my tears away.

"It's fine." I shrug, pretending I'm okay. I'm trying my hardest to hide how upset I am about this. But my father sees everything. He doesn't necessarily respond to it but he definitely sees it. "When's her funeral?"

"A week Monday."

"Where?"

"London. You'll fly with me and Joan. We'll stay in a hotel the night before, go to the funeral and then come back." He states, full of mourning.

"Okay." I am nearly inaudible. I sniffle and wipe another tear, not wanting to cry in front of my father.

"You're allowed to cry, Evelyn." He looks at me, but I can't look at him. I just stare ahead, wiping the rivers coming out of my eyes. But there's no offer of a consoling hug. No warmth. No affection.

"How was your trip to Portree?" My father changes the subject.

"Uneventful." I still don't look at him.

"Have you eaten?"

"No. We were going to but then…" I stop talking, not knowing if I should tell him about the suspicious men in Portree.

"But then what?" He pushes the topic.

"We just couldn't find anywhere to go." I lie, offering him a false smile.

"Where's Joan?" He asks and I just lift my shoulders. He looks uneasy.

"Look, while I've thoroughly enjoyed this little lecture, can I please leave now?"

"Only if it's to go and eat something. You look awful." He frowns and cups my chin with his hand, assessing my face.

"You know, you're the second person to tell me that today." I raise my brows at him as he continues to notice my paleness.

"Well, maybe you should take the hint and eat something." He glares into my eyes. "Evelyn, you need to eat some food. You've lost weight. And I bet you any money I can feel your ribs." He gently pokes at my ribs to assess them. I involuntarily giggle at the feeling.

"Bugger off. That tickles." I jerk away from him. "Look, will you please just get off my back about the whole eating thing? The more you pester me to eat, the less I will." I hold my hands up. He's starting to sound like broken record.

"I will pester you about it as much as I like because I don't want my only child to starve. I'll go and make you a sandwich." My father stands.

"No, Dad, honestly, I don't want one."

"Tough." He opens the door and leaves the room.

"Honestly, just half a slice of toast is fine!" I yell and wait for his response. "Dad, I promise it will be a waste of bread! And with the current cost of living crisis, I don't think it's wise to waste food! Think of the children in Africa, Dad!"

"You're having a sandwich, Evelyn!" I can hear his distant booming voice.

"Okay, just don't use any fillings! Or butter! Or bread!"

It is late afternoon and I've been given permission to walk along the harbourside on my own. I have decided to take Max for a walk. He is a good excuse for whenever I want to leave the house. As I watch him walk ahead of me, I find myself thinking.

My father confessed that he will never be like my mother. In all honesty, nobody ever will. She was the epitome of kindness. She was such a light in my darkness. Whenever I had a nightmare, whenever I was scared, she was there. After a bad day at school, she would be so ready to make the day better. Whenever I was sad, she would sing me a song from my favourite Disney movie. My father will never be as affectionate as she was, but he is slowly changing. He's letting his guard down more and more. He's even sharing a joke or two. I'm blindly optimistic that this is just the beginning of a transformation.

After roughly ten minutes, I am standing at the harbour, watching the boats as they rock. Max is absentmindedly sniffing. I look at the house, noticing how pleasant it looks from the outside. I suddenly shiver, feeling the chill in the air.

"Come on, Max." I pull his lead slightly and he approaches me. I'm ready to go home.

"Oh, shit, look out!" A young male Scottish voice shrieks at me before a bike passes at an alarming speed. I gasp and stumble back, falling right into the harbour, letting go of Max's lead. I scream before I feel the stab of cold water against my back. I feel winded. I choke. I scramble to reach the surface. I can hear distant, muffled barking as Max does his best to reach me. Once I breach the surface of the water, I flail my arms around in panic, gasping and panting.

"Fuck, this is so bloody cold!" I cough and splutter. That's another one for the swear jar.

"Oh, my god, let me help you." That same male voice appears beside me. He is kneeling on the nearby slipway. Max is still barking. Thank god my mother taught me how to swim. I breaststroke to the slipway, trying to ignore the harsh temperature of the water. Once I get to the slipway, the boy helps me out.

"Well… that's one way to… wake up." I can't stop shivering. The boy stands in front of me, looking into my eyes.

"Are you alright, lass?" His Scottish brogue feels welcoming and reassuring. I look at him. He's my age, with dark green eyes and hazel hair.

"Are you insane?!" I shout harshly at him. "Who rides a bike at a million miles per hour that close to a bloody harbour?"

"Sorry, I didn't see you." The boy shakes his head desperately, trying his hardest to apologise for his actions. I scoff and hug myself with my arms. I need to get warm. I begin to walk away but he follows. "Hey, what's your name?"

"Piss off." I snap.

"That's an odd name." He quips. I stop walking and glare at him.

"Evie. Come on, Max. Let's go home." I whistle and Max walks at my side as I continue towards the house.

"I'm Noah, by the way." The boy still follows me.

"Did you lose your ark?" I am in no mood to be pleasant. Noah laughs quietly.

"Oh, you think you're the first to make that joke?" He won't leave me alone. I stop walking again and turn to face him, a mask of indignation on my face.

"Look, Noah, as much as I'd love to get to know you, I am freezing and wet and I want to go home. So get on your rocket bike and leave me alone." I huff and continue to walk. Noah finally decides not to follow me. Before I decide to reach the house, I take out my phone from my jeans pocket, praying to all the gods it still works. It's waterproof, so I would hope so. My fingers shake as I access my contacts. After pressing the call button, I bring it to my ear.

"Evie? Everything okay?" Joan answers.

"Don't ask why, but please get a towel for when I walk in."

Once I walk into the house, there is a flurry of urgency in the air. Max walks ahead of me while I shut the door.

"Evie!" Joan shouts lightly as she enters the hallway. She rushes to me with a towel and wraps it around me.

"Water looked so refreshing so I went for a swim." I quip.

"Tell me what happened." Joan rubs my arms in an attempt to warm me up.

"Some kid with a murderous vendetta. It was an accident. He was on his bike and rode past me. I stumbled back and fell in." I offer her the truth. Joan stifles a smile. I smile back before sneezing.

"Yes, well, you better go and get dry before your father…"

"What the hell happened to you?" The familiar sound of my father's voice fills the house. My eyes widen before I look up at the staircase. He is walking down it, staring at me with a look of confusion, anger and bewilderment.

"Like I said, fancied a swim." I sneeze. "I'm getting changed and then I'm going to crawl into a hole and die. Please do excuse me." My voice is muffled by my new nasal congestion. I sneeze again and pass my father. I can hear Joan giggle softly. I'm going to get a cold. I just know I am. Right as we're supposed to meet my father's ominous client. Maybe we can use it as an excuse for my non-attendance. Maybe there is one massive silver lining to falling into what feels like sub-zero temperatures.

CHAPTER FOUR

Thursday

I haven't stopped sneezing. It's been nearly twenty-four hours since my swim. Joan has me tucked into bed, surrounded by pillows and medicines. I am pretty much bedbound. I am still cold, but also incredibly warm. I'm having cold sweats. I haven't seen my father since I fell into the harbour. I don't think he really knows what to say or do. But Joan has been my nurse, checking on me as much as she can. She's made me soups and sandwiches, but they've pretty much gone uneaten. If I didn't have an appetite before, I definitely don't now.

I am lying in bed, scrolling through my phone. It's the only activity I have while stuck in this room, trying to get well. I need a comforting voice in my ear. I need someone to make me laugh. So I call Sam. I bring the phone to my ear and wait for her to answer. It's after 3pm, so she shouldn't be at school.

"Hey, Evie." Her sweet, warm voice fills my ear.

"Hi, Sam. Sorry I didn't call you the other day." My voice is still a phlegmy mumble.

"Oh, that's okay. I assumed you were busy." Sam responds with her usual understanding. I cough weakly, covering my mouth.

"Are you ill?"

"I've got a cold. The perks of Scotland." I do my best to be funny.

"That's where you are?"

"We're staying with my aunt in a place called Kyleakin. It's on the Isle of Skye, right in the Inner Hebrides." I explain, clearing my throat and still sniffing.

"That's really far. Are you coming back to London?" Her question causes me to feel that familiar disappointment.

"No. Dad said we're not. But I'll try and visit." I've no idea how I will. I'm not even allowed out of the house while my father is away.

"I think my parents would happily pay for a flight, Evie. I'll ask them. And you can stay with me for the weekend. Maybe in a couple of weeks or something?" She sounds so excited by the idea.

"Maybe. I'll have to ask Dad. How are things at school?" I decide to initiate a slightly more casual conversation.

"They're good. We're rehearsing for the Summer show at the moment. Miss Perkins has given your slot to Olivia. She's singing the same song you were going to." This information makes me slightly jealous.

"My song? What a bitch. At least I can play a bloody instrument. She's probably just using a backing track." That's going to ruin my whole week.

"Yeah, I think she is."

"The disrespect." I mutter, making Sam giggle. "Are you still doing your dance?"

"I am. I've got my outfit ready and everything. Do you reckon you'll be able to come and watch the show?" There is so much hope in her voice.

"And listen to Olivia Harris butcher the song I was going to sing? I'll pass." I cough into my hand again. "No, I'd love to come and watch it."

"Good. I miss you, Evie. And if you need me, I'm only on the other end of the phone, okay? We can even do a FaceTime." She offers.

"That sounds good." There is a sudden knock on the door. It makes me jump. "Look, I have to go. I'll call you soon, okay?"

"Okay, Evie. I'll talk to my parents about that weekend." I can hear her smile.

"And I'll talk to my Dad. Bye." I end the call. "Come in." I holler quietly to whoever knocked. As the door opens, I expect Joan to walk in. Or even Francis. But it isn't either of them. It's my father. He's carrying a bowl of something.

"You'll talk to me about what?" My father sits on the edge of my bed, raising a brow at me.

"Oh, I see I got my eavesdropping prowess from you." I'm getting braver with my retorts. I shuffle so that I am sitting up, feeling incredibly weak.

"I've brought you some soup. Joan told me you're still not eating. So I'm here to make sure you do." He offers me the bowl. I hesitantly take it.

"One day, you'll actually come and see me because you want to, not because of some mission to make me eat food." I take the spoon and eat a bit of soup. It's tasty but my body is fighting it. I sneer and put the bowl down onto my lap.

"No. Eat the soup." My father lifts the bowl in my hand, instructing me to eat more.

"Ja, Herr Kommandant." I put on my best German impression and bring the tiniest bit of soup to my mouth. My father gives me a scolding look and rests the back of his hand on my forehead to check my temperature. It's nice to know he cares, I guess.

"You're still a bit warm." He comments and collects something from his pocket. It's a little thermometer. He places it near my mouth and I open it slightly. My father then rests the thermometer in my mouth. I am so confused.

"Since when did you become Florence Nightingale?" I frown in blind bewilderment, my voice distorted by the thermometer.

"Evelyn, I am trying to get you back to full health. And I'd appreciate it if you didn't throw me a sarcastic comment every two minutes." He reprimands. I'm obviously getting too brave.

"Sorry." I look down. My father takes the thermometer out and reads it.

"You've got a fever. And you've inherited that behaviour from your mother. She was always the worst patient whenever she was ill." My father has a look of reminiscence in his eyes. I smile whenever he talks about her. It means he's opening up. "Who were you on the phone to?" The interrogation continues.

"Sam."

"How is she?"

"She's fine. They're getting ready for the Summer show. Some girl at school is singing the song I was going to. The backstabbing bitch." I mutter under my breath.

"Evelyn." My father frowns at me.

"Sorry but I'm bloody miffed about it." I put the bowl on the bedside table. I see the look on my father's face. "I can't eat any more." I shrug and he nods.

"What did you need to talk to me about?" He persists. I feel nervous.

"Well, there's not much point because you're just going to say no anyway." I cross my arms. He gives me an impatient look and clears his throat. "She's going to ask her parents if I can stay at hers in London for a weekend, maybe in a couple of weeks. She's going to see if they can pay for a flight." I speak rather quickly, wanting to get it out as quick as possible.

"No."

"I thought as much." I roll my eyes.

"No, they will not be paying for your flight. Because you'll be using the jet." My father stares at me impassively. I frown, completely perplexed.

"Wait, you're letting me go to London?" I can't hide the hope in my voice.

"I am not a monster, Evelyn. Samantha is your best friend. If you want to spend a weekend with your friend, I will allow it. There will be a million rules that you *will* follow." He scowls at me. It doesn't deter the beaming smile on my face. "But I understand how important Sam's friendship is to you. So, yes, I will let you go to London." He is so quiet. So calm. The air is so relaxed.

"Thank you!" I lunge out of bed and hug him, taking him by surprise and making him stumble back a touch. He very hesitantly wraps his arms around me.

"Just tell me when you're planning to go and I'll get the jet ready for us both." His sudden statement makes me pull out of the hug and stare at him.

"I can't go alone?"

"Absolutely not, you're sixteen years old. If you think I'll let you go to London on your own, then you're in dire need of some psychological help." He raises a brow, a stern look in his eyes. "Besides, sixteen-year-olds aren't allowed to fly without an adult."

"Not even on your jet?"

"No."

"I knew there was a catch." I mutter.

"I'll ring Samantha's parents. Now, get back into bed." My father instructs. I climb back under the covers as he stands up, collecting my half-eaten bowl of soup.

"Dad?"

"Mm-hmm."

"Am I still going to this dinner tomorrow?" There is clearly some reluctance on my father's face after I ask the question. He sighs loudly.

"We'll see how you feel. I would rather you didn't." My father thinks aloud.

"But what Connelly wants, he gets, right?" I ask rhetorically, looking down at my fingers, resting on my lap. I worry that I've put my foot in my mouth again, especially when my father doesn't respond. Instead, he puts the bowl back on the bedside table and sits with me once more.

"Listen to me, Evelyn. Nothing will happen with Connelly. I don't know what Joan has told you but he will not hurt you. I won't let him." My father states firmly.

"But you said so yourself, he's the one thing you can't protect me from." I continue to look down.

"Then I'll die trying." His moving statement makes me look into his eyes, full of solemn surprise. I ponder his words as he collects the bowl and begins to leave the room. Before he gets to the door, he stops and stands for a moment, looking ahead. Surprisingly, he turns and approaches me again. He leans down and kisses my forehead. "Get some sleep." My father gives me a commanding look.

"Ja, Herr Kommandant." I nod as he turns away.

"Evelyn." He scolds.

"Sorry." I mutter as he closes the door behind him. I can't do anything but smile. He's changing. Kissing my forehead before I slept was something my mother would always do. He never did. That's the first time he's ever kissed my forehead. I wrap myself in this feeling. It's euphoric.

I grow bored of the clamminess of my bedroom. So I decide to get out of bed. I have a shower, hoping it will cleanse away some of my illness. It does and I already feel a lot better. I change into a tank top and baggy jogging bottoms before hesitantly opening my bedroom door. Max is lying on the landing outside of my room so I crouch down to give him some love. That's when I see the door open. The office door. I assume he's left it open because he thinks I'm too indisposed to leave the bedroom. I battle with my curiosity. I battle with the endless desire to snoop around things I shouldn't. I open my ears as I stand straight. I can't hear anyone or anything. Oh, god, I really shouldn't do this.

I reprimand myself as I cautiously take silent steps towards the office door. With my ears still on high alert, I push on it to open it wider. I feel like I'm entering some forbidden kingdom. Some secret realm. But it all looks relatively normal. There is a laptop, a desk, some filing cabinets. On the wall is a bookshelf of sorts. I run my hand over the different books. Some old stories. Some more modern. I smile when I see a copy of *The Secret Garden*. My mother used to read this to me all the time. I flick the pages, loving the smell of the paper. But once I get to the middle of the book, I drop it in horror. Nestled in the paper is a handgun. I frown and look at the bookshelf again. I take out another book. *Great Expectations*. Again, there is a pistol resting inside. I check another. And another. And another. Every book has a gun. My heartbeat quickens. I shake my head. I shouldn't be in here. Oh, god, I really shouldn't be in here. I suddenly hear footsteps. "Oh, fuck." I whisper to myself as I approach the door. My father is walking up the staircase. I can't do anything but freeze and panic. But once he gets halfway, he stops and looks down at someone downstairs.

"Gregory, if she still has a temperature tomorrow, we should tell Connelly not to expect her." Joan's distraction gives me a solid chance to escape. Thank god for Joan Norman. I silently emerge from the office, praying my father doesn't look up. I tip-toe to my bedroom. Once I am there, I rush inside and close the door.

I scramble back into bed, making it seem as if I haven't moved. As I lie under the covers and stare at the ceiling, my mind is chaos. Why would he have guns? I'm panting. I can't catch my breath. The adrenaline rushing through my body is making me feel like I'm covered in ants. Either that or I'm still ill. Once I hear the door of his office close, I rest my hand on my forehead and suddenly feel my damp hair. Shit. I can't pretend I've been in bed the whole time. It's obvious I've been to the family bathroom. Think, Evie, think. Find an angle. Oh, god. The book. *The Secret*

Garden. I left it on the floor. Opened. Right on the page with the gun. Oh, god. I can't stop panicking. I'm fretting. I'm nervous. I hear a knock on my door.

"Come in." I appear as casual as I can. My father walks in, carrying a glass of orange juice. I offer him the calmest smile I can manage.

"You've had a shower." He observes.

"Yeah. I felt all… clammy." I sit up, praying that my breaths slow down. My father sits on the edge of my bed. He holds out the glass of orange juice and I take it. He doesn't seem suspicious. But he's been in his office. I know he has. I heard the door close.

"You seem nervous." Oh, god, he knows. Now I can either lie and hope he doesn't notice or tell him the truth.

"I'm fine. I guess I'm just worried about tomorrow." I go for the first option. My father's expression doesn't change. He's stoic. Completely indifferent.

"Yes, I imagine you are." He strokes his chin as I sip some orange juice. "Evelyn, you wouldn't ever lie to me, would you?" Oh, god, he bloody knows.

"About what?" I shrug and drink some more.

"About anything."

"Of course not." I shake my head. There is an interval of silence. My father takes an incredibly long breath. He knows. He's acting so weird.

"Good. I should hope not." I think he's trying to trap me. "Joan has said that if you still have a temperature tomorrow, you will stay here while we go to Skeabost."

"I know." I blurt out. Oh, wait, I shouldn't know that.

"How do you know that?"

"Oh, I could hear you talking on the stairs, that's all." I say a bit too quickly.

"Evelyn Dawn Elizabeth Norman, why are you lying to me?"

"Dad, I'm not."

"Evelyn, I am going to give you one more chance to tell me the truth." His eyes are growing so angry. I'm so deep in this rabbit hole that it's going to be impossible to get out. I know he knows. He's just waiting for me to stop lying and admit what I did. It's all a psychological tactic. He's done it before.

"Dad, look, I didn't mean to go in there, I swear." I drop all my defences and admit the truth.

"Did you mean to open this?" He reaches into his suit jacket and retrieves a book. I know which one immediately. "Tell me, Evelyn, did you see anything you shouldn't have?"

"Dad..."

"What did you see, Evelyn?" He is starting to seethe. I'm taking a very long time to respond. I'm taking too long. "Tell me, Evelyn!"

"Guns." I whimper, full of terror. My father opens the book to the middle page. The gun is missing.

"You saw guns." He mutters pensively. "Might I suggest, Evelyn, that you unsee the things you saw in that room? You will never speak of them again. And if I ever catch you going into that office again, you can kiss this trip to London goodbye. You can kiss ever seeing your friends again goodbye. You can kiss any and all freedom goodbye. Is this in any way unclear?" His voice is menacing. It's sinister and shakes me to my core. I tearfully shake my head. "Good." My father slams the book shut and stands up. I flinch. He approaches the door. "And don't you ever lie to me again." He throws the door closed behind him. I jump. I'm rendered completely speechless. My father has never scared me before. But I'm terrified. That was unpleasant, to say the least. I put the orange juice on the bedside table. I crumble into pieces. I sob, suddenly feeling a new fear. I am fearful of my father. Never in my life have I ever been scared of either of my parents. But I believe him when he says I will never see Sam again. I believe him when he says I will never see any freedom again. I make myself a promise. No more snooping. No more curiosity. I thought he was changing. I thought he was becoming more human. But he never will. I know that now. The realisation hits me like a tonne of bricks. Gregory Norman is a dangerous man. I still don't know what he does. But whatever it is, it's violent. It's maybe even criminal. Finding the guns in that room opened a lot of doors in my mind. I'm not stupid. I can put the puzzle together. Pays well. Flexible. Works for himself. Maybe he's a crime boss. Maybe he's mafia. Whatever it is, I will never lie to him again.

I have joined Joan and my father at the dining table. It's the evening before the mysterious dinner party. My father doesn't even regard me as we sit together. I am poking aimlessly at the chicken on my plate. Again, it looks delicious but I am so full of anxiety that anything I eat will come straight back out again. I don't look at Joan. I don't look at anything but the table.

"Are you okay, Evie?" Joan's voice makes me jump. I'm so skittish. I bring my gaze up to see her, and she is wearing a questioning frown.

"Yeah, I'm fine."

"You're shaking like a leaf." Joan comments. I look down at my hands. She's not wrong. My father finally looks at me. The moment his eyes find mine, I look down again. I'm nearly in tears. "Evie, what's happened?"

"I think it would be beneficial for us to go over the rules of the house again." My father brings a glass of red wine to his lips. Joan stares at him.

"Evie, what did you do?" There is evident fear in her voice.

"Nothing. I just…" My voice is barely noticeable.

"Evelyn went snooping, didn't you, Evelyn?" He is acting so ominously. "So, I merely reminded her of the consequences certain actions would have."

"She went into the office." The penny drops for Joan.

"Yes." My father stares down at me. I feel an inch tall. "And I think we can be confident that Evelyn will not make that same mistake again." His brown eyes don't leave my face. "Can I, Evelyn? Can I be confident you won't make that same mistake again?"

"Dad, just leave me alone." I quickly wipe the tears from my eyes. His expression softens in the tiniest way. "I'm really not hungry. Can I leave?" I look at him in pleading. He nods. The moment he does, I stand and walk out of the room, starting to sob. I'm becoming an expert at crying and rushing to my bedroom.

I slam my bedroom door shut and fall onto the bed, releasing all of my anguish, fear, anger and sadness. My cries are muffled as my face is buried in a fluffy pillow. It isn't long before there is a knock on the door. I know it's not my father. He would never try to have a restorative conversation. I know it's Joan.

"Leave me alone, Joan." I continue to sob. The door opens and I feel someone sitting on the bed with me. I then feel a soothing hand on my back.

"Sweetheart." Her voice is honey. I sit up and hurry into her arms, needing the affection. Needing the feeling of safety. "Oh, my sweetheart."

"I'm so scared of him, Jo." I speak beneath my tears.

"He will never hurt you, Evie." Joan holds my head in her hands. "That man will never hurt you. He's just scared. He's scared of a lot of things. What you found in that room, he never wanted you to find. He's not even angry at you."

"Oh, come on. Of course he is."

"No, he's not. He's angry at himself. He's angry that you had to see it." She sighs and takes my hands. "Your father is an extremely complex man, Evie. But for him, the most important thing in the world is keeping you safe. And sometimes, to keep you safe, he has to be a wall. Remember what I told you; he is not allowed to be vulnerable. Well, situations like today make him vulnerable. You make him vulnerable." Joan speaks so wisely.

"All he wants to do is protect you. Not just from people like Connelly, but from what he does. By now, I assume you've done some thinking about your father's job. He doesn't want you to know the truth. And by finding that room, there was an element of that truth coming out. He panicked."

"Still doesn't give him the right to be an asshole." I wipe my eyes.

"I'll tell him you said that, shall I?" She quips.

"You may as well. I'm in enough shit as it is."

"Look, once this dinner is over tomorrow, you'll see a different man. He's just so anxious about it. And, yes, he is letting that anxiety get the better of him. But this will pass. For now, don't mention today again."

"What if he mentions it?" I frown.

"He won't. He knows it's counterproductive. But I think you should probably steer clear of your father until tomorrow afternoon. Like I said, he's anxious about it and every time he sees you, he is weaker. And tomorrow, he needs to be strong." Joan kisses my head and stands up.

"Thank you, Jo." I whisper sincerely.

"Anything you need, Evie, I'm right here." She winks at me and leaves the room. Her words are true and she's right. I need to steer clear of my father until this dinner. I piss him off. Emotions run high. But tomorrow, emotions need to run low. In roughly twenty-four hours, it will be over. It will all be over. I think.

CHAPTER FIVE

Friday

The dinner is in a couple of hours. I'm full of fear, apprehension and a tiny bit of excitement. I should be terrified of meeting my father's client but there is a dark curiosity within me. It's something I've always had. And we found that out the hard way through my little spy mission yesterday. I'm getting out of the house. I'm learning more about my father's job. It's all quite thrilling. I look at myself in the mirror. Joan has styled my hair into an elegant bun, letting little strands of hair fall neatly down the sides of my face. The dress hugs my body in all the best ways. My father is right, though. I've lost weight. But the elegant, understated make-up on my face hides any paleness. I feel mature. I'm not quite the picture of health yet, but just enough to make this evening possible.

The atmosphere downstairs is a mix of caution and haste. I try not to fall down the stairs in these heels. They're not particularly high but I'm not used to wearing shoes like these. I can hear the distant, muffled voice of my father speaking to Joan in the kitchen. I follow the sound. When I get there, my father is sipping a glass of red wine. He is clad in a black tuxedo, with a straight jetted pocket. There is a black bowtie around his neck. He is the picture of decorum. I then turn my head to look at Joan, who is wearing a dark red, shoulder-less evening gown. Her hair falls into styled waves down her shoulders. Around her neck is a diamond and ruby necklace. It matches my earrings. She's stunning. When she sees me, it almost looks as if she will cry. "Evie." Joan whispers in delighted shock, holding a hand over her heart. I click my fingers on both hands, resembling the Addams Family theme. "Evie, you do not look like Morticia Addams." She scolds humorously, making me giggle. "You look so beautiful." Joan stands in front of me and strokes a strand of hair that falls by my face.

"Thanks, Joan." I smile before looking at my father. He doesn't look pleased but he also doesn't look disappointed. He's just looking at me with a pain in his eyes. Oh, god, I know why. I look like Mum. I look at the floor, feeling an overwhelming sense of guilt. I shouldn't have worn this dress.

"We should get moving." My father walks past me, his voice cold and guarded.

"Gregory." Joan stops him. "Don't you have anything to say to Evie?" She scoffs, displeased with his lack of regard for me. My father just stares at me.

"No, he's right. Let's go." I can't hide the disappointment in my voice as I brush past my father, nearly hitting him with my shoulder. I hear him sigh as I make a beeline for the door. There is clearly still some animosity over what I did yesterday.

Joan and I sit in the back of the Mercedes while my father sits beside Francis, who is driving us to Skeabost. There is quiet classical music emanating from the speakers.

"Evelyn, before we arrive at Skeabost, there are some rules I would like to go through with you." My father doesn't look at me while he speaks. "During the entire course of the evening, you will stay with me. If you need the bathroom, inform me and I will walk you there. You do not speak unless you are spoken to. You do not ask questions. You do not say or do anything out of line. And no swearing under any circumstances. Am I clear?"

"Ja, Herr..." I lean my head back, about make the same old quip. But a look of warning from my father immediately changes my mind. "Yes."

"Good." He once again faces the front. "The event is a dinner, as you know. I am aware your appetite is still weak, but I will encourage you to eat whatever you can. Do you have any questions for me?" There is a cold formality in his voice. I assume he's getting into character for when he sees Connelly.

"Can I drink alcohol?" I begin my questions.

"Absolutely not."

"What do I say if someone asks about our situation?"

"You look at me. I will answer the question. On second thoughts, any time you are spoken to, look at me. And I will decide whether or not to answer for you."

"How many people will there be?"

"Roughly fifteen." My father takes his phone out of his pocket and starts typing. "Other clients mostly. Some family of Connelly."

"Will he talk to me?" I'm suddenly petrified.

"I imagine so." He sounds almost defeated as he brings his phone to his ear and waits. "Yes. We're on our way. We should..."

"Dad, I'm scared." I whisper, interrupting his phone call. My father instantly takes the phone away from his ear and looks back at me. There is a hint of concern in his eyes.

"Don't be scared. You're with me." This is the first time he has said anything remotely comforting. I nod at him and he faces the front of the car again, continuing with the phone call. "Yes, I'm here. Apologies." He waits. "No, I don't think that's necessary…" I feel a hand in mine as Joan clutches it. I close my eyes and lean my head back. I'll be fine. It will all be absolutely fine. I hope.

Skeabost House Hotel is beautiful, tucked away on its own in the middle of a sea of fields and trees. It looks historical, like a mansion from the Victorian era. I continue to sit in the car as Francis approaches my door. Once he opens it, I carefully step out, not wanting to fall flat on my face. That wouldn't be the best start. My father straightens his jacket as he steps out of the vehicle. Joan soon stands with me.

"You're going to be fine." She whispers in my ear. We observe my father as we all stroll towards the building. He is constantly fidgeting with his cufflinks. "Evie, no questions, alright? I mean it." Joan regards me with an unfamiliar strictness.

"Okay." I nod, understanding the sudden seriousness of the situation. The mansion looms closer and closer and my heart beats faster and faster.

Once we enter the lobby, my father looks back at me, making sure I stay by his side. He gently clutches my arm in a gesture of security. I'll admit, in situations like this, he does make me feel safe. I stand between my father and Joan as we wait for something. I'm not sure what we're waiting for. Until a booming voice that sounds like a double bass bellows from the side of us. "Norman!" The voice is closer. I turn my head to see who I assume is Connelly. He is a largely-built man, wearing a tuxedo that looks a size too small. On his right hand is a selection of gold rings. His eyes are a shade of green, hidden beneath bushy, ungroomed eyebrows. He is balding, with only a few streaks of hair behind his receding hairline. He looks like a full-blown crime boss.

"Connelly." My father firmly shakes his hand, still holding my arm. Connelly then turns his attention to Joan.

"Oh, Joan, it's been years." Connelly leans forward to plant two kisses on her cheeks.

"It has." She speaks with a false received pronunciation. Once the welcomes to her and my father are over, Connelly's green eyes look down to me. I instinctively want to stand behind my father, who does notice me cower next to him slightly. But Connelly's stare keeps me in place.

"And this must be lovely Evelyn." His voice is a raspy hiss.

"Evie." I blurt out, immediately regretting it. My father squeezes my arm in warning.

"My apologies. Gosh, you look just like your mother." Connelly asks for my hand so I slowly lift it. He kisses it. My father squeezes my arm again, but this time, I think it was meant as a comfort. Connelly looks back at him. "Come on in. We're all in the billiard room."

"Not waiting for us, I hope." My father comments as we follow Connelly to a side room, connected to the lobby.

"Not at all, Norman." As Connelly leads us through the lobby, I look up at my father and he looks down to me, still gently clutching my arm. He doesn't say anything. He just nods once and squeezes my arm again. It's a small gesture but I know what he's saying. He's going to get me through this.

Connelly pushes a door open and holds it wide, surveying the people in the billiard room. There is an enormous dining table situated in the middle, surrounded by sixteen luxurious wooden chairs. Everything is wooden, apart from the dark green wallpaper on the walls. There is a low light, shining from eight pendant lamps hanging above the table. My father guides me towards our assigned seats, taking note of the names behind the placemats. He stops when he sees ours. I am meant to be seated next to Connelly. My father quickly swaps my name with his and silently directs me to sit down. I sit, practically shaking as Joan sits beside me. I note the other people sat around the table. Elegant, rich people. They reek of elitism. My father is an elegant rich man but he has never once appeared to be arrogant about his wealth. My father isn't really arrogant at all. As he sits on the other side of me, I can't stop my fingers from fidgeting. Joan clearly notices my anxiety as she leans towards me.

"If you get scared, tap my knee." She whispers. I nod. I feel safer, knowing both she and my father are beside me and I'm tucked in between them. My father is a barrier between me and Connelly, who is standing, holding a glass of champagne.

"Welcome all. Beautiful part of the country, isn't it? I must settle down and retire here one day. And please hold all aging jokes until the end of the speech." He remarks, earning polite laughter from those around us. I can tell when my father is faking his laughter. And he is. I know he isn't the biggest fan of Connelly, but right now, it feels as if he despises the man. Before Connelly can continue, the door bursts open. We all spin to face who entered. My mouth lies open. It's Noah, the boy from the harbour. Oh, this is bad news. I'm praying to god he doesn't recognise me.

"Sorry I'm late, Dad." Noah takes a seat in the only empty chair left and it's directly opposite me. Connelly is his father. This is not good. "Harbour girl." He stares at me in delight as he takes a seat. Out of the corner of my eye, I can see my father turn to look down at me. I sink into my chair, feeling that familiar desperation for the floor to swallow me. I offer Noah a smile and look down at the table.

"You know her, son?" Connelly breaks the awkward silence. "We met the other day when she fell into the harbour at Kyleakin." Noah still dons the same Scottish brogue. If he is Scottish, how come his father isn't? God, I have so many questions but I'm not allowed to ask them.

"Well, what a small world it is." Connelly looks down at me, a wide grin on his face. I feel an inch tall. "As I was saying before I was so rudely interrupted…" Connelly carries on with his speech. My father continues to glare at me. All I can do in response is shrug at him. "We are here to celebrate the remarkable work you have all done this past year. I know there have been trials and tribulations. But we've overcome them and now we are performing better than ever. So raise your glasses please." Connelly instructs. The adults around the room raise a glass. "To the partnership of Connelly and Norman. I know we will continue to do great things."

"To Connelly and Norman." The adults toast and take a sip of their drinks. My father is Connelly's business partner. That's news to me. He told me Connelly was a client. I'm so confused about the whole situation. I don't know how long this dinner is going to take, but I will be spending every moment nervous. And Noah being here just throws a whole bunch of spanners into the works.

A few moments of unbearable uneasiness later, Connelly is in the middle of a deep conversation with my father. Several waiters walk in with small dishes. I can't stop glaring at Noah, who is speaking to an older woman next to him. Maybe that's his mother or something. He has a beaming smile on his face the whole time. I am startled by a dish being placed in front of me. Oh, god, I have to eat in front of all these people. I have to force the food down. It does look really nice. A dab of pate with a little slice of sourdough bread.

"Just eat what you can, sweetheart." Joan instructs reassuringly. I am so thankful for her right now. I collect my starter knife and scrape a tiny sliver of pate onto the bread. I sigh before bringing it to my mouth. I chew slowly and resist the urge to gag. This is going to be a long evening.

The main course has been and gone. I ate what I could, which resulted in about three mouthfuls. Joan kept her hand on my back the entire time, stroking it soothingly. She is currently talking to the guest next to her. As I sit in silence, I notice the conversations around the table are getting louder. Bottles of wine are becoming emptier. Connelly laughs often. It's a loud, abrasive sound, cutting any calmness in the air. It makes me jump every time I hear it. After a moment, I lean towards my father, who is taking a sip of red wine.

"Dad?"

"Yes?"

"I have to use the bathroom." I look into his brown eyes. He nods curtly and I stand up. I am perplexed for a brief second when he also stands. But then I remember his comment about chaperoning me wherever I go.

"Norman." Connelly stops us both from walking away. "I was just speaking to Anderson here about our plans for expansion in the next quarter. Sit down and shed some more light for me. You're the brains behind it all." His command irks my father, who then wears a professional smile as he is turning to face him.

"Of course." My father looks down before speaking in my ear. "You come straight back, do you understand me?"

"I will." I calm his worries and make my way out of the billiard room. I feel my father's eyes on me as I walk. I also feel Connelly's. I throw open the doors, making my way out of the room. Once they shut behind me, I feel all of my nervousness reach the surface. I am breathing loudly. I want to leave. I want my mother. I locate the bathroom and hurriedly make my way towards it.

I vomit. My eyes well up as I battle this endless nausea. Not only am I brimming with anxiety, I'm also probably still recovering from my little flu. I can't go back in there. But I know I have to. I also can't spend too much time in here or my father will come searching. I wash my hands and look at myself in the mirror. I look tired. I look scared. Behind all the make-up, I look like a timid little girl. I suppose I am. I'm terrified but I don't even know what I'm scared of. I wipe any wayward patches of mascara away from my eyes and collect all of my courage. I need to be brave. Think of Mum. Think of her courage. She's with me.

Once I am done in the restrooms, I make my way back to the lobby. I briefly glance at a grand piano. I smile at it as I walk, keeping my feet as steady as I can. I'm still not used to heels. My journey is cut short when I bump into someone.

"Oh, shit, I am so…" I look up. It's Noah and he's smiling at me.

"You need to watch where you're going, Harbour Girl."

"Says you." I scoff. "That's twice now you've decided to collide into me."

"Both accidental, I assure you." Noah smirks. I can't help but smile back. "Quite the dinner, isn't it? And you look beautiful, by the way. Last time I saw you, you were climbing onto a slipway in Kyleakin."

"And whose fault was that?" I cross my arms, feeling confident and smug.

"Aye, it was mine." There is an honest charm in his voice.

"So... Connelly is your father?" I don't know what else to talk about. I've already broken the rule about asking questions. And swearing.

"Aye, Noah Connelly." He offers his hand and I shake it.
"Evie Norman."

"So, our fathers are going to be working together, it seems. Maybe we'll see more of each other, Evie. I do hope so." Now he isn't shoving me into open water, I can get a better sense of who he is. He seems charismatic. He seems kind. He doesn't frighten me like Connelly did. Someone else does frighten me when I see him walking towards us, however.

"Oh, bollocks." I look down. My father stands with us, glaring down at me. "Dad, this is Noah Connelly. Noah, this is my father, Gregory Norman. Although you probably already knew that." I offer a calm introduction, trying anything to diffuse the situation.

"Good to meet you, Noah." My father speaks through clenched teeth as he shakes the boy's hand. "Evelyn, would you mind heading back into the dining room?" He wears a fake calm expression but I know he is exploding inside.

"Yep. It was nice to meet you again, Noah." I am taking too many liberties but I don't want to seem rude. Noah takes my hand and kisses it. I blush slightly. My father clears his throat incredibly loudly and I know that's my cue to leave. I spin on my heel and head back to the billiard room. I suddenly feel a hand around my arm.

"I told you to come straight back." My father hisses in my ear.

"I was coming back but he bumped into me. Anyway, what's the harm in having a little conversation?" As I try to defend myself, my father tugs on my arm, stopping me from walking. He looks around us, checking nobody is nearby before scowling at me again.

"Look, so far, it's all been relatively calm. And yes, you're doing well. But you cannot take any more liberties, Evelyn. Especially with Noah Connelly."

"Why? He's just a boy."

"And Connelly's son." He states firmly. "The evening is nearly over. No more slip ups, Evelyn. Nothing. From now on, you are invisible, do you understand me?"

"So just be what I've been to you for the past sixteen years then, yeah? Shouldn't be too hard, I'm probably an expert at being invisible by now." I can't help but say it. His furious eyes almost look wounded.

"Evelyn…"

"Just forget it." I jerk my arm out of his grip and make my way back into the billiard room.

My father is undeniably uneasy as the evening nears its denouement. My little dig is probably still on his mind. It's true, though. The man barely acknowledged me while we lived in

London. I have spoken to him more in the past four days than I ever have before. I think he and Joan are the only adults at this table who aren't anywhere near as tipsy as everyone else is. Connelly is clearly sitting on an alcohol-fuelled cloud nine. He's attempted to speak to me several times already but every time I am about to answer, my father speaks for me. I can see Connelly growing frustrated at that. I know he wants me to do the talking.

"So, Evie, do you have any plans for college?" Connelly leans his head back to see me behind my father.

"Um…" I wait for my father's interruption. It doesn't happen. "I was thinking of doing some A-Levels."

"Business?" Connelly asks.

"No. Business isn't for me. I haven't got the brain for it. I do want to go to uni but I don't really know what I want to do." I mutter shyly.

"You're only, what, sixteen? You still have time to figure it out. Maybe one day, you can come and work for me. We offer roles in marketing, administration." His suggestion comes as a shock. It makes me feel queasy.

"Um, thanks for the offer, but, uh…" I stutter and look into my father's eyes, silently telling him I need rescuing.

"I think Evelyn is better suited to something more skills-based, rather than being trapped in an office." My father interrupts the awkward pause in the conversation. I let out a long sigh of relief.

"What skills does she have? I'm sure we could find a way to utilise them." Connelly persists.

"Her skills are a bit broader than what Connelly and Norman could use. She's more creative than a lot of people her age." My father continues to save the situation. I relax in my seat, thinking it's all over.

"Creativity, eh? What kind of things do you do, Evie?" Connelly takes another sip of his wine. He wants me to talk again.

"Oh, um…" Oh, god, do I tell him? "I'm a classically trained pianist. My mother taught me initially, and she taught me how to sing." My voice is so weak. I didn't want to disclose any of this.

"There's a grand piano in the lobby. Give us a tune, Evie." He commands out of nowhere. My father's face falls. I silently panic. "No, honestly, I haven't played for a while. Or sang. I'll probably sound like a dying cat." I attempt to refuse his instruction with humour. Connelly doesn't smile.

"Nonsense. I'm sure you sound delightful." He smirks. My father sighs. "Sing us a song, Miss Norman." Connelly is clearly quite drunk. "Here, have some liquid courage." He clumsily pours me a glass of white wine.

"Connelly, she's sixteen years old." My father interjects.

"Perfect age for your first sip." Connelly gets to his feet, still holding the glass of wine in his hand. He holds it out in front of me. I glance at my father, who stares at me and shakes his head. If I am going to perform in front of a crowd of complete strangers, I will need the liquid courage. I take the glass from Connelly and drink the whole thing in one go before practically slamming the glass onto the table. My father seethes. All the rules have been completely violated. Connelly wears a delighted expression and silently instructs me to stand, so I timidly do. Once I am stood, he wraps an arm around me tightly. Okay, maybe this was a bad idea. "If you could all head to the lobby, Miss Norman here is going to treat us to some music." After Connelly speaks, all guests get to their feet. Connelly walks away from the table and my father clutches my arm, pulling me down to speak in my ear.

"Don't you dare, Evelyn." He hisses.

"What Connelly wants, he gets, remember?" My voice is smothered in contempt as I jerk my arm out of my father's grip.

"Evie, don't." Joan also tries to stop me as I walk past her. I can do this. Just a quick little tune. Just a bit of entertainment. Oh, god, I *am* the entertainment.

Every guest is stood in the lobby of the hotel, including my father and Joan. I am seated at the grand piano, trying to think of something to perform.

"Any requests?" I ask the room, slightly tipsy. My father is stood with his arms crossed and I have never seen this expression on his face before. It's pure fury. I clear my throat and begin to play the introduction to *Sweet Child O'Mine*. The moment my father realises what song it is, his anger only grows. My mother played piano beautifully and she would play this for me all the time. It was like a little personal tradition. She would always pretend the song was about me, especially when singing the lyrics about sky blue eyes. My blue eyes. But she played a very specific arrangement, and that's exactly what I'm playing now. As I begin to sing, I realise I don't actually sound too bad. I actually sound quite pretty. It must be the liquid courage. It's her own version of the song. It almost sounds gloomy. It's slow and gentle. I completely lose myself to it. The people around me don't exist anymore. I haven't played piano in such a long time but every note is seamless. Perfect. As I play and sing, I am tapping the keys with a certain confidence. A certain power. She's with me. She's sitting beside me on this stool, giving me courage. She is my courage. I finally open my eyes and look at my father. He's drowning in an ocean of fury and sadness, remembering my mother as I do. We are the only people in this room who understand the significance of this song, especially this rendition. I practically sneer at him as I hit the notes in the instrumental. I'm angry and I don't know why. Playing music always has a way of bringing out my deepest emotions. As I reach the end of the song, slowly singing the '*where do we go's*, I notice myself becoming tearful. I stare at my father and power through, until the very last '*sweet child o'mine*', where my tears finally begin to fall. Once I have played the final chord, I just stare ahead, forcing back the tears and breathing heavily. The guests erupt in a pleasant applause. I wipe my eyes and stand up. I don't curtsey. I don't bow. I just look at my father, anger and regret consuming me. I shouldn't have done this.

"She plays beautifully, Norman." Connelly leans towards my father, who is the only one not clapping. "Brava, Evie!" He grins at me. My father briefly looks at him before scowling at me. With a look of angry resolve, my father marches in my direction. I really shouldn't have done this.

"Dad, look, I…" I am rendered completely mute as my father bends down and furiously throws me over his shoulder, causing me to gasp loudly. I tightly clutch the back of his tuxedo in fright. Then all I can see is the floor moving as I'm carried through the lobby. It's so disorientating. It's so terrifying. It's so humiliating. "Joan, we're leaving!" My father's voice is thunderous as he carries me out of the hotel. Well, at least the dinner party is over.

80

CHAPTER SIX

My father walks through the car park, towards the Mercedes. His steps are heavy and his grip on me is tight. I can feel the sheer anger coursing through him by the way he's carrying me. I can hear his furious breaths. I whip my hair away from my face so I can look ahead. Behind us, Joan is rushing to catch up.

"Dad, please put me down!" I shout, my voice jumping with every step my father takes. "Dad, I can walk to the damn car! We're out of the hotel, just put me down!" He doesn't answer me. He just jerks me over his shoulder more, almost as a warning. I can hear the click of the Mercedes unlocking and a door opening. My father then drops me from his shoulder with no fragility and my heels hit the concrete.

"Get in. Now." He glares at me.

"Dad, I…" I am silenced by his mere expression. I tearfully relent and enter the car. Once I am sat on the leather seat, my father slams the door and makes his way to the other side.

"Gregory." Joan's disapproving voice can be heard outside.

"In the car!" My father roars. He has never been this angry. He's even yelling at Joan. I look out the window, resting my head on my palm, trying to hold the tears back. I've never been more humiliated in my life. Joan opens her door and sits beside me while my father takes a seat in the front. Francis then fires up the ignition and begins the journey home. It's going to be the most uncomfortable hour of my life.

Nobody has spoken a word and we're only halfway back to Kyleakin. I've barely blinked. My mind is hazy but busy. As I sit and look outside at the moon-lit mountains, I feel a hand in mine. Joan is offering me a gesture of solidarity. I am desperate to speak. I am desperate to melt the ice in the air. I am desperate to apologise. My father breaks the silence once he brings his phone to his ear.

"Yes?" He snaps. "That's fine. Express my apologies and schedule a meeting with Connelly tomorrow afternoon. I'll sort this mess out." He pauses. "Yes, that should be fine. Tell him I'll meet him at 2pm." He hangs up.

"Dad…"

"Not a damn word, Evelyn." My father cuts me off.

"Not even to say sorry?" I scoff. He twists his head to look back at me. There is still a deep, heavy frown above his eyes.

"Oh, you want to apologise, do you? That'd be a first." He hisses. I do my best to ignore the disdain in his tone. "I gave you rules, Evelyn. No drinking. No questions. No speaking. I told you to be invisible. And to stay with me at all times!"

"Dad, you heard what he said when I needed the bathroom. I had to go alone. And then Noah…" I begin to argue passionately.

"I don't even want to discuss his son." He faces the front again.

"What happened with Noah?" Joan enters the debate.

"Literally nothing." I mumble. My father lets out a livid sigh.

"Evelyn, you will never speak to that boy again, am I clear?" He orders.

"Why not?"

"Do not push me, Evelyn. You know I hate repeating myself."

"No, why are you so scared of Connelly, Dad?! Are you scared he's going to murder me or something?!" My voice fills the car.

"Evie." Joan squeezes my hand, trying to settle me down.

"No! I don't get why I'm the one being completely lynched for this. Dad, you know it wasn't my fault. And it's not my fault that your new business partner's an asshole." I counter.

"Evelyn, I heavily suggest you stop talking. Right now."

"Oh, there's a fucking surprise." I mutter. "Francis, stop at a cash point on the way. I need to make several deposits to the fucking swear jar."

"Evie…" Joan urges.

"No, this is such bullshit." I scoff.

"That is enough!" My father growls.

"Dad, please just listen to me. I'm your bloody daughter."

"Yes, you are, Evelyn, and you are balancing very precariously on the edge of my patience. So I suggest either you stop talking, or so help me, you will find out exactly what happens when I lose that patience." His voice isn't loud but that makes it all the more intimidating. He's eerily calm. I hug myself and twist my body towards the door. I'm full of anger. I'm full of fear. It's an unpleasant mix. I want to get out. I need to get out of this car. Away from him. Away from the man who makes me feel so small, so insignificant. Away from the man who despises me.

After roughly ten minutes, I begin to feel sick. Nobody has said a word. It's horrific. I don't know even know what time it is. I shut my eyes, trying to ward off the nausea building up. It's no use. I need to get out.

"Francis, stop the car." I sit up.

"We are not stopping this car, Evelyn." My father snaps.

"No, seriously, stop the car!" I yell. The car suddenly comes to an abrupt halt. I unbuckle my seatbelt and clutch the door handle before rushing out of the vehicle.

"Evelyn!" I ignore my father before I slam the door shut and sprint away from the Mercedes, up the landscape. The air is freezing but the freshness of it is welcome. I stop about one hundred metres away from the car and vomit onto the grass. Thank God Joan put my hair in a bun. I catch my breath and my eyes water. I spit onto the ground. I soon hear the familiar sound of a car door closing in the distance behind me before I begin to walk away from the area. It's pitch black but I know who is coming to check on me. It's Joan. It's always Joan. I stop walking and look down to the ground beneath me. I decide to take my heels off, not wanting to ruin them and desperate to end the pain in the balls of my feet.

"Look, I'll come back in second, Joan. I just needed to get away from…" I turn around. It's not Joan. "… him." My heart falls into my stomach as I face my father. I can't really see him but I can see the shimmer of the moon against his cufflinks and in his eyes. He is offering me a small tissue. I slowly take it and wipe my mouth, even though there is hardly anything to wipe away.

"Are you alright?" He puts his hands in his pockets.

"Grand." I scoff in derision, stowing the tissue in my sleeve.

"Take a walk with me." He calmly instructs as he passes me. I look back at the car. Francis has parked it safely along the side of the road. "Now, Evelyn!" My father's sudden booming voice in the silent air makes me jump. I swallow all of my pride and follow him through the wilderness.

84

My father doesn't speak for ages. We just wander aimlessly along the bottom of the mountain. Doing it bare foot isn't a pleasant experience; I keep stepping on little rocks. I wince and mutter painfully every time I do. But I would rather leave my shoes off. If I get a heel stuck in the grass, there's no getting it out. And these shoes cost more than a week in the Bahamas.

"Dad, as much as I'm loving this little hike, I keep stepping on rocks and it hurts." I complain. I stop walking when I notice my father has. He still doesn't speak. He just looks ahead, his hands still in his pockets. Maybe he's rehearsing what to say. He's chosen a nice setting for a little heart-to-heart.

"When your mother died, I'd never been more terrified in my life." My father finally speaks. His voice isn't angry or cold. It's low and wise. "I was not prepared to be a single father. I had no idea what I was doing. And to answer a certain question you asked me in the car; Connelly doesn't scare me. No, the one thing that does scare me, however, is having to do this on my own. Having to do this without your mother. I'm not a good father to you, Evelyn, I won't deny that. That's why she was so important." He continues to stroll. I follow diligently.

"Ow." I wince as I am stabbed by yet another rock. My father hears it and stops. He waits for me to catch up before continuing. "But I was always good at one thing. And that was keeping you safe. That's what I brought to the table. She was the one to give you affection. I was the protector." He looks down. "But I couldn't protect her. And now my daughter doesn't have her mother anymore."

"Dad, you can't…" My voice is merely a croak.

"I know what you're going to say, Evelyn. And I *can* blame myself, and I always will." He states slowly and cautiously, turning his head to check that I am okay.

"How did she die?" I ask carefully. My father sighs.

"Not by accident." He confesses. I glare at him, feeling the shock of his words.

"It was Connelly, wasn't it?" A single tear falls down my cheek.

"I don't know. But until I am certain it wasn't Connelly, I cannot drop my guard. I can't lose my focus." He stands directly in front of me, looking down at me.

"Then why are you working with him? Why did you agree to be his partner?" I can't fathom any of this as I look into his eyes.

"Friends close, enemies closer." My father frowns. "I need to hit him from the inside, do you understand me? I need to build trust. To build that trust, I need to work with him. For him." He runs a hand through his hair. "You're in the middle of my mess and I never wanted you to be."

"Is that why you were angry I went into the office? Because I was getting into your mess?" I ask, hoping it wasn't a stupid idea to bring it up. But right now, it feels like I can say anything to him.

"In a manner of speaking, yes." My father nods.

"Well, surely it would just be easier if you told me what you do, then I wouldn't have to…"

"No. I will never tell you what I do."

"Is it illegal?" I can't hide the curiosity in my voice.

"I said no questions, Evelyn."

"Do you kill people?" This question clearly irritates him. "Well, you didn't say no."

"Evelyn." He scolds.

86

"Sorry. No more questions, I promise." I look down, timid again.

"Look…" He sighs. "Tonight was a disaster. You peaked Connelly's interest. And not only that, you played a damn piano and gave us all a tune." The frown above his eyes grows deeper.

"I didn't exactly have a choice, Dad." I roll my eyes.

"Not the point. But that's why I had to get you out of there. I had to get you away from Connelly."

"You could've just said. I don't think the man-handling was necessary." I mumble, still feeling annoyed by it.

"It was necessary, Evelyn. I apologise for it but it was the fastest way to get you out of that hotel. And I didn't you want around Connelly for a second more. See, Connelly has little obsessions, Evelyn…" My father begins to explain.

"I know. Joan told me." I nod slowly. "And you're worried that I might be the next little obsession."

"Yes. I needed you to not attract too much attention, especially his. But that plan well and truly went out the window, didn't it?" I can't really see his face but I feel like he might be smirking. There is a new humorous mood. It's a nice surprise. "I forgot how well you could play piano." He changes the subject.

"Yeah, it's been a while. And sorry for choosing that song. I saw the look on your face when I started playing it." I look at anything but him.

"No, it wasn't an ideal choice." He agrees. I feel that guilt again. I keep forgetting that it's not just me who lost her.

"Dad, for the record, you're not a bad father. You're not exactly going to win Father of the Year any time soon but you're not bad." I shrug, my arms crossed. "Yeah, you've been horrible and cold… but I've never wanted for anything. I've had a good childhood. And, well, my life is what it is because of you."

"Thank you, Evelyn." His voice is full of sincerity. "Come on. We should head back to the car." My father turns and walks away from me. I begin to join him, knowing that this little heart-to-heart may have changed a lot of things. I am smiling to myself until I step onto a sharp rock.

"Ow, fuck!"

"Evelyn, why did you take your bloody shoes off?" He stops walking and waits for me to catch up. I hobble painfully along the rocky ground.

"I wasn't going to traipse through the wilderness in heels, Dad." I offer him a look of mock confusion. "And if I ruin these very expensive shoes, you'll kill me." I shrug. My father sighs and shakes his head before he suddenly picks me up. "Wait, what if I need to puke again?" I rest my shoes on my lap and wrap my arms around his neck.

"Then I'll drop you. Because you are not getting vomit on my tuxedo, Evelyn." He is clearly annoyed.

"Nice to know I'm less important than your tuxedo." I mutter under my breath, making him look down at me with an irritated expression. I immediately cower under it, turning my head away.

"Dad?"

"Mm-hmm."

"Thanks for not being too pissed off."

"The night is still young, Evelyn." I can hear a hint of amusement in his voice.

"Ha, you're pissing hilarious." I mutter under my breath.

"Evelyn, swear one more time and I will leave you out here so you can walk back to Kyleakin. Shoes or no shoes."

"Sorry." I say quickly. I stare ahead, feeling a pang of guilt over something else I recently said. "Dad, I'm sorry for what I said to you back at the dinner party." My sincere apology makes him stop walking. He clearly needs elaboration. "When I said that I've been invisible to you all my life."

"Is that how you've felt? Invisible?" My father's question comes as a surprise. I lose my courage and feel like a scared little mouse again. "Evelyn, answer me."

"Well... yeah." I look away, growing tearful. It takes him a while to respond.

"Evelyn, I know you miss your mother but..."

"It's fine. I get it. She's gone. And she's never coming back." I choke, releasing my tears quietly. There is such a long moment of stillness. My father barely moves. But then I feel a kiss on my head, and stare at him in slight shock. His eyes are full of concern, regret and maybe even a hint of love. I cry and wrap my arms even tighter around his neck, leaning myself into a hug. His grip on me grows tighter. Even though he is carrying me, it's clear he is hugging me back. We don't say anything but we don't need to. He loves me. I feel a new closeness to him that I have never felt before as we stay like this for what feels like hours.

The next morning, as I wake up, I feel something I haven't felt for a long time. I'm hungry. No, I'm starving. I rush out of bed, get showered, get dressed and head downstairs. When I enter the kitchen, Joan is making herself a coffee. I collect a slice of bread and shove it into the toaster. I have a beaming smile on my face. Joan notices.

"Someone's happy this morning." She comments as I collect the butter from the fridge, kicking it closed behind me.

"Just feeling better." I shrug and wait for the toast to pop.

"And you're eating breakfast." Her powers of deduction really are second to none.

"Yeah, I'm bloody starving."

"You're starving!" She celebrates. It confuses me. "Gregory, come to the kitchen!"

"No, no, Joan." I hold my head in my hands, leaning my elbows on the worktop. My father walks in through the doorway. Joan grabs my arm and pulls me to her.

"She's starving!" Joan beams, squeezing me to her. My father crosses his arms, somewhat amused.

"Your elation confuses me." I mutter. Joan giggles. "And don't get excited. It's just toast." My voice is barely comprehensible as my cheek is pressed against Joan's face.

"That's it. Tonight, we're having Mexican night." Joan pinches my cheek.

"Ow." I try to jerk away. My toast pops out of the toaster and Joan finally lets my cheek go. I rub it and turn to prepare my breakfast. "We can go to Kyle of Lochalsh and get some bits. I'll make nachos, fajitas, Mexican rice, some dips…" Joan is in a state of overwhelming joy. It warms my heart. I watch her get a list ready as I spread the butter on my toast. My father stands beside me, making himself a coffee.

"Are you still meeting with Connelly today?" I finish spreading the butter.

"Mm-hmm." He waits for the coffee machine.

"Can I come with you?" I ask cautiously. He glares down at me, wearing a look of disturbed shock. "Not to the meeting. I'll just sit in the car or something." He doesn't reply. He just continues to glare at me. "Okay, that was officially the stupidest thing I've ever asked you."

"It's up there." He frowns and stirs his coffee. I take a bite of toast. "Besides, it sounds like you're going to Kyle with Jo to get some Mexican food."

"Oh, do I have to go? She's freaking me out." We both look at Joan, who is still full of beans as she collects some reusable shopping bags.

"Yes." My father sips some coffee.

"Joy." I roll my eyes and take another bite. My father nudges my side with his elbow. It takes me by surprise. He's never been remotely playful. I stare up at him with a restrained smile on my face. He just raises a brow at me. I giggle softly and eat some more toast.

"Come on. Let's go." Joan stands in front of us, holding her list and some bags.

"What?" I ask, my mouth full of toast.

"We're leaving. Get your shoes on." Joan glides out of the kitchen.

"God, I hate being rushed in the morning. This is precisely why I stopped eating breakfast four years ago." I bring what's left of my toast to my mouth and chew it.

"Is that so? Well, I distinctly remember it being because you always got out of bed too late and never had the time." My father narrows his eyes pensively.

"Yeah, that's not how I remember it." I swipe the crumbs off my hands. "And, I mean, who's going to have the better memory? The teenager or the old man?"

"Oi." He snaps. I smirk and head for the door. "Evelyn." Once he speaks, I stop and slowly spin to face him. "I'm aware it's your birthday in two months and I need to know what you want."

"I don't want anything." I shrug.

"There must be something."

"Well, once I'm seventeen, I can get a provisional licence. And I have always wanted to drive the Merc." I cross my arms, smiling.

"Not a chance in hell." He shuts down the idea immediately.

"No?" I imitate a driver, pretending to hold a steering wheel and beep a horn. "Not even a little jaunt down the country?"

"No." My father is trying incredibly hard not to laugh. It's weird to think he actually finds me amusing now.

"Well, in that case, I don't want anything."

"Come on, Evie!" Joan hollers from the hallway.

"Auf Wiedersehen, Herr Kommandant." I spin towards the door and leave the room.

We're sat around the table. Joan is beyond delighted that we're doing this. Mexican night. My father is sat beside me. It makes a change. He's normally sat opposite me. Francis is with us, rolling himself a fajita. There is a calm, wonderful feeling. It's family. That's what we are right now. A family.

"Oh, Greg, I have some tequila." Joan gets to her feet and approaches a liquor cabinet in the corner of the room. I frown as she comes back to the table with three shot glasses and a bottle of Sierra.

"You guys aren't getting drunk, are you?" I ask in slight horror.

"We're celebrating." Joan asserts.

"Celebrating what?" I ask, munching on a nacho.

"Well, you're finally eating. The dinner party went by without a hitch." She pours some tequila into the three shot glasses.

"Debatable, thanks to a certain someone." My father interjects.

"The hell did I do?" I grimace and look at him.

"You really want me to dignify that with a response, Evelyn?"

"Alright. Point taken." I cross my arms. He chuckles. I've actually made him laugh.

"Now, I just need to grab the lime and salt." Joan makes her way to the kitchen.

"I've never seen you drunk." I comment as my father passes a shot of tequila to Francis. "Are you a miserable bastard when you're drunk?" Drunk Gregory Norman. That's a terrifying thought.

"Well, you're going to find out very soon, aren't you?" He quips, making me smile slightly. I think he's finally starting to relax. Joan did say this would happen after the dinner party. "Oh, I forgot to tell you, I've arranged for a private tutor." My father informs me out of the blue. I look at him in confusion. "He starts next week, while I'm in London."

"I'm going to be home-schooled?" I can't hide my reluctance.

"Just until your exams." He nods as he chews some rice. "Which I'm very aware are only a couple of weeks away. I could also give you some help if you want." This is the first time my father has ever offered to help with homework.

"You sure? Schools have changed a fair bit since you went. We don't use a chisel and hammer anymore, for a start." My little jibe earns an elbow to the ribs. "Ow!" I jolt upright and rub my side.

"Dad, I don't need a tutor. I was top student in most of my classes back in London. You may not have noticed, but I'm very clever."

"Not the point. You still need exam practice." He brings another forkful of rice to his mouth and looks down at me as he chews. I roll my eyes and eat one of my nachos.

"You know, we should do Mexican night more often." I suggest.

"Is that so?" My father leans back in his seat. He has an unusual affectionate look in his eyes as he watches me eat my nachos.

"Ah, jalapeno!" I fret and waft my mouth. My tolerance of spice is unbelievably low. Joan soon comes back with several sliced limes and a tub of table salt.

"Here we are. Let's get this party started, eh?" She has a crazy, excited look in her eyes.

"Actually, on second thoughts, maybe we shouldn't do Mexican night more often." I bite a nacho as I observe my aunt. My father laughs. I've made him laugh again. I have never heard him laugh like this. I feel cheerful. And it greatly improves my appetite.

An hour later, Joan, my father and Francis have consumed a decent amount of tequila and it shows. I sit in blind confusion as they get substantially tipsier. Joan has put away all the food and now it's just a case of enjoying each other's company. My father pours himself, Joan and Francis another tequila.

"Can I try some?" I ask in the hope that his intoxication makes him say yes. He narrows his eyes at me before winking at Joan, who smiles and walks to the liquor cabinet. She returns to the table with another shot glass and places it in front of me.

"Do you know what to do?" My father pours a bit of tequila in.

"I'm not an expert but I'm pretty sure you drink it." I quip as I clutch the glass. My father takes my hand and places a small

94

amount of salt on it. He then puts a lime wedge on the table in front of me.

"Lick the salt. Drink the tequila. Bite the lime." He instructs and leans back in his chair, watching me like a hawk.

"Well, that all sounds incredibly gross." I look down at the salt on my hand. I grimace and lick it, immediately hating the taste.

"Now drink the tequila." My father interjects.

"I know, I know." I take the glass and knock back the liquid. I am instantly rendered breathless. My father chuckles. I pick up the lime and bite it. I shut my eyes tightly before putting the chewed lime in my empty shot glass.

"Tequila isn't the drink for you then, Evie?" Joan giggles.

"No, that was the most repulsive thing in the world." I shake my head in disgust. My father does his own shot. I lean back, still disturbed by the taste.

"Oh, Greg, do you remember that club in Cancun?" Joan gets her phone out of her pocket.

"Yes, I do." My father smirks, nodding slowly.

"Wait, you guys went clubbing in Mexico?" I ask him in disbelief and he nods.

"Oh, Evie, your mother was such a good dancer. We went to this nightclub in Cancun, shortly before your mother was pregnant with you." Joan reminisces fondly.

"Explains a lot." I mutter. My father laughs. Again. I'm on a roll.

"Oh, Greg, what was that one song called?" She scrolls through her phone, obviously looking for the song in question. "Oh, I've found it!" She shouts. At that moment, a Mexican song plays from Joan's phone. It's sung completely in Spanish and it gets Joan to her feet. "Evie, isn't one of your GCSEs in Spanish?" She starts to dance.

"Yeah, biggest mistake of my life." I cross my arms. My father gets to his feet.

"Come on." He grabs my arm, trying to pull me up.

"No, no, no. I'll pass, thanks. You kids have fun." I manage to release myself from my father's grip. He shakes his head at me before walking to Joan and dancing freely with her. I am both disturbed and confused as they imitate traditional Latin American moves, like a salsa. I watch, sitting with my arms crossed. My face is just a picture of bemusement. "You know this is incredibly stereotypical? It's borderline racist." I judge them, making them both stop and look at me.

"Oh, Greg, it seems she is a lost cause." Joan shakes her head in mock disappointment. My father sighs loudly and stands behind my chair.

"Dad, is it too late to ask you to be a miserable bastard?" I stare ahead blankly as he puts his hands on my shoulders.

"I'm so sorry, Jo. I thought I raised her better than this." Out of nowhere, he reaches down and tickles my ribs. I jump instantly and giggle, trying to squirm away. He has never tickled me before. He's definitely drunk.

"No! Dad!" I shout between my bursts of laughter. I do all I can to get away from his hands but they find me. Joan beams at the interaction. "Stop!" I laugh loudly. My father eventually stops and returns to Joan, to carry on dancing. Joan stares at me and gestures for me to join them, using her index finger. I grin and roll my eyes before getting to my feet. We salsa, rolling our hips and giggling. Joan takes my hand and holds another hand around my waist, pretending we're in a ballroom. I laugh. She laughs. It isn't long before Francis approaches us, offering to dance with Joan. She gladly complies. As I watch them, I feel a pair of arms wrap around my neck from behind me. I smile and hold onto them as my father rests his chin on the top of my head. I'm so incredibly happy. I'm in heaven. Nothing could ruin this moment.

The doorbell rings. Joan turns the music off. We all stop dancing and look in the direction of the front door.

"I'll get it." I unhook my father's arms from around my neck.

"Evelyn, wait."

"Dad, I'm the only one here who's sober. I'll answer it." I brush past him, ignoring his attempts to stop me. I make my way to the front door. It's only 9pm. Who could possibly be the worst person at the door? I find out when I open it. Connelly is stood right in front of me. I look up at him in horror.

"Good evening, Evie."

CHAPTER SEVEN

I sit on the staircase, biting my finger as I listen to the conversation between my father and Connelly in the living room. Max sits with me, resting his chin on my knee. I stroke him, finding some comfort in having him with me. He's like my own personal guard dog. I ruminate the possible reasons Connelly is here. My father had a meeting with him today. Maybe it's something off the back of that. Maybe it's something more sinister. Maybe it's because of how I acted at the dinner party.

I lean my head against the wall. They've been in the living room for around an hour. I clock parts of their conversation. It all seems like regular business jargon, nothing out of the ordinary. I can feel my eyelids grow heavy. I'm tired.

"Evelyn." The sudden snapping of my name leaps me awake. My father is stood in front of the staircase. "Have you not learnt the lesson about eavesdropping?" He doesn't sound happy. His voice has reverted back to that stern tone I know all too well.

"Sorry." I stand up, ready to go back to my room.

"Connelly wants to speak to you." My father informs me.

"What? Why me?"

"I don't know. Come on." He isn't drunk anymore. He's magically sobered up. I follow him towards the living room.

"Dad." I sound so fearful.

"You'll be okay. You're with me." My father mutters as he leads me to the door. I can tell there is an element of fear in him too. But unlike me, he has a duty to hide it.

My father walks into the living room first. He acts as a constant blockade between me and Connelly as I make my way inside. Once I am, he silently instructs me to sit on the sofa Connelly isn't sat on.

"Nice to see you again, Evie." Connelly remarks. I just look at my father, who nods reassuringly and closes the door. He stays stood in the centre of the room.

"And you, Mr Connelly." I speak with the utmost respect. Now I know what kind of man Connelly potentially is, I need to refrain from rattling his cage.

"Firstly, I just wanted to thank you for the little show you put on for us at Skeabost. It was wonderful to watch. You have a talent."

"Thanks." I respond unenthusiastically.

"Mr Connelly has some things he would like to discuss with you, Evelyn." I can see the uneasiness on my father's face as he moves the conversation along.

"Okay." My fingers fidget.

"Sorry for barging in like this but it couldn't wait, I'm afraid." Connelly leans forward. "Evie, I am under the impression that you are friends with my son."

"Um, well, I wouldn't say…" I begin but my father clears his throat. I look at him and he frowns at me. "Um, yeah, I guess."

"Good to know. I need you to do something for me." Connelly is about to cut to the chase. "I need this friendship to continue. I need you to, how do I put this? I need you to form a strong friendship with my son." He nods.

"You want me to…?"

"Just keep an eye on him. Give him some attention." He doesn't hesitate.

"Mr Connelly, I barely know your son."

"That's not an issue. He's quite taken with you, I can see that. He wants to get to know you more. I need you to let him." Connelly dons a dangerous look. My father finally sits down next to me.

"Okay." I whisper, instinctively leaning closer to my father.

"Now, Evie…"

"Evelyn." I interrupt. My father looks at me. "My name is Evelyn."

"Very well, Evelyn." Connelly nods. "The reason I need you to do this little favour for me is because I am concerned about my son. He doesn't pay any attention to his college work. He is getting drunk with friends. He needs a good influence in his life. Myself, I am always working and his mother is always dipping into her little hobbies. We have no time for him. I think you could be a very good influence."

"You want me to keep your son in check?" I ask.

"He needs a friend, Evelyn. Maybe even more." There is a dark smile on Connelly's face. My father places a hand on my back. I immediately feel safer.

"Um, then I guess… yeah, I can do that." My breath hitches.

"Fantastic." Connelly nods. "Then that's all we need. I'll see myself out, Norman." He taps his knees and stands.

"No, I'll show you out." My father strokes my back once and follows him. After a moment, I hear their distant farewells as they get to the front door. I then hear the sound of it closing. Before long, the living room door opens and my father stands in the doorway.

"Dad." I get to my feet and rush into his arms. He slowly wraps me in a hug, like he is hesitant to hug me back again.

"It's okay." He whispers.

"Dad, I can't do that." I shake my head, still wrapped in his arms.

"Evelyn, listen to me." He pulls me out of the hug, placing his hands on my arms. "I know it's scary and I don't know what he wants but..."

"He wants to pimp me out to his son, Dad. I think that's pretty bloody obvious." I scoff and pace across the room. "And what do I do about Connelly?"

"Leave Connelly to me. He's going back to London on Tuesday. You won't need to deal with him again, Evelyn." My father stands in front of me, looking down at me, checking I'm okay. After a moment, his face turns into that of deep regret. "Evelyn, I've had some time to think. What with Connelly's unexpected visit tonight and the fact he'll be in the city, I don't think it would be wise for you to go to London to see Samantha." He informs me.

"Wait, what?" I stare at him in alarm.

"I'll be phoning her parents in the morning to cancel the trip." My father puts his hands in his pockets. I just glare at him, full of disappointment, full of shock.

"No, no, Dad..."

"Evelyn, I'm sorry."

"No, you can't do that. I need to see Sam. Please." I shake my head.

"It isn't happening, Evelyn." His patience is wearing thin but I don't care.

"No!" I shove him but he barely moves. My strength is nothing compared to his. "I need to go to London. I need my best friend. She's all I have in the world. You can't take that away from me!"

"Evelyn, I refuse to repeat myself." He begins to glower. "It's already done." That coldness is back.

"I hate you so much." I sob and brush past him, hitting his arm with my shoulder as I run out of the living room, towards the stairs. As I reach the upper floor, Joan is emerging from her bedroom.

"Evie? What's happened?" I ignore her completely, wanting to be in my bedroom. My sanctuary. The one place the world can't make me feel like shit. Once again, I am slamming my bedroom door and throwing myself onto my bed. I think I've done this nearly every single night since we arrived. The common denominator: my father. He's managed to take everything away from me. My home, my best friend in the world. His connection to Connelly may have even took my mother away. I thought I was becoming happier. I thought I was finally starting to love my new life. But I was so wrong. This will never be home.

The next morning, I wake up with a tiredness and irritation in my eyes. I didn't really sleep. It was disrupted. I look at the clock on my bedside table; it's nearly 9am. And it's Sunday. Connelly leaves in two days. I begin to wonder what happens with Noah when Connelly leaves and if I still need to be his friend. It seemed as if Noah lived in Scotland. Maybe Connelly has separated from Mrs Connelly and they live here. It opens my mind up to so many more questions. These are questions I need to keep tucked safely in my head. I'm sure I'll get to ask them soon.

Once I am showered and clothed, I decide to brave downstairs. I haven't seen my father since I shoved him and stormed out of the living room. I also told him I hated him, so I imagine our first conversation will be frosty to say the least. The walk to the kitchen isn't an enthusiastic as it was yesterday morning. Any traces of our little Mexican night have vanished. Joan isn't making coffee. My father isn't anywhere to be seen. And neither is Francis.

"Hello?" I call out and wait for a response. Nothing. Not even Max. I make my way to the refrigerator to grab the orange juice. I pour myself a glass and lean against the worktop, sipping it slowly. After a moment, I reach for my phone from my back jeans pocket. I click on a certain contact and wait for the call to connect.

"Hi, Evie." Sam sounds unhappy.

"I take it you heard the news?" I sit on the worktop.

"Your Dad rang my parents about an hour ago. They didn't tell me why you can't come down." Once she explains, I check the time on my phone. It's only 10am. Jesus Christ, the man doesn't hang about.

"It's all a bit complicated, Sam." I sigh. At that moment, I hear the gentle thudding of footsteps down the staircase.

"I'm sure it is. Has anything exciting happened since we last spoke?"

"I met a boy." I inform her, nearly blushing.

"A boy? Is he cute?" Sam's sadness has made way for excitement.

"He's alright, I guess." My eyes soon see my father walk into the kitchen. When he clocks me, he clicks his fingers and points to the floor, silently ordering me to get off the worktop. I reluctantly do as he approaches the coffee machine. We barely acknowledge each other.

"Is Scotland growing on you now?" Sam asks as I aimlessly walk around the kitchen.

"It's alright. I much prefer London though. I miss the hustle and bustle, I guess. I'll still try and make the Summer show. Actually, you know what, I'll definitely be there." I check to see if my father reacts. He doesn't. He just sips his coffee.

"Oh, that's awesome! I'll reserve you a seat. Is your Dad coming with you? Only I need to know how many seats to reserve."

"No. I'll be coming alone." I state confidently. My father stops sipping.

"Okay, cool. I can't wait to see you, Evie. I miss you."

"I miss you too, Sam. I'll see you soon, I promise. Even if I have to hitchhike all the way to London or something." This definitely got a reaction.

"Alright. Well, call me when you decide to come down."

"Yeah, I'll call you. Give my love to your folks for me."

"I will. Bye, Evie."

"Bye, Sam." I hang up the phone and put it in my jeans pocket.

"Put your shoes on. We're going for a drive." My father finishes his coffee and puts the mug in the sink. Without saying another word, he leaves the room. I stand in a state of confusion. A drive with my father. Where are we even going? Whatever is going on, I'm incredibly reluctant.

I close the front door and my father locks it behind me. As I walk to the Mercedes, I realise I still haven't seen Joan or Francis. Maybe they're both still in bed. It is Sunday, after all. And they did get rather drunk last night. A thought suddenly enters my head.

"Are you driving?" I spin to face my father, who is opening the driver's side door. He nods. "Aren't you, like, too hungover?"

"Just get in the car, Evelyn." He takes a seat and shuts his door.

"Alright, well, if I die, it's your fault." I open the door to the back.

"No. Get in the front." My father orders. I frown before closing the back door and opening the front passenger side instead. I am never allowed to sit in the front. It almost feels wrong. I sit myself in the passenger seat and buckle my seatbelt. It's going to be weird seeing my father drive. Something so normal. So everyday. He's apparently a brilliant driver, as I've been reliably informed by my mother and Francis several times. But seeing him do something so out of character for him, it confuses me. Maybe this is just another way of trying to prove that he's human.

"Where are we going?" I ask. My father doesn't answer. He just pulls away from the house and keeps his eyes on the road. I roll my eyes and look out the window as we drive past the harbour. Maybe this drive is something to do with Connelly. Maybe we're going to visit him or something.

Half an hour later and my father still hasn't said a word. We're not in Skye anymore. We crossed the Skye bridge and made our way to the mainland. I rest my chin on my palm, watching the scenery fly by. I hate car journeys, especially when I don't know how long they'll be and the only other person in the car refuses to speak to me.

"Where's Joan?" I ask and wait. Nothing. "Where's Francis?" I wait again. "Where's your voice?" I still wait. "Dad, just say something." He just drives. I cross my arms and lean against the window. I close my eyes and sigh. I guess I'll just have to get some of the sleep I missed out on during the night.

When I wake up, we're still cruising. It looks like we're on an A-road. I haven't seen a busy road for what feels like ages. I notice a sign for Inverness as we continue to drive. Why are we going all the way to Inverness? I would ask the driver but apparently that's not an option. I sit up and yawn, noticing something in the cupholder. It's a takeaway coffee cup. My father is sipping his own.

"Is this mine?" I point to the cup. He nods. "Thanks." I take the cup and sip some. It's hot chocolate. The man does know me. I sigh and slouch in my seat. "Why are we going to Inverness?" I bite the bullet and ask. Again, he just drives. "Dad." I elongate the word, like a whine. For a split second, his eyes point in my direction. But he's silent. "God, you're such a dick sometimes." Maybe an insult will do the trick. I don't care if he tells me off, at least he'll be talking to me. "Can I at least put some music on?" I continue. My father presses the touchscreen on the centre console, loading up Spotify. I grab my phone and link it to the Bluetooth. I scroll through the options. "Ooh, maybe some heavy metal? Or some K-Pop. I know that's a forty-year-old's favourite. Or maybe something classical like Mozart. Take my father back to his bloody childhood." I smirk and look at him. No reaction. God, he should win an Oscar. I settle for some Nirvana and look out the window. I sing along and pretend to play the drums as I do. I will annoy him. I will make it my personal mission. I continue to play my imaginary drumkit while I sip some of my hot chocolate. My father also sips some of his own drink. Still stoic. Still completely expressionless. "Dad, just saying, it's illegal for drivers to eat or drink at the wheel." He just continues to sip. "Look, are you pissed off at me or something? Have I done something wrong?" I look at him yet again. He shakes his head. "Makes a change." I remark. He isn't amused. I slouch even more in my seat and sip some hot chocolate. "Is it because I said I hated you? Because I don't... not on weekends." My quip earns the tiniest hint of amusement on his face. He clears his throat and immediately removes it. This is tedious.

What feels like hours of torturous silent treatment later, we finally arrive at our destination. My father parks the Mercedes in the short-stay car park at Inverness airport. He turns off the ignition and gets out. I open my own door and stand outside the car, stretching my arms.

"Wait, why are we at the airport?" I ask. My father tilts his head, silently instructing me to follow, so I do. He leads me through the car park and towards the arrivals.

We stand together. My father checks his watch as we stand and wait for something. Or someone, of course. Maybe he's dragged me along to meet a client. I exhale, full of boredom, full of confusion. Some people start to arrive, and I assume a plane has just landed. I look up at my father, who barely notices I'm here. "Dad, come on. Stop being like this. Are you waiting for an apology or something? Because, alright, I'm sorry, okay? I'm sorry for what I said. I'm sorry for being such a..."

"Evie!" My eyes widen when I hear that voice. I instantly look through the arrivals and see someone I recognise, waving excitedly in the distance. She leaves her suitcase with her parents and runs towards me. I look at my father in confused shock. He winks at me in response. My breath shudders tearfully as I look back the arrivals.

"Sam!" I sprint away from my father and towards my best friend. I shuffle through the other passengers, apologising as I do. I just want to hug her. There is nobody else in the world I want to hug more than her right now. Once I finally reach Sam, we throw ourselves into each other's arms. I laugh. I smile. I cry. "Oh, my god, what are you doing here?!"

"Your Dad rang last night to say you couldn't come to London, so instead, he booked us a flight here today. I couldn't say anything on the phone this morning, because he wanted it to be a surprise." Sam explains everything. Her parents, William and Maria, soon stand with us. I gasp at them and they smile. I hug Maria.

"Hello, Evie, my darling. It's so good to see you again." Maria is like a second mother to me. Sam and I have been friends since we were babies.

"Hi, Will." I hug Sam's father. I then look back at Sam. My jaw is hurting from all of my smiling.

"Let's go say hello to Greg, sweetheart." Maria links arms with William and they approach my father. I giggle with Sam and we follow her parents.

"I can't believe this." I pull her to me as we walk. "How long are you here for?"

"A couple of days. Until Tuesday, I think." Sam answers. "I think we're getting the jet with your Dad back to London." As she speaks, I clock eyes with my father and offer him the most heartfelt smile in the world. He doesn't smile back. He just shakes William's hand as he greets him.

After leaving the airport, we all got into the Mercedes. Sam, Maria and I were sat in the back while our fathers sat in the front. Sam told me everything as we sat in the car. She and her parents are staying in Joan's house with us. Apparently, Joan and Francis were in on the whole surprise. Joan is having a little spa experience for a couple of days. Courtesy of my father. And Francis has been given the week off. My father parks the Mercedes outside the house and we all begin to get out. Will grabs the suitcase from the boot as I open the front door for Sam and her mother. I hold it open for Will, who gives me a thankful nod as he enters the house with their case. The moment my father reaches the door, I jump into his arms, catching him off guard. My father holds me tightly and chuckles. I don't say anything. Words won't even touch the surface of the gratitude I feel.

I sit on my bed with Sam, accompanied by Max. It's nearly midnight but we're full of beans. We talk endlessly. We giggle while sharing memories. It feels like the sleepovers I would have back in London and a small piece of home creeps into my heart. We continue to giggle as we look at Sam's phone together. "Does he have Instagram?" She is trying her hardest to find Noah's socials.

"I don't know, Sam. I barely know the dude." I stroke Max's head as I watch her work her best friend FBI magic.

"Noah Connelly, yeah?" She checks and I nod. She then scrolls and scrolls.

"You're not going to find…"

"Got him!" Sam gasps and scrolls through his profile. "Boyfriend check commencing now. Okay, he's cute, he's seventeen, and clearly knows how to have a good time. Oh, my god, okay, you would have the most adorable babies."

"Sam!" I shout in playful shock.

"I'll even be maid of honour at your wedding. Now, your favourite colour is purple, so I'm thinking a purple motif. Of course, your dress will have to be white." Sam looks back at her phone. "Ooh, why don't I message him and ask if he'll rent a tuxedo?"

"Okay, give me the phone!" I reach across Sam to try and grab her mobile but she keeps it away from me. She begins to type a message.

"Hello… Noah… this… is… Sam, Evie's… best… friend…"

"Sam, give me the damn phone!" I laugh and keep trying to take the phone from her.

"She… loves… you…" The moment she types this, I wrestle her. Sam holds out her arm as we roll around together on the bed, giggling and full of playfulness. We are so busy playfighting that we don't notice my wide open bedroom door and the person standing in the doorway. Not until he clears his throat anyway. Immediately, we stop rolling around and look up at my father.

"Guys, it's midnight. Keep it down." He instructs.

"Sorry, Mr Norman."

"Yeah, sorry, we know it's late for you old people." I grab Sam's phone and delete the typing she'd inputted.

"Less of the old, Evelyn. And don't stay up too late." My father instructs.

"Ja, Herr Kommandant." I continue to look down at Sam's phone, scrolling through Noah's Instagram. My father clutches the door handle and begins to close it.

"Evie, just let me message Noah. I need to check he'll be a good boyfriend." Sam says as my father is still walking out. I instantly lift my head and stare at her with the widest eyes, shaking my head in panic. When she sees my expression, guilt and regret wash all over her face. My father stops closing the door.

"Ignore her, Dad. She's just, uh, spent too much time away from the institution. She hasn't had her meds. I don't even know who this Noah geezer is. It's clearly just one of the voices in her brain." I do my best to crawl out of this hole.

"It's true. I am clinically insane." Sam tries her hardest not to giggle. It only makes me want to laugh. I hold it in as much as I can but it isn't long before Sam and I are falling into a pit of held back laughter. The only person not remotely amused is my father.

"Evelyn." His voice instantly stows the giggling.

"Ja, Herr Kommandant?" My voice is slow and quiet.

"Would you come and speak to me in the living room please?"

"Ja…" I close my eyes and mutter a silent prayer as my father leaves the room.

"Evie, I'm so sorry."

"No, it's not your fault. You just forgot to take your meds." I clamber off the bed, making Sam giggle as I leave the room.

The living room is silent when I walk in. My father sits on a sofa, barely blinking. I cautiously and slowly join him. The air is too still. God, I hate his little reprimands. I know what I've done. I really don't need a polemical. And he is taking an exceptionally long time to speak.

"Please tell me…" My father begins. I close my eyes. "That your best friend did not just refer to Noah Connelly as your boyfriend."

"Dad, we were just playing around. It doesn't mean anything." I slouch in my seat.

"I sincerely hope not. Because I'm also praying to all the gods that she was joking when she said she was messaging him."

"Of course she was. I would never let her message him." I'm offended by his low expectations of my intelligence.

"Have *you* messaged him?" His eyes find mine.

"No!" I am so irked. "We were just fucking about." He clears his throat. "Messing about."

"Good. Because this friendship with Noah Connelly worries me."

"We're not even friends."

"Just remember who his father is, Evelyn." He advises.

"Yeah, your scary business partner who looks like a mafia boss from the 1930's." I mutter. My father suppresses a smile. There is an interval of silence before he looks down at me again.

"You seem happier."

"I am." I shrug. "And thank you for organising this little visit. I'm still not entirely sure why you had to give me the silent treatment for the whole car ride though."

"All part of the process." He remarks.

"Would that be the process of pissing me off?"

"Evelyn!"

"Peeing me off." I cross my arms and look down. "You know, when we were in the car, I thought you'd gone back to your old self again. It worried me a bit."

"My old self? Please do enlighten me." He raises an interrogative brow.

"Oh, I'd really rather not." I sink into my seat.

"You've peaked my interest now, Evelyn. Please do illuminate me." He persists. I need to choose my words carefully. I actually think he has gone back to his old self. I feel that same timidity I always used to feel.

"Well... uh... you've always been a bit... um... oh, for god's sake, I've already told you what you were like." I start to become irate.

"Are you referring back to the conversation we had in the kitchen several days ago, where you told me I treated you like shit?" He is so passive. So indifferent. And hearing him swear is like a bullet to the ears.

"Yeah, that's the one." I want this discussion to end.

"But I don't anymore, is that what you're saying?" He keeps the discussion going. I just lean my head back, still not quite knowing what to say. "Evelyn, I'm waiting."

"Fine." I roll my eyes and sit up. "It's like there's two versions of you, okay? Nice Dad and Horrible Dad. Now, Nice Dad is a fun person. I like him. Horrible Dad is just scary as shit, I mean scary as hell. And I never know which one you're going to be. And right now, you're being Horrible Dad." I look away from him. He doesn't reply for a moment and I worry that I've touched a nerve. "Well, which Dad is this?" I suddenly feel an arm around my neck and I'm being yanked towards him. I then feel his fist rub against my head.

"No, get off!" I yell irritably and try to leave his grip but I am nowhere near strong enough to move his arm. "Dad!" I practically growl. My body twists and turns but my head is kept completely still as his fist continues to grind down onto it. "Dad, piss off!" I can't help but laugh.

"Is this not Nice Dad?" He frowns.

"No!" I giggle and he finally stops. He keeps his arm around my neck and hugs me to him. I lean back into him, not able to stop the smile spreading across my face. "Dad?" I look up at him.

"Mm-hmm."

"Can I ask you a slightly brave question?"

"What do you mean by brave?" There is scepticism in his voice.

"Well, it's about your job." I state carefully. He doesn't immediately shut it down. He just lets out a long sigh and nods.

"So, you know you're going to London with Sam and her parents on Tuesday?"

"Mm-hmm."

"Well, Connelly is going back to London on Tuesday too."

"Do you actually have a question or are you just going to continue stating facts?" His retort earns a slap on the arm from me.

"My question is, are you working with Connelly in London?"

"Yes." He answers seriously. "We have some meetings, a couple of lunches to go to, potential clients to meet. Nothing hugely exciting."

"Are you taking one of your guns?" It comes out involuntarily and I regret it. My father slowly looks down at me.

"Now, that *is* too brave."

"Yep." I nod in agreement. My father checks his watch.

"Come on. Go and get some sleep, we've got a lot of walking to do tomorrow." He kisses my head before unwrapping his arm from around me. I shuffle off the sofa. Before I leave the room, I hover in the doorway.

"Dad…" I slowly turn to face him. He looks at me, waiting for me to continue. "When you're in London with Connelly, just be careful, yeah?"

"Are you seriously telling me you're worried about me?" He gets to his feet.

"Well, yeah." I scoff. My father chuckles.

"I'll be fine. Connelly is, for the most part, harmless." My father puts his hands in his pockets, the picture of nonchalance.

"And for the least part?" I can't hide the fear in my voice. He notices.

"Something to remember about Connelly, Evelyn, is that the man has a million weaknesses. You won't understand half of them because you're not in business. But I know what they are. And as long as I do, the man is harmless." He stands right in front of me, smirking down at me. I nod slowly, processing his words.

"Does he know your weaknesses?" I frown up at him.

"I only have the one." That affection in his eyes is back. "Now, go back to bed."

"Goodnight, Dad." I stand on tip-toes but I can't reach his cheek to kiss it.

"You alright down there?" He taunts.

"Dad!" I giggle. My father chuckles and bends down so I can kiss his cheek. He then wraps me in a tight hug.

"Goodnight." He speaks nearly inaudibly as I leave his arms and make my way out of the living room. As I climb the stairs, all I can do is think. Today was amazing. He is amazing. This is not the same man as before. He's really changing.

CHAPTER EIGHT

I can't keep my hair out of my face as we walk up the trail to Coire Lagan, even if it is in a ponytail. Sam and I are walking side by side behind the adults. We are clad in hiking boots, sports clothing, fleeces and we have all got a hiking pole. It's a good job we're all relatively fit or this would be a nightmare. My father has assured us that the destination is worth the arduous walk. Coire Lagan is a corrie, a tiny loch surrounded by rocky peaks. In our backpacks are supplies for a picnic, bottles of water and all the technology we need in order to not get lost. Although, that would be fairly hard considering there are trail marks everywhere. And I mean everywhere.

We're about to approach the final ascent of the trail. It's incredibly short but unbelievably steep and the wayward rocks make it somewhat hazardous. Just before we begin, my father looks back at me and Sam. He gestures for us to walk ahead of the adults. Maybe that's so they can catch us when we inevitably fall on our faces. As we walk up the incline, I can see why they say this is the hardest part.

"Dad, when you said we'd be walking today, I didn't think you meant up a bloody mountain." I catch my breath in between speaking. He doesn't respond. Ever since we got in the car, he's been acting stricter and more distant. More like Horrible Dad with every moment that passes. "Alright, just ignore me then."

"What's at the top anyway?" Sam asks as she walks beside me.

"Oh, it's called a corrie. It's like a tiny loch surrounded by rocks and stuff." I explain as best as I can behind my heavy breathing.

"Have you been here before?" Sam continues to ask.

"I don't think so." I respond as she looks around at the landscape. She loves it, I can tell. And the more I think about it, the more I love this place. As I think and walk, I skid on a rock and nearly completely lose my footing. Sam catches my arm as I giggle and wave my arms out to steady myself. We soon laugh together.

"Evelyn, watch where you're going." My father scolds.

"Oh, quit your worrying, Herr Kommandant." I snap back, focusing on where I walk. If I do fall on my face, there will be no living it down.

"I suggest you change how you address me, Evelyn. And do it fast." His sudden words stop me from walking. Sam just looks at me. I frown in sheer confusion and spin to look at my father.

"What is your problem?" I scoff. His face is the same irritated, angry stare. He sighs before facing Will and Maria.

"We'll catch up to you. I need to speak to my daughter a moment." His voice is calm and stoic. I immediately feel a pang of uneasiness. Will, Maria and Sam all continue to walk. My father's eyes follow them until they are a fair distance away, and then he glares at me.

"Dad, what's going on? You're being…"

"You need to watch how you speak to me, Evelyn." He warns, full of harshness.

"Because I made a joke?" I shake my head, floored by his emotional 180.

"No, because I am your father. And I deserve a little more respect."

"Respect?" I ask in disbelief. "After sixteen years of being *this*, you really want my respect?" I turn away, hiding my tears again as I walk up the rest of the trail.

Not long after we began the ascent, we have finished it. And before us is the corrie, nestled peacefully in the centre of a ring of rocky formations. My father begins to walk ahead with Sam's parents. As he passes me, I catch his eyes. They're still guarded, but it's almost like he's giving me a silent apology. I turn around, greeted by a vista of magnificence. The land goes on for miles until it is broken by the sapphire waters beyond. Sam appears beside me and we lean against each other in a little cuddle.

"Are you okay?" Her voice is so soothing.

"Yeah, I'm fine." I nod, not really fine.

"Well, this needs a photo." Sam states as she gets her phone out of her backpack. As she directs the camera at me, I stretch my arms out to the side and place a wide open smile on my face. Once she has taken it, I take out my own phone and stand with Sam, our backs to the panoramic view behind us. We both wear the most delighted smiles as I take a selfie.

"Send it to me." Sam gleams.

"Sam, you really think I've got 4G here, in the middle of buttfuck nowhere?!" I scoff.

"Evelyn!" My father shouts from the distance.

"In the middle of nowhere!" I correct myself. "Jesus Christ, he's being a prick."

"Wasn't he always?" Sam asks.

"Yeah." I exhale. "Yeah, he was. Probably always will be." I stow my tears as I put my phone away. Sam notices.

"Look, when you send me the photo, we'll make it our backgrounds, okay? And whenever you feel sad or alone, just look at that screen." Her concern is heart-warming. There's so much care. She genuinely gives a damn and it warms my heart.

Roughly ten minutes later, we are all sat on the grass together, tucking into the picnic that we made. I continue to chatter with Sam about a myriad of things from the people in school to our college plans. She wants to go to UCL eventually, to study law. Sam would make a brilliant solicitor. She's patient but also a problem solver. As she discusses her plans, I suddenly remember that I don't have any at all. I don't even know if Skye has a college. I worry that I may not be getting the same opportunities that I would've had if I'd stayed in London. It angers me. There is a creeping feeling of frustration, like my future has been taken away from me and I had no say in it.

"You okay?" Sam's voice takes me out of my thoughts.

"Sorry. I got side-tracked." I take out my water bottle.

"What are your college plans?" She asks.

"I don't know. But I definitely want to go to uni. Get some independence. Meet people." I ponder aloud. I've never really had any independence. I was always driven to school. I've always had my parents floating about wherever I go. I'm looking forward to not depending on my father.

"Maybe we should go to UCL together." Sam suggests. I grin.

"Let's make a pact…" I take her hand, making her giggle. "You and me at uni together. Even if we're doing separate courses, we stay together. And maybe one day, we'll get a little flat and just…"

"Live together." She smiles, finishing my sentence.

"In London. Just us. All the shit food we want. No pissy adults." I nod confidently, making her laugh more. We wrap ourselves in a hug of blissful delight. I love her. I love her to pieces. As we hug, I feel the sting of realisation. She's going home tomorrow. And I'm staying here.

"Who's going swimming then?" Will hollers gently. Sam and I both frown, coming out of the hug.

"Yeah, no, thanks." I shake my head

"No, it's probably freezing." Sam comments. Will stands up and approaches her.

"Well, there's only one way to find out, Sammy." He bends down and picks her up before walking her towards the corrie.

"No, Dad!" Sam screams and laughs before Will puts her down. I smile at the image, sipping some more bottled water.

"I'm going for a walk." I tighten the lid on the bottle as I inform my father. I get to my feet and begin to trek away.

"Evelyn…"

"Not far, just… far enough." There is a palpable irritation in my voice as I trek further and further from the little picnic area.

I found my way to the edge of the peak, sitting on the grass and looking out at the landscape. It's the perfect place for some thinking. And that's exactly what I'm doing right now. Endlessly thinking. About my future. My situation. My mother. I still haven't really grieved properly. I'm not in the depression stage yet. I'm teetering around the bargaining stage. Although, by the looks of it, I'm still in the anger stage.

"We're heading back down in a moment." My thoughts are disrupted by the voice of my father, who is sitting on a rock nearby. I nod in response. "Are you alright?"

"Oh, you actually give a shit." I mutter under my breath. I don't know if he heard it. It was incredibly quiet.

"Yes, I did hear that." He sounds irritable.

"What do I do about college, Dad? There's nothing here."

"We'll figure something out. There are some learning centres scattered across Skye. If we can't do that, then we'll get you some online courses or something." His suggestion doesn't exactly appease me.

"So, that's it? I just sit in Joan's house for the next two years? Not meeting anyone, not seeing anyone. Just sitting at a laptop." I'm full of contempt.

"Evelyn…"

"Do you know what Sam's doing?" I scoff rhetorically. "She's going to Newham college to do her A-Levels. Business, law, English and psychology. She is going to one of the best colleges in London." I mutter spitefully. "Do you know why she's doing that?" I stand up and look at him. "Because, unlike me, she had a fucking choice." I turn and begin to walk away.

"Evelyn!"

"Oh, I'm sorry." I stop and spin to face him. "Did I not speak with enough respect?" I stare at him, full of scorn as I walk away from him. Immediately, he follows me. I don't stop. I'm full to the brim with anger.

"Evelyn Dawn Elizabeth Norman, stop walking away from me."
The moment he uses my full name, I stop. My father stands beside
me, looking down in irritation and concern.

"I've made a choice." I state, holding back tears. "When I'm
eighteen, I'm going back to London. I'm living with Sam.
Because…" I exhale tearfully. "For the next year, I am never
going to experience what I would've been experiencing in
London. No people. No learning how to drive. No underage
clubbing." I huff.

"Underage clubbing?" My father raises a brow at me.

"It's true though, isn't it? I am not going to be a normal
seventeen-year-old. My life has been turned right upside down
and all my opportunities have just gone." I'm getting more and
more riled up.

"You're blaming me for that, are you?" My father is using that
tone again. He's not happy. But for the first time, it doesn't affect
me. I don't cower at it anymore. I'm no longer a mouse staring up
at an eagle.

"Well, who else is there to blame, Dad? I didn't choose this. Mum
certainly didn't choose to die." My words are venom.
Unintentional venom. I realise I'm starting to put my foot in my
mouth again, especially when I see my father's expression.

"Be very careful with your next words, Evelyn." He warns calmly.

"Why? What are you going to do? Dad, I'm not scared of you
anymore." I laugh slightly, finally done with his bullshit.

"What do you mean, scared?" His irritation has now turned into
worry. "Evelyn, are you telling me you're scared of me?"

"How can I not be?" I shrug like it's obvious. "For sixteen years,
you barely spoke to me. You never even hugged me. You barely

even acknowledged I was in the room. And then, my mother dies. And I see this dark side of you. You have guns hidden in the house. You're secretive. You have a business partner who you are nearly certain killed your wife!" I shout at him.

"Evelyn…"

"And I'm supposed to just live every day, not thinking you're dangerous? I'm supposed to not be scared?" Once I have spoken my little monologue, he just stares at me. I can't gauge his reaction. I couldn't even guess which emotion he's feeling.

"I never wanted you to be scared of me, Evelyn."

"Well, that went to plan, didn't it?" I shake my head. He is about to reply but, like clockwork, his phone rings. I scoff and nod slowly as he takes it out of the little pocket of his trousers. He stares at the screen for a moment. "Answer it. Go on. Take it. Because whatever this bloody job is, it's crystal clear that I will never be more important than it." I offer him a look of scorn before walking away.

"What?" He's answered the phone. He's angry. "No, that's not good enough." He pauses. "Well, tell them I said so. That'll soon get their asses in gear." As the tears stream down my face, I look back at him. He is just pacing from side to side, the phone still to his ear. He glimpses at me briefly before looking back down. I sob and continue to walk back towards Sam and her parents.

I lean my head on my palm as my father drives us all back to Kyleakin. Sam's parents discuss the day energetically. Sam is asleep next to me, leaning on my arm. My father and I don't speak. We sit in silence. He keeps looking at me in the rear-view mirror. I don't look at him but I can see him in my peripheral vision.

"I was thinking…" My father finally speaks. "Since you're all leaving tomorrow, we should have a takeaway tonight. I'll buy."

"No, Greg, you've already let us stay with you and you've done all this driving. We'll get it." Will offers.

"That's kind of you. Thanks, Will." My father nods.

"What does everyone want?" Will spins to face the back.

"Well, what is on offer in Kyleakin, Greg?" Maria asks, full of the same energy.

"Not much, I'm afraid. Couple of good Indian places." My father continues the discussion. It's just background noise to me.

"Indian sounds good." Maria comments.

"Yeah, I'm up for that." Will agrees. "Evie?" All eyes are on me.

"Whatever you guys want." I respond with just enough enthusiasm to not seem like the rudest person on Earth.

"Oh, somebody is tired after our long day, it seems." Maria giggles softly. My father looks at me in the rear-view mirror again.

"Why don't you get some sleep, Evelyn?" He suggests. It's the same tone that he always used to speak in. And I feel so despised. I finally look back at him in the mirror. I then twist my body to face the window more, wanting to stare out at the scenery. I force myself not to cry. If I cry, then questions get asked. Questions I am not in the mood for. For now, I'll just sit in silence and let my mind empty itself of all thought. I'll just go numb.

My father parks the car outside the house. Maria nudges Sam awake and she adorably rubs her eyes. I get out of the car and close the door, nearly slamming it. I head straight for the house. I want to lie on my bed. I want to not speak to anyone, for I fear I will grow irritated and shut them all away. Maybe even say something I'll regret. My father watches as I use my own key to unlock the front door. I head straight to my room, not muttering a word to anybody, not even Sam. I want to shut myself away. I'm exhausted, mentally and physically. I land on my bed and shut my eyes. I need Joan's soothing voice. I need her to hug me and tell me everything is going to be okay. I need my mother. She'd know exactly what to say.

About half an hour later, my father, Sam and her parents are in the living room, discussing a variety of things. I can hear them as I walk down the staircase and approach the kitchen. Once there, I take a glass tumbler from the cupboard and fill it with tap water. I didn't realise how dehydrated I was. All that hiking must've really knocked me out. I pour whatever is left in the glass in the sink and turn around. I jump in fright when I see my father walking in.

"Sorry. I didn't mean to scare you…" He pauses after he speaks, clearly remembering our last conversation.

"Poor choice of words?" I raise a brow.

"Quite. Look, I need to know what you want." He doesn't elucidate so I offer him a look of confusion. "Food."

"Oh. I don't want anything." I put the glass tumbler in the sink and rinse it.

"So, we're back to the no-eating thing, are we?" My father crosses his arms and leans against the worktop. I do my best to ignore him while I decide to do some washing up. I hate cleaning but I'll do anything to stop my mind going blank. "You know what's going to happen, don't you?"

"What?" I say with little to no energy.

"You won't order anything and then you'll spend the whole evening stealing bits of mine." He's trying to lighten the atmosphere. I frown. This is the same man who's been a complete and utter tosser to me all day. I think carefully before responding. "No… because you'll order a jalfrezi and that's the most disgusting curry in the world." I tilt my head to the side.

"I demand you take that back." He speaks with a mock anger in his tone. I try my hardest to not smile. "Oh, my god. You're smiling. Evelyn Norman is smiling. Tell the pope." He echoes the words I said all those days ago in the car. I ignore him as I put a newly-washed plate on the draining board. "Okay, something is definitely wrong. You're doing the dishes."

"Dad." I scold, throwing the sponge in the sink. I finally look at him and he is now wearing an expression of concern. All humour has disappeared.

"Talk to me, Evelyn. Be candid. Be honest." He commands.

"No, because I'll put my foot right in it again. And today, you have shown me that I was clearly very, very wrong."

"Wrong about what?"

"You." I scoff tearfully before shaking my head and turning it away.

"Evelyn, talk to me. You asked me, not long ago, if I was someone you could talk to. And I am, Evelyn. That's my job." He explains.

"Ah, yes, your job." I regard him with a hint of spite.

"Don't be contemptuous, Evelyn, it doesn't suit you." My father frowns before letting out a long sigh. "Look, I have done nothing but think about what you said today And I am telling you now, Evelyn, that my work will never be more important than you."

126

"It is, though, isn't it? Your job is the reason we're here in the first place." I counter.

"An element of it is, yes."

"So you dragged your daughter away from her life because of your job? Forgive me if I'm wrong, Dad, but that sounds suspiciously like someone who values their job more than their child's happiness." I snap back with an incredibly good point, staring at him with my arms crossed.

"I'm not arguing about this. And I refuse to dignify that with a response. If you honestly think I value my job more than you, Evelyn, then god help you." That mask of anger is back.

"Let's just agree to disagree then." I call a ceasefire.

"Best idea you've had in a while." He remarks. I offer him a disdainful look. "Now, I will ask you again and you know I hate repeating myself…" He sounds like he's losing his patience, so I get ready for a reprimand masked as a question.

"No, wait. I know what's coming." I am miffed. My father sighs irritably. "It's going to be…" I imitate his low, clear voice. "Evelyn, who do you think you are? Evelyn, why do you keep giving me such disrespect? Evelyn, why can't you just speak to me like I'm your father? Evelyn, why do you always…?"

"What curry do you want?" His question takes me by surprise. It was clearly not what I was expecting. And he asks it with the blankest expression. I can't help but burst into laughter. He seems confused. The more he looks at me in bewilderment, the more I giggle. "Evelyn, answer the damn question. I need to order the food."

"Korma, please." I still can't stop laughing, holding a hand over my eyes. My father continues to glare at me in confusion as he leaves the room.

We all sit around the dinner table. The last supper. It feels ceremonious, celebrating friendship and a good couple of days. Sam and I chatter emptily as the adults partake in a slightly more grown-up conversation.

"When's this Summer show, Sam?" My father asks, bringing a forkful of jalfrezi to his mouth. Sam and I end our conversation.

"22nd July." She answers.

"I'm only asking because I need to make travel arrangements." My father leans back in his seat, an enigmatic look on his face.

"What travel arrangements?" I frown at him in confusion.

"Well, we can't walk to London, can we?" Once he responds in his usual sarcastic way, I clock his meaning. There is a slab of iciness in his voice. It's not a fun sarcasm, but an almost mocking one. I look down at my plate and take a forkful of food, still confused by his demeanour.

"Oh, my god, Evie, why don't I ask Miss Perkins if you can have a slot? That would be amazing!" Sam interjects, full of enthusiasm.

"No." I shake my head, my mouth full of curry.

"Oh, come on, you love playing piano. She'll say yes, I know she will." She persists.

"Sam, I'd love to but it's not going to happen."

"Why not?"

"I don't have a piano. Pitch-perfect performances don't just happen. I have to practice." I shrug, eating another small forkful of korma.

128

"Do you miss performing, Evie?" Maria enters the conversation.

"Um, yes and no. I miss having that creative outlet, I guess. But I know that every time I play, I'll think of Mum. So, maybe I shouldn't play." I become mournful.

"I think that's precisely why you *should* play." Maria continues, offering a wise perspective. I smile warmly at her, appreciating her words.

"Yeah, maybe." The rest of the evening falls into a pleasant collection of ideas and opinions. My father is still acting cold. I don't know why. Maybe he's worried about this visit to London. Joan always said that he takes his anxiety out on other people. Well, he needs to stop doing that. Because I'm getting sick of it.

CHAPTER NINE

Tuesday

Today is the day my father leaves for London. Today is also the day I say goodbye to Sam and her parents. I think back to the previous day. With the exception of my little polemic and my father's constant frostiness, it was perfect. A couple of days spent with Sam, laughing and chatting. And now it's all over and I feel a stab of disappointment. Reality has to crash into us in the end.

Sam and I have decided to climb up to Castle Moil, only a short walk away from the house. I know they will need to make tracks soon. And it breaks my heart. Once we get to Castle Moil, I sit on a stone wall and look out at the sea, trying to keep my hair out of my face through the heavy wind. Sam sits with me.
"I will try and come down to London soon." I mutter aloud. "I miss it so much."
"But this place is gorgeous, Evie."
"Yeah, but it's not home." I look down. "I don't think anywhere will be home ever again, you know." I start to well up. "I'm just glad I have you, Sam. I have my best friend in the whole world with me. Even if it's only for another…" I check my watch.
"Twenty minutes." My candid comment makes Sam giggle. She leans her head against my shoulder, so I rest my head on hers. We sit like this for a while, just looking out at the water, grateful for

each other. It's peaceful. Until my phone rings. I grab it from my jeans pocket and check the caller. I roll my eyes. "Yeah?"

"Where are you?" My father asks.

"Just at the castle."

"Come on back. We need to leave soon."

"Yeah." I hang up and put my phone back in my pocket. I sigh and look at Sam. I can feel the tears building and she notices. In a flash, we stand up and hug. It's tight. It's desperate. It's goodbye. We just stand in the middle of the hill and cry in each other's arms. "I'm going to miss you, Sam."

"I'm going to miss you, Evie." I can hear her tears. "But don't forget. You and me together in London."

"Together in London." I whisper.

I stand outside the Mercedes, giving Sam one last hug. I've already said goodbye to her parents. I'm crying again, but around her, I don't feel ashamed of it.

"Call me, okay?" She speaks in my arms.

"I will." I close my eyes and let her go. As she gets into the car, I wave and let out a long, heartbroken sigh. My father stands in front of me with a frown on his face. It's not an angry frown, it almost looks sympathetic.

"Tutor is here tomorrow at eleven. Joan is back in about half an hour. I'll be back on Thursday, around lunchtime. Pick up the phone if you need me." After his instructions, all I can do is nod unenthusiastically.

"Alright, well, have a good flight, I guess." I shrug, not knowing what to say. My father looks back at the car for a moment. Slowly and unsurely, he pulls me into a hug. It's odd. It's held back. It's distant. It's nothing like the hugs he was starting to give me. After he lets me go, I just stare at him emptily.

"I'll see you soon. Be good."

"Yeah, bye, Dad." I nod as he gets into the driver's side of the car. I watch the car as it rolls away, still stumped and disappointed as Max sits by my side. I look down at him and tap my knees. He jumps up at me and give me little kisses on my cheek. "Come on, let's go inside."

I lie on the sofa, flicking through channels on the TV. I'm bored. I check my phone; Joan isn't back for another twenty minutes. That gives me some time. Some completely unsupervised time. I scramble to my feet and rush to the staircase. I climb it, feeling that adrenaline again. As I approach the office door, I endlessly chide myself. I am dumb. I am a moron. But this is the one chance I have to check this room without being caught. If it's even unlocked, of course. Holy crap. It is. I think for a second before pulling the handle down. If Joan catches me, it's not the end of the world. And I am free of my father for two days. With a smile, I push the door open. I won't check the books again. I already know what's in those. No, I want something else. Files or something. Something with actual information. I sit in the large black leather office chair and open one of the drawers in the desk. I pull out an A4 ring binder and aimlessly flick through it. It doesn't look like much, just accounts and some business jargon that I don't understand. I put it back in the drawer and find another ring binder. Only this time, there is a title on the front: TARGETS.

"What the hell?" I frown and open it. It's profiles of people. Mainly middle-aged men, but some women. Maybe it's just a collection of potential clients. I am about to close the folder but one of the profiles is different. Stamped across the page in large, red capital letters is the word 'deceased'. Okay, maybe it's just a way to keep track of which clients are no longer an option. I put the file away in exactly the same place I found it and lean back in the office chair. I rack my brain for all possibilities. I look down at the laptop. I know I won't be able to access it. My father isn't an idiot and passwords are a thing. But I know him well. I open the laptop and I am immediately greeted by a sign-in screen. Maybe my mother's name is the password. I type in the name Elizabeth but no luck. Maybe it's his own mother? I type in Dawn. No luck. Maybe it's me. In blind optimism, I type Evelyn. It works. Dad, that's damn insecure. I thought you were an intelligent man. I feel a rush of fondness knowing I'm his password, though. His desktop background makes me smile too. It's a picture of me, him and my mother when I was a baby. Oh, god, this feels so wrong. I shouldn't be doing this. Flicking through files was one thing. But I've just hacked into his work laptop. No, Evie, stop. I slam the laptop shut. Know when to quit. Know how far is too far. And I have just gone too far.

Wednesday. I'm currently saying goodbye to my new tutor. Colin, his name is. He taught me all about language and structure in *A Christmas Carol*. My father got him up to speed on what I was learning in London before we moved. The irony of me learning about a money-hungry, miserable, nearly inhuman man isn't lost on me. No, that's not fair. My father isn't necessarily money-hungry. He just earns a lot of it. And he's not miserable. Nearly inhuman? Depends on his mood. And he does do a lot for charity. And he bloody loves Christmas. I follow Colin to the front door and bid him farewell as he leaves. As I wave at his car driving away, I spot someone near the harbour. It's Noah. He's sitting on his own.

"Joan, I'm just popping out for a second!" I know she's somewhere in the house. When I don't get a response, I just shrug and put my shoes on.

I make my way over to Noah. He is sitting on the edge of the harbour, looking down at the water. I decide to sit next to him, exhaling loudly and flashing him a warm smile. I know Connelly is essentially forcing me to be his friend, but I think I genuinely want to. He is the only other person my age in this mountainous, grassy wilderness.

"Hi, Evie."

"Hi, Noah." There is a calmness in the air as we sit together. I can't help but notice his expression. "What's wrong?"

"You don't need to be nice to me, Evie. I know all about my father's plan and what he asked you to do." He confesses. "I overheard him talking about it with my Mum."

"Are they together?" I ask, genuinely curious.

"No." Noah shakes his head. "They divorced ten years ago. Dad moved to London and Mum stayed up here with me. I only live down the road. That's why I like to cycle down here. It's beautiful."

"Yeah, it is." I lean back on my hands, soaking in whatever sun is cracking through the clouds. "Look, I don't want to be your friend just because your Dad asked me to be your friend. I do honestly want to be your friend, Noah." I offer him a sincere look. "I had to leave all my friends behind when I came here. It'd be nice to have at least one." I scoff. Noah chuckles.

"Aye, that sounds good." He smiles at me, so I smile back. "Do you want to go for a little bike ride? You can sit on the handlebars." Noah stands up and offers his hand. I grab it and he pulls me to my feet. We approach his bicycle.

"I've never ridden on handlebars before. What if I fall off?" I'm full of anxiety about this.

"You won't fall off." Noah laughs. "Come on." He mounts his bike. I sigh loudly and stand in front of it. Using whatever strength I have in my arms, I haul myself backwards onto the bike. So far, so good. "Now, just hold the bar. I won't go too fast."

"Not like last time then?" I spin my head to smirk at him.

"No, nothing like last time. I promise." He gives me a smile, making me giggle.

Noah takes us through the landscape, cycling along the single-lane A-roads near Kyleakin. It's a wonderful experience, seeing Skye like this and not through a car window. I can feel the bite of the wind against my face. And my hair flutters uncontrollably. Poor Noah is probably being whipped by it. As we cycle, something catches my eye, just perching on a wooden post on the side of the road.

"Noah, stop. Stop." I instruct hastily but quietly. I grin and get off the bike before silently crouching near the wooden post. "It's an eagle." I comment as Noah sits beside me. Perched on the wooden post is an eagle with a bright yellow beak and a mosaic of brown feathers. It's majestic. "What is it, a golden eagle?"

"Yeah, you find them a lot around here. If you're lucky." He whispers. I carefully take my phone out of my pocket. I take a few pictures and giggle quietly.

"This is going to make Dad so jealous. He loves eagles." I open up WhatsApp and send the picture to my father. I'm surprised there's 4G.

"Where is your Dad?" Noah asks.

"London. Business stuff." I continue to watch the eagle. I could watch it for hours. My phone vibrates so I check my messages.

I told you to stay in the house while I was away.

My eyes widen. Oh, god, he did. I completely forgot. I go cold. "Oh, shit, I need to go home." I hurriedly stand up, making the eagle fly away. As I approach the bike, Noah follows.

"What's the hurry?" He mounts the bike so I can climb aboard.

"I was technically grounded." I explain. Once I have safely tucked myself onto the bike, we both look up at the sky. We see the eagle, gliding around. We don't move for a moment. We just stay at the side of the road, watching the eagle soar. Such a powerful, free animal. I can see why they're my father's favourite. If reincarnation exists, I'm coming back as one of these.

After I have waved goodbye to Noah from the front door, I close it and smile to myself, full of a giddiness I haven't felt before. Oh, god, maybe I do like him. Maybe Sam was right. I'm going to marry him and have his babies.

"Evie? Where did you go? You know you're not allowed out while your father is away." Joan appears from the kitchen with an incredibly apprehensive look on her face.

"Sorry, Joan, I forgot." I take my shoes off.

"Well, best not forget again." There is a fear in her voice and I have no idea why. I communicate with my eyes, secretly asking what's wrong. She just tilts her head, instructing me to follow her back into the kitchen.

Every step as I walk to the kitchen is filled with unease. I'm genuinely scared but I have yet to find out why. Joan takes my hand as we walk through the house. I start to breathe quicker. Once we reach the kitchen, the situation becomes apparent. I gasp when I see two men standing in the kitchen, wearing designer suits. But they're not businessmen. No, they're something dark. That's when I realise where I recognise them from. They're the men we saw in Portree.

"Ah, there you are, Miss Norman." One of the men talks. The other just watches.

"Who are you?" I ask.

"We work with your father." Even I can tell that's a bunch of bullshit. I nod slowly in response, my hand still resting in Joan's. "Before we begin, do you mind if I make myself and my colleague a coffee?"

"Help yourself." Joan nods. The first intruder approaches the coffee machine. While they are both distracted, she squeezes my hand. "Evie." Joan whispers. I look up at her. "Secret Garden." She stares at me. I frown in confusion. "The key is in my trouser pocket. Secret. Garden." Oh, god. I know what she's saying. She wants me to get a gun. I nod, telling her I understand. I silently reach into her trouser pocket and collect the key. I take small steps backwards, making my way out of the kitchen.

I hurry upstairs, trying to not make any noise. I reach the office and my fingers shake uncontrollably as I unlock the door. The key nearly falls from my fingers multiple times. Once I am inside, I look up at the bookshelf. After I reach up and grab the book, I open *The Secret Garden* and the handgun rests inside. I hope she doesn't want me to use it. I wouldn't have the faintest idea what I was doing. I stow the gun in the back of my jeans and leave the office.

When I get back to the kitchen, the intruders are leaning against the worktop with their coffees in their hands. I slowly and carefully take the gun from my jeans and hold it behind my back as I walk in.

"Where did you go, Miss Norman?" The first intruder asks with a suspicious look in his eyes.

"Bathroom." I do my best to act casual. I stand behind Joan, who is holding a hand behind her back. I place the gun into it. The moment she has it, she cocks it and points it at the intruders. She isn't scared or even the least bit nervous. She looks like something from an espionage movie.

"Get out of this house. Or I shoot." Her voice is so clear, so confident. "Cover your ears, Evie." She is so calm. I hold my hands over my ears. The intruders reach for their own guns but Joan doesn't give them a chance to. I scream as two bullets are fired. The men fall to the floor, lifeless, before Joan takes the magazine out of the gun. She is hasty and poised. She really knows how to handle a weapon. I don't think I can take any more family surprises.

"What the...?" I whisper in shock, slowly taking my hands away.

"Evie, are you alright?" She stows the gun in the back of her trousers. She's so composed and casual. It's unnerving.

"Am I alright?! I've just watched my aunt shoot two people to death! Am I..." I scoff in utter disbelief. I feel sick. It's either the absurdity of the situation or the fact I've just seen two people get killed. I rush to the sink. Joan strokes my back as I heave vomit into it.

"Completely normal response, sweetheart." She attempts to comfort me. I just wipe my mouth and wash my hands, rinsing the vomit into the drain.

"Joan, what the hell is going on?" I shake my head, full of shocked confusion.

"Listen to me, Evie, there are things happening that you are completely unaware of. I need you to not ask questions." Her voice is full of urgency.

"Are you a bloody assassin or something?"

"Evie, what did I just say about questions? But no. I'm not." She strokes my arms.

"Then why have I just watched you kill two people?! Why were they even here in the first place?!" I continue to ask questions.

"Evie!" Joan holds my head in her hands. "Listen to me. No more questions. You cannot ask questions about this, alright? It'll open the biggest can of worms in the world. All you need to know is that you're safe. You'll always be safe."

"Okay, I won't ask questions." I shake my head, still catching my breath.

"Good girl." Joan pulls me into a hug. "Are you alright?"

"I think so." My voice shakes.

"Look, why don't you go upstairs and have a lie down? I'll sort these two out." She is clearly referring to the two dead bodies in our kitchen.

"Sort them out?"

"Questions, Evie. No more." Joan warns.

"Okay." I can't do anything but whisper. "Are you going to tell Dad?"

"No, I don't want to bother him with this." She explains. "I can sort this out. Just leave it to me, don't tell him. Honestly, Evie, go to bed. I'll bring up some brandy or something. You're probably in a bit of shock."

"Yeah, no shit." I nod. Joan giggles. She is being way too nonchalant about this. It's only lunchtime and I've already seen two people get killed. I smile unsurely at her before I make my way out of the kitchen. My legs feel like jelly. I can barely walk. I need to lie down. I feel all light-headed and weird. God, I hope I'm not sick again.

I wake up the next morning, but it's involuntary. Something wakes me up. It feels like there is someone in the room with me. My eyes sting as I drowsily open them. It's early, I can tell. I turn my head slowly and what I see makes me jump. My father is sitting on the edge of my bed, a glass of water in his hand. He doesn't look happy to see me, but his expression is a wall. I honestly couldn't take a guess at his current emotion. And he looks more frayed than usual, like he's had a sleepless night. His hair, for the first time, is out of place.

"What time is it?" I groan and pull the duvet over my face.

"A little after 6am." Once he informs me of this fact, I grimace.

"Come back in, like, three hours." My voice is just a tired drone.

"Drink some water." He instructs.

"No. Dad, go away." I roll onto my side. I am too tired for this nonsense. "What maniac wakes his child up at six in the morning, unless it's to go to an airport?"

"Evelyn, it wasn't a polite request." His words make me open my eyes. He's still acting like his old self. Maybe he knows what happened yesterday. I slowly pop myself out of the covers before sitting up and cautiously taking the glass of water. I take a small sip, still feeling incredibly sleepy.

"I thought you said you weren't going to be back until lunchtime."

"I got the jet and came back early." He is still a wall. I glare at him in confusion.

"Why?" There is a curiosity in my tone. I need to know if Joan has told him.

"Because I missed my little girl and I wanted to make sure she was safe." This isn't him. His overly affectionate words send a massive warning.

"Look, Dad, is this because I went out yesterday? Because, I swear, it was literally just down the road. I wasn't even gone for long." I rush to explain myself.

"No. Although, we will be discussing that later." He clears his throat and reaches into his suit jacket. I take another sip of water while he retrieves a device and holds it in front of me. "Evelyn, what is this?"

"It's a camera."

"Correct." He's acting weird again. "Helpful, these things are. Motion capture. HD video, and I can monitor it with this." He takes his phone out of his pocket. "If the camera picks something up, it sends it to my phone."

"21st century technology. Isn't it incredible?" I quip, full of apprehension. My father chuckles slowly, but it's not genuine. It's almost mocking.

"It is, indeed. Let me ask you one question, Evelyn. Where do you think I might have put two of these little cameras?" His brows furrow. His mouth is a hard line. The penny drops right as I am taking another sip. I hover the glass near my mouth.

"Shit." I whisper almost inaudibly. My father puts his phone and the camera back into his suit.

"You see, the first time, I let slide, because you weren't aware of why you're not allowed in there. This time, you knew why. It's a matter of safety, Evelyn. Your safety. And I take your safety very seriously." He is acting too calm. It's unnerving. "Now, I find myself having to make a difficult decision. Because I clearly need to remind you of the rules." He stands up and paces slowly. "Last time, I told you what would happen if I found you in there again."

"Dad, wait, you need to listen…" I get out of bed.

"Sit down, Evelyn!" He roars. It's loud. It's terrifying. It instantly sits me down. I start to cry. "I said I would remove all freedom. I meant it, Evelyn. I cannot trust you. You will not step foot outside this house again. You will not see your friends again. You will not leave my sight ever again!"

"Dad, please. Listen to me!" I release the floods from my eyes and my father falters for a millisecond.

"Evelyn, you didn't just enter my office. You opened my files. You hacked into my laptop." He's trying so hard to stay calm. I have no excuses. "You took a gun. Where is it, Evelyn?" He must've seen footage of me grabbing the gun for Joan.

"Joan hasn't told you?" I whisper.

"Told me what?" He seethes.

"Nothing." I shake my head. I need to concoct a lie. "I went into your office and I got a gun." Oh, god, this is going to land me in so much shit. But I need to protect Joan's confidence. "I didn't do anything, I just took it. Then Joan found me with it and I think she still has it." I explain, knowing exactly what to expect. There is a deep, dark fury in his eyes. One that I have never seen before. He has never once hit me. But his mere expression makes me wonder if he might.

"You took a gun from my office. Evelyn, are you out of your mind?!" The sheer volume of his voice crumbles me. "And you had the gall to sit here and pretend nothing happened!" Regardless of the situation with Joan, I still went into his office after meeting with Noah. And I left the house when he told me not to. I am not innocent, by any means. He has a right to be angry.

"Dad, please don't... don't turn back into Horrible Dad."

"You don't exactly leave me with much choice now, do you, Evelyn? You still expect me to be nice to you after you pull a stunt like that?" My father walks towards me with a rage in his stare. He clutches my arm. It hurts. "Evelyn, I told you never to lie to me again. Why do you keep lying to me?!"

"Because I'm fucking terrified of you!" I shriek. It comes out of nowhere. He releases my arm, a look of remorse on his face. "You know I am! This is precisely the reason why I am so bloody scared of you. So, do what you want, Dad. Keep me trapped here. Never let me see my friends again. I don't give a shit about your stupid threats and your cold words anymore. For sixteen years, I have had this. And I am done." My fear has turned to rage.

"Evelyn..."

"I haven't given a shit about anything since she died. For several days, I didn't even give a shit about myself. I wasn't eating and I didn't even care." I take a pause from my little outburst. I've

143

rendered him speechless. I've needed to say all of this for a long, long time. And now I finally have the courage. "All my life, I have felt so hated by you. But you were starting to change. And then when Sam was here, you hated me again and I don't know why. Because you refuse to tell me why and I never know who you're going to be. So pick one or the other. Because I am so done with the endless flips of this massive coin. And I can't take it anymore. I'd rather you just be cold to me all the time and not give me hope." My words fall apart beneath my tears.

"Evelyn…" His expression falls into something I rarely see. It's sheer sympathy.

"You once said that you will never be anything like Mum. But you were. You were really starting to become her. But now that's gone, and it's never coming back, is it?" I tearfully shake my head. "You said so yourself; your job is to be my father, not my best friend. But when I need you, when I really, *really* need my Dad… you turn straight back into this. And you will never be her." When he doesn't respond, I lie back down on the bed, burying myself under the covers and sobbing. He doesn't leave the room. He doesn't say anything. I do, however, feel him sit on the bed. The moment I feel a hand on my shoulder, I flinch. "Evelyn." His voice is so soft, so warm. It's miles away from what it was a moment ago. I stay beneath the covers, sobbing into nothing. "Evelyn…" I still don't respond to him. I just jerk his hand off my shoulder. I then hear him sigh. "Oh, what did your mother used to do when you were sad?" He ponders aloud. He's so quiet. "Whenever you were crying, she did something."

"Dad, don't." I can't hide the irritation in my voice.

"She used to sing you something when you were younger, didn't she? Oh, what was it?" He's clearly pretending he doesn't remember. It only irks me further.

"Dad." I warn.

"Something from your favourite Disney movie. Oh, I remember."

"No, you don't." I drone.

"Oh, yes, I do." I feel him lean against me, so his head is near mine. I'm still hiding under the covers and I am never coming out. He doesn't care. He just wraps his arms around my little Evie-shaped duvet pile and starts to sing *You'll Be in My Heart*. I'm surprised he actually knows the words.

"I am not four years old anymore, Dad." He doesn't stop. "Dad!" I begin to giggle.

"You're the classically trained musician with perfect pitch. So tell me, do I sound good?" He quips.

"No." I reply honestly. "I think if Phil Collins were dead, he would be rolling in his grave right now." After my comment, my father laughs and carries on singing. When he gets to the chorus, I start to find it unbearable, knowing I will never hear her sing it to me again. I sob. My father hears me and instantly stops singing. "Evelyn?" He strokes my arm over the covers. I rush out of them and hug him so rapidly, so desperately, squeezing my eyes shut. He holds me as I cry. He doesn't say a word. He just lets me release all of my pain.

"I miss her, Dad." I cry loudly. I cry like I haven't cried before.

"I know. I miss her too. And I am sorry. I am so, so sorry." All he does is hold me tighter. I don't know if he's crying. I've never seen him cry. But this is not the same man who was sat on my bed when I woke up. This isn't the man who was yelling at me only

145

moments ago. All of that malice has gone. This is the first time we've both properly grieved together. It's cathartic. And it's going to be life-changing. We've both been as strong as we can, but now we both realise how important we are to each other.

CHAPTER TEN

Sunday

It's my mother's funeral tomorrow. We have to go to London for the ceremony, and I am currently sat on the jet next to my father. Joan is sleeping in her seat nearby. We're staying at a hotel overnight, watching the funeral in the morning and then taking the jet home. It's going to feel odd, being in London again. I want to be excited but the reason for this trip slightly dampens that.

As I sit in the cream leather seat on the jet, I glance over at my father, who is reading his phone. It's only been just under two weeks since we left London, but I still have an endless list of questions. I know he won't answer questions about Connelly or his job, but there are some questions he will definitely answer. He hasn't turned back into Horrible Dad since he came back from London a few days ago, the morning I cried like a five-year-old in his arms. So I pluck up my courage and wonder if now is the right time to ask them.

"Dad?" I look down shyly.

"Mm-hmm." He still stares at his phone.

"Why did you sell our house?" It's a question I've been meaning to ask for quite some time. Once we left London, I assumed he'd sold our big townhouse in Notting Hill but never explained why.

"I haven't sold it. It's being temporarily rented." He answers, still looking at his phone. I want to snatch it from his hand so bad.

"You rented out my childhood home?" I stare at him blankly, clearly unimpressed.

"Yes. It's good business. Passive income." My father finally tucks his phone into his pocket and raises a brow at me.

"Is everything business to you?"

"I'm a businessman." He shrugs.

"Allegedly." I mutter under my breath, earning a certain look from him. I giggle at his expression, making him smirk.

"I also didn't sell it because I'm hoping we can live in it again one day." He gazes out the window.

"Wait, what?" Hearing my obvious confusion, he looks back at me. "I thought you said we were never living in London again."

"That was back when I was Horrible Dad, I believe." He winks, making me roll my eyes and shake my head. "And besides, if you are going to live in London on your own or with Sam, I want to be nearby."

"Oh, there's always a fucking catch." I mumble to myself.

"Evelyn!"

"Dad, we're on a private jet, who the heck is around to hear me swear?" I straighten my back, looking at the rest of the plane. My father chuckles. "Oh, yeah, nobody. We are literally the only people in this plane, and Joan is asleep." I slouch in my seat again, crossing my arms. "Anyway, who cares if I say a few colourful words? It's 2023."

"Me. That's the point." He glowers at me playfully. I stifle a laugh.

"Well, I blame the parents." After a while, I think about the other question I was meaning to ask him. "Dad?"

"Yes, Evelyn?" I think he's getting bored of these questions but I don't care.

"Why did we drive to Scotland? Why didn't we fly?" This question clearly ignites a spark of concern within him. He doesn't initially respond. He just strokes his chin and contemplates the words to say.

"Safety." Just one very vague word.

"That's it? Just safety? That's all I'm getting?"

"Yes."

"What, was Connelly going to blow up the plane or something?" I scoff. This does not amuse my father. And for a moment, he looks incensed.

"That's enough questions." He doesn't look at me anymore. He just gazes out the window, clearly full of thought, full of worry.

"I'm sorry. Foot in mouth disease." I mutter sincerely and lean my head back. I then feel a hand in mine, making me smile. When I feel my phone vibrate in my pocket, I frown and retrieve it.

"Who's that?" My father asks.

"Oh, it's probably Sam, checking details for tomorrow." I look at the message. It's not Sam. It's Noah. He's messaged me on Instagram. I immediately hold my phone to my chest, concealing it from the man beside me. "I, uh… I'll be back." I scramble out of my seat, wanting to find a more private place to read this message.

"Where are you going?"

"Christ, Mr That's-Enough-Questions. For a man who hates questions, you don't half ask a lot of them." I offer him a look of mock scorn and walk away. I can hear the faint sound of my father chuckling as I do. I hide myself away in the on-board lavatory and check to see what Noah's written.

Hi Evie
Sorry for the outreach. I heard you were in London for your mother's funeral and wanted to just say I'm thinking of you. If you need anything when you come back, a pleasant bike ride perhaps, let me know and we can do something. I really enjoyed our little bike ride the other day.
And thanks for being genuine.
Noah

Being genuine? I assume he's alluding to the potential agreement I have with his father and how I refuse to let that be the one reason we're friends. And he said he's thinking of me. That's sweet. But how does he know about the funeral? How does he know I'm not in Scotland?

With apprehension, I saunter back to my seat. My father is, again, typing away on his phone. Once I am sat down, I direct my eyes to the screen. It isn't long before I'm leaning over and peeping at it.

"What's a requisition?" I ask, staring at the screen. My father looks at me in annoyance, seeing that I've been prying. "Sorry." I sit up straight again and look ahead. He continues typing.

"When a business requests goods for a specific purpose." He relents and mutters, not once looking away from his phone.

"What purpose?" I lean against his arm, full of curiosity.

"Depends on the business." My father raises a brow at me. I grin at him, silently asking him to elaborate. He chuckles. "An example would be a health insurance company needing to buy training supplies and so on. It would have to go through a requisition process."

"So what are you currently requisitioning?" I can't hide my interest. He looks up thoughtfully, noticeably deliberating how much he wants to disclose.

"Stuff." My father nods.

"Stuff?" I give him a blank look.

"Stuff." He reiterates.

"Does this stuff include guns?" I persist.

"Evelyn, remember that day I told you that your questions were becoming a smidge too brave?" His question is clearly rhetorical, used as a warning.

"Yeah, sorry." I take the hint and sit up straight, holding up my hands in surrender. He isn't quite ready to tell me everything I want to know but he is opening up more and more. The thought pleases me.

"Before we land, I want to go through some rules for when we're in London." He puts his phone away and waits for my usual protest. I just nod at him. "You're being uncharacteristically compliant." My father observes sceptically.

"Come on, let's hear them." I lean back, crossing my arms.

"You do not leave the hotel without me or Joan. You do not have any phone contact with anyone apart from me, Joan or Sam. You go to sleep when I tell you to go to sleep. You stay close while we're walking around. No wandering off on your own…"

"Christ, how many are there?"

"And most important of all…" He is clearly not entertaining my quip. "Tomorrow, whatever you need, you tell us." There is a sincere look in his eyes. "I'm being serious, Evelyn. If you think you're not coping with it, tell me. Please."

"I will, Dad." I smile sadly at him.

"Get back here." He tilts his head, gesturing towards him. He then opens his arm. I grin as I snuggle into him and he wraps his arm around me, squeezing me to him reassuringly. I smile and close my eyes when I feel a kiss on my head. Two weeks ago, this would've been unthinkable. But now, it's almost predictable.

It's nighttime and I am lying on my bed in my hotel room. The TV is broadcasting quietly as I scroll through my phone. I re-read Noah's message. In a moment of madness, I send a reply.

Hi Noah
Thanks for the message. And thanks for thinking of me. I'm in the hotel in London, and the funeral is tomorrow. It's weird being back in London again.
How are things in bonny Scotland?
Evie x

I press send. Oh, god, I put a kiss. I never put kisses in messages. They're immature and redundant. But I just sent a kiss to Noah Connelly, the son of the man who potentially murdered my mother. I scroll through his Instagram, looking at his images and I realise what Connelly meant when he said his son needs a good influence. There are images of Noah drinking, smoking weed, raving. It seems like such a contrast to the boy I met at the harbourside. Soon enough, there is a gentle knock on my door.

"Evelyn, turn your light off and go to sleep." My father instructs from outside. I check the time on my phone.

"Dad, it's not even midnight." I complain.

"Evelyn, sleep when I tell you to sleep, remember?"

"Fine." I holler back before switching the TV and side lamp off.

"And your phone." He continues.

"I'm not on my phone." I respond, still scrolling.

"Yes, you are."

"What, have you got cameras in here too?" I retort. He doesn't reply. "Too soon?"

"Go to sleep." My father says slowly and firmly.

"Fine. Phone is off." I place my phone on the bedside table.

"I'll be ringing to give you a wake-up call at 8am."

"Gute Nacht, Herr Kommandant." I shuffle to get under the covers. God, I love hotel bedding. It's always better than home.

"Goodnight, sweetheart." My father walks away from the door. That's the first time he's ever given me a sentimental pet name. Maybe it's because he knows tomorrow is going to be incredibly difficult and he wants to give me all the comfort he can. As I lie in the covers, I wait. Once I know he has definitely gone, I grab my phone. There is a message waiting for me.

Hi Evie
Things in Scotland are bonny, alright. I don't know if you're interested, but in the summer holidays, me and a couple of friends are getting together. Just taking some blankets up the road and chilling by the coast. BBQ, some drinking. You're welcome to join us if you want. I know you said you wanted more friends here. We're happy to oblige. We're thinking Saturday 5th August.
Noah

I widen my eyes. I'm being invited to a gathering. For the first time since arriving in Scotland, I have people my own age inviting me to a little shindig. It fills me with the most incredible excitement. So I reply.

That sounds amazing. I'll definitely be there!
Look, I have to get some sleep and you may not hear from me
tomorrow, but I'll text you if I can. Goodnight.
Evie

After a while, once I have sent the message, my phone vibrates and a little goodnight message comes through from Noah. I put my phone back on the table and lie on my side. I can't stop the giant smile spreading across my face.

I am rudely awoken by the shrill ringtone of my phone. I groan and reach my arm out of the covers to pick it up, keeping my eyes closed as I answer the call.

"Yeah?" My voice is just a tired cello.

"Wakey-wakey."

"Yeah, I'm up." I drone, covering my face with the covers.

"Evelyn, have we established the rules around lying to me?"

"Dad, I promise I'm up." I yawn.

"Meet us in the lobby in an hour."

"Rendezvous in t-minus sixty minutes. Got it. Bye." I hang up the call and drop my phone onto the bed. I've still got time for ten minutes of snoozing.

I've showered, dried my hair and changed into my black dress for my mother's funeral. Being nearly the end of May, I've opted for a black knee-length frill-trim dress with short sleeves. On my feet are a pair of black pumps with a bow on the front. My hair is understated, falling into long, elegant waves. And my make-up is neutral. Not too much mascara. Not today; it'll just slide down my face. I take a look in the mirror before leaving my hotel room. I give myself a pep talk. I can do this. I've just got to get through the next few hours.

My father and Joan are waiting in the lobby for me. He's wearing a black suit and tie, with a white shirt. He doesn't really look any different to how he usually does. And Joan is wearing a lovely ankle-length, long-sleeved black dress with a belt. The moment my father sees me, there is a look of pain in his eyes. I don't think he was expecting to see his daughter dressed for a funeral so soon. Not just any funeral. The funeral of her mother. "Morning." I stand with them.

"Enjoy your ten-minute snooze?" My father asks, checking his watch.

"How do you know these things?" I grimace in confusion.

"Because I know you, Evelyn Norman. You've hated mornings since you were nine years old." It's odd hearing him reminisce about my childhood so freely. But maybe today, he's feeling a tad sentimental. "The car is picking us up in ten minutes. Are you hungry?"

"Not in the slightest. Where's the funeral?"

"Brompton, where the service will be held and where she'll be buried." He tries to run through the itinerary as stoically as he can, but I can hear the restrained anguish in his voice.

"Yeah, I have no idea where that is." I offer him a shy smile.

"London." He winks.

"Oh, my god. No shi…" My words are cut off when I feel Joan cover my mouth with her hand. My father raises a brow and I roll my eyes.

"Evie, this is a very sophisticated establishment. So, please refrain from your usual vocabulary in here." She scolds.

"I will limit my vocabulary, Aunt Joan." I surrender, my voice muffled by her hand. Joan takes her hand away from my mouth and gives me a look of warning. She also has that hidden anguish in her eyes.

"Any questions before the car turns up?" My father puts his hands in his pockets.

"How many people will there be?"

"Fifty, I believe. Family, friends, some work colleagues. Sam and her parents will be there too." He informs me.

"Nana and Grandad?"

"They'll be there." This information makes me smile. I love my mother's parents. "Also, I didn't ask you to in the end as I didn't want to put any pressure on you, but there is some time slotted for you to give a speech. But only if you want to."

"Are you giving a speech?"

"Yes."

"Then I want to as well." I nod, trying to appear confident. Inside, I am crumbling. I have never been one for giving speeches, but I want to say goodbye to my mother.

I am pleasantly surprised by the amount of people at my mother's funeral. My father was right; there must be fifty people here. Some I recognise, some I don't. I offer Sam a gentle wave as Joan and I stand at the front of the pews in the chapel.

"Evie." A voice I haven't heard in weeks appears next to me. It's my maternal grandmother, Caroline. I smile and spin to face her. "Hi, Nana." I close my eyes as she pulls me into a hug, a grandmother's hug.

"How are you, poppet?" Nana kisses my cheek as the hug ends.

"I'm okay, I think. Where's…?" My words are cut off by a pair of arms wrapping around my waist from behind me. I know who it is instantly. These hugs were always his speciality. "Hi, Grandad." I giggle as I'm squeezed.

"Oh, my little angel." Grandad spins me to face him, planting a long kiss on my cheek. "Whatever you need, we're here. If you want to come to the house, then the door is always open. Nana will cook you one of her famous roast dinners." He pinches my cheek, making me laugh softly.

"Oh, that would be amazing. I'll ask Dad." I nod.

"Where is your father, darling?" Nana asks.

"Caroline." My father's voice appears behind us. Nana instantly spins and gives him the warmest hug. My parents were married for two decades, and she became his second mother. He adores both of my mother's parents.

"Oh, Gregory." Nana kisses his cheek.

"Franklin." My father shakes my grandfather's hand.

"My boy. Anything you need." Grandad nods firmly, making my father visibly appreciative.

"Evie, sit with me, sweetheart." Joan instructs from beside me. I sit down next to her.

"We'll see you afterwards, alright?" Nana bends down and plants another kiss on my cheek before walking to another seat with Grandad. I exhale shakily, my fingers fidgeting on my lap.

"Evelyn." My father sits beside me. I look at him. "Remember, if you're not coping, you need to let me know."

"I will, Dad."

"Good. I'll be back in a moment." He nods before standing.

"Where are you going?"

"The coffin." He gives me a gentle, reassuring look before walking away, back towards the door we came in from. Once he is gone, I feel a pang of loneliness. I'm surrounded by people I love but it's all becoming very real.

After a few moments, subtle music begins to play; a piano arrangement of *Tears in Heaven* by Eric Clapton. Of course, it's a piano version of a song by one of her favourite artists. And it's being played incredibly beautifully. As we all stand, my legs begin to feel weak. My heart feels heavy. I see something out of the corner of my eye. My father and several others are carrying a coffin, walking slowly towards us. The moment I see it, I begin to lose it, my eyes to the floor and tears flowing out gently.

"You're alright, sweetheart." Joan takes my hand but it doesn't do a thing to stop the tears. I breathe loudly and rapidly. When I finally look up, I see someone to my right. The moment my eyes meet my father's, he gives me a look. A look I have never seen before. It's a look of unconditional love. It's a look that tells me he is going to get me through this. It calms me. Once the coffin has been placed onto the platform at the front of the chapel, the men that carried it approach their assigned seats. My father stands next to me as some kind of pastor stands before us, at an elevated podium.

"Please be seated." He instructs and we do. The music fades away. My breathing is still not normal. "We have gathered here today to celebrate the life of Elizabeth Louise Norman. A loving wife. A devoted mother. A daughter. A friend. A treasured colleague. We are joined today by Elizabeth's husband Gregory and their daughter Evelyn." The moment the pastor says my name, it all comes crashing down and I begin to breathe rapidly again.

"Dad, I'm not coping." I whisper tearfully. I then feel my father take my hand and squeeze it.

"Gregory and Evelyn are two people who I know miss this woman terribly and feel the wound her departure left behind. Gregory has lost a wonderful wife and Evelyn has lost her dear mother." The pastor looks sympathetically at me. I listen to every word he says as he continues to speak fondly of my mother.

After a couple more minutes of listening to the pastor, he gazes at my father, who still hasn't let go of my hand. It's time for my father to give his speech. He looks at me reassuringly before getting to his feet and I watch him as he stands at the elevated podium. He looks poised and calm as he clears his throat.

"Firstly, I would like to express my gratitude for your messages of condolences. They've given me the courage necessary to be the man I need to be today. Not just for my wife, but for our daughter, Evelyn. I was thrown into single fatherhood rather unexpectedly. And I battled such a harrowing loss. I had no idea what to do. I'd lost the woman I loved. The mother of my child. I told myself I needed to be strong, to not show any vulnerability. But Evelyn, these last few days, has taught me a lesson. Vulnerability around those we love is crucial. Exposing our heartbreak is imperative. Because it's the people we love that get us through that loss. They are the ones that rescue us from the darkness. And Evelyn has rescued me from that darkness. She has been the one thing that's got me through this. I've had to turn her life upside down, but she never fails to smile. She never fails to find an opportunity to laugh. At me, most of the time." There is a ripple of laughter around the attendees. I giggle softly. "And If I'm to make my wife one final promise, it's this. I will make sure our daughter feels her mother's love every day. She'll feel that love through my sister, Joan. Through her friends. I'm aware her best friend, Sam, is here with us today. But Evelyn will also feel that love through me. I will try my hardest to be everything her mother was. I will rescue her from her own darkness. You have my word, Evelyn." As he looks at me, I can't believe I'm hearing him say these words. My heart feels like it will explode. "Lizzy was unlike anyone I've ever known. She was the warmest, kindest person in existence. And she shouldn't be gone. She should still be here with us, playing piano or making our daughter laugh. The house, without her, isn't a home but we're trying our best, aren't we, Evelyn? For a woman like Lizzy to fall in love with and marry a cold-hearted bastard like me, it was a surprise. But I adored her. I adored her like I have never adored anyone. Well, with the exception of one person. Because the lovely woman I adored gave me a child. A child who reminds me of her every day. A child who I would move the world for. Who I would kill for and die for. Being a father is the most wonderful thing, and I owe it all to my beautiful, musical, kind and loving wife." His words are so honest, so completely from the heart. "Goodbye, Lizzy. Put in a good word for us and enjoy all the pina coladas in the sky. And we'll keep going, just like you'd want us to. We love you. Our baby loves you. I love you."

After hearing his words, I now have no doubt. The man loves me. The man loves me more than anything else in the world. It's been a few moments since my father gave his speech, and he is now sitting beside me, holding my hand again.

"And now, I believe Elizabeth's daughter Evelyn would like to say something." The pastor smiles tenderly at me. I suddenly go cold.

"Are you sure you want to do this?" My father whispers in my ear. "Yeah. Yeah, I'll be fine." I shake away the nerves and stand. My father offers me a comforting nod before I walk to the podium. I suddenly see a hundred eyes staring at me. I focus on the eyes I love. Joan. Nana. Grandad. Sam. And my father.

"Hi, everyone. I'll add an immediate disclaimer and say that this speech is not going to be as good as my father's. Because, well, he had more than twenty minutes to think about his." My quip earns a gentle wave of laughter. My father winks at me. "I wasn't going to speak to you today. I didn't think I had it in me. But every time I think of Mum, I gain a little courage. Because I know that she always wanted me to be brave. Even if it was just stage fright before a piano performance. Or when you start at a new school. I was always brave, because of her. And when she died, I didn't think I was ever going to be brave again." My tears threaten to take over but I don't let them. Any time I feel like I'm struggling, I just look at my father. And I feel like a million soldiers are standing with me. "But I am brave. All the time. Just getting through these last two weeks has been a brave thing to do. Living in another country. Living away from my best friend. Starting a brand new life. It's brave. But it hasn't just been Mum. I need to mention this person because he'll kill me if I don't." I smirk, making my father chuckle. "But Dad has been the one thing I needed. I know he talked about rescuing people from darkness just now… well, Dad, you don't need to make any promises that you'll rescue me, because you already have." I nod tearfully, trying to compose myself. "And at the beginning, I was so scared that you weren't going to. But I've seen more of your... humanity in the last two weeks than I have ever seen in you. And every time I look at you, I know I'm going to be okay. There's a part of me that just feels at home." My tears finally take over. "But I miss my Mum. I miss her hugs. I miss the way she would play me a song. I miss her little traditions, like watching a scary film on Halloween. Little picnics in Hyde Park. Making cakes together and just ending up being covered in flour because of our silly little food fights." I giggle mournfully but the tears soon come back. "And I'm just really scared I'm going to forget her voice. I'm really scared that I'll forget what she looks like. I'm just really scared..." I can barely speak anymore. I can't get the words out. I'm crumbling. In front of all these people, I am turning into a sobbing mess. I feel like I'm going to stop breathing. But then I see someone rushing to me. He's walking but with such a determination in his step that he may as well be running. And he runs to me. He doesn't care about the fifty people in the room. He doesn't stop for anything. I am his goal. I whimper and sob as I am pulled into the most loving hug I have ever felt. He holds me in his arms in front of everyone as I cry against him.

"You're okay. I've got you." He whispers as he strokes the back of my head.

"Dad." I choke.

"I'm here, sweetheart. I'm here." The attendees don't exist anymore. It's just me and him. Against this feeling. Against this grief. And it will always be just me and him against the world. This is it. His transformation is complete. And I know he will never go back to the way he was. My heart explodes. I feel so precious to him, stood at this podium, wrapped snugly in the arms of my father.

CHAPTER ELEVEN

Two months later

Grief is still taking its sweet time to leave me alone but it's getting better. That day changed everything. After the initial ceremony, my mother was buried in the cemetery. Joan and my father didn't let go of my hands. We're back in Scotland. I haven't been back in the office. I'm never going in there again. I don't think my father's heart could take it. And I don't want to kill the man. Joan still hasn't told him what happened with the intruders. I have no idea what she did with the bodies. Maybe they're in the garden. I told her about the lie I told my father, covering the truth about why I had the gun. She was incredibly grateful and will probably hate herself for a while for putting me in that position. But I told her everything was fine. I finished my exams. I found them all a breeze, apart from Spanish but that's only because no hablo español muy bien. I don't even know why I took it as a GCSE. Nevertheless, I came out of each exam feeling a sense of accomplishment. Even after all of the grief and my life getting turned upside down, I still did it. And I'm pretty sure I smashed it.

"Evie!" Joan sings my name like an opera singer as she walks up the stairs. I groan as I lie on my stomach, checking the time on my phone. It's only 7am. Soon enough, I hear the sound of my door opening. Joan rushes in and sits on my bed.

"Why do you and Dad have such a vendetta against letting me sleep?" I bury my face in my arms, still lying on my stomach.

"Because it's someone's birthday today." Joan speaks with a childish excitement.

"I haven't died yet. Good for me. Now leave me alone." I mumble, my voice muffled by my arms. I scream when I feel a pair of hands tickle my sides. I giggle and twist, trying to get away. She stops tickling me and stands up.

"Come on. Up you get. Change out of your PJs, shower, dressed, brush teeth and meet us downstairs." I don't know how she's this energetic at seven in the morning.

"I'm not allowed a PJ day on my birthday? Seems incredibly unfair." I complain as I sit up and yawn.

"Your father's orders, not mine. If you're going to moan about it, do it to him and not me." Joan winks before she clutches the door handle and leaves the room. I sit in a state of tired confusion. I then smile to myself. It's my birthday.

Even after a shower, getting dressed and attempting to look human, I am still rubbing my eyes as I walk into the kitchen. My movements are slow as I approach the coffee machine. My father is stood against the worktop with his own coffee in his hand. I don't usually drink coffee but I need to wake up. I don't look at my father as I wait for it to brew, but he is smirking at me.

"Happy…"

"No. Don't speak to me." I hold up a hand, silencing him. "You're the reason this crazy woman woke me up at some ungodly hour. On my birthday, when I should be allowed a lie-in and to stay in my PJs for as long as I want."

"Well, sorry to disappoint. But I couldn't let you stay in bed because we have a long drive ahead of us." My father states enigmatically before sipping some coffee. I frown and look at him, silently asking for some elaboration. He just briefly raises both eyebrows.

"More family secrets. How exciting." I mutter, my voice laced with sarcasm. Even after being rudely awakened, my wit is still ready and raring to go.

"We leave in ten minutes." My father informs me before finishing the rest of his coffee.

"Are you actually going to talk to me in the car this time?"

"If I feel like it." He shoves me playfully as he passes me to approach the kitchen door. I giggle and watch as he leaves the room. I hate surprises. I hate secrets but I'm not dumb. I assume it's a birthday thing and I suddenly feel excited.

Joan, my father and I approach the Mercedes. Francis has been told to stay and watch the dog while we travel to wherever the heck we're going. My father opens his door and I begin to enter the back of the car.

"Front, Evelyn." My father orders as he sits in the driver's seat. Joan winks as I stare at her in confusion. I soon sit in the front passenger seat as Joan settles in the back.

"Why am I in the front?" I ask as I buckle my seatbelt.

"I don't know. I think you were born today or something." My father's obvious quip makes me laugh. He fires up the ignition and drives away from the house.

"Am I allowed to know where we're going?" I yawn.

"No."

"Am I allowed to sleep?"

166

"Yes."

"How long is the journey?"

"About four hours."

"Four hours?! Where the hell are we going, the moon?" I grimace in sheer scepticism. "Can you at least tell me something about where we're going?"

"Christ, how many more questions are you going to ask me?" My father asks, mocking irritation as he steers the car.

"As many as I want, it's my birthday." I lean my head back, smiling to myself. "Are we stopping for coffee on the way?"

"I imagine so. Now, go to sleep. You're going to give me a migraine." He glances at me briefly before continuing to drive.

"Can we have the radio on?" Once I ask, he taps the touchscreen on the centre console. BBC Radio One fills the car. "Can I be the resident car DJ?"

"Evelyn Norman, go to sleep." He repeatedly strokes his fingers down my forehead and nose. It instantly makes me feel sleepy.

"Dad, that's not going to work." I mumble within a long yawn, closing my eyes.

"It worked for your mother. It'll work for me." He continues to stroke my forehead.

"Fine. I'll go to sleep. Stupid Dad superpowers." I surrender to my new Dad-induced sleepiness and twist my body to offer myself a more comfortable sleeping position. I can hear my father chuckle softy as his hand comes away from my face. These past two months, he's been my rock. My safety net. Ever since the funeral, I haven't seen a glimpse of Horrible Dad. I have yet to see him cry and he still has yet to call me by my preferred name, but I'm hopeful. I'm hopeful that he will drop those walls completely.

I hear my father whisper my name as my eyes open. The car has stopped and I look around. I recognise where we are from when we initially drove to Scotland. The shop in Fort William. My father unbuckles his seatbelt and looks at me.

"Joan and I are popping into the shop to get a coffee. Do you want anything?"

"Just a coffee, please." I answer, still half asleep.

"Food?"

"Uh-uh." I shake my head and close my eyes.

"Evelyn, please eat some food."

"Not hungry."

"I'll grab something just in case you are."

"Okay, Herr Kommandant." I respond with no enthusiasm, my eyes still closed.

"Have to pee?"

"No, Dad." I drone, just wanting some peace.

"Stay in the car." My father orders before leaving the vehicle. I open my eyes a smidge and watch as he and Joan walk towards the supermarket. If we're in Fort William, we must be roughly halfway. As I lean my head on my palm, I look out the window. I squint, thinking I see something. It may just be a sleep-induced haze. But I definitely see someone I recognise. Sat in a black BMW is Connelly. He isn't looking at me but he definitely knows I'm here. I collect my phone from my pocket.

Noah, is your Dad in Scotland?

I continue to glare at the BMW as I wait for a reply. My phone vibrates.

168

Yeah, he's driving up from the airport as we speak. Why?

It's definitely Connelly. Maybe it's coincidence. But the journey from Inverness to Skye doesn't pass through Fort William. You'd have to go majorly out of your way. I message Noah yet again.

He's in Fort William. I can see him in his car.

Noah replies.

Oh, he said he had some business in Fort William. Didn't say what it was. Why are you in Fort William anyway?

It's my birthday. Dad is very enigmatically driving me somewhere.

Oh, happy birthday! And I hope the enigma is broken soon.

I giggle at his reply. As I continue to watch Connelly, I notice he is picking up the phone and answering a call. He twists his head to look around before turning on the ignition and driving away. I frown. That was not coincidence. I suddenly jump when I hear a couple of doors opening on the Mercedes. My father sits beside me, a couple of takeaway coffee cups and small brown paper bag in his hands while Joan takes a seat in the back with her own beverage.

"One coffee." My father holds out one of the coffee cups.

"Thanks." I take it.

"And I got you a croissant." He places the little bag on my lap.

"That's brave, knowing I might get crumbs in your car." I open the lid of my coffee to cool it down.

"That's why you're the one hoovering them up." He quips. I giggle softly but I still feel apprehensive about seeing Connelly. I ponder whether to tell my father but he might change course and turn back. I don't want anything to ruin this little mystery trip. So I offer him a smile. I do my best to make it as authentic as possible but I know the man reads me like a book. He frowns at me as he turns on the ignition. "Is everything okay?" He knows something's up.

"Grand." I carefully sip some coffee. My father slowly pulls out of the parking space to continue our journey. As he drives through it, I continue to look for Connelly. But his BMW is nowhere to be seen. I do my best to make sure it doesn't ruin my day.

Nearing the end of our journey, I notice signs for Glasgow appearing more frequently and I assume we're travelling to the city. I try to think of what could possibly be in Glasgow that isn't in Kyleakin. A myriad of things. Large buildings. Cars. Young people. People in general. A McDonald's.

"Why are we going to Glasgow?" I ask my father, who is cruising confidently. I have also finally decided to eat the croissant he bought me.

"To be revealed soon." He keeps the enigma going.

"You know, this whole keeping stuff a secret thing is getting stale now. First it was your job. Then it was your business partner. Then the forbidden office." I am still cautious when discussing the office. I know it's still a sore spot for both of us.

"All of which, including this, need to stay a secret." My father remarks, navigating his way into the city.

"Just letting you know, I hate secrets." The irony of my statement isn't lost on me. I'm currently actively keeping two secrets from my father. Three, if you include the secret messages between me and Noah.

"I think you'll like this secret." My father glances at me and smiles. I've never seen this look on him before. It's like he's giddy about something. Again, I have the art of deduction and I assume it's birthday-related. I spin my body to see Joan, who just winks at me and stays silent. I huff and look ahead again, making my father chuckle.

He parks the car at an Arnold Clark dealership in Glasgow. Joan is the first to step out of the vehicle and she immediately heads for the entrance to the dealership. I clutch my door handle before noticing my father isn't leaving the car.

"Do you need me to stay here?" I ask slowly and suspiciously. He just nods. I let the door handle go. He reaches into his suit and pulls out a birthday card, wrapped in an envelope. Without saying a word, he gives it to me. I narrow my eyes in sheer scepticism before opening it. Once I pull the card out, I look at the cover. There's a humorous message about teenagers and their stereotypical traits. I giggle at it and open the card. A smaller card falls onto my lap. I take it in my fingers and study it. It's a provisional licence, with my details, picture, everything. I glare at my father and his eyes gesture to the birthday card. I read it.

Dear Evelyn

I know you said you didn't want anything but, sorry, that's just not good enough. I also know you said that you want to feel like a regular seventeen-year-old. And what are all seventeen-year-olds legally allowed to do, apart from piss their fathers off?

I laugh.

It's time for that thing called independence to start. To me, that's a terrifying notion and I know I will be spending the next few weeks looking at life insurance quotes.

I laugh again.

But this is it. Be the regular seventeen-year-old you want to be. Capture your independence. Starting with this gift.

Happy birthday.

All my love
Nice Dad

"Dad, what...?" I close the card and look at him in sheer puzzlement. He doesn't say a word. He just opens his car door and leaves. I put the provisional licence back in the birthday card and rest it on my seat once I get out of the car. My father walks ahead with his hands in his pockets. Joan is waiting for us at the entrance to the dealership. My father gives her a mysterious wink and she smiles. Holy shit. I know what's happening and I'm not ready for it. Soon enough, a man walks out of the dealership and greets us. "Welcome, Mr Norman, I presume?" The salesman approaches my father, holding out his hand for him to shake.

"Yes, that's me." My father shakes the man's hand.

"It's all ready to go." The salesman gestures for us to follow. My father raises both eyebrows at me before walking away. Joan and I join him.

"Dad." I look up at him, feeling a nervous panic.

"Yes?" He is indifferent to my distress.

"You haven't." I shake my head, fearing that he has.

"Haven't what?" My father looks at me with an overdramatic confusion. I scoff and frown at his lack of seriousness. He smirks and wraps an arm around my neck, pulling me to him as we walk.

About half a minute later, I realise that he in fact has. Standing in the middle of the dealership car display area is a light blue 2023 Fiat 500. It's gorgeous. It's stunning. The salesman throws the keys at my father, who nods thankfully.

"Paperwork is done. Logbook is inside. You can drive it away whenever you're ready." The salesman informs my father.

"Thank you." My father smiles professionally before the salesman walks away. The moment the salesman has gone, he slowly turns to look at me. Without saying a word, he throws the keys at me and I catch them awkwardly. "It's yours."

"No. No, no, no. You can't." I shake my head, floored by the whole situation. "Dad, that's a fucking car."

"A *fucking* car?" He puts his hands in his pockets and looks at the Fiat. Joan giggles softly. "I sincerely hope not, there are children about." My father looks back in my direction, a hint of amusement in his eyes.

"Dad!" I shout in cheerful annoyance and shove him. He chuckles before I jump up and give him the most grateful hug in the world.

"Happy birthday." He mutters softly as we hug, lifting me off the ground.

"Thank you, Dad." I begin to cry. It's gratitude. It's elation. It's the knowledge that my father understands exactly what I need.

"You're welcome, sweetheart." He kisses the side of my head and puts me down. "Don't get too excited, though. You're not driving it today. You haven't had a single lesson."

"Then, how…?"

"Joan is driving it back." My father explains. I look back at Joan and she is walking to me, her arms open and inviting. I rush into them, smiling widely.

"Can I sit in it?" I ask once the hug has ended.

"Of course you can." My father watches me as I use the keys to unlock the car. I giggle like a little kid and rush to the driver side door. My father joins me, opening the passenger side. Once I am sitting in the driver's seat, I look around at the interior. The steering wheel is so sleek and I take note of all the buttons on it. Some are for music controls. Some are for in-built calling systems. I then notice the touchscreen panel on the centre console. I put my foot down on the different pedals, laughing in glee as I experience what it feels like to be a driver for the first time. My father just observes as I explore the car.

"This is so cool!" I yell, making him smile.

"It's hybrid. Manual transmission." He begins to describe all the necessaries.

"Transmission is gears, yeah?" I place a hand on the gearstick.

"Correct. This model has six of them. Handling is light. Really nice size engine as you don't want anything too big for your first car." The moment he says this is my first car, my awareness of what's happening hits me even more. It's suddenly very real. "Dad, this is… no, this is too much. You can't do this." I smile in disbelief.

"Well, it's a bit late to tell me that. I've already paid the man and put your name in the logbook." My father quips, making me giggle more, if that was even possible. "If she could see you now, Evelyn, I hope she'd be as proud of you as I am." He turns serious and it catches me off guard in the most moving way.

"Dad, don't make me cry." I sniffle and succumb to my tears, quickly wiping them away.

"If you don't want to cry, then I'm afraid you're in for some disappointment when you see what's at home. Because if that doesn't make you cry, then I have failed spectacularly." The enigma is back.

"What's at home?" I ask, a mix of hope and dread.

My father walks up the staircase first, still not having told me any more information about what's waiting for me. Even during the four-hour car ride back to Kyleakin. He stops at the door to the spare bedroom in the house. Before he opens the door, he gives me a look. It's not a smile or a frown. It's just a seemingly empty expression but full to the brim with affection, and maybe a little pain. To anyone else, it would be unreadable. After a long sigh, he opens the door and holds it wide so I can pass him. Once I see what's in the room, I feel my heart skip a billion beats. I am immediately rendered a tearful, emotional mess. It's a walnut wood medium grand piano, sat right in the centre of the room. I have no words. I don't even know if I can breathe.

"It's a Steinway." I whisper breathlessly and tearfully.

"This is why Francis stayed home. It was delivered while we were in Glasgow." My father's voice is incredibly soft. I break down completely and spin before resting my forehead against his chest. He wraps me in his arms yet again. But this isn't the same enthusiastic, gleeful hug we shared at the dealership. It is full of sombreness. I am beyond happy with this gift, but a piano is a symbol. It's a physical representation of her. The woman we both adored to the ends of the Earth. "I thought about the conversation you had with Sam's parents the night before I left with them." He speaks as he holds me. I close my eyes tightly. "Obviously, I didn't plan it in time for the Summer show next week, but it's here now. And it's yours."

"Dad." I sob against his chest. "Thank you."

"You're so welcome." He plants an incredibly long kiss on the top of my head. I wipe my eyes as I step out of his arms. I sigh as I walk to the piano, sitting down slowly on the stool. I stroke my fingers along the keys. My father just stays in the doorway, watching me with his hands in his pockets.

"Any requests?" I chuckle softly. He echoes my tender laughter, slowly walking towards me and the piano.

"Something she played." My father instructs as he stands beside me. I smile, knowing the perfect song. I play *Sweet Child O'Mine*. The same rendition I played at the dinner party with Connelly. But this time is different. There's no anger, within either myself or my father. There's just sentiment. My singing isn't driven by irritation. But it's softer, more careful. Lighter. My fingers and feet touch the ivories and pedals like they're made of porcelain. My fingers float between each chord. I close my eyes, focusing on nothing but the memory of my mother. I suddenly notice my father perching himself on the edge of the stool I'm sitting on. I offer him a heartfelt smile before looking back down at the keys. As I reach the incredibly slow and soft '*where do we go's*, I hear something extraordinary. My father sniffles. I look at him as I sing and a single tear rolls down his cheek. It only fuels my own tearful state as I begin to play and sing with more force. More passion. I crescendo into the final '*sweet child o'mine*' and lose all control. Water runs down my cheeks like rivers. Until I play the last chord. Once I am done, we both sit in silence, remembering her. There is nothing but true love in this room. We don't say a word and we don't have to. We both know what the other is thinking. I rest my head on his shoulder and he rests his head on mine. The walls have collapsed.

CHAPTER TWELVE

A couple of days later, I am sat at my Steinway, plucking little notes as I go. I want to write something. I've always played arrangements but I've never once created anything original. I probably could write a piece of music if I put my mind to it; maybe I can treat it like a little project. As I aimlessly press keys and take note of which ones work and which ones don't, I find myself thinking about the Summer show. We're still going to it. My father has prepared the jet for London and made arrangements with Sam's parents. I'm excited but I feel like I'll just be regressing, unable to get closure from the life I had. I need to move on. I need to start enjoying Scotland.

I play a little song to myself, practicing the finer details of my skill. I am a confident musician but my mother had a certain flair. She was flawless and could design a melody with no real effort. I want to be her. I want to be at her level. Once I hear a knock on the door, I holler for them to enter. As I see my father appear in the doorway, I start playing the *Imperial March* from Star Wars. He crosses his arms, trying his hardest not to laugh. His attempts to look intimidating just make me smile more as I play the ominous chords.

"Very funny." He remarks and I stop playing, still smirking at him. "How is it?" My father asks as he walks towards me, looking

down at the piano. There is a certain gloom to his movements, like
something is on his mind.

"Perfect." I nod, stroking the keys. He sits himself on the edge of
the stool with me.

"I found you a driving instructor." My father informs me. I widen
my eyes in excitement. "Obviously you can drive your car
whenever you want with either myself or Joan, but I'd like you to
get some proper tuition."

"Thanks, Dad." I mutter sincerely.

"Our trip to London next week is all sorted. I just need to finalise
some plans and sort some bits." He looks at me carefully for a
split second, still shrouded in thought.

"What?" I frown. He sighs loudly.

"Come with me." My father gets to his feet and approaches the
door. I sit in confusion for a moment before making the executive
decision to follow him.

My father leads me to another room upstairs. It's his office.
I can't help but feel suspicious about his actions. He's quiet and
the uneasiness coursing through him is palpable. Once he has
unlocked the door, he walks inside. I stay in the doorway, not
wanting to enter. My father notices.

"You can come in, Evelyn." He states gently. It feels like he's
angry at me. But I have no idea what I've done. I take a timid step
into the ominous space. I cautiously look around the room in
general, still not knowing if I'm allowed to.

"Where are the cameras?" I ask, feeling a smidge of bravery. As
my father collects a book from the bookshelf, he gestures to the
corner of the room using his head. I look up to see a camera
mounted under the ceiling. I then spin to see another, opposite the

first, situated in the corner of the ceiling behind me. They're really quite obvious and I feel silly having missed them when I snooped around. My father suddenly breaks the tense silence in the air as he clears his throat. I look at him and he's holding a book.

"Take a seat." He tilts his head towards the black leather office chair. I slowly do as I'm told, a tiny speck of fear in my heart. I'm not scared of him. I never will be again, but I'm scared of what he's potentially discovered. Maybe it's Noah. Maybe he knows that I've been messaging him. I won't assume anything until he states outright why I'm in this room, supposedly about to be reprimanded. "Evelyn…" He exhales. "I need you to think back to when you came in here."

"Which time?"

"The third, technically." My father elucidates. He is referring to when I grabbed the gun. "I need you to remember exactly what happened and what you did." His voice is low and patient, but it's clear he is concerned about something.

"I remember." I nod, speaking quietly.

"Good." My father looks down at the book in his hand. "Please tell me, in detail, what happened when you came in here."

"Um, I came in. I grabbed *The Secret Garden*. I took the gun out of the book." This is still a bit of an open wound for me. "And then I left."

"Then what?"

"Nothing. I told you. I just took the gun and Joan found me with it." My fingers fiddle with each other. I'm anxious as hell.

"Evelyn…" My father crouches in front of me. He isn't angry. He looks worried. "I need complete and utter honesty when you answer my next question."

180

"I won't lie to you, Dad." I shake my head.

"Good." He pauses for a moment, like he's trying to stay calm. "Evelyn, did you shoot that gun?" My father asks, full of apprehension. I instantly frown, rendered perplexed by the question.

"No."

"Evelyn…"

"Dad, I didn't." I urge gently. He nods slowly before standing straight and opening the book to the middle page. He takes the gun out. Oh, god, is he going to shoot me? I would make a joke about that but something tells me now is not the time.

"The reason I'm asking, Evelyn, is because…" My father removes the magazine of the handgun. "There are two bullets missing from this gun. And I haven't used it." He elaborates. I remember why the bullets are missing. Joan.

"Okay." I exhale loudly. I need to tell him. "Dad, before I explain, can you promise me that Horrible Dad won't make an appearance?" I request as he puts the magazine back in the gun.

"I'll try my hardest." My father puts the gun back in the book and closes it, waiting patiently for me to continue.

"Here goes. Um… I lied to you." I speak so carefully, checking his reaction now and again. He's stoic, wearing a flawless poker face. "I didn't just come in, grab the gun and that was it. Joan never found me with it." I sigh, gathering all the courage necessary. "When you were in London, I went out for a bit, as you know." I look at him. He nods slowly, following my discourse.

"And when I came back, Joan seemed upset about something. She seemed scared. Then she told me to follow her to the kitchen and when I got there, there were two men in suits." Once I disclose this, my father loses his poker face slightly. "They were just stood in the kitchen but Joan seemed scared of them at the start. When the men were getting a coffee, she said to me 'secret garden' and told me the office key was in her pocket. She used 'secret garden' as a code, I guess. But I knew what she needed me to do." I lean back in the chair. "I unlocked the door and grabbed the gun from the book. When I got back to the kitchen, I secretly gave the gun to Joan. She shot the men and told me to go to my room." As I speak, the shock of the events comes back and I begin to cry. "I lied to you, Dad. When I woke up and you were sat with me, I had to lie to you. Joan didn't want you to know or worry or panic. So I made a lie." I can just about get the words out through the tears. I quickly wipe my eyes. "And that's it. That's the whole truth. That's what happened." I cross my arms, unable to look at him.

My father lets out a long, loud sigh and I immediately assume he's enraged. But he crouches in front of me and gently places a hand on my cheek, using his thumb to wipe my tears away.

"Evelyn, look at me." He breaks the silence. I sniffle and look into his eyes. They're not full of rage like I was expecting. They're full of affection. "Thank you for telling me the truth."

"No problem." I nod, trying to seem as relaxed as I can.

"Has Joan told you anything about why those men were here?" He asks.

"No. She told me not to ask questions. And then I immediately asked about five." I narrow my eyes thoughtfully, making my father chuckle.

"Alright. I will speak to Joan. She can shed some light on what happened in more detail, but Evelyn…" When he says my name, I listen intently. "If anything like that ever happens again, I need you to tell me. Anything that seems remotely not right, I need you to tell me immediately, do you understand?"

"There's something else." I confess. "When we were in Fort William on my birthday, and you and Joan were in the shop, I saw a black BMW. And Connelly was sat in it." The moment I say this, a mask of fear and anger wash all over my father's face. "He didn't do anything. But just before you got back, he answered a call and drove away."

"Evelyn, why didn't you tell me?"

"Because I knew you'd probably drive us home. I didn't want to ruin everything." I hurry to explain. My father just closes his eyes and shakes his head. He then stands up, rubbing the bridge of his nose. My father seems more concerned about Connelly being sat in a car than the two men who tried to kill me and Joan. I know there's more to Connelly than meets the eye. There's something darker going on.

"Alright, here's what's going to happen. From now on, you are not left alone." My father begins to turn back into his old self. But not the angry, cold part of him, just the focused, tactical part. "I am going to limit your contact with people. Whenever you are not in this house, you are with me or Joan. Nobody else."

"What?" I stand up in protest.

"For your safety, Evelyn." He starts to explain.

"But what about my driving lessons?" I cross my arms and shrug. I don't want to lose my one chance at independence. My father stares at me for a moment, clearly thinking deeply.

"I will teach you how to drive." There is so much reluctance in his tone. "I'll get dual controls put in the Fiat and I will teach you."

"Can you have dual controls if you're not an instructor?" I am
sceptical.

"You can if you're Gregory Norman." He winks at me. His job
obviously allows him some kind of authorisation that the public
doesn't have.

"And you're really okay with teaching me how to drive?" The
scepticism lingers.

"I'll be honest, Evelyn, I don't scare easy. Men like Connelly,
they come and go. For the most part, I'm not scared of them. I've
seen and experienced a lot of terrifying things. But listen to me
when I say that nothing in this world scares me more than the
prospect of being your driving instructor." My father raises a
brow. I am offended. I am miffed. I scowl at him but it only
makes him chuckle. In a gesture of playful violence, I lunge at
him, about to punch his chest but he manages to block my attack,
holding my fist in his hand. Jesus Christ, his reflexes are
ridiculous.

"Oh, I don't think so. Come here, you!" My father bends down
and throws me over his shoulder.

"No, no, no! Dad!" I yell loudly as he carries me out of the office.
He locks the door and begins to carry me down the stairs. "No,
Dad! Put me down! This is bloody terrifying!" I giggle and my
words jerk with every step he takes. I clutch the back of his suit
jacket tightly. "Dad, please don't drop me!" I'm in a state of sheer
terror but it's hysterical. He doesn't mutter a word as I am carried
through the house, still chortling. Once we enter the kitchen, it
sounds as if my father is collecting a set of car keys. As he turns to
head out of the kitchen, I lift my head up and swipe my hair away.
I see Joan, cooking something on the stove. "Joan! Help me!" I

plead desperately and laugh as I am carried away. She shakes her head, clearly very amused at the sight. "Traitor!" I shriek as we travel down the hallway.

As my father carries me out of the house, through the front door, I am still giggling uncontrollably. I have no real sense of where we are but I see the familiar concrete of the front porch as I am endlessly staring at the ground. He walks for a few paces more once we have made our way further outside. Until finally, I am put back on my feet right beside my new Fiat. I get my bearings, feeling incredibly disorientated.

"Get in." My father tilts his head towards the car after pressing the button to unlock it. I grin and open the driver's side door. My father makes his way to the front passenger side. I clutch the steering wheel, all giddy and happy. My father closes his door and clears his throat. "Now, I'm not letting you drive today but I may as well show you the basics before we get started." He explains and I know it's important that I listen.

"Okay." I try to stow my excitement.

"First things first. Seatbelt."

"Dad, we're not going anywhere." I argue.

"I don't care." He frowns. I roll my eyes and buckle up. "Now, your cockpit checks." He gestures to the different mirrors. "Rear-view mirror and side mirrors. Make sure you adjust them every time you get in, to make sure you can see clearly out of them." I clutch the rear-view mirror and shimmy it slightly to a better position. "Can you see the curb and the side of the car in your side mirrors?" He asks and I check.

"Yes."

"Good. Now, headrest. Lean your head back." He instructs and I do, feeling the headrest against the back of my head. "Top of the headrest should always be above your ears."

"It is." I nod once.

"Good. Push the clutch down for me."

"Is that the left one?"

"That's the one." He nods. I push down on the left pedal. It feels very far away. "Now I know you're a short-ass and this…" He squeezes my left knee. "This is way too straight. Roll your seat forward."

"How the bloody hell do I do that?" I look around for the lever.

"Front of your seat." He explains. I look down and reach for the lever. I pull it and roll myself forward slightly. I check the pedal again. "Bit more."

"Dad, I'm not that bloody short."

"Bit more." He repeats slowly, clear amusement in his voice. I sigh and roll myself forward some more. My father nods. "That's your cockpit checks done. These need to be done before every lesson, understood? I'm not letting you turn the ignition on until you've done them." There is a hint of enjoyment in his tone, like he's secretly having the time of his life. I know he loves cars. I know he loves driving. And now he's teaching me.

"Understood." I smile.

"Good. Now…"

"Dad." I look at him with a sincere expression.

"Yes?"

"Thank you for doing this. I know it can't be easy, not being able to share this with Mum. I know you're probably also fearing for your life." I giggle to myself, making him smile. "But it's the little

186

things, you know? Teaching me to drive. It's such a Dad thing to do. And before these last two months, I never even imagined that I would be sat in a car and you're teaching me how to drive. So, I appreciate it." I think back to who he was yet again, and the changes within him only seem more apparent. The old Gregory Norman would never have done this with me.

"Don't mention it." My father nods. "Now, your pedals." He gestures to my feet and I look at the pedals. "You know left is clutch. Middle is brake. Right is accelerator. Put your foot down on the clutch again for me. All the way." I press my left foot down. "Keep the clutch to the floor. These are your gears. You can only change them when the clutch is all the way down." He rests his hand on the gearstick. "First." He changes gear. "Second and so on." He puts it back into neutral. "Have a go at changing gears. Release the clutch between each one."

"Okay." I take my foot off the clutch and then press it down again. I pop it into first, second, third, fourth and fifth. "What's sixth gear?"

"Just an added gear to save fuel. Means you're not revving at high speeds. I'll teach you more about that later on as we won't be worrying about sixth gear for a while."

"Aw." I groan in disappointment.

"Turn the ignition on." My father passes me the key. I place it in the ignition and twist it. The car purrs to life and I grin. "I'll go through the other parts of your dashboard in the future. But one thing I really want you have a good long look at is this." He leans towards me and rests an index finger on the speedometer. "This is called the speedometer. You see the little numbers? That's how fast you're going. And I don't know if you're aware but there are rules as to how fast you can go."

"Dad." I giggle and roll my eyes.

"They're speed limits, not targets, Evelyn. Understood?"

"Understood." I drone. My voice suggests irritation but in actuality, I'm having the best time. We're doing something so normal. So everyday.

"I will get the dual controls fitted in a couple of days. I'll ring a mechanic on the mainland and get them done. Skye is not the easiest place to drive through, so I'll probably take us somewhere a bit safer for your first couple of lessons, and then you can take over. Maybe drive us back."

"Okay."

"Turn the car off." My father crosses his arms and I turn the ignition off. He sighs loudly. "Look, I know you probably never will, but don't ever drive this car without me or Joan." I'm offended at the notion.

"I won't."

"Good." He offers me a sincere look.

"Dad, can I ask you a brave question... again?" I aimlessly fiddle with the key and stare at the dashboard as I ask.

"Of course you can."

"Am I in danger?" I continue to stare at the dashboard. There is an incredibly long pause so I gaze at my father, who is once again glaring at me in deep thought. His eyes narrow slightly as he contemplates what to say.

"The problem is, Evelyn, if I say yes, then you'll become worried and scared. And I don't want you to be scared. I want you to enjoy your days without any fear of not being safe. But... if I say no, then you'll possibly put yourself in harm's way. So I am at a slight impasse."

"You know that was just an unnecessarily long way of saying yes?" I frown. My father suppresses a smile before that familiar gloom appears in his eyes.

"You're too smart." He remarks and I feel smug. He then lets out another long, thoughtful sigh. "Evelyn, you are potentially in danger."

"Connelly?"

"Yes. Like I told you before, Connelly is a dangerous man. And when you told me that he was in Fort William, something became very clear." My father leans back in his chair and exhales. "Let's go for a walk."

My father walks ahead of me as we approach Castle Moil. Being the middle of July, the weather is incredibly pleasant and I feel real rays of sun for the first time since we arrived here. I think about what he said in the car. I'm potentially in danger, and Noah has invited me to a mountainside get together. I wonder if I should go. But I also remember what Connelly has asked me to do. I need to be friends with his son, and refusing an invitation like that would not be fitting the brief. Once we reach the ruins of the castle, my father stops walking.

"Last time we went for a little father-daughter heart-to-heart in the country, my feet were being stabbed to death and you were angry with me." I state as I stand beside him, looking out at the panorama.

"You don't need to be sick, do you?" My father looks down at me with his arms crossed, clear humour in his tone. I nudge his arm with my elbow, making him chuckle softly. We both look out at the loch, the mountains and the sheer beauty of the Inner Hebrides. "Evelyn, any questions you have about Connelly, feel free to ask them. Because the thing that's become very clear to me is that I need to trust you with some truths. All part of the mission to keep you safe. So ask away. Anything." He is finally giving me something. I rack my brain for a question.

"Did he kill Mum?"

"Still unsure."

"Does he want to hurt me?"

"Yes."

"Does he want to kill me?"

"I don't know." My father puts his hands in his pockets. I notice he does this when he is incredibly contemplative. "But remember what I said. That isn't going to happen. I won't let it."

"I know, Dad." I nod. "So, do you know why he wants to hurt me?"

"Not quite. Now, I do have to be careful. Some questions and answers could lead to potential information about my job. So if I don't respond in detail, that'll be why." He elucidates.

"I understand." I am the most mature I've ever been. No quips. No sarcasm. It is of the utmost importance that I take this seriously. I realise that now. "My friendship with Noah, what do you want me to do with that? I can't avoid him but…"

"Stick with it for now. But don't ever put yourself in a position where I can't get to you, Evelyn." My father finally looks at me. I feel so small when he does. I used to feel meek and scared. But now I feel like his eyes are a shield. A suit of armour.

"Like what?" I ask.

"Well, as an example, I'm away in London for a week in August, and while I am away, I want no contact with Noah Connelly."

"Which week?"

"I'm leaving on the third." He answers. Shit. Noah's get together is on the fifth. I feel a pang of apprehension. I want to go. I really want to go. But my father will be all the way in London. "Is that going to be a problem?" He clearly sees that I'm dealing with an internal dilemma.

"No." I respond a bit too quickly.

"Evelyn."

"No. It's just so I know when to avoid him if he asks if I'm free on a certain day, that's all." My cover up is flawless. Even I'm surprised at how believable that was.

"Alright." He seems satisfied with my answer. I feel a wave of relief.

"Um…" I look down, ready to ask another question. My father directs his eyes towards me. "You said I could ask any question about Connelly, right?"

"Correct."

"Okay. So I have one more. And it's… brave."

"Ask away."

"You said you want to bring Connelly down from the inside and that's why you're working with him." I begin, incredibly shy. My father nods. "And you said he's dangerous. So, does that mean you're planning to… kill him?" There is a long pause after I ask this. I fear that it was too far. Too brave. Too curious. Until my father sighs.

"Yes."

CHAPTER THIRTEEN

It's the day of the Summer show. My father hasn't said a word to me since we got on the plane. Joan elected to stay home and look after Max. Francis is helping her with little house chores. It's just me and my father, visiting London. Our home. After our talk on Castle Moil, he seemed different. Not regressed, per se, but more guarded with his emotions. He hasn't been playful. He's been affectionate but it's like he's hesitant again. But I understand why now. I imagine he's terrified.

We land in half an hour. I am sitting in silence next to my father, who is still tapping away at his phone. I'm surprised the thing hasn't fused to his hand in some weird evolutionary mutation. I collect my bottle of water from its holder and take a long, thoughtful sip. I keep thinking about Noah. Not in a romantic way, but I'm endlessly battling the decision to go to the get together. Anyone with half a brain would avoid it like the plague. But sometimes I only have quarter of a brain. And I'm desperate to be with people my own bloody age.

"Dad?"

"Mm-hmm." He still looks at his phone.

"Are you okay?" The moment I ask, he looks at me, full of concern and confusion.

"Of course I am. Why wouldn't I be?"

"Well, could you please alert your face of that fact? Because ever since the walk on Castle Moil, you've been a miserable bastard." I candidly offer him my opinion. I'm waiting for the glimmer of amusement in his eyes but it doesn't come. He just goes back to his phone.

"I'm fine, Evelyn."

"Oh, it seems you need to alert your voice as well." I mutter under my breath, crossing my arms and looking away from him. He sighs loudly, locking his phone and popping it in his trouser pocket.

"It's nothing that concerns you." He eventually explains.

"Job stuff?" I am getting too curious. But again, to my surprise, he nods. "Okay, if I ask you just one little, teeny-tiny question about your job, will you get angry at me?" I twist my body to face him, looking up at him with a hopeful smile.

"Well, in order for me to ascertain whether or not I should be angry, I will need to hear the question in the first place. So you've dug yourself rather a large hole there, Evelyn Norman." He frowns at me. I open my mouth to respond but I stop myself to think carefully. His blank expression offers no assistance.

"That is very true. But please may I ask it anyway?" I smile innocently.

"Go on." My father rolls his eyes.

"So, you said you need to work with Connelly, yeah?"

"Mm-hmm."

"Well, my question is, is your work with Connelly your real job, or is there some kind of side hustle going on?"

"That's two questions." He's irritated.

"Technically it's the same question just broken into two." I smirk smugly. For the first time since our talk at Castle Moil, he chuckles.

"And I'm not answering either of them." My father winks at me. I slouch in my seat, full of disappointment. "Evelyn, my job is something I would like you to never have any knowledge of. So any question you have about it, just think twice first." He retrieves his phone again and continues to type away.

"Yeah, yeah." I mutter, looking away from him.

"Evelyn, are you okay?" He asks, still staring at his phone.

"Yeah, why?" I continue to mumble.

"Well, it seems you need to alert your voice of that fact."

"Oh, look, you're still bloody hilarious." I roll my eyes, still looking away. I then jump in surprise and giggle loudly when I feel fingers at my ribs. He is still staring at his phone with no expression as he tickles me, but he's playful again. This offers me some hope that I haven't completely lost him.

We take our seats in the theatre at Kensington Hall Academy, waiting for the show to start. I'm looking forward to it. I really am. But a small part of me feels like I'm still mourning for the life I had. Being back here, seeing the stage I would've performed on, I feel disheartened. My father is sitting beside me. I'm sure he would rather be anywhere else in the world right now. I don't think he really wants to watch two hours of teenagers singing, dancing and playing instruments. But he's here to support my friend and I'm grateful for that. I flicker through the programme that I picked up as we entered. I scan it for the setlist to see when Sam is performing. I raise my brows in pleasant surprise and lean towards my father.

"Hey, Dad." I smirk.

"Mm-hmm."

"Sam's is the fifth performance. So, if you want, we could leave after she's done. It means we'll only be here for about half an hour." I raise an eyebrow at him, offering up my suggestion. He just stares at me with a look I haven't really seen before. I think it's a mix of relief and appreciation.

"Evelyn, I love you." His overly affectionate statement makes me laugh. "Honestly, maybe I did raise you right."

"Of course you did. I'm a delight." I read the rest of the programme. "Although, let's be fair, Mum was really the one who raised me…"

"Evie!" A warm, middle-aged female voice makes me jump out of my skin. I spin my head to see a woman, standing beside my seat.

"Hi, Miss Perkins!" I stand up, dropping the programme onto my chair, and enter her arms. She rocks me from side to side, clearly very happy to see me.

"Oh, my dear, how are you?" She scans my face after we hug.

"I'm fine. How are you?" I can't stow my smile.

"I'm very well, thank you. Oh, and I must say hello to your father." Miss Perkins turns her attention to my father, who is standing behind me, offering his hand.

"Good to see you again, Angela." He shakes her hand tenderly. She was always a firm favourite of my mother's, mainly because she gave such a damn about my piano tuition.

"Gregory, it's wonderful to see you too. And you have my deepest condolences." Her voice is so sincere.

"Thank you." He replies. Once the handshake is over, Miss Perkins just gleams at me.

"Oh, I miss you, darling. I miss roaming around the corridors and hearing you playing my grand in the music room." Again, there is no pretence. She's a wonderful woman.

"I miss it too, Miss P." I mutter sentimentally.

"And do forgive me for giving your slot to Olivia. I'll be honest, she pestered me so much for it that I don't think I had a choice in the end. And she's singing your bloody song too." There is an element of infuriation in her voice and it delights me.

"That's okay. Sam and I both agree that's she's a little…" I am about to say what I really want to say but my father clearing his throat stops me. I look down at him as he sits in his seat, giving me a cautionary stare. "Oh, get off my case, I was going to say pitchy." I snap, making him stifle a chuckle.

"Well, I best get backstage." Miss Perkins' speech makes me face her. "But Evie, if you ever wanted to enrol in the sixth form here, I'd be more than happy to give you anything you need. And I need a good pianist for the orchestra. Nobody so far can pull off an accelerando like you can. Honestly, darling, they're never on my tempo."

"No?" I raise my brows, utterly amused by her words. "And thanks for the offer but we're in Scotland now. I don't think it's really possible."

"Oh, I didn't know that, dear. Well, if you're ever in London again, this place will be your home. Musically too, I hope." She offers me an affectionate wink.

"Thanks, Miss P." I speak softly before she walks away. That stabbing feeling comes back. Almost like the fear of missing out. I feel tearful, knowing I would've had a place here if I wanted it. The sadness starts to creep up. I can feel it tugging at my heart.

"I'll be back in a sec." I mutter before walking away from our seats.

"Evelyn, stay here!" My father calls me back but I don't stop.

I look down into the sink as I stand in the bathroom, breathing loudly and trying to hold back even more tears. When I look in the mirror, I see what my tears have done to my face. There are tiny specks of mascara under my eyes and it's so obvious that I've been crying. I need it to go away. I need to look stronger than this. I know I'm not worried about crying in front of my father anymore. But it's for me more than anyone else. I can't let every little disappointment get to me like this. So I exhale and wipe the mascara away, forcing the sadness back. When I am happy I will pass as looking relatively okay, I leave the bathroom. The moment I step out the door, I stop, looking ahead in fear. More men in suits. Four of them. They haven't clocked me yet. They don't seem to just be working for the security here either. It's a public event, they've obviously bought a ticket and managed to get in that way. I take cautious steps backwards, pushing the bathroom door back as I do. Once I am back in, I lock myself in a cubicle and stand on the lid of the toilet. I try my hardest to stow my panic when the main bathroom door flies open. I've never been this scared in my life. I go cold. I start to breathe loudly. I cover my mouth with my hand, trying to be as soundless as possible. There are heavy footsteps as the unknown person walks around.

"No sign of her, sir. There's a locked door but I didn't see anybody come in. Must be out of order or something." The unidentified man must be speaking into some kind of phone or earpiece. Wow, he's a bit stupid. Doesn't even check the cubicle.

"Is her father there?" Another voice comes through the speakerphone.

"Too public, sir. Can't get a clear shot." The man in the bathroom's words make me feel sheer, unbridled terror. A clear shot? I hope to god that doesn't mean what I think it means. He's here to kill us. Assassinate us.

"We'll get another chance. Get back to the office." The person on the call orders. I recognise that voice. It's not Connelly. But I recognise it.

"Sir." Bathroom man snaps. I then hear the distinct sound of the main door opening and closing. I melt, shaking in relief and fear at the same time. I sit on the toilet lid and try my hardest to just breathe. I'll need to brave the outside soon.

After roughly five minutes, I ascertain that it's safe to leave the bathroom. I unlock my cubicle and very carefully head for the main door. I'm still skittish. I'm still being incredibly cautious. Before I open the main door, I take a deep, courageous breath. Once it opens, I immediately scream in fright and let out a loud exhalation when I see someone. But it's not an assassin. It's not a man in a suit. Well, he is in a suit. But it's my father, standing before the doorway with a furious look on his face.

"We're leaving. Now." He scowls at me. I haven't seen this look in a while. But it's all too recognisable. I try to follow his broad, angry steps as he walks away from the bathroom.

"But, Dad…"

"Evelyn, we are leaving." He doesn't look back at me but his voice suggests a plethora of negative emotions. I try my hardest to keep up.

"But Sam's performance…"

"I don't give a fuck about Sam's performance, Evelyn!" He roars as he spins to glower at me. His face and voice are enough to instantly halt my steps. And he said the F-word. God, he's livid. "I am driving us back to the airport and we are getting on that plane. Then we are flying back to Inverness and I am driving us home. Is this in any way unclear?!" Horrible Dad has rejoined the chat. Well, he clearly never really left.

"No." I speak beneath the tears forming in my eyes.

"Good." His mouth barely moves. God, he's outraged. I don't know if it's at me or not. No, it can't be at me. All I did was go to the bathroom. He must know about the men in suits. I stand still for a moment as he continues to storm away. My arms hug my body as the adrenaline calms into a gentle shock. "Evelyn!" His impatient hollering is just background noise as I look at the floor. I'm petrified. I'm frozen, coming to the realisation of what nearly happened. They nearly found me. They nearly killed my father. I slowly lift my gaze to see him. "Evelyn, for fu…" As he spins to face me, I sprint towards him. There is a look of confusion and concern on his face as I forcefully run into his arms and sob.

"Dad, he was looking for me." I cry loudly.

"It's okay, sweetheart." He strokes the back of my head, whispering so quietly.

"I was so scared." I choke against his shoulder.

"I know you were. But I've got you." Again, he is such a contrast to who he was only moments ago. When he sees me this vulnerable, this afraid, it instantly smashes the glass in his heart. "Come on. We need to go."

I sit in the seat on the jet as my father paces back and forth, roaring commands and insults down a phone. I don't look at him. I just stare at nothing, my mind completely blank, like you do on a mode of public transport.

"It needs to be sorted! Now!" He bellows down the phone. I can't help but feel sorry for the person on the other end of it. "This cannot happen again, do you understand me? And you better have a good excuse if it does, or so help me, you will live in a state of constant fear after I'm done with you." My father hangs up the phone and drops it angrily onto the cream leather seat nearby. Remind me never to piss him off. God, I want to say something witty. I would've done if this was in any other context. But what happened at the school was harrowing and I don't think I've completely processed it. My father doesn't sit down or look at me. He paces, full of endless thoughts, I imagine. After a moment, my father finally stares at me. He must notice my fingers constantly fiddling and my eyes seldom blinking because he approaches the little mini bar. When he has finished making whatever he's making, he walks back to me with a glass of an amber-coloured liquid in his hand.

"The fuck is that?" I look at the glass in confusion.

"Brandy." He states, surprisingly calmly. "Drink it and I'll pardon your Latin." He instructs and I take the glass from his hand. Once I sip some, I splutter and choke.

"Ew." I croak and shake my head.

"Evelyn, drink it. You'll feel better." There is still clearly some paternal need to look after me in there somewhere. I take another sip and grimace. "Do you have any questions for me?"

"Do you know what happened? In the school?" I rest the brandy glass on my lap.

"Not all of it. I was hoping you could illuminate me as to what happened after you left the theatre." He's speaking in that distant, cold tone again.

"I went to the bathroom. And when I came out, there were some men. They looked iffy so I went back inside." I'm surprisingly nonchalant. Or just numb. "And then one of them came into the bathroom. I locked myself in the stall."

"They followed you in?" My father's face falls. He looks terrified.

"No. They were just aimlessly searching. I happened to be in it at the time." I take another swig of brandy.

"Evelyn, I told you to always stay by my side." His voice is softer but he's still clearly irritated by my wandering off. I just scoff derisively.

"So you're just going to chaperone me every time I need a pee?" I ask, my voice reflecting the absurdity of his notion.

"Listen to me, Evelyn..." My father crouches in front of my chair as I take another sip of brandy and suppress a gag. "I called for you to come back. And you didn't. God, if you'd have left that theatre five minutes later..." He closes his eyes and shakes his head, looking down to the floor. He's right. I'm incredibly lucky with my timing.

"Dad, I'm sorry." I whisper. His brown eyes find mine.

"Forgiven." He kisses my forehead, offering me some much-needed reassurance. "Did anyone say anything?" He clears his throat and stands straight, pacing again.

"Um, yeah. The guy who came in made a phone call. He was following orders, speaking to someone higher up. They were clearly looking for me. Although, I didn't really make it difficult. He didn't even check the stalls." I frown, taking another swig of brandy. "Literally the stupidest henchman ever. I could've done a better job at finding me and I can't find my shoes half the time."

"Evelyn, take this seriously."

"Sorry. Um, he told his boss that he couldn't find me. And then the boss asked if you were there... but he said..." I am suddenly rendered mute by tears. My father stops pacing and looks at me.

"What did he say?"

"That it was too public. And they couldn't get a clear shot of you." I let the tears fall as I, again, come to the realisation that I nearly lost my father. "Dad, they were in a school with children and people and..." I begin to have a panic attack. My father crouches in front of me again, staring into my eyes.

"I know, okay? I know. I am sorting this, Evelyn. I promise you."

"Dad, they wanted to kill you." I shake my head.

"Am I dead?" He asks rather casually for my liking.

"No."

"Then drink your brandy and calm down." After my father's incredibly *helpful* suggestion, I take another sip of brandy. He stands straight and paces yet again.

"Cheers, Dad. Absolutely stellar advice. I will now magically calm down." I speak dryly, full of irritation. I can see his lips very slightly tilt up into a smile. He then sighs and sits in the seat next to me.

"Maybe I shouldn't go to London for the week." He rests his fingers against his chin as he gazes out the window. "It's too soon to leave you on your own."

"But Joan..."

"Yes, Joan will be there. But she isn't me. I trust her unequivocally with your life, but when it comes to protecting

202

you…" His words make way for another sigh. "I once said that I would die trying to protect you." I listen to him, still drinking my brandy. It's nearly all gone. "And I would, Evelyn. Any father would. I know I've been cold for the past sixteen years but parenthood is still parenthood. And people make unbelievable sacrifices for their children. That's been the case for me ever since the day your mother spent eighteen very painful hours in St Barts."

"Eighteen hours?" I ask in slight shock.

"Mm-hmm." He raises a brow.

"Christ. Sorry, Mum." I mutter to myself, knocking back the rest of my brandy and placing the glass on a side table. My father chuckles. Hearing his soft, low laughter makes me smile. I lean against his arm and he doesn't hesitate to wrap it around me, planting a kiss on my head.

"Evelyn, you need to do what I say, alright?" My father brings the seriousness back. "I need you to stay with me when I tell you to."

"I know, Dad." I roll my eyes, still leaning against him.

"And I'm sorry we had to cut the performance short. I'm sorry we had to leave and miss Sam's dance." His heartfelt apology evokes a funny thought. I suddenly start laughing to myself. Unable to stop. "What's the joke?" I can't answer his question. I shake my head, too far gone into this wheezy, uncontrollable laughter. "This isn't a laughing matter, Evelyn."

"I'm sorry. It's just…" I snicker again, starting to sound like Donald Duck. "If you really didn't want to be at that show, you could've just said. You didn't have to hire four hitmen to kill you." I surrender to my laughter again, checking his reaction. He's trying so hard not to entertain it.

"That's not funny, Evelyn." My father shakes his head, forcing himself to stay apathetic.

"Yes, it is!" I laugh silently with my eyes closed, making my chest pulse rapidly, the occasional high-pitched wheeze coming out. I haven't laughed like this for a long, long time. After a second, I can hear the familiar sound of an amused Gregory Norman. He's laughing. I can feel it, leant against him.

"Evelyn…" He stops laughing, and it's to reprimand me. But the clear humour in his voice only makes me laugh more.

"Dad, am I drunk?" I giggle. Maybe it was the brandy.

"If this is you drunk, then we're all fucked." I can hear the smirk on his face.

"Pardon your Latin." I chastise, making him laugh loudly. My own laughter eventually calms into a soft hum. "Dad?"

"Mm-hmm." Flickers of chuckling still come through. My own chuckling has disappeared and made way for something fearful. "The man that the guy in the bathroom was talking to, it wasn't Connelly. I recognised his voice though. Do you know who it was?"

"Yes, I know who it was." He confesses. I look up at him, opening my mouth to ask something, "And no, I'm not telling you." My mouth immediately closes. He's still not completely giving when it comes to specific information, it seems. But he will be. I nearly died tonight. I deserve to know why. And I deserve to know who wants me dead.

CHAPTER FOURTEEN

August 2ⁿᵈ

I'm driving around in the Fiat. I'm not the most confident driver
in the world but that will take time. My father is sitting in the
passenger seat, ready to use the dual controls if I need him to.
Hopefully, he won't need to. I haven't yet had any close calls or
instances where he's needed to take over. I'm currently cruising
down the A87, back towards Kyleakin after going to Portree for
the day. It's a stunning drive and I can see why my father takes
any opportunity he can to get behind the wheel. I also haven't had
any bad weather while driving. There was the odd spittle of rain
but nothing to render me the least bit nervous.

"Stop at Broadford. I need to pick up some stuff for Joan." He
instructs and I nod. "While we're there, we could start practicing
some manoeuvres."

"Do you know what they are?" I ask, quickly glancing in the rear-
view mirror.

"Yes. There are three, four technically, if you include the
emergency stop."

"What are they?"

"Reverse around a corner, reverse parallel park, reverse bay
parking and, like I said, emergency stop."

"That's a lot of reversing." I comment. I'm getting really good at speaking while driving. I don't get distracted in the slightest.

"It is. But they need to check you can do them." He takes his phone out of his pocket and brings it to his ear. I'm not really sure he should be using the phone while teaching me to drive. "Hi, Jo, we're on our way home. Remind me what you need." He pauses. I assume she's speaking. "Uh-huh." He listens again. "Yeah, she's doing fine." My father looks at me. "She's no Lewis Hamilton but we're still alive."

"Oh, ha-ha." I fake laugh.

"Yes." He listens again. "Alright, see you soon. Bye." My father hangs up the call and puts the phone back in his pocket. As I drive, I notice I am approaching a tractor. My tummy turns. I need to overtake. "This is easy, alright?" My father obviously knows I need to as well. "Trick to overtaking is gear use and knowing when to do it. Wait until you have a clear, straight road. Check your side mirror, indicate, pop it down a gear and move into the other lane. Get it done quickly but safely."

"Okay." I mutter to myself as the stretch of road becomes straighter. "Now?"

"This seems good." He nods and I pop the clutch down, changing down into fourth gear. My acceleration picks up and I move into the other lane. It's clear as day and I have nothing but time to pass the tractor. Once I am past it, I gently move back into my lane. A massive smile spreads across my face as I seamlessly change the gear back up to sixth. "Your first overtake. Well done."

"Thanks. You know, you're a really good instructor. Maybe when you want to retire from your secret job doing whatever the hell it is you do, you could do this instead." I suggest.

"Evelyn, teaching one reckless seventeen-year-old to drive is more than enough experience for me." My father comments.

"Reckless?" I frown and briefly look at him.

"Speedometer." He raises a brow. I glance at the dashboard.

"Shit, sorry." I ease off the accelerator. My father shakes his head and chuckles.

"What do I always say about speed?"

"It's a limit, not a target." I drone.

"Correct. And remember that, Lewis Hamilton." His little remark makes me giggle. I love this. Moving to Scotland is turning out to be one of the best things that ever happened to me. My relationship with my father is perfect. I'm driving around the most gorgeous terrain in the UK. Thoughts of London and the life I had dwindle away more with every day that passes. I think I'm starting to be happy.

I park the car at the little Co-Op in Broadford. Once I know I am straight and within the lines, I pull the handbrake and put it in neutral. My father opens his door and I do the same. I can't remember the last time I went food shopping with him. It's yet another one of those everyday things that I rarely see him do. Once we are out of the car, I lock it and follow my father into the shop. He grabs a basket and we begin to mooch around.

"What does Joan need?" I cross my arms as I walk beside him.

"Just some extra stuff for tonight." He scans the shelf. I find myself growing a tad bored. I hate grocery shopping. It's soul destroying. I aimlessly take steps away from my father. "Stay with me." He orders and I stop. I roll my eyes and walk backwards, back towards him. Once he has what he needs from this aisle, we walk to another.

"Can I not even walk around a shop on my own?" I ask.

"No."

"But we're in the same building. I'll just shout Marco and you can shout Polo. It'll be fine. We'll even form a secret code. Maybe I can shout 'secret garden' if I'm in trouble." I suggest, earning an unamused look from my father.

"Evelyn, we were in the same building nearly two weeks ago and remember what happened. You stay with me." He reiterates firmly.

"Fine."

"Speaking of secret garden, I had a chance to talk to Joan about the intruders." He picks up a bag of pasta.

"Oh?" Finally, an interesting conversation.

"Mm-hmm. All taken care of. Police are aware. We don't need to do anything." He clears his throat as we make our way to another aisle.

"So, she killed two people and that's it? No police? No questions asked?" I frown, slightly confused by the situation.

"That's it, and keep your voice down." He picks up a garlic bread, obviously not willing to divulge any more information. I nod in understanding and continue to follow. As we pass an aisle, I see someone and smile. He's in the beers, wines and spirits aisle, staring at the shelf in deep thought. I reverse away from my father and approach Noah, nudging his arm with mine.

"Oh, hey, Evie." Noah gleams when he sees me.

"Hi." I am shy for some reason.

"Just grabbing some essentials for Saturday. You're still coming right?" He puts a bottle of vodka in the basket.

"Don't ask that too loudly but yes, I should be. Um, you're seventeen. How are you buying alcohol?"

"Dad got me a fake ID." He confesses.

"Oh." I nod slowly.

"He's in the car, waiting." This information comes as an unwanted surprise. Noah frowns when he notices my expression. "You alright?"

"Yeah, fine. I just…"

"Polo!" I hear the distant loud voice of my father.

"Who's that?" Noah asks.

"Dad. Marco!" I holler back, letting him know where I am. I don't mind if he sees me with Noah. He told me to stick with the friendship. Eventually, my father appears in the aisle and stands in front of me. When he sees Noah, he frowns.

"Noah." My father greets the boy with a fake politeness.

"Oh, hi, Mr Norman." Noah is being genuinely polite. My father sees the contents of his basket and narrows his eyes. "Anyway, I need to go. Was good to see you, Evie, and let me know if you want to hook up sometime." His poor choice of words makes my father practically snarl. Noah notices. "Oh, sorry, Mr N, not like that." He chuckles awkwardly. "And that's definitely my cue to leave. Bye, Evie."

"Bye, Noah." I offer him a smile before he walks away. That smile grows as I watch him. Until I face my father and it disappears completely.

"Evelyn, what did I just say?" His voice is restrained.

"What? I saw him. I said hello. Dad, it's a free country, I can say hello to people." I begin to grow agitated. He doesn't respond with words, just a deep frown.

"We're going home." He states firmly before walking away. I follow diligently.

I'm driving along the A-road. We're only ten minutes away from home. For the first time since I started learning how to drive, I'm distracted. I clutch the wheel at ten and two and watch the road, but it's like I'm on autopilot. I'm not really thinking about my driving.

"Evelyn, watch your speed." My father instructs. I glance at the speedometer and come off the accelerator a touch. I'm still mute. I haven't spoken a word since we got back in the car after paying for the shopping. I assume my father has noticed. He hasn't really said anything to me either. We sit in silence. The only time he speaks to me is to offer me tuition while I'm driving. "Alright, go on. What's wrong?"

"Nothing." I'm barely audible.

"Something's wrong, Evelyn." My father persists. It only makes me more irritated.

"Nothing's wrong. I'm fine." I glance in the rear-view mirror briefly. I see a car behind me and I focus my eyes on it. A black BMW. Just like the one in Fort William. I study it. I try to make out the driver but he's a good 100m away.

"Evie!" I suddenly feel the car jerk as my father grabs the steering wheel, pulling us back into our lane and out of the way of an oncoming car, which beeps its horn incredibly angrily as it zooms past. Once we are back in our lane and safe, my father tries to stay calm. "Pull over. Now." I follow his command the moment it is safe to do so. I press the indicator and settle us down along the side of the road before pulling the handbrake up and sighing in relief. The BMW drives past. "Are you okay?" He asks coldly and

I nod. "What the hell was that, Evelyn?!" My father sounds angry but I know he is trying not to be. I know he doesn't want to scare me away from driving forever. "Evelyn, answer me!" The moment his voice remotely resembles Horrible Dad, I scowl and turn off the ignition. I check my side mirror and open my door, wanting out of the confined space. "Evelyn!"

I slam the door and make my way across the road, standing on the other side. I'm still getting over the fright of what happened in the car. I'm still getting over the uneasiness of seeing that BMW. I'm still getting over the fact that someone wants to kill me. It's been nearly two weeks since what happened in London, but I'm still terrified. Only a psychopath wouldn't be. As I stand with my arms crossed, I hear the familiar sound of a door closing. I quickly wipe my tears as the footsteps across the tarmac appear closer. My father doesn't say anything as he stands beside me. We just look at the mountains together.

"Are you alright?" He mutters, significantly calmer than he was. I nod. "What happened, Evelyn? You were doing fine."

"I don't know." I shrug sulkily, kicking little rocks with my foot, refusing to look at him.

"You've been off since Broadford. You haven't muttered a word to me. Ever since you saw Noah, you've been angry." My father does the one thing he does best; reads me like a book. "Tell me what's wrong."

"No." I shake my head and walk forwards, into the grassy landscape. To my surprise, he doesn't follow me, like he knows I just want some space. He stays where he is, watching me like a hawk. But he allows me some time to collect my thoughts. And I do collect them. I collect them and process them. Until Connelly is dealt with, I do not leave my father's sight, that much is clear. But that's too much. It's too smothery. I can't even be in a different aisle in a shop. That shit isn't going to last long. I refuse to be shepherded for the rest of my time here.

Once I have had my five minutes of careful contemplation, I decide it's time to face the music and my father again. I spin and walk towards him. He is, yet again, stood with his hands in his pockets as he waits patiently for me.

"Are you done with your teenage sulking?" The humour in his eyes is palpable. I don't know whether to be annoyed or amused by that comment.

"Yep, and you've still got a year of it to go." I retort. He chuckles as I walk past him. Before I pass him fully, I feel a gentle hand around my upper arm. I face him.

"Do you want me to drive?" He asks solemnly, understanding I may still be a bit shaken up.

"No. Back on the horse." I nod firmly and confidently.

"Right answer." He smiles, a deep layer of pride in his eyes. He then pulls me into a hug. "Sorry for getting angry in the car."

"It's okay. I was being a…" I frown in realisation and pull out of the hug, looking into his brown eyes. "You called me Evie." This is it. That final wall has collapsed. He's trying so hard not to get sentimental about it.

"It's just quicker to say in an emergency." My father shrugs casually. "I regard myself as an intelligent man and I'm fairly certain Evelyn has more syllables."

"Oh, shut up."

Nearly home. My father and I have shared pleasant conversations. All teenage sulking, as he puts it, has gone. As I laugh at one of his jokes he thinks is hilarious, I briefly glance in my rear-view mirror. It's back. The BMW. We're only a couple of minutes from home but I don't want it to follow us there.

"Dad." I try to stay calm, ready to tell him.

"I see it." My father is looking out of his own mirror. He's also switched onto the fact we're being followed. "Alright, listen to me. Stay in control, stay composed. Just drive. Don't overthink and I'll do what I can."

"Okay." I whisper, my palms feeling sweaty as I grip the steering wheel.

"Evelyn, you do what I say when I say it. Don't question what I ask you to do. Just do it, am I clear?"

"You're clear." I nod.

"Stay on the A87." He instructs incredibly calmly. The BMW still follows. "Alright, when I tell you to, put your right foot to the floor."

"What?" I ask in horror. I assume dual controls only have a brake and clutch.

"Evelyn, what did I just say about questioning me? When I tell you to, put your foot down." He stares at me seriously. I nod. My father presses down on the clutch using the dual controls and changes down a couple of gears. His movements are so swift and calm. Right now, he's Horrible Dad. But I don't mind, because I know he's going to get us out of this mess. "Now." The moment he snaps, I put my foot down. We race forward. "Just keep going." He switches between looking out of his mirror and facing the road ahead of us. I keep the steering steady as we near 80mph. I suddenly feel a hand on the steering wheel as we charge down the road. "Let go of the wheel." I do. At that moment, my father steers us away from the A-road, onto the grassy landscape. I scream and panic. "Keep your foot down, Evelyn." He spins the steering wheel like it's made of feathers. He doesn't even need to think about what he's doing. The car shudders. "Just focus on that pedal. And when I tell you to, take your foot off the accelerator." "Okay." My voice is shaky, breathy.

"If you want to close your eyes, you can." My father steers us through the landscape. The BMW is still behind us but falling. I close my eyes tightly as we ride along the wilderness for what seems like an eternity. My father stays cool and composed. "Take your foot off." He orders and I lift my right foot. At that moment, my father slams down onto the clutch and pulls the handbrake up, steering us so that we drift at a 90° angle. I open my eyes. His movements are rapid. I gasp and close my eyes tightly as the car spins to the side. Once he is happy that we have drifted far enough, he takes the handbrake off and changes gear. "Foot down!" He shouts and I press my foot down hard on the accelerator. We lunge forward and the BMW is left behind, grappling with the terrain. My father continues to control the car until we reach the A-road. Once we're on it, I continue to press my foot to the floor. "Don't slow down." He continues. I'm reaching 70mph. My father takes one last look behind the car and lets out a small sigh. "Alright, slow down." I barely notice his instruction behind my terrified sobs. He places a hand on my shoulder. "Slow down, slow down, slow down." He repeats so calmly. I take my foot off the accelerator and let the car fall to a lower speed, until it's only doing about thirty. "When I say, pull over." He twists to look behind us once more. I do all I can do stow my rapid breathing. "Okay, pull over." I breathe shakily and press down on the indicator. We're only a stone's throw away from Kyleakin but he obviously wants us to stop for a reason. The moment I stop the car and pull the handbrake, he is opening his car door and unbuckling his seatbelt. He leaves the car, a determination in his movements. My fingers shake as I unbuckle my own seatbelt. I jump in fright when my car door flies open. Once I see who opened it, I am out of the car and throwing myself into his arms. I can't stop shaking as my father hugs me. I'm hyperventilating. I am shivering, trapped in this fight or flight, adrenaline-fuelled nightmare. "You were brilliant, Evelyn. You were so, so brilliant." He does his best to console me. But I'm quivering with fear.

"Dad." I sob.

"It's okay. It's okay." My father strokes the back of my head. I close my eyes. My legs feel like jelly. I can barely stand up anymore. "Go and sit in the passenger seat." He lets me go. I step out of the hug, immediately feeling light-headed and sick.

"Dad, I think I'm going to pass out." I stare ahead, barely able to hear my own voice.

"Come on, I've got you." My father wraps an arm around my waist and guides me around the car. I stumble but he doesn't let me fall. Once we get to the passenger side, I clumsily sit down and he shuts the door next to me. I reach for the seatbelt but it takes a couple of tries. I buckle the seatbelt just as my father sits in the driver's seat and closes the door. He then proceeds to drive us home. "If you need to pass out, then let it happen, okay?" My father rests a hand on my shoulder as he drives. I just lean my head on my palm, staring outside, doing all I can to stay awake as black envelopes me.

CHAPTER FIFTEEN

I open my eyes. I'm not in the car. I'm lying on my side on the
sofa, covered in a blanket. I'm in the recovery position. I look
around woozily but there is nobody in the room. I do notice a
glass of water on the table beside the sofa though. I sit up,
immediately feeling a stabbing pain in my head as I reach for the
water. I chug nearly the whole thing. I'm either dehydrated or
what happened in the car really knocked me out. Literally. I just
remember feeling nothing but fear. I remember not being able to
breathe. I suppose oxygen starvation will do this to a person. I
must've passed out in the car. I was hoping I wouldn't. Passing
out is not my idea of a fun time.

As I stagger through the hallway, I can hear a muffled
conversation in the kitchen. It's my father and Joan and it seems
to be quite a heated discussion.

"I have to, Jo. I don't have a choice. If I don't go to London,
Connelly will get suspicious and we can't risk that!" My father
practically yells as I lean back against the wall to eavesdrop.

"Your daughter was followed today, Gregory. Almost two weeks
ago, she was nearly killed and you want to abandon her to go to
London?" Joan is equally as vocal.

"Don't say it like that. I'm not abandoning her. I will never
abandon her. But I still have a job to do. You know that."

"She is your job, Greg! She is your daughter! She is your only purpose in this world, not this job. Not the team. Not the objective."

"What am I supposed to do, Jo? Just sit here and play happy families while Connelly gets more suspicious of me? Don't forget why we came here in the first place."

"Gregory…"

"She will be safe. As long as she doesn't leave this house, she will be safe. I'm only needed in London for a week. Once my work with Connelly is done, I will get on the jet and come home. Joan, please understand what I need to do."

"I understand perfectly, Greg. And so does she." As Joan speaks, I look down. "She knows that you will always value this job more than her. And it's wrong, Greg. For sixteen years, you put this job before her. Look, I am loving this new connection that you both have and I am so incredibly happy for you. But you need to open your eyes."

"They are open, Jo. Because if I don't finish what I started sixteen years ago, it all falls to shit." There is a pause in the conversation. "Is she awake yet?" Joan asks, calming the air.

"I'll check." My father responds. Oh, fuck, shit, bollocks. I spin on my heel, hoping to make my way back to the living room.

"Evelyn." The moment I hear my name, I grimace and close my eyes. I spin slowly and open them.

"Sorry." I mutter.

"It seems you need some more lessons on eavesdropping." He crosses his arms.

"Or a crash course." I hope to redeem myself with humour. It works. My father smiles faintly but then frowns in concern.

"How are you feeling?" He walks to me and cups my chin to study my face.

"Grand. Like I didn't just pass out in a car." I stare ahead blankly, speaking in an incredibly dry tone. "How did you even get me into the house?"

"Carried you. And you're too light." He gives me an admonishing look. "Come on, there's some food in the kitchen." My father turns away and walks into the kitchen.

"Dad…" I whine.

"You are eating food, Evelyn! This no-eating bollocks has gone on for long enough!" I can't tell if he's angry or not as I hear his distant, booming voice. I never can. At least I knew where I stood with Horrible Dad. This guy is a bloody yo-yo.

I stand, leant against the worktop, clutching a bowl of tomato pasta. My father paces back and forth as Joan sits at the table by the French doors, resting her chin on her interlocked fingers. I have no choice but to just observe and listen while I take little forkfuls of pasta.

"Evelyn, how much of that did you hear?" My father asks, still pacing. I finish my mouthful and swallow.

"I heard you arguing about you going to London tomorrow. And then the rest of it." I nod. "Dad, you guys really need to be more careful with how loudly you have your secret conversations." I stab some more pasta with my fork and take a bite. He just looks at me and I smile at him while I chew.

"Or, here's an idea, you could learn to not listen in on those conversations and be such a nosey rosey." He raises a brow. I giggle softly, making him smirk. "Alright, the cat is precariously close to being out of the bag." He thinks aloud. I stop chewing in

218

the blind hope that he is finally going to tell me what he does.

"Now before you ask, no, I am not telling you what my job is."

"Aw." I look down, full of disappointment.

"But I will listen to your questions and answer the ones I am willing to." My father places his hands in his pockets.

"That's hardly fair. You could choose to answer none of them." I protest, about to eat another mouthful of pasta.

"That's my only offer." He states. I roll my eyes. "Go on then, throw them at me." He orders. I put my bowl and fork down, thinking of what to ask.

"Are you actually working for Connelly?" I cross my arms.

"No."

"Did you learn to drive at the James Bond School of Motoring?" I ask in mock curiosity. It amuses him greatly. He stifles a laugh so he can answer.

"No."

"Are you going to London tomorrow?"

"Yes." He answers hesitantly.

"Am I allowed out of the house on my own?"

"No." There is no hesitation this time. I hold back the urge to roll my eyes, deciding to accept his answers.

"Why are we in Scotland?"

"Next question."

"But, Dad…"

"Next question." He repeats slowly and firmly. I need to think of a different angle.

"Are we ever living in London again?"

"Next question." My father's expression doesn't change. I, on the other hand, am riding a rollercoaster of disappointment, frustration, fear, apprehension and hope.

"How long is this going to last? How long am I going to not be allowed out on my own? How long until I can see Sam again?"

"Until further notice."

"Dad, you can't say that." I argue.

"I just did. And please ask one question at a time."

"No, you can't keep me in the dark like this. You bought me a car and made this massive deal about me capturing my independence. But now what? That's just gone?" I look away from him, trying to hide my incredibly obvious annoyance.

"Evelyn, that was before I became aware of how much danger you were in." He answers honestly. "I apologise but your safety is slightly more important than your ability to drive and your friendships."

"Speaking of friendships, am I *ever* going to see Sam again?" I am becoming more and more irate. My fuse is about to blow. Tears are building.

"Yes, you will see Sam again."

"When?" I snap.

"I don't know." My father seems genuinely remorseful. I shake my head, forcing back the tears.

"So, this is my life now? Stay in this house. Be monitored and chaperoned by my father and aunt. No college. No friends. No bloody freedom." I take a second to compose myself. "Look, Dad, I am so grateful for everything you've done. You bought me a car. You bought me a gorgeous Steinway & Sons piano. You are endlessly trying to keep me safe. And I know that all you want in

220

this world is for me to be happy. But I need to know why this is happening. Please just give me that." The tears fall as I crumble into pieces in front of him.

"Because you're my daughter." My father places a hand on my cheek. "Like I told you, my job is risky. And because of who I am and what I do, some unfavourable people want to hurt me. And the best way to do that…"

"Is through me." I nod in understanding.

"I only have the one weakness, Evelyn. It's you. It's always been you. Even when I was cold and distant. Do you know why?"

"Because I'm such a burden and a massive waste of your time?" I ask in mock interest. "Oh, wait, no. That's all finished now, hasn't it? You magically found your humanity." I smile. My father pinches my ear. "Ow!" I jerk my head to the side as a reflex, pressing my ear to my shoulder.

"No." He frowns. I also frown and rub my ear. "Because you're my baby and I am your Dad. So you will always be my weakness. You are the very centre of my heart, Evelyn." His confession moves me in the deepest way.

"Should put that on a Hallmark card." My dry response is clearly not well-received.

"Will you stop…" My father puts me in a headlock. I thrash in his grip as he grinds his fist down onto my head and rubs it. Joan laughs. "… being a sarcastic little twat?!"

"Dad!" I shout as he continues. "Alright, alright! I'll stop the bloody sarcasm!" I can't contain the laughter in my voice. My father releases me. I immediately stroke my fingers through my now-frizzy hair. "So, what am I supposed to do now then? Just grin and bear it?"

"I'm afraid so." My father puts his hands back in his pockets.

"What time are you going to London tomorrow?" I lean against the worktop again.

"Early. I have a lot to do in London during the day. Now, this nicely leads us to my rules." He smiles. I scoff, shaking my head. "The obvious ones are stay in the house, no going out on your own, no Noah, including messages."

"I don't message..."

"Yes, you do." My father frowns deeply. How the hell does he know that? "No staying up too late. No whining. No complaining..."

"No breathing." I raise my brows. My father gives me a look before taking a step towards me. I immediately hold my hands up defensively. "Okay! Okay! I take it back. No more noogies." My desperate plead stops him.

"You will listen to Joan. You will do exactly what Joan says without hesitation. Call me if you need to. I'm incredibly busy this week, so if I'm not reachable, I'll try and get back to you."

"Dad, I get it."

"Good." He nods slowly before sighing. "I mean it, Evelyn. You can't break any of these rules." There is a turmoil within him and I know he's battling the decision to go to London in the first place. So I stare into his eyes and nod, silently giving him my word. I can't see Noah. I won't. It'd break my father's heart.

I am rudely awoken the next morning by the sound of a knock on my bedroom door. After a moment, it opens and closes. I frown and look at who has entered. My father sits on the edge of my bed and smiles down at me. I don't smile back.

"What time is it?" I groan.

"5am."

"Jesus pissing Christ, Dad. This has to stop." I pull the covers over my face, making my father chuckle quietly.

"Evelyn, I'm relatively certain I could fund a small business with the swearing money you owe me." He quips. I giggle under the covers.

"Just don't force the employees of this small business to wake up at five in the morning and you'll have a low staff turnover." I join the joke.

"That's impressive knowledge, Evelyn Norman. Maybe you should go into business after all." He compliments.

"Yeah, you really sell it with the endless death threats we're getting." There is a silent moment after I say this. "Sorry, that was probably too soon."

"I'll let it slide." My father mutters. "Look, I'm leaving in a moment. Just wanted to say goodbye."

"Goodbye." I drone, still under the covers. "There you go. Have a good flight."

"No, a proper goodbye." There is a warm affection in his voice. I reluctantly take the covers away from my face.

"And what would constitute a proper goodbye, pray tell?" I close my eyes, just wanting some peace. All of a sudden, I feel an endless multitude of kisses on my cheeks and forehead. He doesn't stop. "Okay, okay, Dad!" I squint my eyes shut, trying to get away. "Your stubble is stabbing me in the eye!" I giggle. He finally stops kissing my face. "You know, I think I'm actually starting to prefer Horrible Dad. That geezer never woke me up stupidly early." After my statement, my father wears a look of mock woundedness. I roll my eyes and clamber out of bed to give him a hug, making him laugh softly.

"See you in a week, okay?" He holds me tighter.

"I'm going to miss you."

"I'll miss you too. Be good." My father kisses the side of my head and lets me go.

"Auf Wiedersehen, Herr Kommandant. Text me when you land and all that crap." I get straight back into bed and snuggle into my pillow.

"I will. Goodbye, sweetheart." I can hear the door close. I smile to myself. The last time he left me to go to London, he treated me coldly. But that was the nicest goodbye I've ever had. It was the way my mother usually said goodbye.

It is the afternoon, the day before the get together. I sit at my piano, still trying out different notes and scribbling them down. The melody is picking up. It's becoming something I'm proud of. My ability to read sheet music helps a great deal as well. I am in the middle of practicing a few bars when my phone vibrates in my jeans pocket. I stop playing and look at the message.

Tomorrow, I'll pick you up at seven in my friend's car. We're not going far, just a few miles down the road from your house. Bring something warm to wear as it can get quite chilly where we're going. I'm really looking forward to it.
Noah

Oh, Christ. I sit and stare at the keys of my piano. The get together. I desperately want to go. I want to be with people my own age. I want to sit around a BBQ and laugh with other teens. I want to spend the evening under the crystal clear sky, sat on the coast. I want to get to know Noah. It's decided. I'm going.

Noah arrives in five minutes. I'm pacing across my bedroom, wearing my usual jeans, t-shirt and a leather jacket. But I've made my hair pretty. I've put some understated but attractive make-up on. I just need to find a way to get out of the house. I could wait until Joan is in the shower or far away from the front door. Or I could climb down a pole. But that seems unnecessarily dangerous. I perk my ears up, trying to figure out where she is. I think she's in the kitchen. This is my chance.

I have my keys and phone. Surely, that's all I'll need. I've never been to a coastal get together with friends before. It's exciting. I silently open and close my bedroom door, constantly listening out for Joan. I descend the staircase, each step at a time. When I get to the hallway, I panic. Max. He always goes mental when the front door opens.

"Max, foodies!" Joan hollers from the kitchen. Max instantly gets up and patters away. I smile and clutch the front door handle before I make my escape.

Noah is waiting for me outside in a nice, if slightly neglected, Ford Fiesta. He waves as I run to the car and open the back passenger door. Once I am in, I grin like a kid at Christmas. Noah sits in the front, next to a male driver and there is another person sat next to me. They both look slightly older than me. "Evie, this is Luke." Noah gestures to the driver. We nod at each other in greeting. "And this is Amelia." He points his head to the girl beside me.

"Hi." I gleam.

"Oh, my god. Another girl, finally!" Amelia wraps her arms around me in unbridled glee. It surprises and delights me.

"Yeah, Amelia is a hugger." Noah explains as Luke puts the car in gear and drives away from my house. Now we are setting off, the anxiety is starting to creep up, but I'm still full of excitement.

"How've you been?" He asks me. I pause for a moment like I haven't had threats made against me, nearly crashed my car, been followed by his father, watched my father drive a car like he was in a rally stage, and been told I'm never allowed out of my house unsupervised again.

"Grand." I smile.

Luke has parked the car at the side of the A-road, near a small township called Ashaig, and we are trekking further into the wilderness, near the coast of Skye. I check the GPS on my phone to see exactly where we are. And I have five missed calls from Joan. I lock my phone and stow it in my jeans pocket. I can deal with Joan later. She's understanding. It'll be fine. I think.

"Here is fine." Noah states as we find a nice spot. Luke and Amelia each gather a blanket from their backpacks and rest them on the floor. Noah opens a shopping bag and starts laying bottles on the ground. He has it all. Vodka, gin, cider, whiskey, rum. No BBQ in sight though. I guess that was just a placeholder for getting absolutely off our faces. Noah collects some plastic cups from his shopping bag. He better put them in a suitable recycling receptacle when he's done.

"Come and sit with me, Evie." Amelia grins. I smile and sit next to her on the blanket she has laid out.

"What's your poison, Evie?" Noah asks, pouring Amelia a cup of vodka. Luke has opted to not drink, being our designated driver.

"Anything but tequila or brandy." I nod. He chuckles and pours me a whiskey.

"Give that a try. It's quite a nice, mild one." Noah explains as he passes me the plastic cup. I lift it in the air and take a sip. It's delicious.

"Oh, that's nice, thanks." I sip some more. Once we all have our drinks, Noah raises his cup in the air.

"We now commence the 2023 Summer splashdown." He states loudly, making us all laugh. We then all take a sip of our drinks.

About two hours later, the night is getting slightly darker and we're all getting tipsier. I feel cold, so I wrap myself in my leather jacket more. Noah, who has been standing and talking to Luke, sits beside me and exhales loudly, pouring some more whiskey in my cup. I look up at Amelia, who is waving her arms around, apparently listening to silent music.

"She's having... a good time." I giggle, gesturing to Amelia. Noah chuckles as he finishes pouring my drink. "Thanks." I take a sip immediately. After a moment, there is a ringtone and Noah grabs a phone from his pocket.

"Yeah?" He snaps, kind of professionally. If I wasn't so drunk, I'd find it suspicious. "Uh, yes." He pauses. "Yes. All fine." He pauses again. I frown. "I'll let you know. Thanks. Goodbye." He hangs up and puts his phone away.

"Who was that?" I ask.

"A mate of mine."

"It all sounded very curt." I comment, sipping some whiskey.

"Alright, look, Evie, don't tell anyone but I, um, I deal now and again." He confesses.

"Drugs?"

"Just a bit of weed. That was my supplier." After Noah explains, I feel slightly uneasy as I drink even more whiskey. "You know you should go steady with whiskey, aye? Really sneaks up on you, that stuff." He remarks, drinking his own vodka.

"Nah… whiskey is… fine." I'm sure I'm slurring my speech.

"I've done some thinking, Evie." Noah suddenly drops a serious note into the works. I look at him intently. "I've really enjoyed being your friend."

"Oh, that's nice. Well, me too, but about being your friend… obviously." I wear a thoughtful expression. He chuckles at me.

"My father confessed everything. How he asked you to be my friend. And he told me it was because he was worried about me. All my going out with friends and stuff. He said I was going off the rails slightly." He explains.

"Well, you are technically a drug dealer so maybe… he's not wrong." My words are incredibly slurred. "And he told me to be a good influence on you, but I think that's backfired on him a bit." I take another sip.

"How so?"

"Because rather than me being a good influence on you, you've been a bad influence on me." In probably my maddest of moments, I kiss him. I hold my whiskey in one hand and rest my other on the ground as we kiss. It's a young, inexperienced kiss but a kiss all the same. I don't really know if he's kissing me back. But this will definitely be something to tell Sam. Maybe I am going to marry him and have his babies.

"Maybe that should be your last whiskey." Noah nods.

"Maybe you should pour me another one." I comment back. He chuckles again and shrugs unsurely before pouring a tiny bit in my cup. The whiskey has given me courage. I feel attractive. I feel free. I feel… incredibly drunk.

I stagger out of the Ford Fiesta outside my house and check the time on my phone. It's just gone midnight. I also glance at the several missed calls and messages from Joan. I'll have to apologise for that when I speak to her in the morning. I brush the guilt away and tuck the phone in my back jeans pocket as Noah steps out of the car to say goodbye. I turn to face him, smiling.

"I'll see you soon, Evie. I'll message you, okay?"

"See you soon, Mr Connelly." I slowly punch his shoulder.

"Pushing you into this harbour was the best day of my life." Noah confesses. I give him a sentimental look and place a hand against his cheek, patting it.

"Or you're just off your face right now and don't know what you're saying." I giggle and turn to head to the house.

"Bye, Harbour Girl!" Noah hollers from behind me, making me laugh more. I then hear him get into the car and they drive away. I take my house key out of my pocket and very silently place it into the front door.

Once the door is open, I do all I can to make sure I don't wake Joan. I lock the front door and slowly take my Converse off. I walk to the kitchen, needing to put my keys in the fruit bowl. I'm wavy and I realise that I am actually quite drunk. Once I get to the kitchen, I choose not to turn the lights on for fear of waking Joan. But then I freeze. Stood in the dark, at the open French doors, is a man, looking out into the garden. I can't see his face but I know exactly who it is. I turn the light on. Upon noticing the light, he turns around and my heart falls into my stomach. His face is one I didn't think I would see again for a long, long time. It's a picture of fury. A canvas of anger, disappointment but also poise. If there is one thing he's good at, it's being calmly furious. He doesn't say a word and, yet again, I'm the mouse, staring up at the eagle. Staring up at my father.

CHAPTER SIXTEEN

I'm a moron. I'm an idiot. I'm officially the stupidest person on the Isle of Skye. I know exactly how this conversation is going to go. And I do wish I was slightly more sober for it. But something tells me this discussion won't wait. After I discovered my father in the kitchen and he discovered me, walking drunkenly into our home after midnight, the atmosphere was frosty. But behind all of the rage and resentment, the only emotion in his eyes was relief. And guilt hit me like a train. And now here I am, sitting on the sofa as my father stands in the centre of the room with his hands in his pockets, contemplating exactly what to say to me.

"Do you have anything to say to me?" His voice is a lot softer than I was expecting.

"How did you know I was gone?" My speech is still a bit slurred.

"Joan does possess a mobile phone, Evelyn." My father snaps, clear irritation lacing his voice. That softness has gone. "She rang me. About eight o'clock. And I'm also very aware she tried to ring you several times. But did you pick up the damn phone? No, you did not. And by not picking up that phone, your aunt, a person who loves you more than anything else in this world thought you were dead!" His volume is increasing. I'm waiting for the inevitable roar of his voice as he gets more enraged. "Where the hell have you been, Evelyn?!"

"Near Ashaig."

"Ashaig? So, all this time, you've been seven miles down the road?" The shock and disbelief in his voice are palpable. "While your aunt sat here and suffered, thinking you were dead, you were seven miles away?! She went out looking for you, Evelyn. She only just got back home an hour ago. But if you'd have picked up your damn phone, just to tell her you were alive…"

"Dad, I'm sorry." I don't hesitate to apologise. Not this time. He sneers angrily and shakes his head, doing his best to calm down. "Evelyn, you are not stupid. But this was incredibly stupid! You were followed in your car two days ago! You are not safe out there without me!"

"Dad, I know that."

"Then tell me why the hell I received a phone call from Joan, in tears and convinced you'd been kidnapped. Or worse." I don't know if he actually wants a response or if it was rhetorical. "Who were you with?" He asks the one question I was hoping he wouldn't.

"Noah. And a couple of his friends." The moment I say the name, my father begins to lose his cool again.

"And you've been drinking."

"Yes."

"In the middle of nowhere with people you barely know."

"Yes."

"Fully aware that someone wants to hurt you."

"Yes." I look down, riddled with guilt. "Dad, I thought you were in London." I shake my head, still crying gently.

"I came back."

"Why?" I finally look up at him.

"Oh, I don't know, Evelyn. Maybe it's because my sister rang me to tell me that my daughter was missing!" He glowers at me. I instantly look down again, transformed into the meek, scared little girl I am. "So, I got on the plane and Francis picked me up from Inverness."

"Dad, I'm so sorry." I quickly wipe my eyes. My father lets out a long, irritated sigh and rubs his eyes.

"Evelyn, I'm not furious about the fact you went out. That's part of your age and it's something I know I will have to deal with again. I was seventeen once, I know the drill." His words are warm, but his tone definitely isn't. "What I am furious about is the fact you didn't tell us, either of us. So not only did we think you were dead, Evelyn, but I have also had to abandon a week of very important work. You can't even begin to comprehend how important that work was. All because you didn't pick up your phone."

"Dad…" I choke. My tears don't assuage his anger. But his expression does soften a touch before he looks out the window. "Take a glass of water and go to bed. Get out of my sight." My father doesn't look at me, he just gazes out the window, his hands in his pockets. I burst into tears and run from the sofa. I throw open the living room door and rush to the kitchen to make myself that glass of water.

As I climb the staircase, water in hand, I can't fight the tears. I climb each stair with a guilt-riddled pain in my step. And then I reach the upper level. Joan is stood in the doorway to her bedroom. This is the first time I haven't seen any warmth in her eyes. This is the first time I've seen nothing but coldness. She closes her bedroom door and I feel a wave of shame. I feel sick as

I walk into my bedroom. I put the glass of water down and stare ahead for a moment. Nope. It's coming.

Within a flash, I am rushing to the family bathroom. I barely notice my father walking up the stairs as I run into the room and vomit into the toilet. I then feel pair of hands collect my long hair and take it away from my face. My first time getting drunk and I've chundered. This isn't a good way to start. I breathe heavily and make sure the nausea has gone before I grab some tissue to wipe my mouth. All the while, my father is stroking my back. I throw the tissue in and close the toilet lid before I just sit, catching my breath. I burst into more tears.

"I'm so sorry, Dad." I sob.

"It's okay." He continues to stroke my back. The anger has gone. Now he knows I'm alive and safe, he's allowed himself to calm down. I push away from the toilet and flush it. I approach the sink and collect some toothpaste and my toothbrush. I brush frantically, wanting to get any trace of vomit out of my mouth. My father just waits patiently. Once I have brushed my teeth, I instantly feel better. I still feel drunk and disorientated but at least I don't have to puke again.

"I am never getting this bloody drunk again." I remark as I look down at the sink.

"We all say that, Evelyn. And then a week later, we're back in the toilet bowl. Like I said, I was seventeen once." My father echoes the humour in my tone.

"Yeah, back in the middle ages, drinking mead." I smile slightly, knowing the tension in the air is starting to vanish. As my father chuckles, I turn to look at him, still trying to ward off tears. "I'm sorry, Dad."

"Come here." He opens his arms and I enter them. He rests his chin on my head. "You will never scare me like that again, am I clear? Anytime you want to go off and do something completely reckless, you will tell me first."

"I will. I just wanted to go out and have some fun." I mumble against his chest.

"I didn't realise vomiting into a toilet was your idea of fun." My father quips, making me laugh. I then close my eyes and sigh.

"I'm going to bed." I step out the hug and open the bathroom door. I want to lie down. I want the room to stop spinning.

I have changed into my pyjamas and I am sitting cross-legged on my bed, checking the messages on my phone. I read the ones Joan sent me and my heart instantly drops.

Evie, where are you?

Pick up the phone, Evie.

Evie, please tell me where you are. I'm worried sick! I'm in the car so please call me and I will come and pick you up.

Evie, this isn't a joke, I need to know where you are!

I've called your father. He's on his way home. Please just let one of us know you're okay.

I scrunch my eyes closed, not willing to read anymore. Her sheer panic is so evident. And it breaks my heart. As I rest the phone pensively against my mouth, there is a knock on my door. I holler

235

for them to enter and my father walks in, holding a packet of medicine. I place the phone on my bedside table as my father sits on the edge of my bed.

"Some painkillers for the morning." He explains, putting the pills on the table.

"Is it going to be that bad?" I frown.

"Oh, you bet. Drink your water." He tilts his head to the glass of water I made. I collect it and take a tiny sip. "No, drink the whole thing, Evelyn."

"Do I have to?"

"Not unless you want a magnificent headache in the morning." He raises a brow and I reluctantly chug the entire glass. "I have some questions but I think they'd better wait until you're a bit less, for want of a better term, shit-faced." His sudden cursing makes me nearly choke on the water in laughter. I swallow and nod slowly before putting the glass down.

"Yeah, I will answer your questions when I'm not shit-faced."

"Yes, you will. But there is one question that cannot wait." He clears his throat and deliberates how to ask it. "Noah. Now, I don't know how you feel about him. But I know how he feels about you. And I have to ask, as much I don't want to…"

"Dad, hang on. Are you about to give me the talk?" I grimace in horror. "No, no, no. This definitely can wait, Dad." I shake my head desperately.

"Look, all I'm going to ask is if anything happened." He's taking this so seriously and I need to do the same.

"Okay. Alright. We, um, we kissed. That's it. Nothing else." I confess. My father sighs loudly and drops his head to face the floor. Once he brings his head back up, he nods slowly and thoughtfully.

"Thank you for telling me. Now, I know that Connelly asked you to be a friend of his son and to be a good influence on him, essentially. But it ends now. I am ending that arrangement. Noah is bad news. He may not be a problem but his father is."

"Wait, are you banning me from seeing Noah?"

"For a while, yes."

"Dad…"

"Evelyn, after the stunt you pulled tonight, you're lucky I'm ever letting you out of the house again. And I explicitly told you not to message him anymore." He has a good point. I'm in no position to demand certain freedoms.

"Fine." I roll my eyes.

"Right, interrogation over. Get into bed." He stands up. I scramble under the covers and wrap myself in them, lying on my side.

"Goodnight." I close my eyes.

"Goodnight, sweetheart." My father plants a kiss on my head before approaching the door. I suddenly sit up.

"Dad?"

"Mm-hmm." He turns to face me.

"I'm sorry you had to come back from London." I mutter sincerely. My father exhales and makes his way back to the bed, a new disappointment in his eyes as he sits down.

"Yes, it's not ideal. But the moment I got that call, nothing else really mattered."

"You dropped everything for me?" I ask, full of doubt. This is a man who has always chosen work over me. Every time. Even by just answering a phone call when I'm trying to speak to him.

"Of course I did. You sound surprised."

"Well, that's probably because I am?" I offer him a look of mock confusion, making him chuckle.

"Evelyn, when we were on Coire Lagan, you accused me of valuing my job more than I value you. And I told you that you were wrong. Because you were. It doesn't matter what my job is. The moment I hear that you're in trouble, that's it. I come running. And that will always be the case, do you hear me?"

"I hear you."

"Good. But do please refrain from interrupting a very important business trip in the future. I love you, Evelyn, but if this continues, I might need to start seriously rethinking this whole father business. I hear orphanages are very accommodating these days. You like gruel, don't you?" He asks with a mock curiosity.

"Sorry, but you seem to have me confused with that Oliver Twist geezer." I stare blankly before closing my eyes and lying back. I just want the room to stop spinning.

"Well, forgive the confusion. But he was skinny. And…" He elongates the word before he suddenly tickles my stomach. I laugh and try to get away. "Yep, you are too."

"No, I'll puke!" I giggle. He stops. I look up to see him smiling and looking down at me in amusement and with all kinds of affection. Three months ago, I wouldn't have even been able to visualise this look in my head. I never knew he could even look at me like this. But now I see it every day. And his ways of telling me he loves me have changed. The looks of sheer warmth. The hugs. The kisses. The playfulness. The noogies. The tickling. The jokes. It's like a whole new love language. It was my mother's love language. It's a father's love language. And now he's fluent.

238

"Get some sleep. You'll feel better." My father stands up and approaches the door. I climb back into bed. "Take your painkillers in the morning. And you *will* be apologising to Joan."

"Can you be there when I do?"

"Nope." He opens the door.

"Dad!"

"Goodnight, Evelyn." He leaves the room. I smile to myself, knowing that Horrible Dad is never coming back. And in his place is this funny, warm, affectionate person. I used to hate him. There was even a point at which I wished it was him who died and not my mother. But now he's my favourite person in the world.

My head. Jesus Christ, my head. And I'm tired. Still disorientated, even after a fairly deep sleep. I still feel drunk. The room is still spinning slightly. I sit up in bed, scrunching my eyes closed. I notice the little packet of pills on my bedside table. I need to take them but I drank all my water before going to sleep. That means I need to brave the rest of the house to get some more. And it also means I'll see Joan.

I change into a clean outfit of jeans and a t-shirt. My eyelids are still to the floor as I leave my bedroom with the empty glass in my hand. I feel like death personified. And I am never doing this again. As I pass my father's office, the door opens and all I can hear is the low, amused chuckle of my father. I wear a look of annoyance and slowly turn to face him. He is leaning against the doorway with his arms crossed.

"Good morning, Evelyn."

"Is it?" I remark, full of contempt. My father laughs.

"Your first hangover." He states.

"Yeah and my pissing last." I mutter under my breath.

"Evelyn." He chides. I give him an apologetic smile. "Joan is in the kitchen, by the way." He informs me casually.

"That's nice for her." I spin away, ready to make my way down the stairs.

"Go and apologise, Evelyn." He instructs firmly.

"Yeah, yeah, yeah." I grumble as I descend the staircase. I am full of that timidity again. I feel terrible for what I did to Joan and I know I need to apologise. But she is the one person I never wanted to make feel this way.

Once I enter the kitchen, I see her. She is sat at the little table by the French doors, her hands wrapped around a mug of coffee. I saunter to the coffee machine and make my own. She doesn't look at me. And for the first time, the atmosphere between us is icy. I'm used to this atmosphere. I've had it with my father dozens of times. But never with Joan. We were allies. As I take my mug of coffee to the table, I ponder what I want to say. I sit down and she still doesn't look at me.

"Joan." I croak, barely able to speak. There is a flicker of change in her expression but she is still shrouded in apathy. "I am so sorry. I never wanted you to feel like this, and I am so sorry that I made you panic and…" I force the tears back. "I should've called you. I know I should've. And I will never do that again. Please look at me." I practically beg and she does. There is no warmth in her gaze. "Joan, I am so, so sorry. I mean it. I am. I saw your messages after I came home, and Dad told me that you went looking for me. And I can't imagine what you were thinking."

"Would you like me to enlighten you, Evie?" Joan regards me with a shade of spite. Listening to it come from her breaks my heart. "As your father has probably made you aware, I thought you'd been taken. I thought you were dead, Evie. I am not going to digress about that, however. It's unnecessary. But I will express my complete and utter disappointment in you." That stings. "And I hope this will never happen again."

"It won't. I swear." I shake my head.

"Good." The warmth in her gaze slowly starts to come back. "Would you like some breakfast?"

"No, thank you." I reach into my jeans pocket and take out the paracetamol my father gave me last night. I swallow a couple with the coffee. There is a glimmer of amusement on Joan's face. "Headache?" She asks.

"Mm-hmm." I close my eyes and look down.

"Well, I have the perfect remedy for those."

"I will sell you my soul if you could give me that remedy." I respond with complete seriousness. Joan chuckles and stands up.

"Give me a hug." She requests tenderly. I well up and get to my feet, rushing into her arms and holding her tightly. "Don't scare me like that again, Evie Norman."

"I won't." I whisper, giving her my word. And I will keep my word. No more stupid decisions. No more potentially reckless ideas. From now on, I follow the rules. I stay in this house.

I am lying on the sofa, doing all I can to ignore the throbbing pain in my head. And watching pointless daytime TV doesn't seem to be working, so I switch it off. I should have a nap or something. I close my eyes, ready to go to sleep but my phone rings as it sits near my face on the sofa. I frown and pick it up before seeing the unrecognisable mobile number. I hesitantly answer it.

"Hello?" I mumble.

"Ooh, you sound how I feel." Noah chuckles.

"Noah? How did you get my number?"

"You gave it to me last night, ya wee muppet." Oh, did I? I have no memory of that.

"Oh. Look…" I close my eyes. "I really enjoyed myself last night. And I really enjoyed that little kiss. But, um… I'm so sorry, Noah, we can't be friends anymore. I can't see you anymore." There is so much disappointment in my voice.

"What's brought this on? Did I do something wrong?"

"No, no, no. It's just… I need to make more decisions that are good for me. And, well, you're not good for me. Not right now, anyway. Not for a while."

"Oh, okay. I get it, I guess. And thanks for telling me, Evie. But if you ever need me, I am always available." He is so genuine. It only makes this more difficult.

"Thanks, Noah. All the best, I guess."

"Yeah, and you." He hangs up and I put my phone down. I start to well up. I am also ready to crawl into a little hole and die. I meant it when I said I am never getting drunk again. I don't want to feel this way ever again. But these are the lessons we learn as we grow up. And I learnt another lesson today. Always tell your family where you are, and don't catch feelings for guys who have dangerous fathers. All the feelings I've caught for Noah, I need to throw them away. And it devastates me.

CHAPTER SEVENTEEN

November

It's been three months since the little get together with Noah. I haven't contacted him. And I haven't had a single message from him either. I've also kept good on my promise to stay with my father and Joan whenever we go out. I had my GCSE exam results. Six 9s, one 8 and a 5. Bloody Spanish. *Joder española.* But nevertheless, I am over the moon with them. As is my father. Not bad for a girl whose life did a complete 180. We celebrated, of course. And my father, Joan and Francis drank even more tequila. After my little drunk session, I refused even a sip. I think I'm going to be teetotal after that night. My father and Joan seem more relaxed. More ready to put all of that nastiness behind us.

I'm currently not with them, however. I am sitting in my little Fiat, taking a practical driving test. It's going well, I think. My father is waiting back at the test centre in Portree, probably more full of nerves than I am. I do everything as he instructed. I mirror, signal, manoeuvre. I check blind spots. I hold the wheel at ten and two. My speed is fine. My hazard perception is fine. Everything is going fine.

"Right, now I would like you to park along the side of the road somewhere safe please. Behind this red car, not too close or far away." The examiner instructs. I look in all necessary mirrors and tilt the indicator down. Once I come to a stop, I pull the handbrake and put it in neutral. "Thank you. Now, I am going to ask you to perform one of the manoeuvres. I would like you to perform a reverse parallel park and park behind the car in front of us." Oh, god, this isn't going to be fine and the examiner is like a robot. I nod and smile, acknowledging the request. This is my worst manoeuvre and I blame my instructor. I complete the MSM process and check my blind spots before pulling away from the curb. I do all I can to remember how my father taught me this as I pull up alongside the red car. I check my blind spots again and commence the manoeuvre, constantly checking around me. Constantly keeping an eye on where I am. Once my side mirror is level with the car's back door handle, I check my blind spots yet again and spin the wheel to position myself to reverse towards the curb. I do all I can to steady my breathing before checking my blind spots one final time. Once that's done, I begin the final part of the manoeuvre, praying to god I don't hit the curb. So far, so good. I finish the manoeuvre as the examiner makes notes on a little iPad. "You can now pull away when it is safe to do so."

I drive back into the test centre in Portree, completely unaware of how that went. I feel even more nervous when I see my father, stood outside the test centre with his hands in his pockets. His expression is stony. I know he's probably feeling all the anguish I am. Once I am directed to, I park in one of the bays. Oh, god. The apprehension is killing me. I don't care if I've failed. I just want this constant anxiety to end as I pull the handbrake. "Please turn off the engine." The examiner instructs and I do. He taps his iPad a bit more and I close my eyes. "Thank you, that was a very good drive today, Evelyn. And I am pleased to say you've passed." Holy mother of bollocks. "Now that you'll be driving on your own, I'd like you to be aware of a few things…" He offers me some feedback and takes me through the five minors I received. I don't care about them. I don't even hear them. I'm on the highest on cloud nines. "May I see your driving licence again, please?" I pass him my provisional license and he takes a blank certificate out of his folder. He jots down my driver number and details. I can't stop my heart from beating rapidly. This is pure happiness. This is relief. Hope. Freedom. The adrenaline is so delightful. Once the examiner has jotted down my details, he passes me the certificate. "Thank you, Evelyn. Your new licence will be with you within two weeks, but you are free to drive until then. Well done."

"Thank you." My voice is just a weak murmur. The examiner opens his door and leaves the car. I place the certificate on the backseat before doing the same.

I don my most disheartened look. I do all I can to stow my smile and pretend I'm heartbroken as I walk towards my father. I even pretend to wipe a tear or two. He instantly looks concerned. I know he's probably feeling a wave of disappointment but he's also supportive. I am so looking forward to this.

"Oh, Evelyn. You'll get them next time." My father tries to comfort me.

"It's not that." I shake my head, feigning tearfulness.

"What's wrong?"

"I'm just going to really miss our little lessons together, you know. I'm really going to miss you constantly barking at me about my speed." As I continue the charade, the penny drops for my father, who does his best to stow a smile. "And most of all, I am going to miss the cheap as shit insurance."

"Evelyn Norman." My father snaps.

"I passed, Herr Kommandant!" I yell loudly and full of such happiness, jumping into my father's arms. "Ja! Ich passed!" I shout, still donning the German accent.

"You absolute superstar!" He spins me around. I giggle like a little kid in his arms. This feeling is one I'm going to remember for the rest of my life.

My father drives the Fiat back home. I wasn't allowed to. Apparently there's a rule about learners not driving home after a test, whether they passed or not. I don't care. I'm still smothered by all this euphoria. I am full of beans. I am shaking like a leaf but for the best possible reason.

"How many minors did you get?" My father asks as I stare at my certificate.

"Five. Although, if I'd have gone to the James Bond School of Motoring like you, I probably would've got none." My comment makes him chuckle.

"Well, we can't all be me." He winks. "Proud of you, sweetheart."

"Thanks, Dad." I gleam. "So what happens now?"

"Sort your insurance out. Burn the L plates. And celebrate. I'm thinking Mexican night." He smirks at me.

"You read my mind, padre." I lean back in my seat. I haven't stopped smiling since I was told the result of my test.

"Look, Evelyn, I don't want to dampen the bliss you're feeling right now but..." My father clears his throat. "Now you are a full driver, there are some things I want to run by you before I let you go off on your own."

246

"Okay." I frown patiently.

"My partial lockdown is still in place. If you go for a drive, it's with me or Joan."

"But, Dad…"

"Evelyn, the whole point of this is to keep you safe. Now, I know it's been three months and nothing has happened, but Connelly is still out there. You are potentially still in danger and I don't want to take that risk." He elucidates. That euphoria I felt is gone. I am qualified to drive but I'm not allowed to.

"Dad, I promise I will be so careful. I'll be vigilant, I swear. For the past three months, I have done everything you said. I haven't left the house without you guys. I haven't contacted Noah. I haven't snuck out. I've been so bloody good." I argue. My father is clearly battling some indecision.

"Evelyn…"

"Please just let me go for a tiny drive on my own. I won't ask you for anything ever again, I promise." I spin to face him, holding my hands in a praying motion. "Please. Dad, I am begging you." My voice is desperate. I am literally begging. He raises a brow and briefly directs his eyes at me.

"One tiny drive. And I mean a mile." He states firmly. I want to hug him but he's driving. So instead, I just flash him the biggest grin of my life.

"You're the best!" I exclaim. He chuckles and shakes his head.

"Don't make me regret that, Evelyn."

"I won't. I'll be good. I'll be amazing." I'm so full of excitement. In my head, I decide where to go. The world is my bloody oyster.

We've sorted out my insurance. I am now legally allowed to drive. I'm nervous. I'm excited. For the first time in weeks and weeks, I'm free. That spark of independence flashes brighter and brighter. I sit in the driver's seat, ready and raring to go. My father bends down to speak to me through the window.

"Ashaig and back, Evelyn."

"Ashaig and back." I nod, grinning like a mime.

"Be safe. Have fun." My father steps away from the car, his hands once again in his pockets. I feel for him. The amount of uneasiness he must be feeling, it only makes this all the more impactful.

"They may take our lives, but they'll never take our freedom!" I yell in an overdramatic Scottish accent. My father rubs the bridge of his nose, looking down and shaking his head. This is it. Independence. Liberation. I shift the car into first. I push the accelerator down. I bring the clutch up. I find the bite. And I stall. The only sound I can hear is the uncontrollable laughter of my father outside the car. I switch the engine back on and press the button to roll the window down.

"How's that freedom going, William Wallace?" My father quips.

"Meant to do that."

"Of course you did." He winks. After successfully setting off, I gleam as I drive through Kyleakin.

I sit in my parked car in a layby, just watching the mountains through the open window. I know he said Ashaig and back but I really want to enjoy this freedom before I have to go back home. As I smile to myself, my phone rings. I frown and retrieve it from my jeans pocket. It's Sam.

"Hi, Sam." I answer.

"Hi, Evie." She sounds scared. Her voice is shaking.

"Sam, you okay? You sound a little…"

248

"Evie, I need you. I need you to come to London. I don't know where Mum is and something's going on with my Dad. There are men in our house and they won't leave." Sam practically whispers.

"Sam, are you in danger?" My heart falls.

"I don't know. They've been here for a couple of days. Evie, I would never ask you to do this but I really need you right now." She's panicking. I'm panicking. I check the time on my phone; it's only just gone 2pm. I build a series of events in my head. I could potentially drive to Inverness. It's all A-roads. I have enough money in my bank to get a flight to London. Oh, god, am I really doing this? "Evie?"

"I'll be there as quick as I can." I hang up the call and turn on the ignition. Yes, I am really doing this.

I am on the mainland. I've been driving for about thirty minutes. I do all I can to stay calm. I know this is crazy. I know I've only just learnt how to drive but this is precisely why I wanted this independence. To see Sam. And not just to see her, but to potentially rescue her from a scary situation. I don't know what I'll do when I get there. If she is in danger, I could sneak her out of the house and get us a taxi to the airport, and then fly to Inverness. Then I'll drive us both back to mine. It's a good, solid gold plan. I jump in fright when the touchscreen on the centre console alerts me to a person calling. And guess who it is. Nevertheless, I can't do what I did last time. Telling my father what I'm doing is more merciful than having him believe something happened to me. I can't put him through that again. "Dad…"

"Where are you?"

"Please don't hate me. Look, when I come back, you can ground me for life. You can cut my driving licence up into little pieces but first, you need to let me do this." I have never spoken so quickly in my life.

"Evelyn Dawn Elizabeth Norman, where are you?" We're in full name territory.

"Uh... currently driving to Inverness." I try to sound so casual.

"What?!"

"Look, I need to fly to London and go to Sam's. She's in trouble. She rang me and she's really scared. Dad, I need to do this. I'm alive. I'm safe. Please." I beg.

"Evelyn, you will turn that car around and you will come home right now or, so help me, you will never see the light of day again." Horrible Dad is back. But this time, he doesn't scare me.

"I'm sorry, Dad. I really am." I sigh.

"Evelyn, you are not going to Sam's! It's not..." I hang up the call. I begin to cry. This will break his heart. All of the trust that has been building has completely vanished. He will never trust me again. But it's alright. Everything will be alright.

I stroll through departures, trying not to seem like a panicking mess. My father is wealthy. He's powerful. He could already have his army of corporate goons looking for me. So I need to be invisible. I've done it before. I did it for sixteen years. I know how to be invisible. I know what it feels like.

The flight was full of anxiety. I got through departures without a hitch and I was expecting a lot more obstacles. I know what resources my father has access to. He's one of the wealthiest CEOs in the UK. But he chose not to use them and I don't know why. I'm now in the cab on the way to Sam's house in

Kensington. I've been full of adrenaline for the past several hours and it won't go away. Not until I know she is safe. The cab comes to a halt outside Sam's house and I pay the driver before rushing out and sprinting to the black wooden door. I knock and knock like a crazy person. Until I see someone approaching through the little stained glass window. It's not Sam. It's not her mother. The door flies open.

"Evie, what the hell are you doing here?" Will asks, slightly stunned.

"I came to see Sam." I need to concoct a lie. "She was just feeling really down, so I thought I would surprise her."

"That's kind of you. She's upstairs. I'll call for her." He smiles slightly. "Come in, come in." Will opens the door wider for me and I enter the townhouse. "Samantha!" Oh, that's odd. He always calls her Sammy. "Samantha, come down!" Not long after his hollering, I hear the patter of feet on stairs. Soon enough, Sam glides down them and rushes into my arms.

"Sam." I whisper desperately, closing my eyes.

"Hi, Evie." She whispers back. Will doesn't walk away.

"Is there somewhere we can speak?" I ask in incredibly hushed tones. Sam nods in my arms and I sigh in relief. Once the hug is over, she takes my hand.

"We'll be in my room." She smiles sweetly at her father, who nods curtly.

Sam paces across her room, holding a hand against her forehead. I sit on the bed, completely flummoxed by what is happening.

"Okay, listen to me. Firstly, thank you so much for coming and just being the best. Secondly, what the hell do I do? I can't leave the house." She panics.

"Where are the men you talked about?"

"All over. Scattered around. Evie, he is acting so weird. He's like a completely different person." Sam clearly needs a brandy.

"Yeah, I heard him call you Samantha. Seemed odd." I nod slowly.

"Will you stay with me? Please? Stay the night or something and we'll just figure something out in the morning." Sam sits beside me on the bed, taking my hands.

"Sam, we could go back to mine. Get a taxi to the airport and I can see if Dad will let us use the jet…"

"No, no, no. Not while my father's in the house. He's at work tomorrow, all day. We can sneak out, past the men." She establishes a plan.

"Where's your Mum?"

"I don't know." Sam bursts into tears. I put a comforting hand on her shoulder. "I'm so sorry I asked you to do this but you were the one person I needed."

"What are friends for?" I shrug and smile. Sam wraps her arms around my neck, giving me the most desperate hug in the world. Something is wrong. I can feel it.

I'm wide awake, lying in Sam's bed next to her. I'm still fully clothed. I didn't really have a chance to pack any overnight essentials. I'm restless and full of frayed nerves. I lean my hand out to check the time on my phone. It's just gone 2am. After a long sigh, I sit up, my mind clouded and busy at the same time. I think all of the stress of the past day is taking its toll. I'm so in need of some water too. I haven't eaten or drank a thing since leaving Ashaig. I assume it's safe to go and grab a glass of water. For all Sam's father knows, I'm just a friend coming to stay. Even if the men are down there, surely they won't do anything. I have barely seen any of them since arriving. I tuck my phone in my back jeans pocket and head out of the bedroom.

The darkness downstairs is disorientating but I know Sam's house well enough to know where the kitchen is. As I walk through the hallway, I am extremely vigilant. I don't know if these elusive men are still here, or where Will is. For the most part, I know I probably can't trust him anymore. Sam seemed terrified of him.

"Evie?" His sudden voice makes me stop walking. I turn to look at him as he emerges from the living room.

"Hi, Will."

"What are you doing awake?" It's too dark to see his face.

"Just needed a water, that's all." I am timid. I am afraid. I've known this man all my life. He is my best friend's father. But right now, he seems like a villain.

"Look, I don't know what Samantha told you today, Evie. But I really…" His words are struck by a silenced gunshot, landing right in his head. I scream and instantly cover my mouth as his body falls onto the floor in front of me. I freeze on the spot. My breaths quicken. I need to get back upstairs. I need to get Sam and leave this house. But where is the gunman? It's too dark. Too pitch black to see anything. The only light is the slight crack of the streetlight through a window. I sprint into the kitchen, thanking all the gods I'm wearing socks. My steps are soundless. I need to grab a knife or something. This is Connelly. Oh, god, maybe he found out I was coming to Sam's. Maybe he's here to kill me. I tuck all of those thoughts away. For now, I just need to concentrate on not being killed. I am alone in the darkness of this house. And I have never been more scared.

I open drawers and drawers in the kitchen. I'm panicking as I look for a knife. I find one, a chef's knife. I can't turn a light on. I can't compromise my location. But footsteps are coming closer. The gunman is in the hallway. I stand with my back to the wall, beside the kitchen door, holding the knife out. I am breathing so loudly. So quickly. I am sobbing silently. The footsteps are coming closer and there is absolutely nothing I can do. My lips shudder as I cry defencelessly, rendered a shaking, trembling mess. I scrunch my eyes closed, succumbing to the fear spreading through me. This isn't just fright. This is pure, unbridled terror. Until the footsteps appear further away. My eyes open, my vision blurred by the sheer volume of water in them. I drop soundless tears as I decide whether or not this is my chance to escape. It has to be. I push away from the wall and sprint through the kitchen door. I forget all about Will's dead body as I rush through the hallway. I trip over it and groan painfully as I land on the marble floor, dropping the knife. I feel like I've hit my head. I frantically shuffle backwards, shaking uncontrollably as I scramble away from the dead body. With all the courage I have, I stand up and spin. I gasp in sheer terror when I see the gunman. Right in front of me. I freeze on the spot, my mouth agape in shock as I stare up at him. I don't blink. I barely breathe. He is wearing black leather gloves and a silenced pistol rests in his hand. I can just see the outlines of his black business suit. My shaky breath is the only sound in the air, fear and alarm smothering my heart. I look into his eyes, which are practically hidden in the darkness. But his tall frame and his hair, I instantly recognise.

"Dad?" I can't breathe. I feel pain in the back of my head. I feel sick. I pass out.

CHAPTER EIGHTEEN

There is an aching in my chest as I wake up. I feel a cold sensation against my left temple as the side of my head rests against the window of a car. I'm groggy. My head feels like a million bricks. There is a dull ache in the back of it. I can still feel the dried tears on my cheeks and they sting. It takes all of my strength to move my head but I do, trying to get a better idea of exactly where I am. I'm in a car but it's not the Mercedes or my little Fiat. A bottle of water lies in the cupholder just to the right of me and I turn my head even more to see who is driving, wincing in pain. My father is still wearing the same black leather gloves I saw earlier as he steers us through the streets of London. I have no idea where we are. I have no idea how I'm in this car with him. I assume he must've carried me into it after I passed out. But he killed Sam's father. And what's happened to Sam? She's in that house all alone. As I stare at my father's impassive, cold expression, I don't know whether or not be scared. Until he finally looks at me. And for some reason, all of that fear washes away.

"Drink the water, Evelyn." He gestures to the bottle beside me. His tone is back to how it was when we first left London, all those months ago. This is the same icy tone he used when we left my mother's body at the Royal London hospital. I slowly reach out to grab the bottle of water and gradually drink some. My movements are careful and unbearably slow. My father reaches an arm back to grab something from the back seat. I recoil at the sudden movement. He then holds up a prepackaged sandwich. I hesitantly take it but I don't open it. "Eat it, Evelyn."

"Dad…"

"Eat it." His brown eyes find mine again. I don't know if he's angry or not. I don't think he is. But he has definitely reverted back to the man I spent twelve hours in a car with not long ago. I swallow all of my uncertainty as I open the sandwich packet and take out one of the halves. I take the tiniest bite, knowing that I'm probably starving. I have a million questions but I know my father is in no position to answer any of them. My father moves his arm again and his hand travels towards the back of my head. I flinch and wince the moment his hand touches it. He notices and takes his hand away, wrapping his fingers around the steering wheel as he drives us through London.

Roughly ten minutes later, my father is driving us towards our private jet near Terminal 4 at Heathrow. As the plane comes into view, I see Francis stood next to it. I sit and ruminate as my father pulls up next to the plane. But he doesn't open his door. He doesn't tell me to get out. Instead, he just sits and stares ahead. I can't imagine what he's feeling. His daughter ran away from home and flew to London by herself. And he has also just killed a man. Oh, god, I've just watched my father murder someone in cold blood. The realisation hits me and I begin to breathe rapidly. "Evelyn." His voice is so soft, so quiet. I instantly turn my head to face him. "Are you alright?" His eyes are filled with that gentle affection again. Those eyes tell me one thing and one thing only; he won't hurt me. So I nod. I then immediately burst into tears.

My father unbuckles his seatbelt and gets out of the car as I crumble into pieces. I then hear the familiar sound of my car door opening. My father reaches past me and presses the button to release my seatbelt. Once I am unbuckled, he collects me in his arms and I tightly wrap my own arms around his neck as he carries me towards the jet.

My father places me down onto one of the cream leather seats. I am still crying as he approaches the mini bar, just as he has before. I'm sure he's going to make me drink another brandy. "Everything set, Mr Norman?" Our pilot, Alistair, asks from the cockpit. My father responds with a curt nod and the door to the jet closes. It isn't long before I can feel the engines hum to life. My father walks towards me and offers me the glass but it's not brandy. It's water. I hesitantly take it. He then sits himself in the opposite leather chair, interlocking his gloved fingers on his crossed knee. Not a strand of his hair is out of place and that familiar frown rests above his eyes. I still can't read his expression, however. He's a wall again as he reaches for something in his pocket. Once he has taken the pill packet out of his pocket, he pushes two little tablets out and offers them to me. With my free hand, I take them and look down at them. "Evelyn, you have a mild concussion. Please drink the water and take the Paracetamol." He commands softly as he takes the black gloves off. His voice is so guarded, almost clinical. I slowly bring one of the tablets to my mouth. I take the tiniest sip of water and swallow them one by one. A few moments pass and as we taxi towards the runway, my father's phone rings. He retrieves it from his trouser pocket and answers the call.

"Hi, Joan." He pauses. "Yes, I've got her. She's fine. She's a bit shaken up and she's got a mild concussion but she's fine." He pauses again. "She fell back and hit her head on the floor." Another pause. "Yes, that's all sorted too. I'll let you know when we've landed in Inverness." Another pause. "Alright. See you soon." My father hangs up the call and puts his phone back into his pocket. I look down at the glass in my hands and stroke it aimlessly. I feel the sudden acceleration of the jet as it takes off. This was always my least favourite part. "Evelyn, I need you to speak to me."

"What do you want me to say?" I mumble, still staring at the glass.

"I just need to hear your voice." He states, almost sentimentally. I finally look into his eyes. They aren't cold anymore.

"Is Sam okay?" I ask, practically whispering. My father smiles ever so slightly.

"Sam is fine. When we get home, I will spend a very long time explaining all of this. I won't answer any questions now as you're still in shock." He describes the plan. I nod in understanding. "But for now, I just want to make sure you're okay."

"I'm okay." I answer, very confident that I'm not okay.

"Evelyn." Yet again, he reads me like a book. "I need you to tell me the truth." He pauses for a moment. "Are you scared of me?" There is a worried look in his eyes after he has asked the question, almost terrified. I think carefully for a moment.

"No. I'm not scared of you." I shake my head.

"Because, regardless of what you saw, I will never hurt you. You know that, don't you?" His voice is like butter.

"I know." I nod tearfully, putting the glass down on a side table.

"Good. Because I'm desperate to do this." My father rises from his seat and crouches in front of me. He then urgently wraps his arms around my waist, pulling me into a forceful, desperate hug. I lose all composure and cry in his arms, tightly holding onto him. After a moment, he swaps with me and sits on my seat. I don't unhook my arms from around his neck for a second as he sits me on his lap and holds me. His fear is evident. It's like he thought he was going to lose me. Maybe he was. He strokes the back of my head and I feel so wonderfully buried in this feeling of safety. I've seen him kill a man right in front of me but right now, I feel so incredibly safe. It's like I'm four-years-old again. But to him, I always will be. No matter how old I am. No matter what independence I have. I am his little girl. We stay like this for what feels like the entire flight home.

It's been several hours since we arrived at the house, at roughly 7am. Joan was incredibly relieved to see me, if still a little miffed at the fact I left in the first place. After saying a fond hello to her, I went straight to bed, to empty my mind of everything and to get a couple more hours of sleep. It's now mid-afternoon and I am sitting at my piano, still working on that song I started to write. It's a good way to calm my still slightly frayed nerves. Soon enough, my phone vibrates and I check it. There is a message from my father.

Dining room.

I walk into the dining room, feeling a certain apprehension after that incredibly enigmatic message. I have no idea what this is going to be about. Well, there are a plethora of things it could be about. But I don't know which one. As I walk in, I see my father stood on the other side of the table, his hands in his pockets. It all seems very professional.

"Evelyn, take a seat." My father instructs. I slowly sit in a chair directly opposite him, staring at him with a look of pure uncertainty. "Now, I think it's time I told you what my job is but I need you to stay calm. Can you do that?" Oh, my god. It's happening.

"Yeah."

"And you'll take it seriously?"

"Yes."

"Then stop smiling." My father raises a brow at me. I've been grinning like a banshee since I found out what was going on.

"I don't think I can." I respond honestly. "But I will take it seriously, I promise."

"Good." He nods slowly and chuckles. "Evelyn, as you may be well aware by now, my job is slightly unconventional. And the truth is, I work for a very specific division of the Secret Intelligence Service, commonly known as MI6." The moment he says this, there is a unique exhilaration and confusion rattling within me. I take an exceptionally long time to process his words. Once I do, my mouth lies open.

"You're MI6?!" I practically yell and he nods, calm as ever. The next words that come out of my mouth aren't really even words, just a croaky stuttering.

"I can see that you are slightly dumbstruck." My father observes. After a second, I laugh loudly, rendered completely stunned. He is doing all he can to hide his amusement at my reaction.

"Dumbstruck?" I laugh again. He clears his throat. "Dad, you just told me you're a bloody secret agent!"

"Not quite. That's not exactly what MI6 is. We're just a very discreet homeland security unit. There are a lot of misconceptions around what we do."

"But you are technically a secret agent though, right?" I ask, still in disbelief. My father takes a long breath.

"Yes." The moment he says it, I jolt up in excitement. But when I see his expression, I compose myself.

"Okay. I am calm, I promise. And as you can imagine, I have a trillion questions." I lean back, unable to stow the massive smile on my face.

"I'm sure you do." My father smirks.

"Number one of my trillion questions; what the fuck?"

"Evelyn." He scolds.

"Okay. Sorry." I stifle a laugh. "Number two of my trillion questions; what the *actual* fuck?"

"Evelyn." He can't help but chuckle.

"No, come on." I giggle. I then pause for a moment, knowing I may need to take this a little more seriously. "Okay, okay, a real question. When did you decide that this was the career for you?" I ask, almost like an interviewer.

"Before you were born." My father is amused.

"So you decided, at the grand old age of twenty...four...?

"Twenty-two. It was a couple of years before we had you."

"Okay, so you decided, at the grand old age of twenty-two, to be a bloody spy? Dad, I think you watched too many James Bonds in your childhood." My eyes widen. "Oh, my god, please can I start calling you 007?!"

"Call me 007, Evelyn, and you will spend the rest of your days wishing you hadn't." My father adjusts his cufflinks. His demeanour is so calm.

"Sounds like something 007 would say…" I mutter under my breath.

"Evelyn, this is your last warning. Just because I am telling you the truth, it doesn't give you license to take the piss." He states firmly.

"Okay, but do you have… a license… to kill?" I close my eyes as I stow my laughter. Once I open them again, I gauge his reaction. His stoicism falters for a millisecond.

"I will let that one slide. Because that was funny." My father narrows his eyes. "And for the last time, MI6 is not like you see in movies. It's just a secret organisation." He's being so patient.

"Do you have, like, a code name though?" I lean forward.

"I do."

"Am I allowed to know what it is?" I continue to smile. My father takes a very long time to respond.

"It's Eagle. And, on the topic of code names, if you are ever in a position whereby you cannot directly call me 'Dad', then use that code name."

"I will. Should I have a code name?"

"How about Pain in the Ass?" He asks impassively. I just look at him blankly for a moment.

"That'll do." I nod and he nods back. "Okay so, twenty-two years old, you decide to be James Bond." I shrug. "That's fine. I'm following. And Joan…"

"Joan doesn't work with me. I just taught her how to handle a gun, that's all." My father sighs thoughtfully. "When I was in school, my parents started to notice little skills of mine."

"You were a secret agent in school?!" I ask, clearly sarcastically.

"Evelyn." He scolds yet again. This time, he means it.

"Sorry." I smile.

"They saw my skills, my mental capacity, my problem solving, my discretion. And they liked it. So, when I was eighteen, they sent me to Cambridge to do a business degree. I was approached by what we might call a talent spotter. I went through an intense recruitment process. Started off as a standard intelligence officer. Over time, made my way up. Did some more training…"

"James Bond training?"

"Yes." He says slowly. "And that's how it all started."

"Okay. So, how does Connelly fit into all of this then?"

"Finally, a good question." He raises a brow. "Connelly has been on our radar for a long time. Just over seventeen years. He's a bit of a consulting criminal. He is the highest of the high. He is untouchable. Which is why I was incredibly uneasy about the dinner party. Which is why I have done everything in my power to keep you safe." He frowns at me in deep thought. "If Connelly got even the slightest whiff of who I really was, he would end you, do you understand me? If Connelly ever found out what I was really doing, he would find you and he would use you to destroy me. I couldn't have you find out the truth. It terrified me. Because every time you nearly found out the truth, you were exposed to Connelly more. And then this thing with Noah started…" He lets out a long sigh. "And when Connelly said he would like you to seek a friendship with Noah, I knew exactly what he was doing. He was

264

trying to trap you using his son. And unfortunately, you fell into that trap. Not as far as I feared but you did." As he speaks, I ingest every word. "Remember our little talk after the dinner party, I told you that I needed to build trust. Work with him, destroy him from the inside. Well, it all required an element of, for want of a better term, spying." His raised eyebrow makes me giggle. "Evelyn."

"Sorry."

"I had to think how businessmen thought. Especially a man like Connelly. So, I did some business bits on the side and started my own company. My company back in London is completely legitimate, I will add. The money I've made, it's all lawful. But in order to gain Connelly's trust and respect, I had to have my own established company. The SIS paid for the startup and I took it from there. I didn't realise how well the company would do. And it made me a lot of money. Now, I've never once killed for money and I never will." He pauses for a moment. "But I have killed, Evelyn. I will tell you now. I have killed dozens of people and you need to take this so seriously." He sighs and I nod. "While I'm killing dozens of people, I'm also making enemies. Moving to Scotland was a last resort until your mother died. Then I had no choice. I needed you away from London. London wasn't safe for you anymore. And then Connelly came to Scotland and it all went a bit wrong."

"Dad, can I ask you another question?"

"Of course you can."

"Sam's Dad, why did you kill him?" I shake my head.

"When you discovered me in Sam's home last night, that was unfortunate. Incredibly unfortunate. But I had to. That night at the Summer show, you said you recognised the voice coming through the assailant's phone. It was William, Sam's father." He explains so carefully. I widen my eyes.

"So, this whole time, my best friend's Dad has been a…"

"Yes. He was working for Connelly."

"Did you know that the whole time?"

"Yes. And when you told me you were travelling to Sam's, I had to make my way there as well. I had to get to William before he got to you. And he nearly did." I can see a hint of admonishment on his face. I feel small again. "Now… Connelly is unfortunately starting to become suspicious. That's why I've been taking trips to London. To keep up appearances, and it did work for a while. However, Connelly is a very intelligent man. But like I said, I know his weaknesses. So myself and my team, if you will, are trying to find the right time to strike. It's taken us seventeen years but we're close. Closer than we have ever been before."

"So, you are… undercover?"

"Mm-hmm."

"To take down Connelly because he's this… what, he's just a problem? What is he?"

"Connelly isn't just a problem. He is actively involved with and provides financial support for various terrorist organisations."

"What?" I ask in shock. "Is that the reason we drove to Scotland, and didn't fly?"

"Yes, I didn't want to take any chances. And it's also the reason why I wasn't all that impressed with your comment on the way to London for your mother's funeral." My father states, still clearly unimpressed. I rack my brain for the comment I made.

"Oh, the one where I asked if he was going to blow up…?"

"Mm-hmm." His voice clearly expresses his disapproval.

"Yeah… but in my defence, I had no idea. Because someone has kept this a secret for seventeen years." I cross my arms.

"For a good reason. The thing is, Evelyn, he also dips into human trafficking now and again." His expression falters a touch, like he is suppressing a feeling of disgust. "And when you fell into his… interests, shall we say, I was terrified. Human trafficking, Evelyn, it scares me. And I don't want to imagine what would've happened if he got to you. If he had managed to get to you, you'd be sat in the back of a truck right now, headed to god knows where. Starving. Dehydrated. Surrounded by several other people, equally as scared, equally as young." He closes his eyes and shakes his head, pushing the intrusive thoughts away. "That's the kind of man Connelly is."

"Alright, I get it. And I get the need to keep this from me. I understand everything now. I understand the guns. I understand the secrecy. I understand the forbidden office. But I can't understand… there's a file that I read, as you know because of your bloody cameras…" I roll my eyes. "There's a file and it says targets on the front. What are they? Who are they?"

"Another good question, well done." He winks at me. I smile, proud of myself. "They are others who are also on our radar. Some of them work with Connelly. Some don't. I'm sure you saw the word 'deceased' on one of them. Well, they are active targets. People we need to, for want of a better term again, take care of."

"Who were the two men that Joan killed?"

"I don't know yet. We're assuming they were working for Connelly."

"Wait a second. Why didn't Joan tell you about them? I mean, you're MI6 and she could've told you…"

"She did tell me, the moment you went to your room. She had to, so I could organise removal of the bodies."

"But… you got angry at me. Like, really angry. And then after my birthday, you asked me about the bullets."

"I apologise, Evelyn, but I have been throwing little tests your way, without your knowledge. I needed to know that I could trust you if you ever found out the truth. Joan also told you to keep it a secret, because I need to be confident that you will keep what I do a secret. We're not called the Obvious Intelligence Service."

"Okay, well, did I at least pass these ridiculous tests?" I shrug, a bit miffed by the whole situation.

"Not initially. But that day, when I asked you about the missing bullets and through keeping Joan's confidence, you passed with flying colours. So, well done." My father sighs and looks down. "The problem is, Evelyn, Connelly is not my first shark. And he won't be my last. Telling family members can be risky. So, constantly, my family and I are exposed to retaliation."

"Did Mum know you were working for MI6?"

"Yes. Your mother knew everything. And your mother was flawless. She was discreet and incredibly understanding." His expression turns regretful as he chooses his next words. "The reason I was so cold towards you for sixteen years, and like I said, your mother knew what I was doing… well, all of that detachment… I did it to protect you. If I acted cold around you, and rarely acknowledged you, it kept you safe, Evelyn. Because like I said, I only have the one weakness." There is such a fondness in his stare. "And I couldn't allow them to see that. But unfortunately, William did."

"When?"

"At the funeral. He was there, as you know, with Sam and her mother. And he saw me walk to you when you couldn't finish your speech. And he knew, at that moment, exactly what you meant to me. Situations like that are what I've been trying to avoid for sixteen years." As my father explains, a horrible realisation comes over me.

"That's why you changed. When Sam and her parents were here and you treated me like you used to, it was to stop Will from seeing…"

"Mm-hmm. It was to stop William from seeing how much you meant to me. I acted coldly again because I needed him to think that…"

"You hated me."

"Essentially."

"So the past sixteen years of you being a heartless prick, that was all just a ploy? That was all just a cover up?" I scoff, almost tearful. He looks wounded. "Dad, for sixteen years, you made me feel like you hated me. Do you realise how cruel that is?"

"I know it's cruel, Evelyn. But it was necessary. You had your mother, and she was a million times the parent I was. She was the one to give you the love, the hugs, the affection. I was the protector and by keeping you at a distance, I kept you safe."

"Fine. I get it. So, what changed then?"

"She died. And when she died, I didn't cope with it very well. Better than I thought I would, but still not well. I still tried to keep that distance from you. But every time I saw you, I saw that you needed her. I saw that you needed me. And you and I were spending a lot more time together. I got to know you more. And I fell in complete and utter love with you, Evelyn." His poignant words cause the rivers of tears to fall. "I started to see who you really were. I always thought you were this timid, scared little thing. But you're not. You're brave. You're clever. You're funny. You're a pain in the ass but you're funny."

"That's accurate." I laugh tearfully. He chuckles in response. "Every day, I kept telling myself to stay distant, to not grow too attached to you. I kept trying to revert back to…"

"Horrible Dad?"

"Yes. Because keeping you at a distance, it was safer that way. But every time I tried to stay distant and not grow to love you, I would see you cry, I would see you laugh. And that's why I've always made you believe you couldn't cry in front of me. It weakened me. Because all I wanted to do was hug you and make you feel better. But I couldn't. I had to stay strong. During our time here, I grew to love you more and more. Until finally, I cracked."

"Dad…" I close my eyes and let out a long breath. "You made your daughter think she wasn't allowed to cry… so that you wouldn't catch feelings?" I nod slowly, trying to wrap my head around this. "Yeah, I'm going to need a very long minute to come to terms with that. And do you happen to have the number of a very good therapist?"

"Evelyn, I apologise profusely for this. For not being the father you needed for sixteen years. I've given you a good life and you know that. You've always been humble about our wealth, so well done. You got that from your mother. But no amount of money in the world can make up for the absence of love. And there has been an absence of love from me. But not anymore. I am no longer keeping my distance. I haven't since the night of the dinner party, where we had our little heart-to-heart on the mountainside. That was the moment I decided to really try to make up for the last sixteen years. I love you unconditionally and I always have. I need you to know that."

"I know you love me now, Dad. But for sixteen years…" I begin to sob.

"Evelyn…" He rushes to me and crouches beside me. "Look at me. Sweetheart, look at me." I finally do. "There is nothing in this world I regret more than the last sixteen years. Your aunt was right. For sixteen years, I put this job before you. This objective. But that ends now. And I will do everything I can to make up for it." He places a hand on my cheek, wiping my tears away. "And the SIS can get you that therapist." I can't help but giggle at his joke. It breaks away some of the sadness I feel but I need to figure out if I'm willing to forgive him for this. "Don't hate me. Please don't hate me. I can't lose you, Evelyn."

"You won't lose me, Dad. I promise." I whisper. He wraps me in his arms. I close my eyes and hug him back. "So…" I continue and he slowly lets me go. "All the business stuff, was that all fake?" As I ask, he stands back where he was and puts his hands in his pockets again.

"Yes and no. The business stuff you saw, all the paperwork, the phone calls, the requisitions… they were a bit of a front. The company is very real. And always will be. But it was an act. All part of the…"

"Undercover?" I smirk, wiping my eyes.

"Yes." He wears a humorous scolding look, making me giggle.

"Okay, I'm with you. So, um, what happens now then? Now that I know?"

"I have to kill you." He nods once, completely serious.

"Wait, you just told me I had to be serious, so why do you get to make jokes and I don't?"

"Who says I'm joking?" His mouth tilts up into a playful smile.

"Dad!" I laugh, making him chuckle. His expression then turns serious again.

"You knowing what I do is territory I haven't yet encountered. The SIS are aware that I am telling you the truth. And as long as you are discreet, it's fine. The plan was for you to never know any of this. I never wanted you to. Because the moment you know…"

"I'm not safe, I get it."

"That's why every time you went into that office, I was furious with you. You were close to finding out the truth. That's why I became Horrible Dad. And Horrible Dad is MI6 Dad, I'm afraid, and he may come back periodically. Because there are times where I worry about your safety more than how you feel. And why, when Sam was here…"

"I get it. You had to turn into MI6 Dad. Um, speaking of Sam…"

"Mm-hmm."

"You said that her Dad worked for Connelly. How long has that been going on?" I can see a hesitation in his eyes after I ask this.

"The whole seventeen years."

"Okay, well, isn't it just a massive coincidence that she's my best friend? The daughter of one of the men you've been trying to take down." My confusion is obvious. It's as clear as the remorse on my father's face.

"It's not a coincidence, Evelyn." He states. It takes me a while to clock his meaning, but I do. And I am distraught.

"What?!" I yell.

"I've known about William's connection to Connelly ever since we started this assignment. So I needed access to him. The best way to do that was through you and Sam. I set up play dates, found out where he lived and moved closer. Pulled some strings and made sure you both went to school together. Exactly the same classes. Paired together on field trips, school projects, that sort of thing. Of course, I made sure you were safe. Evelyn, I am deeply sorry to tell you this, but your friendship with Sam was completely my doing." After he speaks, I feel cold.

"No." I stand up, shaking my head.

"She's still your friend, Evelyn." He can clearly see my emotional fuse is blowing.

"You're telling me that my entire friendship with Sam is a lie? It was just a part of this plan to get Connelly? It was all just part of your job?" I rest a hand over my forehead.

"Yes, Evelyn. But it's authentic. You love Sam."

"Yes, I do love Sam! But it's not real! And it's really nice to know that I have had literally no say in anything that has happened in my life, not even my fucking friendships."

"Evelyn, calm down." He slowly walks to me.

"No, don't tell me to calm down, Dad. You have controlled every single aspect of my life. All because of this job." The tears fall as I try to compose myself. "Where is Sam now? You just blew her father's head off so where is she?"

"Once I dealt with William and carried you to the car, I rang my team. Sam is going to be taken to a Protected Persons Unit. She's currently with my people."

"Your people?"

"I'm relatively high up."

"What about her mother? Where is she?" Once I ask, there is an incredibly long pause.

"Sam's mother is missing."

"What?"

"We're trying to find her. But Sam is safe, I assure you. William used Sam, Evelyn. I should've seen it coming. He knew that your friendship with Sam was strong. He knew that if she rang you in a state of panic, then you would come running. And you did. There were no men in the house. Sam lied to you."

"So, Sam's also…"

"No, Sam is innocent. But she was forced to make the call."

"That's why he was calling her Samantha; he was scaring her into doing what he needed?"

"Mm-hmm. Then when you got to the house, she had to find a way to get you to stay. And again, you did. Your loyalty to Sam was used against you."

"Yeah, because of you." I scoff.

"What?"

"Well, if this friendship hadn't been designed by you in the first place, none of that would've happened."

"I told you a long time ago, I'm not a fortune teller. I had no idea it would lead to that." He narrows his eyes slightly. He is so incredibly pensive right now. I begin to sob, finding it all a bit too much.

"Am I ever going to see her again?" I ask tearfully. "When you're done with Connelly, is she even going to be my friend anymore?"

"Evelyn, of course she is. Don't be absurd."

"Well, forgive my absurdity, Dad! But you've just told me that my father has been living a double life. You've just told me that my best friend in the whole world was just a fabrication so that you could get a job done! You made me believe you hated me! For years, Dad! My whole life has been a fucking lie but at least you're earning a decent pay cheque!" I storm out of the room, crying uncontrollably.

"Evelyn!" I ignore him. I feel like I loathe him. I know the truth and it all makes sense now. Everything makes sense. My friendship with Sam was just a tactic by him to get what he needed. All my life, he made me feel like he hated me because his job was dangerous. But he chose to make me feel that way. He's controlled and manipulated every element of my existence. Where I lived. Who my friends were. What choices I had or didn't have. It's because of him that I may never see my best friend again. It's because of him that I won't go to college where I want to. It's because of him that I was dragged to Scotland the day my mother died. And I hate him for it.

CHAPTER NINETEEN

It's only been a couple of hours since I found out the truth. And I'm still furious. I'm still filled with endless questions. Some things still need clearing up, like why we moved to Scotland in the first place. He said it was for my protection but I can't help feel there's something more to it. I need to know what happens next. I need to know if we are ever going back to London. Bloody MI6. I knew his job was something unimaginable. And it sounds like he's incredibly high up the ladder. Maybe he even works directly with the government. I always thought he was just a suave businessman. I always assumed our wealth came from his companies. Apparently not. It's all been one massive cover up. My whole life is a lie.

I am lying on my side on my bed, still sniffling and trying to keep the tears at bay, when I hear my door open and close. Three months ago, I would've always assumed it was Joan walking in. My father never did the restorative conversations. But now, I know it's him. And it will always be him who comes to check on me after we've had a falling out. I do still love him. But what he told me changes a lot of things. As I continue to look away, I feel him sit on the bed and then I hear the very recognisable sound of him sighing loudly.

"Dad, can I ask you a question?" I mutter tearfully.

"What is it, sweetheart?"

"Has anything in my life been real?" I close my eyes and let the tears fall.

"Evelyn…" He sounds so sympathetic. It catches me off guard. I feel movement on the bed. I feel him shuffling to a certain position. "Come here." His voice is right behind me. I twist and face him before he wraps his arms around me and pulls me into a sideways hug. I cry against him, feeling so precious to him and protected. "Evelyn, there are so many things in your life that are real. Your family is real. How much we love you is extremely real. Your friendship with Sam is real."

"Am I ever going to see her again?" I sob.

"Evelyn." He places a kiss on my head. "Look at me." I refuse to, shaking my head. "Evelyn, look at me." He repeats and I reluctantly lift my eyes to see his. "I am so sorry you had to find all this out. It was a lot, all of that information. But I promise you, that you will see your best friend again. Because when this is finished, we're going back to London." This information comes as a surprise. I frown at him. "Skye, as gorgeous as it is, isn't the place for you. I can see that. But we came here for safety, among other reasons. We also came here because I thought you could use Joan. When your mother died and I was thrown into being a single father, I knew I needed someone to help me with you. Joan rejoiced at the prospect of us living with her. And it meant you had a bit of a mother. And I had the time to concentrate on work without worrying about you."

"There's a surprise." I roll my eyes.

"But…" He ignores my comment. "That was at the beginning, when I had no idea how to be your father. Now, I'm bit of an

Evelyn expert." There is humour in his tone. "I now know your favourite curry. I now know how to make you laugh. I now know what to do when you come home absolutely off your face." His words make me giggle.

"Dad, I think there's a bit more to fatherhood than that."

"No, that's utter bollocks." He says it with such confidence, I can't help but laugh. "I am well and truly prepared to be your father, Evelyn. I'm not terrified of doing it alone anymore, which is why we are closing in on Connelly as quick as possible. We're getting it done. And then you and I can go back to London. We'll live in our home in Notting Hill. And you can choose any college you want." The moment he mentions college, I frown and sit up, wiping my eyes. He sits up too.

"Wait, you're being serious."

"Of course I am. I want you to have the future you want. If you want to go to Kensington Hall Sixth Form to do your A-Levels, you can. If you want to join the orchestra that Miss Perkins mentioned, you can. And then if you want to be at UCL with Sam, I'll always be nearby. You made a very good point, Evelyn. I have taken some choices away from you. These choices were never mine to take away. So, you and me, we're going back to London. We're going home." He nods. I instantly leap into his arms, full of gratitude, full of love. He laughs and holds me so tightly.

"Thank you."

"You're welcome, sweetheart."

"I can't wait." I smile, still in his arms. "I'll get to do my music. I'll get to go to nightclubs with Sam."

"Don't push it." He warns. "I don't want any phone calls from you at 3am, asking me to pick your drunk ass up from a club in the middle of Soho."

"I won't." I giggle. My father sighs as the hug ends.

"Listen to me, Evelyn. These next couple of weeks are crucial, and they're going to be rocky. There is still a lot of work I need to do. Now, you know nothing, alright? You don't know my job. You don't know about Connelly. You don't know what I'm doing, is that understood?"

"Understood." I nod.

"The office is no longer forbidden but use caution. There are still some things in there that I don't want you to stumble upon. If you need or want to go in there, please ask me first. Don't just walk in, unless I ask you to get something." He reaches into his trouser pocket and pulls out his phone. "Give me your phone."

"Why?"

"Please." He raises a brow. I grab my phone from my jeans pocket and place it in his hand. I watch as he taps on both his and mine. Once he is done with my phone, he hands it back to me. I look down at it in confusion. He has downloaded and opened a new app. "As you know, my company in London is mostly telecommunications. So I had my team develop an app."

"What does it do?" I aimlessly navigate my way through the app.

"It's called Secret Garden." He informs me. I smile at the reference. "It's a bit of a baby monitoring system for teenagers."

"For me, you mean." I can't hide the smirk on my face.

"Initially." My father nods slowly. "But I'm going to expand it and make it available to the public. There is a button…" He taps an index finger onto my phone screen. On the app, a large circular red button comes up. "Essentially, if you are ever in trouble or scared, press that button. And it sends me a message. It's discreet and means you won't have to type. There are preset messages to choose from. For example, if god forbid, you are in the boot of a car, there is a preset message telling me that. Scroll through them." He instructs and I do. There are lots of different choices.

I'm scared. Can you pick me up?
This person won't leave me alone.
I've been taken by someone.
I'm lost and I can't get home.
I'm in trouble.
I need picking up.
I think someone wants to hurt me.

"They range from needing a pick-up to kidnapping." My father explains while I read. "And once you press that button..."
"It tells you my location?" I look at him. There is a glimmer of pride in his eyes.
"Correct. You choose the message. You press the button. Takes two seconds."
"So when the kid downloads the app, all the parent has to do is pop their phone number in? And then the kid decides whether or not to press the button?"
"Correct. It'll send the chosen message to their parent. You can add your own custom messages too. Give me your phone." He holds out his hand again and I pass the phone to him. I watch as he types something into the app, I assume to create a custom message. He then passes it back to me. "Press the button." He

nods and I do. His phone then pings. My father clears his throat and looks at his phone, a veil of amusement on his face before showing me the screen.

Herr Kommandant, I've been a colossal idiot and I need you to come and get me.

I stifle a laugh, trying to take it seriously as I nod. My father winks at me before pocketing his phone.

"Dad, this is really clever."

"I *am* really clever." He crosses his arms.

"Oh yeah, you're right, Mum was the humble one." I quip. He chuckles softly. "But seriously, this could save people's lives."

"There's really only one life I'd like it to save. But yes, the idea is to create a new blanket of security for young people. Imagine you're in a position where you're not allowed to type a message. You see it in nightclubs all the time. Bar staff are trained to identify certain codes, if someone is being harassed and so on. And it also means that young people feel safe without their parents becoming…"

"Overprotective?" I raise a brow.

"Yes. Now, Evelyn, I am praying to god that you are never in a position where you'll need to use this. But like I said, the next two weeks are going to be dangerous. And I need you on your absolute best behaviour. No driving without us. No leaving the house without us." He frowns at me.

"Speaking of overprotective…" I raise my brows.

"A very necessary protective." My father counters. I suppose he is right. We are in danger and I need to do what he says.

"Okay." I take his hands. "I swear to you that I will stay in the house unless it's with you or Joan. I won't drive. I won't go on any more insane journeys to London…"

"Ah, yes, we haven't discussed that yet." He states. I widen my eyes.

"And we don't have to." I lean back and cover myself with the duvet.

"Yes, we do, Evelyn." I can hear the smirk on his face.

"No, we don't. I have had a lot of information thrown at me today. I found out my father was a double agent. I saw my father shoot a man I've known since I was a baby. I found out that my friendship was all a load of bollocks. I haven't slept properly. Emotions ran incredibly high. I really can't deal with any more mental stress." I hope my reasoning is enough to get me out of this. It takes an incredibly long time but he finally responds with a heavy sigh.

"Alright, well played. Evelyn, I really do think you should go into business. I might just throw you at my Board of Directors, that'll soon shut them up."

"Yeah, I'll sort them out for you, Dad."

"My hero." He chuckles and gets to his feet. I take the covers away from my face and see him approach the door.

"Dad."

"Mm-hmm."

"If I'm not discreet about what your job is, will you really have to kill me?" I ask, completely seriously. My father stares ahead for a moment before turning to look at me. He then looks up in mock contemplation.

"Yes."

"Dad…"

282

"Don't worry. I'll wait until after Christmas." He winks.

"Alright, well, just make sure my death's not boring. I want to go out in a really cool way, you know." I join the joke.

"Oh, I'm sure I'll think of something." He quips as he clutches the door handle. "Be downstairs for dinner in an hour." My father closes the door behind him. I lie back and look up at the ceiling. I smile to myself. My father is a bloody spy.

A week later, I am watching as my father unlocks the door to the office, a room that once filled me with terror but now fills me with such an excited curiosity. He pockets the key after opening the door and I look around. It all looks the same as it did. But it doesn't feel the same, knowing what the contents of this room actually are. My father allows me the freedom to explore, crossing his arms and leaning back against the wall.

"Do you have, like, funky spy sunglasses that give you x-ray vision?" I ask as I mooch around.

"No."

"Do you have a microscopic camera that you can insert into someone's eye?"

"No."

"Do you have a little taser gun disguised as a pen?"

"No."

"Oh, speaking of guns, can I…?" I grin at him.

"Absolutely not." My grin disappears.

"Can't I just hold one?"

"No."

"Why not?"

"I'm not even going to answer that question."

"God, when you told me you were a secret agent, I thought it would be a bit more thrilling than this. Do you actually have anything remotely exciting?"

"No." His expression is dead serious. "Evelyn, I told you, MI6 isn't like the movies. Do you want to know the most exciting thing I have?"

"Yeah." I smile in anticipation.

"Paperwork." My father winks and sits himself down in the black leather chair. I stare ahead vacantly as he signs into his laptop and brings up an electronic document.

"What's that?" I look over his shoulder.

"A report from the events in Sam's house. I need to fill it in." He answers as he types.

"Wow, that is, uh, incredibly high-octane." I remark sarcastically.

"This is how exciting my life is, Evelyn. Actually, while you're here, it would be good to get a bit of a statement from you." His eyes don't come away from the screen.

"Statement?"

"Yes. Anything you think I should be made aware of. Anything else unusual that happened that night."

"You mean apart from the fact I saw a mysterious gunman shoot someone I've known for years, and then I spent an incredibly long time absolutely shitting my pants, tripped over a dead body and hit my head, only to find out that the gunman was my father the whole time?" Once I have given my little discourse, my father looks back at me, so I offer him a smile.

"Sorry, could you repeat that? I wasn't listening." He raises a brow. I giggle and wrap my arms around his neck from behind him, making him chuckle. I stay like this as I watch him.

"Dad, can I ask you a question?"

"Mm-hmm." He continues to type.

"At Inverness airport, you didn't send anyone to stop me. I expected some kind of, I don't know, corporate security of yours or something. But I sailed through."

"No, I didn't send anyone. Do you want to know why?"

"Yeah." Once I have answered his question, he frowns and stops typing. He then clutches my arm affectionately.

"Because I don't trust another damn soul with your life. I have men on my payroll at the company. But they have no idea who I really work for. And when it comes to protecting you, I am the only person I trust. Evelyn, my job puts you in danger. It always will." He starts to become disheartened. "I wasn't there when your mother died. I should've been. I was supposed to protect her..."

"Dad." I wrap my arms around him tighter, offering him some consolation. "You can't blame yourself for Mum. It wasn't your fault." I urge him to listen. "And if anything does happen to me, it won't be your fault either."

"Evelyn, that's not the point. *Nothing* should happen to you. Just as nothing should've happened to your mother." His voice trails off, like he's becoming tearful. I can tell he's holding it back.

"You're allowed to cry, Dad." I echo his words to me from all those months ago. He just chuckles mournfully. "You said so yourself; exposing your heartbreak is imperative."

"Oh, so you do actually listen to me?" He continues with his typing.

"Of course I do. I love you." A massive realisation dawns on me once I have spoken those three words. That's the first time I've said them to him. He's said it to me so many times but I have

285

never said it to him. And I feel an extraordinary stab of guilt. All those years of thinking he was a cold, distant monster. All those years thinking he didn't have an ounce of humanity. All those years thinking he didn't love me. But then I realise something. He did make me feel like he didn't love me. And the more I think about it, that's the cruellest thing he's ever done. That's the one thing a parent should never do to a child. And he did it. I've spent sixteen years receiving no love from my father and for what? A job. I know he's explained it already. I know he did it for a good reason. But right now, I feel devastated. I feel almost betrayed. I've been so wrapped up in my thoughts that I barely notice the tears falling down my cheeks. My father hasn't noticed; he's still facing his laptop. I just stare ahead, in blind realisation that actually... he is a monster. He is cruel. He is heartless. He is all of those things I thought he was. Because he made me believe he didn't love me. He may love me now, but he will never make up for sixteen years of neglect and abandonment. The man didn't even let me cry. I was a child, just a baby in this harsh world, and I needed the love of my father. But I never got it. I slowly unhook my arms from around his neck and take tiny steps back, reversing away from him and the office.

I hurry down the stairs. I need to be away from this house. I am so emotionally overwhelmed that I can't be in the same building as him. Seeing his face would crumble me and I need to release this anger, this pain, this devastation. I rush to the kitchen and collect my car keys from the fruit bowl.

"Evelyn?" I hear the distant sound of my father's low voice as I walk briskly down the hall, towards the front door. "Evelyn?!" I continue to ignore him, putting my Converse on. I have only one goal and that's to get away. "Evelyn?!" He sounds closer but I am already out of the house. I hurriedly unlock my Fiat and throw open the driver's side door. I check my rear-view mirror as I turn the ignition on. My father is rushing out of the house. I throw the gearstick into first and drive. "Evelyn!" He is yelling frantically, sprinting after my car. I don't stop. "Evie!" I can just about hear the distant shriek of my name as I race away from Kyleakin. I will come back. I will. I just need some space. I need some time.

I still haven't stopped crying as I pass Ashaig. I look at the touchscreen on my centre console, battling a decision. After a moment of contemplation, I use the touchscreen to open my contacts. I press a specific one and wait for it to connect.

"Evie? Are you okay? I thought you wanted space."

"Noah, I need to see you. Can I come over?" I sob.

"Yeah, of course. I live in Upper Breakish. Look for the white house with the red van outside, just off the A87."

"I'm almost there. I'll see you soon." I hang up the call using the touchscreen. Another call tries to come through but I ignore it. I'll apologise for this. But I can't speak to him. Not right now. I'm too overwhelmed, too distraught.

I find the white house with the red van. I indicate and pull into the driveway, coming to a stop just in front of one of his double garages. I turn the ignition off and sit in silence for a moment. Noah is emerging from the front door of the house so I offer him a smile. I open and close my car door, popping my phone in my back pocket. Noah opens his arms and I throw myself into them, needing the comfort.

"Are you okay?" He regards me with such a concern in his eyes.

"Not really. I'm sorry for the emergency outreach."

"Not at all. Come on in. I just need to grab something from the garage." Noah strides towards one of the garage doors. I look out at the panorama as I wait for him to collect whatever he needs. I'm going to miss this place when we go back to London. I giggle slightly, thinking about my time in Skye. It's been wonderful but I'm ready to go back to my real home. I am still smiling when I spin to face the garage. My smile immediately disappears when I see what's inside it. My eyes go hazy. My mind goes blurry. All I can feel is the cold, unsettling nausea rising in my stomach. A black BMW is parked in the garage.

"Noah, is your Dad here?" I ask, my voice probably shaking from the terror. Noah walks to me causally.

"No. No, this is my car." He informs me so nonchalantly. I can't process all of my thoughts at once. They fight each other, like gang warfare. I am rendered speechless as I do nothing but think.

"Evelyn, you okay?" He called me Evelyn. No. Something is definitely not right. I reach for my phone in my back jeans pocket in what feels like slow motion. I can't spook him.

"Yeah, I'm fine." I smile, doing all I can to mask my fear. "Um, I'm actually feeling a little unwell. I've been on a plane and I haven't really slept." I giggle awkwardly, hoping my terror isn't completely obvious. "Sorry for this… I'll, um… I'll call you. Yeah… I'll… call you…" I turn around, to head back to my car. I open the Secret Garden app. I am just about to press the button when I feel a cloth around my mouth, being pressed against my face. I scream into it. My cries are muffled. I'm becoming so weak. I do all I can to focus on that one button. But my phone drops from my hand as I can no longer feel my fingers. The last things I see are the distant mountains as a blanket of darkness smothers my vision.

CHAPTER TWENTY

I wake up. I don't know where I am. I'm freezing. I'm thirsty. I'm
hungry. I hear a distant dripping but other than that, it is silent. I
feel like I'm drunk all over again. It only makes me feel more
nauseous as I try to open my eyes. They hardly do. I squint, seeing
a piercing luminescent light above me. My head feels so empty
and I can barely string a thought together. It feels like it weighs
ten tonnes. I lean my head back but the heaviness of it makes me
hit the wall harder than intended. I immediately grimace after
feeling what appears to be stone behind my head. It's not daytime.
I can sense it, even though I have no clue where I am. But I study
the room. It's just an empty, stone hole. I need to get out. I try to
move my hand but my right wrist is tied to something. I slowly
turn my incredibly heavy head to see what I'm tied to and how. A
cable tie lies around my wrist and around a pole against the wall.
Suddenly understanding the severity of my situation, I begin to
sob. There is a new fear within me. It's the same fear as when
you're a child and scary thoughts won't let you sleep. You're
suddenly aware of how alone you are. It's the same fear as when
you've watched too many scary movies, and you constantly feel
like there is a presence in your bedroom whenever you shut your
eyes. It's that, but times a thousand.

I don't know how long it's been since I woke up. I don't know how long it's been since I arrived at Noah's. Holy shit. Noah. He's the one who drugged me. He's the one who owns the BMW. Not Connelly. It's going to be okay. I'm still crying and I am still the most terrified I have ever been, but it's going to be okay. I want Joan. I want my Mum. I want my Dad. My thoughts are cut off by the sound of a heavy metal door slamming, and then harsh footsteps down a stone staircase. I sit back against the wall as much as I can as Noah appears in the room with me. He stands directly before me, pulling on a pair of white cotton gloves.

"Hi, Evelyn." Noah greets me casually. I don't respond. I just stare at him. "I guess you probably have questions. Do you want to ask any?" I have a million questions I want to ask, but I can't speak. "I'll just imagine an FAQ, shall I?" His voice has changed. It's almost slurred. "Basically, we'll start with the obvious. I am the driver of the BMW that followed you a fair amount of time ago. I am one of my father's best employees. Though, he'll never admit it." Noah chuckles scornfully. "Maybe he'll finally be proud of me. Who knows? Sorry, I'm digressing and I know that's irritating. I'm not going to tell you where you are because, well, the reason why is glaringly obvious. And, I mean, where's the fun in that, right? I can tell you some vague information about where you are. You're far away from Kyleakin."

"How far?" My voice is just a croak.

"Oh, shit. She can speak. That's good to know. And to answer your question; roughly one hundred miles away. Give or take." He obviously sees something on my face as he grimaces. "God, you're pale. I suppose I better give you something." He reaches into a pocket and pulls out his phone. He waits for the call to connect and rolls his eyes. He even mouths 'sorry' to me. I just stare at him in pure confusion and shock. "Yeah, bring it down please." Noah hangs up the call. "Sorry about that. Any more questions while we wait for the delivery?"

"What delivery?"

"Well, my father wants you alive so… food, I'm guessing." His demeanour is so unsettling. He's so casual, so nonchalant, like this is just one of his hobbies. His father wants me alive. That's good news. Buys me some time. After a moment, I hear more footsteps coming down the stone staircase. Two people enter the room. One is carrying a plate of something and the other is carrying a bottle of water. It's Luke and Amelia. They settle the refreshments down next to me before walking back up the stairs. I can't even begin to comprehend what's happening. Well, apart from the obvious fact that trusting Noah Connelly was the biggest mistake I ever made.

"This whole time… it's been you." I speak almost breathlessly.

"Not all me. My father, mostly. But, yes, the friendship, the get together, seeing you in the shop… it was all my doing."

"The harbour? When you pushed me in?"

"All planned. I waited and waited for you to leave that house. I was just scouting the area mostly. We knew vaguely where you lived. And then wham. Everything just fell into place."

"The dinner party…"

"I saw you go to the bathroom. So I followed, to bump into you again. Basically, until you turned up at my house three days ago…" Three days?! "It was all relatively planned. The get together near Ashaig, the shop, the BMW, the messages. My father basically said 'stalk that bitch' so I did. And, uh, it worked."

"Three days." I don't say it out loud for his benefit, but more for mine. "I've been here for three days?"

"Yeah. And don't worry. I chucked your phone away." Noah smiles. That hit of nausea comes creeping back. "See, it's funny, Evelyn. Because the plan was to force you to be friends with me. To get access to you. My father thought it would be difficult to keep you interested. But you just wanted a friend so much, that you just attached yourself to me. Even after I followed you and we had that little car chase, you still came to that get together. It was astonishing. You were so desperate for friendship and people your own age, that you actively fell in love with a murderer."

"Murderer?" I whisper in dread.

"Your mother, Evelyn. It wasn't my father who killed her." Oh, god. No. "It was me." I puke. All over the stone floor, I vomit. I haven't eaten in three days, but apparently there was enough in my stomach to bring up. Noah throws me a tissue, almost like I'm a lesser being. I clutch it with my free hand and wipe my mouth. All I've done since moving to Scotland is vomit.

"You killed… my Mum?" Silent tears fall down my cheeks.

"My father's orders, essentially. But I pulled the trigger."

"Why?" I sob.

"Has your Dad told you what he does? What he really does? Because we know. We had an inkling for a while, only an inkling. I killed your mother because of that little inkling. We were never completely sure. But then I followed you that day. And the way he drove that car… well, I assume it was him who got you out of that. You hadn't passed your test, so I highly doubt those mad skills were you. That's when I figured it out, that he was a little bit more than a businessman. And when William couldn't get one of his men to kill the bastard, then we had to rethink. See, William knew you were both going to be at that Summer show. So we ordered him to put a hit out for you and your father. It was a touch too public, though. Although, it would've been a Summer show they'd never forget." Noah suddenly and loudly imitates gunshots. It makes me jump. And he still hasn't answered my question.

"But... why? How long have you known about Dad?"

"Since I killed your mother. We had to be careful. While your father was trying to make sure we didn't know the truth about his job, we had to make sure he didn't know that we knew. It's all quite confusing, but you're not stupid, Evelyn. It's all been one massive double crossing. Bluffing. Gregory Norman had no idea."

"My Mum... why did you kill my Mum?!" I scream. At that moment, there is a darkness in Noah's eyes, like a hidden violence I've never seen before. He strides to me, his steps heavy. I cower immediately before he tightly clutches either side of my face, making my jaw ache.

"Let's get one thing straight." He speaks quietly, like a hiss. It's so unsettling. "You do not talk to me like that again. And I would suggest you drink that water. The body can only survive for so long without it." Noah pushes my head back as he lets go. I start to sob again. He stands in front of me, watching me fall into pieces. I look over at the water and grab it with my free hand. Using my teeth, I unscrew the lid. I chug the whole thing and drop the empty bottle onto the floor. "Good girl." As I look at him, I notice his appearance. He looks different. He looks older.

"How... how old are you?" I ask so slowly.

"Twenty-one." Noah nods. I stay silent, my mouth agape. "I've had fun playing the role of party-loving, weed-smoking seventeen-year-old Noah. The Instagram is fake, Evelyn. All those pictures, we made them. We made it look like I was a messy teen. It had to be believable. Also, it made sure your father was less suspicious of me. He assumed I was just Connelly's son. Completely innocent." As Noah explains everything, the puzzle starts to come together.

"But why are you doing this?" My voice barely breaks my tears.

"It's good business." Noah shrugs. I just glare at him with all kinds of fury. "Ooh, I wouldn't do that if I were you. It'd be a very good idea not to provoke me. And to answer the question you shrieked at me, I killed her... because of your father."

"What?"

"My father has been working with yours for, oh, a long time now." Noah places his hands behind his back. He's still incredibly casual. "And fair play to the man, your Dad... we thought he hated you." Noah laughs. "We thought he absolutely despised you. That was a man who could not give two shits about his child. He gave a lot of shits about his wife, though. So, I got a call from my father, telling me to take her out. We wanted Gregory Norman wounded. Like an animal that'd been shot in just the wrong place. And then you stalk that animal until it dies. Maybe wound it some more on the way. Your father was wounded. But not quite fatally. And there was only one other way to wound him some more before the kill. And when William told us what he saw at that funeral, we knew how to fatally wound your father."

"That's how you knew I was in London. That's how you knew about the funeral..."

"William was incredibly resourceful. Until your father got rid of him. Made things a bit more difficult. So now, we wait. We wait for the inevitable moment. We wait for the fatal wound. We're expecting a call from him. Any moment now. We've told him who we have and what we want."

"What do you want?" I shake my head.

"Him dead." Noah stares at me. "Like a prize stag."

"Why?" I crack under my tears again.

"Your father kept a lot of secrets from you, didn't he? Did he tell you what he's done to my father's company? Evelyn, he's dissolved it. He's wiped the accounts. Connelly and Norman is now just a name. We have nothing. Of course, that was all part of his little side plan. All part of the plan to destroy my father's empire. The real plan, and his real job, was to assassinate my father. And he was close, to be fair. Your father's a smart man. Just not quite smart enough."

"What's going to happen to me?"

"That's why you're being kept alive. We have no need for you dead. It's not you we want. And we have recently become very aware of the sacrifice Gregory Norman is willing to make for your life." His words cut me in all the worst ways.

"No! No, please!" Just as I am pleading for my father's life, Noah gets a phone call. He holds up a finger, silently instructing me to pause before he brings it to his ear. "Yeah? Oh, hi, Dad." He listens and nods. "Oh, good." He pauses again. "Alright, I'll let her know. Thanks." Noah hangs up the call. Once he does, he puts his hands behind his back again and offers me a smile. "Your father is on his way."

Noah is escorting me to a vehicle, his black BMW. My hands are bound by the cable ties behind my back. It's pitch black and I dread to think what time of night it is. I don't even know where we are. He said one hundred miles from Kyleakin, so we're still in Scotland. He's informed me that we're going to a secluded area so the swap can take place in private. The swap. My father is trading his life for mine. I do all I can to stow that sick feeling as I'm shoved into the back of the same BMW that followed me. Noah reaches over to buckle my seatbelt. His proximity to me is gut-wrenching and I grimace at the scent of his cologne. Once I am buckled in, Noah makes his way to the driver's seat and starts the engine. I watch the mountainous terrain as he cruises us down a narrow country road.

"Oh, I almost forgot." Noah snaps suddenly, making me jump. He slams on the brakes and gets out of the car before walking around it. I listen intently to his footsteps on the pebbly road until I hear the click of my door opening. I spin my head to see him holding a cloth. I shake my head in panic, thinking he's going to knock me out again. But he wraps it around my eyes, blindfolding me.

"Can't have you seeing where we're going. Sorry, Evelyn." His apology is, of course, not sincere in the slightest as he slams my door shut. All I can see is black. But I can still hear. I hear him get back into the car. I hear him put a seatbelt on. I can feel the car as we continue to drive. I can hear my ragged, terrified breaths.

"Don't worry, Evelyn. It's only about a ten minute drive." Yeah, the longest ten minutes of my life.

True to his word, Noah stops the car ten minutes later. I hear him turn it off. I hear him get out. I hear my door open. I smell his cologne. I hear the unbuckling of my seatbelt. I am dragged out of the car, not gently either. Under my feet, I feel stones and grass. The November air is freezing. Once we have walked for about a minute, I feel a harsh hand against my shoulder, pushing me down. I land on my knees, feeling the stabbing pain of the stones against them. I wince. I cry against the blindfold. Until it is suddenly taken away. I shake the hair out of my face and look around. We're in a rocky, grassy wasteland. The moon is full and offers a relatively good blanket of light as I sit here and wait. Noah stands next to me, constantly looking at his phone. I hate this feeling. It's a constant dread and I know it won't go away. Because at the end of this dread is grief. All over again. I've only just finished grieving my mother. Now I have to grieve my father.

My knees feel like a pin cushion as I sit and wait, each moment more agonising than the last. Until two cars appear in the distance. One I don't recognise. It's hard to see in this light, but I can tell it's a saloon, long and luxurious. Possibly a Jaguar. But the other car, I do recognise. My father's Mercedes. I shake my head, desperate for this not to be happening. I try to stand but I instantly feel that same harsh hand on my shoulder. The unrecognisable car parks relatively close by, only a few metres away from Noah. And when the door opens, my heart falls at who walks out. It's Connelly. And he looks delighted to see me. "Evelyn." Connelly offers me a malicious smile. I look down to the ground, closing my eyes as tight as I can to release the tears. Connelly stands beside me and I hear a sound I've only heard once before. The cocking of a gun. He points it at my head just as my father's Mercedes comes to a stop, roughly twenty metres away. The moment the gun is pointed at me, I feel helpless. I feel like all the strength within me has vanished. I'm terrified. I'm cold. I'm alone. Until I see him. He is getting out of the back of the Mercedes, straightening his suit jacket. I am immediately rendered a sobbing mess. My father inaudibly says something to the person who chauffeured him here. Francis, I assume. Once he is done speaking to the driver, my father directs his gaze to where I am kneeling. He visibly takes a deep breath and begins to walk towards us. I'm praying he stops. I'm praying he changes his mind and turns back. I want so much for him to get back into that car. But he doesn't. Just like at the funeral, his only goal is me.

"That's close enough, Norman." Connelly snaps. My father stops walking about ten metres away. He doesn't look crestfallen. He looks expressionless. Stoic. Completely placid. And I remember what he told me. Horrible Dad is MI6 Dad, and he will periodically make an appearance. It's all part of his act. The part he was playing for sixteen years. His eyes are lit by the moon. The spikes of stubble on his face create their own shadow on his neck. I can see the outline of his hair. Again, not a single one is out of place. "Thank you for coming, Norman. I won't make this too long as it's rather cold here this time of year. And little Evelyn is shivering, poor thing." Connelly strokes a finger down my cheek, almost wiping my tears away.

"Don't touch me." I grimace and turn my head away from him. I don't know where this courage has come from, but I'm bursting with it. My mother is with me. My father is with me. And nothing scares me anymore. Nothing except losing the man stood before me. Connelly immediately chuckles and looks down at me, almost like he's impressed.

"Oh, Norman, she's brilliant. You've done a good job." He hisses, bending down to clutch my jaw and pressing the barrel of the gun against my head. I can hear the sound of my father trying to keep his cool. "Do you remember our deal, Norman?"

"Yes." My father's voice is low and careful. I feel like I haven't heard it in years.

"Good. I just need certain assurances before I let Evelyn go."

"Check the accounts. The money is all there." My father places his hands in his pockets. I wish I could see his face. Out of the corner of my eye, I see the glow of a phone screen. Connelly is tapping away. I don't stop staring at my father, the gun still pressed against my head.

"Ah, good man, Norman. The whole ten million too. You certainly are a man who keeps his word." Connelly praises and puts the phone away. My father doesn't respond. "Alright, Norman, you know the drill. You've been doing this long enough now." After Connelly's statement, my father reaches his arms to the side. Noah approaches him and pats him, checking for any weapons.

"Clear, Dad." Noah nods and makes his way back to us.

"Now that we have established that I am unarmed, would you kindly take that gun away from my daughter's head?" This is the first time my father has acknowledged my presence since arriving. Connelly doesn't immediately remove the gun and I hear the familiar sound of my father growing impatient.

"Of course. My apologies." Connelly mutters and stops pressing the gun against my head. I let out the biggest sigh of relief once he does. "You get two minutes. Then we finish this." After Connelly speaks, I feel a tug at my wrists until my arms are suddenly freed. Noah has cut the cable ties. I rub my wrists and look up at Connelly. He just nods at me. I whimper and sob as I push myself up from the ground. I sprint to my father. I run to him like he's air to a drowning man. He doesn't hesitate to open his arms and I leap into them. I wrap mine around his neck so tightly and desperately that I worry I'll strangle him.

"Dad." I cry loudly. It completely breaks the silent wilderness.

"Hello, Pain in the Ass." My father chuckles. I giggle tearfully as he kisses the side of my head while stroking the back of it. I scrunch my eyes closed. I never want to let him go. "Alright, listen to me. Joan is in the car…"

"No, no, no. Dad, you can't…" I shake my head desperately.

"Evelyn, listen to me. You do what I say when I say it, is that understood?"

"No, they're going to kill you. They said…"

"I know." My father releases me from his arms. He gently rests his hands on either side of my head as he looks down at me. I can see his eyes. There's pain in them, but beyond all of that pain, there is just love. Pure, unconditional love. "Evelyn, it is so important that you do everything Joan says. Don't question it, just do it, alright?"

"What about you? What's going to happen to you?" I can barely get the words out.

"You let me worry about that."

"Dad, they're going to kill you. No, I can't lose you too. Please." I close my eyes tightly, releasing each agonising tear.

"Evelyn, look at me." His sudden harsh command makes me open my eyes. "Do you trust me?"

"Of course I trust you."

"Then go to Joan. Do everything she says. And I mean everything." I try to hear his voice but my mind is too smothered by the realisation that he is going to die. "You need to go. You need to run to the car. Get out of here, go on."

"Dad." I fall apart. My father hugs me again. And something tells me this is the last time. I cry loudly, utterly heartbroken. "I love you, Dad."

"I love you too, sweetheart. I love you so much. Now, please go. Run, Evelyn." He releases me and stares into my eyes once more. I nod and sob as I rush away from him, my legs barely able to carry me. I do all I can to not fall to the floor in a heartbroken mess. I don't know what's happening behind me. As I sprint, I can see the Mercedes come closer and closer. Joan appears, opening the back door. I land in her arms but she soon lets me go.

"Evie, get in the car, sweetheart." Joan's voice is laced in a panic I haven't heard before. I attempt to look back at my father. "Evie, get in the car right now." Once Joan's tone becomes firm, I remember what my father said about doing whatever Joan told me to. I nod and sit on the cream leather seat. Joan rushes around the car and sits beside me, closing the door. "Now, Francis." She snaps. At that moment, Francis spins the car around and accelerates us away. I sob and tell myself not to look behind us. But I do. I twist my body to look out the back window. "Evie, eyes front." The moment Joan speaks, I stop and look ahead. After a few seconds, I hear a very distant gunshot. I crumble to pieces. I sob loudly and painfully. "Come here, sweetheart." Joan is also in tears. I shuffle and lean against her, releasing all of this pain. I thought I'd never feel it again after my mother. I thought I was done feeling this. But I was wrong. Those months I spent grieving, they're all coming back. This feeling is not elusive to me. He's gone. He's never coming back. The realisation hits me right in the chest. And I know I will never come out of this feeling. I'll be trapped in this darkness forever. And my Dad isn't here to rescue me from it anymore.

CHAPTER TWENTY-ONE

It's been two days since the swap. I haven't stopped crying. I haven't really spoken to Joan since we came home. I've been lying on my bed, barely sleeping. Barely thinking about anything but that night. I haven't eaten. I've been drinking water when I've needed to, but other than that, I am just existing. I haven't played the Steinway. Just thinking about touching that piano makes my chest hurt. Joan comes and checks on me now and again, just a little peep through the door. Just to make sure I'm alive, I imagine. She keeps telling me to eat. I can't eat. I'm back to how I was all those months ago. I miss my father. I miss his voice. I miss his warm, snuggly hugs. I miss his playfulness. I miss his little sarcastic jokes. I miss his brown eyes, which always made me feel safe, even when he was angry. I miss the father he became. He was so perfect. So wonderful. And I barely had any time with that part of him. Because the mouse has lost her eagle.

It's been five days since the swap. I played the piano for the first time. The notes were not seamless. Not perfect. They were scattered and I didn't really follow a rhythm. I just mindlessly pressed keys until I couldn't take anymore. Joan has persisted in her mission to make me eat food. I think I've eaten some toast. I still haven't stopped crying.

It's been eight days since the swap. I'm eating more. But I don't really have a choice. Joan reminded me that he would've wanted me to eat. So I did. I did for him. I still haven't stopped crying.

It's been ten days since the swap. I still haven't stopped crying.

It's been twelve days since the swap. Joan is wonderful. She is patient. Understanding. We are putting up the Christmas tree when I hear a knock on the front door.

"I'll get it." I mutter. I think those are the first three words I've said in days. I drag myself to the front door and open it. Stood before me is Francis, but he's wearing a tailored black suit. I hadn't even noticed he wasn't in the house anymore. I've been too wrapped up in getting over what happened. Beside him is another man, with his arms loosely crossed. Francis smiles at me sympathetically.

"Good afternoon, Evelyn." I am no longer Miss Norman, it seems. "Francis?"

"My name is not Francis. May we share a conversation?" He seems very clinical, no longer my father's friendly driver. I nod and open the door wider. Joan approaches us and smiles warmly when she sees not-Francis.

"Evie, go into the dining room with Mr Wilson. I'll make us all a coffee. Go on." She nods reassuringly. I am incredibly confused as I lead Mr Wilson and his colleague to the dining room.

Once we are in, Mr Wilson and his colleague take a seat. I sit opposite, my fingers endlessly fidgeting. Mr Wilson clears his throat and takes his mobile phone out of his trouser pocket. It all seems very professional and cold. I'm used to it; he's acting like my father. But this is a man who always used to be sunny and friendly. It's slightly unnerving, especially when he holds the phone to his ear.

"Afternoon, sir." He pauses. "Yes, we're at the Norman household in Kyleakin now. I am just speaking to Evelyn Norman." He pauses again. "Yes, I'll let you know. Goodbye." He hangs up and puts the phone away.

"Who was that?" I ask, not knowing if I should. Mr Wilson smiles slightly.

"Yes, I remember you always being a fan of questions. But that was just a member of our team. I have to update them periodically." He interlocks his fingers on the table and lets out a sigh. "The main reason I'm here, Evelyn, is to shed some light on what happened nearly two weeks ago. And to inform you of next steps."

"Are you MI6 too?" As I speak, Joan comes in with three mugs in her hands.

"Sorry for interrupting." She apologises as she places the mugs down, one for each of us.

"Not at all. Thank you, Joan." Mr Wilson collects his mug. Joan places an affectionate hand on my shoulder before leaving the room. I want her to come back. "To answer your question, Evelyn, I worked with your father, yes. Now, Evelyn, I am sure you have questions about Connelly."

"Where is he?"

"Detained. We've got him. Connelly will spend the rest of his days in a maximum security prison. Noah will be placed somewhere away from his father and with less security. But they are both dealt with." Mr Wilson sips some coffee.

"Where's Sam?"

"Still in a PPU."

"And her mother? Dad said she was missing." There is a profound hope in my voice.

"We found her. After we interrogated Connelly, he disclosed the location of the warehouse where she and several other women were being kept. Before he died, your father made a deal with Connelly. In exchange for you, obviously, he gave himself up. If he hadn't, you would be in that warehouse right now, with Sam's mother." This all comes as a bit of a shock. My emotions are juggling. I'm happy Sam's mother is safe. But I'm reminded of what happened to my father, and how close I was to being in serious trouble with Connelly. "Now, your father, as you probably know, had several enemies. Many attempts have been made on his life in the past. But of course, that won't really be a problem anymore…" Mr Wilson is suddenly careful with his words. "I do apologise. That was unnecessarily blunt."

"It's okay." I shake my head.

"Now, as your father worked with us for a long time, we have a duty of care towards you. And we need to make sure you are safe. But before I begin all the administrative stuff, shall we say, I just wanted to tell you that you have my deepest sympathies, Evelyn." He pauses for a moment. "You now have a choice ahead of you. You can either stay here with your aunt, or we can arrange for you to live with your grandparents in London. But we will be keeping surveillance on you for the next couple of weeks. Cars following yours and so on. And then after those two weeks, we will still be offering some security, but I will tell you more about that when the time comes." He leans back and takes another sip of coffee. "How long do I have to decide?"

"Within the next ten minutes if you could. Just so I can alert the relevant people who need to know. So they can set up the…"

"Surveillance. Yeah, I get it." I sigh and scoff, finding this all ridiculous. "I think I want to stay here for a bit. Joan and I are getting ready for Christmas. And I don't want her to be alone for that. London can wait." I nod.

"Thank you, Evelyn. I'll let the relevant people know." Mr Wilson takes yet another sip of coffee. "Is there anything you need in the meantime?" His question comes as a surprise. I chuckle at the absurdity of it.

"Uh, yeah. My Dad back. To travel back in time, you name it. But I am very aware there is only so much the SIS can do." I slouch in my seat.

"Yes, we haven't quite mastered time travel, I'm afraid." I know he's trying to make a joke but he almost sounds like my father and it catches me off guard. I burst into tears right in front of him. I try to compose myself as quickly as possible. "Evelyn, that's all we really came here for. But take this." Mr Wilson reaches into his pocket and retrieves a business card. "My personal number." He passes it to me. "I know I'm not who you thought I was. But I've known you since you were a baby, and I do care about you. A lot. So if you need anything, please let me know."

"Thank you, Francis… um, Mr Wilson." I smile sadly. He offers me a comforting nod and looks at his colleague. They then both stand. Mr Wilson begins to walk out of the room but I leap from my chair and hug him. "Thank you for everything. And thank you for being a friend when she died."

"Of course, Evelyn." Mr Wilson hugs me back. "Take care of yourself, and like I said, my number is on that card." He briefly strokes my cheek before leaving the room with his colleague. I am alone. I'm glad I have some awareness of what happened with Connelly but it was all a bit too much. That fear comes back.

"Evie?" Joan appears through the doorway. "Sweetheart, are you alright?" She strokes my cheek. I shake my head and burst into tears, falling into her arms. "Oh, sweetheart, it's going to be okay, I promise." She strokes my head as she holds it. "Do you need anything? What do you need me to do?"

"I just... I can't..." I fall apart and let go of her, stepping out of her arms and rushing out of the dining room. Once again, I am tearfully running to my room. But it's not because of my father and it never will be again. He will never be there to cheer me up after we've had a falling out, and the thought destroys me.

A couple of hours later, I am still in my room, lying on my side on my bed, crying softly onto my pillow and hugging it. Joan is downstairs, finishing the Christmas tree. She asked if I wanted to help but I couldn't. I can't do anything. The thought shatters me into pieces and I cry into the pillow even more. Soon enough, my door opens. I really am not in the mood for company right now. Especially when I feel her sit on the edge of the bed. I know she just wants to help me and give me a distraction but nothing will help. I don't have the energy to do anything.

"Joan, I'm really sorry. I know you're just trying to make me feel better but I just really want to be alone."

"I don't recall the name Joan being on my birth certificate." It's not Joan. My eyes widen in shock, hope, disbelief and confusion. It's a gut-wrenching but incredibly heart-warming mix. It's a very confusing mix. I continue to stare at the wall as I try to fathom what I just heard. "Evelyn Norman, you're being incredibly rude right now." The voice comes back and I break down into tears, too scared to look. I'm too scared to have that hope. But I need to. I slowly turn around and sit up to see him. He's just sat there, with a playful, bemused frown on his face, wearing the same old black business suit. Not a hair out of place.

"Dad?" I croak. He just winks at me. "Dad." I sob and wrap my arms around his neck, crying like I've never cried before. I hold him so tightly, my eyes closed and my heart nested in this feeling of pure, overwhelming happiness. My father doesn't say anything as he hugs me, stroking the back of my head. He just lets me slowly come to terms with what's happening. He gives me all the time in the world. "Dad, what the fuck is going on?" I still cry.

"I see your Latin hasn't improved." My father scolds, making me giggle. I don't care about my language. I don't even think about anything. I just stay in his arms for what feels like eternity. He finally releases me from the hug and holds my head, his thumbs wiping my tear-covered face. He then places a long, affectionate kiss on my forehead.

"Dad, what is going on? I thought you were dead." I'm still doing all I can to stop crying.

"I'm so sorry, Evelyn, but I had to make you believe I was dead for a while. Until we were certain that all of Connelly's men were taken of, I had to be dead." My father tries to explain.

"But… when we were… I heard a shot." I can barely string a sentence together.

"You did. But it wasn't at me." He strokes my head as I wipe my eyes. I feel like a confused little girl again.

"Is Connelly dead?"

"No. The shot wasn't fatal."

"Okay…" I frown, just trying to understand everything. "So, what happened?"

"That night, as you know, the swap happened. And I had to die, but not in the conventional sense. That was why Joan kept telling you to get into the car and she told you not to look back. You had to think I was dead, Evelyn. Because if you knew I wasn't, then it meant you weren't safe for a while. Remember I told you that things were going to get complicated. Well, what I neglected to tell you was that Connelly had several small groups, little militias, if you will. They had to think I was dead. And so did you. Then, when they were sorted, I could come back to you."

"So, is Connelly really in prison?"

"Yes and no. He's still injured and there are many processes that have to happen before his sentence. But he will certainly be sent to a maximum security prison. The evidence against him is overwhelming. That night, my whole team was there, waiting. The moment you were safe, they got to action."

"So, wait, who's Francis?"

"Ah, yes, Wilson. He's my partner. He has been since the beginning." There is a new mischievous look in his eyes. "The person he called when he was sat with you in the dining room a couple of hours ago…"

"No." I snap, knowing exactly what he's going to say. I shake my head rapidly. "No, no, no. Dad, no."

"Yes." He raises a brow.

"No…"

"Yes." My father chuckles. "It was me."

"You are such a…"

"He had to inform me that he was here and that he was speaking to you. Also, I am the 'relevant people' that he had to inform about your choice of where to live. Mostly because I needed to know where you were, and so I could arrange for little personal things." My father's expression is so nonchalant, so casual. It makes me want to kill him.

"I bloody hate you… so much." I point a finger at him, clear humour in my voice. He laughs and looks at me with that same affection. I try so hard not to giggle. I am miffed. I am over the moon. I leap into his arms again, making him laugh even more as he holds me. "Nearly two weeks, Dad. I have done nothing but cry and, to top it all off, I haven't been eating, so your little fake death idea has backfired on you, hasn't it?"

"Yes, Joan told me all about your little hunger strike." As he holds me, I suddenly feel his fingers at my ribs. I giggle and jerk but I'm locked in his arms.

"No, Dad!" I laugh and try to push away. He chuckles as he stops, still holding onto me. I squeeze my eyes shut and wrap my arms around him even tighter. "Dad, I thought you were…"

"I know, sweetheart. But I'm here." His voice is that same low, buttery sound. "I've got you and I'm here. I am so sorry I had to put you through that." He strokes the back of my head.

"I still hate you." I mumble. My father lets me go and places a hand on my cheek.

"Yes, and I'm afraid you're going to hate me a bit more when I tell you the next part." The enigma in his voice is concerning.

"What next part?" I ask in dread.

"That night, Wilson, while he was sat in the front of the car, had to alert my people that it was time to close in. And he used this." My father retrieves something from his pocket. I frown in confusion when I see it's my phone. "That Secret Garden app. By using your phone to send the message, it reached mine. My messages are monitored by the SIS. Wilson pressing the button sent a message to every single person on my team, telling them it was time." My father holds out my phone and I slowly take it, scoffing at the series of events in my head.

"Wait, your messages are monitored?"

"The ones from you are, yes. Just in case I'm unavailable and you need me. The SIS will be aware." He explains.

"Well, that's annoying." I mutter. He chuckles. "Wait, how did you get my phone back? Noah threw it."

"And that is why you're going to hate me. Come with me." My father gets to his feet and gestures for me to follow. I am full of confused terror as I do.

My father leads me down the staircase, towards the front door. I am silent. I am the mouse again, following the eagle, full of feelings of dread. As we reach the front door, my father sighs loudly before opening it. I continue to follow as he enigmatically walks away from the house with his hands in his pockets. When we reach the harbour, a man in a suit similar to my father's is standing there. His hair is sleeked back and he is the picture of formality. As I look up at him, I stop walking, full of fear and breathing shakily. My father notices.

"Evelyn, it's okay. He won't hurt you." He reassures me. I slowly take more steps and we approach the man. I clutch my father's arm. "Evelyn, let me reintroduce you to Noah Connelly, intelligence officer… in training." He nods. Noah looks down at me, placing a careful smile on his face. I don't speak. I don't know if I can. They both wait so patiently for me to understand what the hell is happening.

"Sorry, what?" I look up at my father, making him chuckle.

"Noah has been working with us for about two years. Before him, accessing Connelly wasn't easy. He is Connelly's son but he's been helping us take down his father. That friendship between you and him was essential to earning Connelly's trust. Noah had to do a lot of acting, didn't you, Noah?" My father smirks.

"I should get a BAFTA." Noah quips. I just stare at him with my mouth open. My brain is going into hyperdrive.

"Evelyn, I can see that you're slightly confused." My father remarks.

"No." I shake my head casually, feigning complete and utter understanding. "No, I am fully with you. I am very, very not confused. I am…"

"Evelyn, I am your father and I know when you're bullshitting me." He clears his throat, needing me to be honest. I look at both him and Noah.

"Okay. So, Noah is Connelly's son?"

"Yes." My father nods.

"And he's secretly been double-crossing his father and working with you?"

314

"Yes."

"While also pretending to be friends with me?"

"Yes."

"And he is not seventeen? He's twenty-one?"

"Yes."

"Then, why the hell was I kidnapped?!" I shout loudly and angrily. My father and Noah burst into laughter.

"Evie…" Noah speaks this time. "I apologise for how I treated you. And you weren't trapped with me for three days. I lied. You were trapped for, oh, maybe a few hours. After you rang me to tell me you were driving to mine, I got straight onto the phone with your father. And our plan changed. You changed the plan, essentially. I then used the whole situation to bait Connelly, who jumped at the chance to organise a swap. My father told yours that we had you. And when I checked to see if your father was unarmed at the swap, he actually wasn't. But earning Connelly's trust guaranteed that I was the one to check. That's why it was successful."

"Did you shoot Connelly?" I spin my head to see my father.

"I did, indeed. I had to incapacitate him so my team could safely move in." My father crosses his arms.

"So, the shot I heard was you?"

"That's the one." He nods. It's all becoming a lot clearer. I shake my head and look back at Noah.

"You drugged me and knocked me out." I am seething.

"I did, yeah." Noah confirms, full of regret.

"You tied me to a pole in a freezing cold room."

"Uh, I did, yeah."

"Luke and Amelia…"

"Also on my payroll." My father interjects. I offer him a look of loathing and he winks at me.

"Okay, but why the hell did you follow us then?" I address Noah again. "That day, when Dad had to take over the car."

"That wasn't me. I lied to you." Noah explains. "When you saw the BMW at my house, it was there because Connelly let me borrow it. But by the time you arrived, your father and I had already established the new plan, and I needed to scare you. I needed you to think that I was dangerous. Because if you did, Connelly did too. It was all about trust, Evie. I had to lose yours to gain my father's."

"So, your father followed us?"

"Yes. It was him, not me." His expression turns remorseful. "And, obviously, it wasn't me who killed your mother. I had to lie to you about that as well. I had to make you believe I was a monster who wanted to hurt you." Once he says this, I look at my father, who wears a sympathetic expression.

"Dad, do you know who killed Mum?" My voice is soft and scared. My father rests his hands on my upper arms and stares into my eyes, full of compassion.

"Yes, I do. It was one of Connelly's contracted killers. He walked into the estate agents she worked in. Then he took out a gun and killed her. Connelly has confessed everything." His voice is also incredibly soft. I shake my head, feeling overwhelmed. "Evelyn, look at me." He orders firmly, seeing my distress. "I am so sorry about all of this. But it's done, you hear me? It's all over, I promise."

"Dad, I feel sick." I breathe heavily.

"That's to be expected." He nods in understanding. "You're probably in a fair amount of shock. And when we get back into the house, you are having some food." He offers me a smile, his paternal instincts completely taking over. I roll my eyes but soon, I am staring ahead in realisation.

"Wait, speaking of feeling sick, the get together by the coast, when I got drunk. Noah was there and we... oh, my god, we kissed." I grimace.

"Something I'd like to forget." My father raises both eyebrows.

"But surely Noah would've told you that I was out. Dad, did... did you know? The whole time, did you know?"

"Yes." He sighs. I glare at him. "Evelyn, any interaction you've had with Noah, I have been made aware of. The messages, the get together. Now, please stay calm and take this seriously..."

"What?" I ask behind clenched teeth.

"I organised the get together." My father clears his throat, giving me a moment to absorb his words.

"What?" I snap in disbelief.

"I did it for several reasons. I had to teach you a lesson about communication. I knew where you were and what you were doing. Like I said, Luke and Amelia are on my payroll. I needed to see if I could trust you to tell me everything, Evelyn. And it seems I couldn't at that moment in time. You didn't tell either me or your aunt where you were. So I reprimanded you for it. As did Joan."

"She knew?"

"She knew, yes. But you learnt that lesson, because you chose to call me when you decided to drive to Inverness. And I'm incredibly proud of you for that. That one phone call to me saved your life, Evelyn." The more he speaks, the more I understand.

"The other reason was so that Noah and I, and you, could fulfil our obligations to Connelly, regarding your friendship. We kept up our end of the bargain, keeping that trust in place. Noah kept his father's trust and that was essential to taking him down."

"But you were pissed off with me because you had to come home from London. You made me feel guilty as hell."

"Yes. I also wanted to prove something to you. I wanted to prove that this job is not more important than you. I told you the importance of that week in London. And when Noah told me where you were, I came home. I was waiting for his call…"

"The call." The penny drops. I spin to see Noah. "You told me it was your drug supplier. And the whole time, while I sat next to you, it was him?!"

"Yeah. Obviously the drug dealing was a lie." Noah nods. I just hold my mouth open, floored and confused.

"No, this is… this is not okay!" I take a couple of steps back, resting my hand on my forehead.

"Evelyn, listen to me." My father stands in front of me, trying to bring me back to reality. "I had to prove to you that you are the most important part of my life. And by using this get together, I had a chance to do just that. I left London because of you. And I will always abandon everything else for you. I needed you to know that." His brown eyes are full of honesty.

"I want to be mad at you… but I don't know if I am." I state, narrowing my eyes. My father chuckles.

"You're allowed to be mad at me. But I also wanted you to have some fun. I am very aware that being here meant you had nobody your age. And, granted, Noah isn't your age. But I wanted you to have… oh, what did you call it? Seventeen-year-old experiences. I wanted you to have some normality, to drink with potential friends, to have a laugh. And I knew you were safe, because you were with my people."

"Dad, while I'm deeply touched by your reasons for it, this is textbook entrapment." I can't hide the disapproval in my voice, making Noah laugh softly.

"I am aware." My father smirks.

"You told me off. You made me feel so guilty…" I begin to argue.

"Evelyn, you still went out without my permission. You still left the house when I explicitly told you not to." My father crosses his arms. "Like I told you, I wasn't furious that you went out. I was furious because you didn't tell me, or Joan. So, this telling off was completely necessary. It taught you a very valuable lesson about communicating with your father." As he glares at me, I feel a bit less self-assured than I did only moments ago. I look at my father for an incredibly long time. His expression doesn't change.

"Yeah, okay." I relent. My father chuckles and looks at Noah.

"Noah, thank you for everything." He shakes Noah's hand. "I'll see you back in London."

"See you soon, Greg. I'll get started on the reports."

"Top man." My father pats Noah's arm.

"And Evie…" Once Noah speaks my name, I can't help but glare at him. "Again, my sincerest apologies but you have been fantastic. Maybe your father could get in touch with recruitment."

"Yeah, thanks, but I think I've had enough MI6 bollocks to last a lifetime." My dry, candid response causes them both to laugh.

"Alright, well, all the best." Noah holds out his hand. I stare at it for a moment before shaking it. The moment we've said goodbye,

Noah strolls away, towards a black Jaguar. I cross my arms as my father and I stand together and watch him leave.

"You know, just once…" As I begin to speak, my father looks down at me. "I want one of my relationships to be real. My best friend was fake, crafted by you. A man I thought would be a potential boyfriend not only turned out to be very fake, but he was also way too old for me." A sudden thought pops into my mind and I stare at him, full of scepticism. "Are you even my real father?" He just laughs. "Oh, I'm glad all of this confusion amuses you. I'm glad that the last four months have rendered me so perplexed that it's damn hilarious." As I look at him, full to the brim with anger, annoyance, disbelief, shock and rage, he just continues to laugh.

"I don't know, Evelyn. You tell me." At that moment, my father wraps his arm around my neck, forcing me into a headlock. He then grinds his fist down onto my head like he has done several times before. And again, I do all I can to get out.

"Dad! No!" I shout. He doesn't stop. "Dad, I mean it. I will run away and never come back. You will never see me again."

"Sorry, Evelyn, but that's not really your choice until you're eighteen." He finally stops but I'm still in a headlock. I crane my head to look up at him, still wearing a deep frown.

"I can't bloody wait. Now, let me go." I spit irritably, trying to pull myself out of his grip.

"No." He jerks me forward and walks me back to the house, still holding me in a headlock.

"Dad!" I clutch his arm tightly, trying not to laugh. "Have I told you that I hate you?" My voice is muffled by his arm.

"Only several times, Evelyn." My father clears his throat.

320

"For the last time. Evie. My name is Evie."

"Evelyn."

"Evie!" I giggle as we approach the house. The moment we reach the front door, my father lets me go and takes the handle. "Dad, wait." Once I speak, he stops and looks at me, letting the handle go. "I need to say sorry."

"What for?" His eyes are full of concern.

"The day I was kidnapped, even though it wasn't real, I left the house because I thought you were this monster. I started thinking about how you made me feel for sixteen years. I thought about the whole Sam situation. And I panicked." As I speak, he listens to every heartfelt word. "God, I hated you." I start to cry. "I really hated you for what you'd done. And then when I was with Noah and he told me what you were willing to do for me…" My tears take the words away. "That all went away, and I'm just really sorry for thinking you were this horrible person. I'm so sorry that I ever doubted how much you cared about me."

"Evie." My father rests a hand on my cheek. "Of course I was willing to do that. I know it was all part of the plan, and not necessarily real, but even if it was real, I still would have done it, and I always will. Do you know why?"

"Because you're my Dad." I sob.

"Correct. Now, come here." He orders firmly. I leap into his arms, wrapping mine around his neck. I adore these hugs. They used to be elusive and unheard of, but now they're my favourite thing in the world. All of my anger about the past sixteen years has vanished into thin air. I will never feel angry again. I forgive him. Completely. And I will never doubt his love for me ever again.

CHAPTER TWENTY-TWO

December 25th

I am woken up by a sound I have never heard before. Christmas songs, but sung by my father, who is joyfully walking up the staircase. It's downright disturbing. I reach my arm out to check my phone; it's 8am. This man is really trying my patience when it comes to sleep. Within seconds, my door is flying open and I rest my face against my pillow. My father clears his throat as he sits on the edge of my bed.

"Dad, I swear to god…"

"Ah, ah, ah. Before you moan at me, this isn't my fault." He interrupts.

"Then who the hell's fault is it?" I mumble into the pillow.

"Your grandmother's." After he speaks, I frown in confusion. I groan in sheer annoyance and sit up. Once I have rubbed the sleep out of my eyes, I immediately see two things; my father holding up his phone, on a video call with my grandmother. And his jumper. His Christmas jumper.

"That is vibrant." I blink rapidly.

"Why, thank you. Come on. Speak to your grandmother." He offers me the phone. I take it and wear my best smile.

"Hi, Nana." I grin through the tiredness.

"Merry Christmas, poppet. Oh, I can see that you're still not a morning person." She laughs in evil delight.

"No. I'm not." I practically clench my teeth. My father chuckles as he watches. "Merry Christmas, Nana. How's Grandad?"

"Oh, he's fine. He's just preparing the turkey. Has your father given you my card?"

"No, he…" At that moment, my father holds out an envelope for me. "Oh, as if by magic. It's almost like he's in the room." I raise my brows sarcastically as I take it. My father suppresses a laugh, trying his hardest not to kill me as he holds the phone up so I can open the card. My grandmother giggles.

"I wanted to watch you open it, poppet." She elaborates.

"Did this have to happen at 8am?" I wear a look of mock confusion as I open the envelope.

"Yes, now shut up and do as you're told." My grandmother snaps, using a fake admonishing tone. It makes me smile.

"Yes, Nana." I take the card out of the envelope. Once I open it, a twenty pound note falls out. "Ooh, money!" I start reading.

"Have you read it yet, dear?"

"Hang on, I'm getting there. Christ, how fast do you think I read?" I ask playfully before I read the rest of the card. My father watches like a hawk. As my tired eyes scan the words, I suddenly become very aware of what's happening. She's booked us three tickets to a West End show tomorrow night. I gasp loudly and stare at my father, who just nods slowly. "Nana, this… really?!"

"Yes, poppet. Your father has already prepared the jet. And we'll see you tomorrow afternoon. Then you'll stay at ours for a couple of days." She elucidates. I hold the card to my chest.

"I want to hug you." I state sentimentally.

"You'll get your chance tomorrow, poppet. For now, have a wonderful Christmas, alright?" My grandmother blows me a kiss.

"Merry Christmas, Nana." I pretend to catch the kiss and place it on my cheek.

"Merry Christmas, darling. Merry Christmas, Greg."

"Merry Christmas, Caroline. Give my love to Frank and I'll be in touch about arrangements for tomorrow." My father turns the phone to face him.

"Speak soon, my darlings." She bids us goodbye. My father smiles before hanging up the video call. I just look at him in a state of delighted shock.

"You can go back to sleep now." He winks. I just lunge at him and throw my arms around his neck, grinning like a banshee. My father chuckles and hugs me back.

"Wait a minute." I frown and look at him. "You hate musicals."

"The third ticket isn't for me." He shakes his head. I close one eye as I think.

"Grandad hates musicals."

"It's not for your grandfather either."

"Then… who's it for?" There is a long pause after I ask.

"It's for Sam." Three words that fill my heart. Three simple words that bring me more joy than anything else in the world.

"What?" I whisper.

"She's out of the PPU. She's going with you and your grandmother. And she will be staying with us there." His words cause me to fall apart. I wrap my arms around him again, full of such gratitude. Full of overwhelming, unequivocal happiness.

"Merry Christmas, Evie."

"Merry Christmas, Dad." I hold him tighter. As I hug him, a thought enters my head and breaks through the happiness. "Dad?"

"Mm-hmm." He kisses my head as I let go of him.

"This is our first Christmas without Mum." I look down, not able to stop the tears. She was always the best at Christmas. All these little traditions that she brought to life. The smallest action like playing a board game or drinking a certain tipple, they had meaning because of her. And a certain song she always used to play on the piano.

"I know." My father's wise voice cuts through my thoughts. "But that is why it is so important that we have a good day. She's with us, you know she is. And she's going to be with you for the rest of your life. Whenever you're scared or unsure, she will be there. And so will I. That is the essence of parenthood." He places an affectionate hand on my cheek.

"Should, uh... put that..."

"Don't you dare." He warns, knowing what I'm going to say. I pause for a second.

"... on a Hallmark card." I smile at him. The moment he is about to lunge at me, I recoil back. "I'm sorry!" I cover myself with the duvet. "No more sarcasm! From this moment on, I am mute!"

"Best news I've heard all day." I can feel him standing up.

"Asshole." I snap back. I then hear him laugh before shutting the door as he leaves. I take the covers away from my face and smile to myself. It's Christmas.

Once I am showered and dressed in normal clothes, I glide down the staircase. I am full of excitement. I am full of happiness. This is going to be a good day, I can feel it. I grin as I enter the kitchen. My grin turns into doubtful surprise when I see who is

325

standing at the stove. My father raises a brow at me, still wearing that jumper.

"I have never, in my life, seen you cook." I comment as I walk up to the coffee machine.

"Well, it's Christmas. And you know how much I love Christmas." He stands to the side and begins peeling potatoes.

"You do bloody love Christmas. Actually, you know what?"

"What?"

"You are a bit like Scrooge, actually." I observe as I sip some of my coffee. My father turns to face me, obviously needing me to elaborate. "Well, you're rich. You were miserable. You seemed to utterly hate everyone. And then you had a change of heart." I smile. "And that is why I got a 9 in English Lit."

"Please tell me you didn't draw parallels between myself and Ebenezer Scrooge in your exam." He sounds almost angry.

"No." I giggle, shaking my head. "No. No, I didn't. No…" There is a silent interval before Joan bursts through the French doors. I immediately grin.

"Oh, she's finally out of bed!" Joan yells in sheer happiness as she wraps her arms around me.

"It's 9am." I frown.

"Precisely. Merry Christmas, sweetheart." Joan nods once and kisses my cheek. I look down to see she is also wearing a Christmas jumper.

"Oh, I see the Christmas jumper virus is spreading." I state dryly.

"Yes, and here's yours." My father walks to the table beside the French doors and picks up a jumper. Without warning, he throws it at me. I catch it awkwardly and glare at him in horror.

"No, Dad." I whine.

326

"Evelyn Dawn Elizabeth Norman, I am your father. You will do what I tell you. And I am telling you to put the jumper on." He crosses his arms. I wear an expression of sheer reluctance before I wrap the jumper over my head. I poke my head through the hole and straighten it.

"God, this is the itchiest thing I've ever worn in my life." I complain, flicking my long hair out of the collar. My father chuckles. I look at my arms, noticing that the sleeves are far too long. It's at least four sizes too big.

"It's all they had, I apologise." My father continues preparing potatoes.

"Well, at least I won't get cold." I collect my coffee mug.

"Okay. Norman Christmas." Joan claps her hands together. It's too early for all of this enthusiasm. "Plan of action. Drink lots. Eat lots. Laugh lots." As she speaks, I lean towards my father.

"Is she drunk already?" I whisper to him. He suppresses a laugh.

"Evie." Joan snaps.

"Yes, dear?" I immediately stand straight.

"I will need your help setting up the dining room. Then, you and I are taking Max for his Christmas walk. And then, you can help me put cards in all of the neighbours' letter boxes. All before lunchtime." She practically flies out of the kitchen. I close my eyes and shake my head.

"Is there a way you can save me from this?" I address my father while I sip my coffee.

"I'm afraid not." He raises his brows.

"Nothing at all? Can't you pretend there's, like, a hostile terrorist takeover down the road and you need me with you because... of a reason I've yet to come up with?"

"Go with your aunt, Evelyn." My father kisses my forehead as he passes me to approach the worktop.

"Not even a tiny national emergency?"

"Now, Evelyn." His fuse is blowing.

"Ja, Herr Kommandant!" I put my mug down and begin to leave the room.

"Evelyn." When I hear him, I stop and spin to face him. "Don't even think about taking that jumper off. And I will know if you do. Take it off and you can kiss goodbye to London tomorrow."

"Dad." I whine. "But I have to go out in public." I mock cry.

"I don't care." He tries his hardest to hide his amusement.

"Ja, Herr bloody Kommandant. " I sigh. Just before I leave, I hear him chuckle. I smile as thoughts go through my head. Something feels different about this Christmas. And I realise it's him. It's my father who is different. I am different. I am no longer a timid child, worried about angering him. I am no longer a mouse staring up at an eagle. Not anymore. I am the eagle.

It's early afternoon. We've eaten lunch. We've played some games. But there's only one other thing I need to do to tick all of the traditional boxes. I sit at my piano, stroking the keys. I haven't played it in what feels like such a long time. I grab my phone from my pocket, needing to read the chords before I start. Once I have pretty much memorised them, I put my phone back in my pocket. I roll my incredibly long jumper sleeves up, clear my throat and begin playing *O Holy Night*. One of my mother's favourite Christmas songs. She would always play it for us back home. Every Christmas without fail. It's a difficult song, but I want to remember her. It isn't long before my father appears next to me, watching me as I press the various keys and sing softly. The verse isn't the hard part. I am not looking forward to the high *divine* near the end. But so far, so good. I even smile a couple of times, especially as my father sits beside me. I give him a look and continue playing. Again, he doesn't speak. He just watches. I wonder if he'll cry again. He probably will when I get to the high note and destroy his ears. For now, I sound nice. The piano sounds nice. It's all just calm and gentle and full of love. By the time I get to the second verse, I begin to cry. I sound like her. And she always sounded beautiful. I have her voice. I have her talent. Oh, god. The high note is coming. I'm a bloody alto. My range is incredible but that note is high. I could dodge it. But that's for wusses. Screw it. It's happening. And it's not nearly as awful as I thought it was going to be. When I look at my father, he raises his brows and gives me an unsure look. Maybe it was as awful as I thought it was going to be. I struggle to sing through my giggling. By the end of the song, I'm a laughing mess. My father chuckles next to me and nudges my arm. The moment I have played the last chord, I lean my forehead against his shoulder and giggle uncontrollably.

"Stunning. Just stunning." He comments dryly.

"Shut up." I mumble against him.

"Utterly… divine." He is trying to rattle my cage.

"Dad!" I burst into more laughter as he wraps an arm around my neck and pulls me to him, chuckling with me.

"It was beautiful. She would be so proud of you." As he kisses the top of my head, I know he's being genuine. And it warms my heart. I'm in my favourite place in the world. Sat at a piano, in my father's arms. "There's a gift for you downstairs." He gently breaks the silence.

"What?"

"Come on." My father continues, keeping up the enigmatic tone I know all too well. He gets to his feet and gestures for me to follow with his head.

"Can I take the jumper off?" I ask as I stand.

"No." He looks back at me as he leads me out of the room.

"Is that not the gift?" My sarcastic question makes him laugh. I hate this feeling of being completely oblivious. But he has a calm excitement in his eyes. Last time he had this look in his eyes, he was showing me a Steinway piano in the spare room. I don't think it's another one of those, however.

Once we have entered the living room, my father leans against the doorway with his arms crossed. I frown at him and he tilts his head down, gesturing to the Christmas tree. I follow his silent command and approach it, noticing a golden envelope nested in the branches. I reach up to grab it. He just had to put it on the highest branch. Once I have it, I look at him again and he nods for me to continue. I sceptically and very slowly open the envelope. There's no card but something drops into my hand. A house key.

"Now…" My father is clearly going to offer some illumination. I continue to frown in confusion. "You are not touching the place until you are at university. And in the meantime, it's being rented out. The rent money is going into a bit of a trust fund, to pay for university."

"Dad…"

"It also means I know you're in a good area. I know that the place is of good quality, well-built and so on. And it's a stone's throw away from where I will be." My father stands in front of me,

looking down into my very confused expression. The penny is
starting to drop.

"No…" I stutter. "Dad, no…"

"Yes. I have purchased an apartment. Two bedrooms, near
Kensington. For you and Sam. I know it's another choice I've
taken away, essentially. But remember what I said, due to my job,
I need to know where you are. Always." He sighs. "And it means
you're not struggling to pay rent. Because I know how much you
don't want to lean on me for things like that. Even though I am
incredibly wealthy. So this allows you to be completely
independent, without terrifying me too much."

"Dad." I begin to well up.

"You'll pay your bills on time. You'll pay your council tax on
time. If you ever do need money, please ask me. If you're going to
have parties, do not damage the property and make sure you…" I
don't give him a chance to finish. I leap into his arms, holding him
so tightly. It's a place for me and Sam. Our little dream of living
together is going to come true. Because of my father.

"Thank you." I squeeze my eyes closed.

"My pleasure, sweetheart. I mean it, though, no going mad."

"We won't." I giggle but a thought pops into my head. "Wait." I
step out of the hug. "You said it would be close to you…"

"That's the second part of this gift. In a week's time, you and I are
moving back to London, back to our townhouse in Notting Hill.
The house is all ready, it just needs some more preparation. The
reason I'm coming with you to London tomorrow is so I can go
and inspect it. Make sure it's ready for us."

"Can I see it too?"

"Of course you can. I've scheduled some time in the afternoon, before we arrive at your grandmother's. You and I will go and see it together. Now, I know you haven't been there since your mother died, so I just wanted to make sure you're ready." His expression is one of concern. Deep concern.

"I'll be fine." I nod, already feeling the tears. "It's going to feel different, though."

"How so?"

"Because you are." I let the tears fall. "I'm not going to walk through the hallway and feel timid when you pass me. I'm not going to be crying and feeling like I can't talk to you. We can cook together and watch TV and stuff. It's going to be weird." My bluntness makes him chuckle.

"Evelyn, I will warn you, though. Sometimes, when I have colleagues over or I'm meeting with potential…"

"Sharks?"

"Correct. Sometimes, I will need to be…"

"MI6 Dad." I nod. "It's fine. Honestly, now I know why, it's completely fine." I offer him a genuine smile and he pulls me into another hug. I feel such a warmth in me. We're going home.

My father twists the key in the lock to our front door. I'm doing all I can to not burst into tears. I haven't worried about crying in front of my father for a long time, but I still want to be strong. Not just for him, but for me. As my father opens the door, I take a deep breath. He steps in first and collects some letters from the floor. I take tiny steps inside. He watches me as he flicks through the letters. The house feels different but it still feels like home. Especially when I notice the smell. It still smells like her. The perfume she used to wear. The little lavender candles she used to light. My eyes begin to fill with tears but I do all I can to suppress them as I walk into the living room. Whoever rented this place in our absence kept it wonderful, and the place is so clean. So homely. There are going to be reminders of her everywhere and every time I see them, it's going to break my heart.

As I reach the upper floor, the smell of my mother lingers. It lingers until I reach my bedroom, a room where I spent so many nights crying. Most of it was usually teenage angst, but a lot of it was also because of my father. And I realise I will never cry in this room again, not because of him anyway. I sit on my bed, feeling the familiar sheets beneath my hands. After living in Scotland for so long, it feels bizarre. As I sit here, I can't hold back the tears anymore. She won't be walking in to check on me. She won't be singing to me until I stop crying. All of that is gone. "Evelyn!" My father hollers from downstairs. I immediately wipe my eyes as a reflex, something I always used to do before Scotland. I need to remind myself that I don't need to do that anymore. Not since his emotional transformation.

My feet patter down the stairs and I see my father in the hallway. He offers me another enigmatic look and I frown at him. "There's someone at the door." He puts his hands in his pockets. I scowl sceptically, yet again, as I make way to the front door. I slowly open it and once it's open, a massive tearful smile rests on my face.

"Evie." Sam rushes to me and I pull her into a forceful hug. I stumble back a touch and bury myself in this feeling.

"Sam, what are you doing here?" I whisper.

"Some men in suits brought me here. Said it was of national importance or something." She giggles, clearly perplexed but I'm not. I slowly give my father a look but he just winks.

"National importance, huh?" I laugh as I hug Sam again.

"Look, Evie, I am so sorry about that day. But my Dad, he was crazy. He was telling me that I had to call you and force you to come to the house." Sam shakes her head desperately.

"It's okay, Sam. I know everything." I nod to reassure her.

"He was killed that night." She states out of nowhere. My heart falls, because I know the truth. "They told me that it was an intruder with a silenced pistol. And I had to be taken away for my own safety. They said they found you in the house and took you away as well."

"Yeah, I was taken to the airport. When I got there, Dad was waiting for me. He got a… call." God, I hate lying, especially to her. "But your Mum…"

"Mum is fine. She was kidnapped. Apparently it was connected to the people who killed my father. But she's back and she's doing better."

"I'm glad, Sam. You both deserve to be really happy." I smile tearfully, holding her hand in mine. "Can I tell her?" I look back at my father, who must have a telepathic link with me, as he nods.

"Okay, Sam, I need you to stay calm, okay?"

"What the hell is going on?" She frowns.

"You know our little plan? Our little live together, do what we want, no pissy adults plan?" As I gleam at her, my father clears his throat. "Uh, I stand by that statement." I nod at him before looking at Sam again. "Well… me and you, we're going to live in an apartment together in Kensington."

"Near Kensington." My father interjects.

"Near Kensington." I repeat.

"What?!" Sam's mouth is agape.

"I know!" I grin like a little child. "Dad got us an apartment and it's just me and you, together. Fully independent. Fully able to do what the hell we want! It's really happening, Sam."

"Oh, my god!" Sam wraps her arms around me and we giggle. I squeeze her so tightly, so full of love, so elated. From now on, it's me and her. Independent. Free. Totally alone in our own little home. No Connelly. No danger. Nothing but sheer unbridled joy.

CHAPTER TWENTY-THREE

One month later

I pace across the hallway, waiting for the postman. I keep checking my phone for the time. I'm full of anxiety, but it's the same anxiety I felt before my driving test. Speaking of driving, my little Fiat has been picked up from Scotland and sent to the house. It's now parked outside our house in Notting Hill. But the thought of driving in London makes me nervous. I haven't even attempted it yet. As I stand here and wait, I think of what I'm waiting for. I have applied to start at Kensington Hall Sixth Form, studying Psychology, English Lit, Music and History. It's what my father calls an eclectic mix. He's not wrong. But it's what I've chosen. Because I now know what I want to do. If the last several months have taught me anything, it's that our brain is a very delicate thing. I want to be a psychiatrist, specialising in child and adolescent psychiatry. I think I've had enough experience with emotional neglect to be good at understanding the effect it has on the mind. My father wasn't necessarily neglectful, but there was definitely an emotional chasm between us. So, I want a PhD. I want to help people through their issues, and work with them for the best outcome. The brain fascinates me. How fragile it is, how much information it can retain. It's astounding how much the brain goes through. I have suffered so much mental stress, and I came out of it okay. Because I had the right support. And I want to give that support to whoever I can. Children, teenagers, people who were just like me.

Just as I start to lose my composure, I hear the letter box. My heart is beating a million times a minute as I see a letter addressed to me. I pick it up and hold it in my hands. I close my eyes. I am about to open it but it is snatched from my fingers by someone stood behind me. I spin to see my father, who is raising a brow, holding the letter.

"Dad, come on. Don't be a twat." I reach for the letter but he keeps it away from me with no expression on his face. "You know, just because I'm short, doesn't mean you can be bellend." I try to reach it again, and he keeps it away, stifling a smile. "Dad, I am warning you. I am not in the mood for this bollocks. I have been waiting. Agonising…"

"Oh, I know you have. But you want to be a psychiatrist, don't you? So, tell me, Dr Norman, why am I doing this?" Oh, I have not got the patience for this.

"Because you're an asshole."

"Not quite."

"Because you hate me."

"Definitely not. Take this seriously."

"Oh, I am." My fuse is starting to blow. I try to reach it again but he continues to keep it away. "Dad!" I giggle. "Please give me the letter." I hold out my hand. He doesn't comply. "Fine. You want me to use my brain, yeah?"

"Would make a change." My father quips. I hold back a laugh.

"Alright." I sigh. "When we look at the deep-rooted psychological ripples that certain stones can cause in the river of our minds…" I am talking utter bollocks. "Then we can ascertain that parents are sometimes dicks. And they want to watch their children suffer. Exhibit A. Gregory Norman, loving father to one child, only loving for the past seven months, though." I cross my arms.

"Watch it." He warns humorously.

"But even though Gregory Norman loves his daughter deeply, he likes to play little mind games, thinking she will fall for his bullshit, such as keeping information from her. Not only in the form of letters he refuses to give her, but endless secrets. And because of these secrets, Evelyn must now live a life of utter chaos. Mental chaos. And she still hasn't heard from this elusive therapist that the SIS offered her. So Evelyn must now deal with her father's idiocy completely and utterly on her own." I finish my little discourse. I can't gauge my father's reaction.

"Evelyn Norman, please join my company." His remark makes me hold back yet more laughter. But his expression is serious. Oh, god, I think he's being genuine. I see this look all the time. I used to see it every day, back when he was Horrible Dad.

"Wait, what?" I frown.

"Regardless of what this letter says, Evelyn, I need someone with a decent mind. If you do get into Kensington Hall, I will work with you to form a work pattern that suits you. But I would like you to work for my company." He clears his throat.

"You're being bloody serious."

"Yes. I know you're not eighteen for a few months, but there are certain internships I can offer you while you study at Kensington Hall." My father elaborates.

"This is the telecommunications company?"

"That's the one, yes."

"Doing what?"

"Whatever suits you. It's your choice, Evelyn. But it will put a gold star on your CV and you'll pretty much have the option of whichever university you want. My company is and always will be very highly regarded. So if you were to work for me, it would set you up for the rest of your life. But like I said, it's your choice." My father nods. I narrow my eyes slightly, seeing if there is an ulterior motive.

"I know why you want me to work for you." I am full of scepticism, yet again.

"Enlighten me. Use that brain."

"It's just one massive baby monitor." I state. "You want to keep an eye on me." I frown. My father's expression falters slightly and I know that I'm right.

"There is an element of that, yes. You would have the freedom to work like any of my employees, and I will never treat you as my child. I will treat you as a member of staff. There will be no kid gloves. No let offs." He wears a stern expression, and I already feel like I'm speaking to my boss's boss's boss.

"But you work for MI6. How can you keep track of me in your company when you have to do that?"

"My company is still managed by me. I still have to run it, maintain it. Yes, it was used to get Connelly, but I still enjoy being a CEO. I spend my time equally between the company and the SIS. But if you choose to do this, it will start your professional life. Somewhere safe. Somewhere I can... keep an eye on you."

"Okay, I understand." The more he describes it, the more interested I am. I would like to start working, and his company is incredibly well-regarded, like he said.

"But first, we need to see what's in this envelope. So open it." My father holds the letter out and I take it, still full of doubt. But that anxiety creeps back again as I open it. I close my eyes briefly before I scan the page. After reading it, inside, I am celebrating. I am overjoyed. The anxiety disappears like raindrops in a flood.

"I got in." I mutter softly. "And they want me to start next week. I don't have to wait until September."

"Congratulations." My father smiles. I look at him and his smile disappears when he sees my new expression. I am doubtful and incredulous as I glare at him.

"Dad, did you do this?" I hold up the letter. "Did you pull any strings so that I would get in?"

"Evelyn, I don't have the power to influence college admissions."

"No, but you... you have the power to influence people. Did you email anyone?"

"Do you want a lie or the truth?"

"Dad, what did you do?"

"I emailed the admissions team. I explained your circumstances, nothing more."

"What circumstances?"

"Evelyn, I need to know where you are. If you weren't at college, I wouldn't know your location every day. You being at Kensington Hall means I can keep an eye on you and know where you are." The moment he explains, I can hardly look at him.

"Oh, my god. Dad..."

"I know it seems a lot. But you need to remember who I am and what I do, Evelyn. I am not a normal man. And you being at Kensington Hall means you're safe."

"I can't believe this." I scoff and shake my head.

"I thought you were happy to get into Kensington. I thought that's what you wanted." His ignorance is infuriating.

"Happy?!" I practically yell. "Dad, I don't even know if it was really me who got in!"

"Of course it was." My father frowns.

"No, it was you. It will always be you! My friendships, Scotland, college… all my life, it is going to be you who decides what happens. Not me. That apartment that I am so grateful for. It's just another surveillance technique, isn't it? Because you're terrified that I am going to do some things on my own. And this job, again, it's just another way of monitoring me."

"Evelyn, listen to me." My father places his hands on my upper arms, urging me to pay attention. "If I was anyone else, I wouldn't be doing this. Your mother was killed when she was supposed to be under my protection. How do you think I would feel if something were to happen to you as well?"

"Things will happen to me, Dad! It's life! Yeah, some creepy guy will try to pull me in a club. Some mugger might decide it's me who's the target that day. But that is life, Dad. And you need to let me live it. On my own." I am full to the brim with anger. I understand his intentions but he has gone too far.

"Evelyn, everything around me needs to be planned, to the absolute, finest detail. Everything that happens to us, I need to be in control of and it is so important that you understand that. You are going to Kensington Hall."

"And know I'm only a student there because my father is Gregory Norman? I'll feel like such a fake. I'll feel like everything I do only happens because of you. Any grades I get, any endorsements, any special treatment. All of my accomplishments will never be my own, will they? I wouldn't even be surprised if you tipped off my driving examiner." I shake my head.

"Listen to me!" His volume shuts me up. "Just because this assignment with Connelly is over, it doesn't mean you're safe."

"I will never be safe, Dad! As long as you have this job, I will never be safe. So, what are you going to do? Keep me working in your company for the rest of my life? Put trackers in my car? I want to be a psychiatrist, Dad. And I will be meeting people. I will be travelling to different hospitals all across the country." I am getting more incensed with each word. "And I highly doubt you are willing to quit your job."

"It's not as simple as that, Evelyn, you know that. You are seventeen-years-old. You know nothing about the world. You have no idea the lengths people will go to... to hurt you." He rubs the bridge of his nose. "Go to Kensington Hall. Join my company, just until I know that you're going to be safe. Or I fly us straight back to Scotland."

"You wouldn't."

"Try me." He scowls at me. He means it. He really would drag me back to Scotland, kicking and screaming.

"I will never have a choice, will I?" I gently release my tears. "I will never have autonomy." I wipe my eyes. "Now, I am going to my room. And I will be checking for cameras. Because, who knows how far you will go with this ridiculous, overprotective bullshit?!" I rip the letter up right in front of him.

"Evelyn!" He shouts as I rush up the stairs. I haven't done this in a while. But I am now. And I am enraged.

The next morning, I am getting ready for my first rehearsal with Miss Perkins' orchestra. When we got back to London, I rang her and told her I was available. She was overjoyed. As was I. Once I am ready, I hesitate before opening my bedroom door. I haven't spoken to my father since my little outburst. And I don't particularly want to. I'm still miffed. But I collect all of my courage and throw the door open.

I can hear the tapping of a laptop keyboard as I make my way downstairs. I saunter into the kitchen and see my father, sitting at the breakfast bar, typing away at his laptop. I don't even acknowledge him as I collect my house keys from the fruit bowl. I grab my satchel from a chair in the kitchen before heading towards the hallway.

"Where are you going?" My father asks, still staring at the screen.

"Out." I snap right as I get to the front door.

"Evelyn!" Right as he hollers my name, I slam it and march away from the house. Once I see my little Fiat, my heart breaks. He's done so much for me. The car. The piano, which is now in our home. The apartment. His heart, for the most part, has been firmly in the right place. But right now, knowing all of my accomplishments aren't my own, it's hard to forgive him. I will. I know I will. We'll patch things up when I get home. But I need space. I need people who aren't Gregory Norman.

I walk into the theatre at Kensington Hall. The moment I see the orchestra, setting up and tuning their instruments, I smile and feel a rush of excitement. As I walk towards the stage, Miss Perkins spins and is visibly full of delight when she sees me.

"Evie, my darling!" She opens up her arms and wraps me in them.

"Hi, Miss Perkins."

"Oh, I am so happy you chose to join us." Miss Perkins claps her hands together. I just raise my eyebrows and offer her an almost false grin. I'm still in a bad mood about yesterday. "Why don't you go and set yourself up on the piano? Get used to it. It might need a bit of a tune." She suggests and I nod. I spot the large black grand piano in the corner of the stage. I sit myself down on the stool, gently checking the pedals.

"Hi, Evie." A sweet, weary voice appears in front of me. I stand and look over the lid to see Olivia Harris, the girl I always thought hated me.

"Oh, hi, Olivia." I mutter unsurely. She gleams and walks around the piano as I sit back down.

"I hear you're coming back here." She begins a conversation.

"Mm-hmm." I nod, not quite knowing how she knows that.

"Is that for A-Levels?"

"Uh, yeah."

"And then what's the plan after that?" Olivia doesn't stop asking questions. It's quite off-putting.

"Um, I don't know. Uni, I guess. I don't know which one." I shake my head, floored by her friendliness.

"I hear Sam wants to go to UCL."

"Yeah, she's hoping to. Um, Olivia, I don't want to seem rude but why are you talking to me? You hate me." I grimace.

"Who told you that?" She seems equally as confused as me.

"Well, Sam did."

"I don't hate you, Evie. I've never hated you. Why would she tell you that?" Olivia scoffs. I rack my brain. Why would Sam tell me that?

"I don't know…" I continue to stare at her in confusion. My forehead is a permanent frown, completely bewildered.

344

"Olivia, your father is on the phone, dear!" Miss Perkins hollers, cutting through the conversation.

"Coming! Look, Evie, why don't we try and be friends? I've always loved your playing." Olivia seems genuine. It continues to confuse me.

"Sure." I respond slowly. Olivia smiles and spins, heading to Miss Perkins to take that phone call. Something doesn't feel right. Sam told me that Olivia hated my guts. Olivia always started rumours and treated me with such contempt, that I believed it. But after seeing her today, my brain is rattled. And how the hell did she know I got into Kensington Hall? I only just got the letter yesterday. I think about what my father said. Everything around us needs to be planned. And that was definitely not planned. I listen to her conversation while I prepare the piano.

"Dad, what's wrong?" Olivia asks, the phone to her ear. "No, I'm at school. I can't just come home, Dad." She drops her shoulders in disappointment. "I'm on my way." Olivia speaks briefly to Miss Perkins and then leaves the hall. Family emergency, I guess.

Half an hour later, we have already finished a segment of the orchestral piece Miss Perkins wants us to perform at the Spring show. I listen to her as she gives us all some feedback. "Jason, tighten the screws on the drums please." Her voice is so clear. "Evie, a bit more tempo in that middle section." She is obsessed with me increasing the tempo. I know I'm not on her tempo today. My brain is too focused on all the confusing things going on in my life. "But in general, everyone, that was wonderful. Shall we take it from the top?" I flick the sheet music back to the beginning. I stretch my fingers and rest them on the keys. My eyes watch Miss Perkins as she conducts us. As I play, I find myself remembering the song I wrote using the Steinway back in Scotland. I'm a terrible lyricist so I'll leave that to someone else, but the melody was really something I was happy with. I must rehearse it more at home. "No. Everybody stop." Miss Perkins suddenly snaps. We all stop playing. "Can we all please just try to be on my tempo? Evie, that includes the accelerando in bar eight." She is losing her patience. This isn't like her. At that moment, I hear my phone ring. I widen my eyes and gasp, scrambling to turn it off. Miss Perkins despises phones during rehearsals. "Evelyn!"

"I know, I know. I'm turning it off." I look at the screen. It's my father. "Actually, Miss P, I need to take this."

"Hurry." Once she has given me permission, I stand and make my way off the stage. I wait until I am in the corridor before answering the phone.

"Yeah?" I roll my eyes.

"Where are you?"

"I'm at college, doing orchestra rehearsals. Why?" I aimlessly look through the door window into the theatre. Miss Perkins is checking something inside the piano. Maybe it does need a tune.

"You need to come home. Right now."

"Dad, I can't just leave. They need me."

"Evelyn, it was not a polite request." That sentence. That tone. A tone that I have heard so many times before. Horrible Dad. No, it's not Horrible Dad anymore. It's MI6 Dad.

"Dad, what's going on?" There is a hint of fear in my voice.

"Get your stuff and come home. Now."

"Okay, okay. I'm leaving." I nod and hang up the call.

As I stroll through the theatre, acting like that wasn't the most ominous phone call of my life, Miss Perkins watches me. I timidly approach her.

"Hi, Miss Perkins. Look, I need to go home." I smile and shake my head apologetically.

"But we need you for the middle section." She argues.

"I know. This is so unprofessional but something's come up and I need to leave. It's, um, a bit of an emergency, I think."

"Well, fine. But I will remember this. And before you leave, you could at least tune the piano for me." Her usual warmth has gone and she is speaking to me differently. This is not the same woman I reunited with at the Summer show. Remind me not to piss Miss Perkins off in the future. I nod obediently and walk back to the piano. "While we wait for Miss Norman to tune the piano, why don't we have a go at practicing the middle section without her?" There is so much contempt in her voice. It's baffling. It's a college orchestra, not the bloody London Philharmonic. I roll my eyes and begin pressing a few keys to see if it actually does need tuning. One note does sound a bit off. I sigh and grab my tuning lever from my satchel. It's such a boring job but someone has to do it. I get to work, pressing each key to see which one sounds buzzy. My pitch is nearly perfect so I'll know which one needs adjusting. I finally get to the middle C.

"Got you, you little bugger." I mutter to myself and stand, looking into the lid. I tighten the string, pressing the key repeatedly and quickly, like you should when you tune. As I speed up, I notice a little red light turn on inside the piano. The more I look at it, the more terrified I get. I immediately stop pressing the key before I collect my phone from my back pocket and call my father.

"Evelyn, no phones!" I ignore Miss Perkins. But I am very aware she didn't call me Evie.

"Come on, Dad. Pick up." I whisper to myself, closing my eyes, muttering a silent prayer.

"Evelyn, you better have left that school or so help me…"

"Dad, just shut up and listen to me!" As I snap, all the other members of the orchestra stare at me. "Dad, what does a bomb look like?" I ask so carefully, so full of terror.

"What are you talking about?" I can hear the fear in his voice. I can hear the restraint in his tone. He knows something I don't. I shake my head, still staring at the red blinking light of the unidentified object.

"Dad… Secret Garden." My voice is a terrified croak as I speak our little code, telling him I'm in danger. "Secret Garden!"

"Get out of there now!"

"Out!" I shriek to the rest of orchestra. "Out! Now! There's a bomb! Get out!" I rush away from the piano as the rest of the people in the theatre scurry away from their own instruments. They all scream. It's a harrowing sound. It's a sound that makes my skin crawl. I keep the phone to my ear as I run, not looking back for a second. And then it happens. The piano erupts in a storm of splintered wood and broken strings, filling the entire theatre with a deafening boom. My ears ring as I fall to the floor. I scream. I panic. I cry. There's heat coming from behind me. I scramble forwards as all of the instruments catch alight. The room suddenly feels dark. But it's burning. I slowly and painfully twist my head to look around me. My vision is blurred. Several people are on the floor, just like me. The ringing in my ears won't go away. I cough emptily. My lungs feels so tight. I feel winded, like I've been sucker punched in the chest. I can't breathe.

"Evelyn?! Evelyn, talk to me! Evie!" The terrified, frantic voice of my father coming out of my phone is the last thing I hear before everything goes black.

Printed in Great Britain
by Amazon